Praise for Adrian Goldsworthy

'Goldsworthy's grasp of military history and his intriguing story-line combine to keep us on the very edge of our seats'
Daily Mail

'Goldsworthy is a fine military historian ... exemplary'
Independent

'Goldsworthy tells this story with great skill and narrative force'
Wall Street Journal

'Compelling'   *Financial Times*

'Mr Goldsworthy is a rising star on the historical scene'
Washington Times

'A superb achievement'   *Literary Review*

Adrian Goldsworthy has a doctorate from Oxford University. His first book, *The Roman Army at War* was recognised by John Keegan as an exceptionally impressive work, original in treatment and impressive in style. He has gone on to write several other books, including *The Fall of the West, Caesar, In the Name of Rome, Cannae* and *Roman Warfare*, which have sold more than a quarter of a million copies and been translated into more than a dozen languages. A full-time author, he regularly contributes to TV documentaries on Roman themes.

Visit www.adriangoldsworthy.com for more information.

Also by Adrian Goldsworthy

FICTION
All in Scarlet Uniform
Send Me Safely Back Again
Beat the Drums Slowly
True Soldier Gentlemen

NON-FICTION
Augustus: From Revolutionary to Emperor
Antony and Cleopatra
The Fall of the West: The Death of the Roman Superpower
Caesar: The Life of a Colossus
In the Name of Rome:
The Men Who Won the Roman Empire
The Complete Roman Army
Cannae: Hannibal's Greatest Victory
The Punic Wars
Roman Warfare
The Roman Army at War, 100 BC–AD 200

RUN THEM ASHORE

Adrian Goldsworthy

WEIDENFELD & NICOLSON

A W&N PAPERBACK

First published in Great Britain in 2014
by Weidenfeld & Nicolson.
This paperback edition first published in 2015
by Weidenfeld & Nicolson,
an imprint of the Orion Publishing Group Ltd,
Carmelite House, 50 Victoria Embankment,
London EC4Y 0DZ

An Hachette UK company

1 3 5 7 9 10 8 6 4 2

ISBN 978-1-7802-2792-4

Typeset at The Spartan Press Ltd,
Lymington, Hants

For Robert

Come, cheer up, my lads, 'tis to glory we steer,
To add something more to this wonderful year;
To honour we call you, as freemen not slaves,
For who are so free as the sons of the waves?

Chorus:
  Heart of oak are our ships, jolly tars are our men,
  We always are ready; steady, boys, steady!
  We'll fight and we'll conquer again and again.

We ne'er see our foes but we wish them to stay,
They never see us but they wish us away;
If they run, why we follow, and run them ashore,
For if they won't fight us, what can we do more?

(Chorus)

They say they'll invade us these terrible foes,
They frighten our women, our children, our beaus,
But if should their flat bottoms, in darkness set oar,
Still Britons they'll find to receive them on shore.

(Chorus)

We still make them feel and we still make them flee,
And drub them ashore as we drub them at sea,
Then cheer up me lads with one heart let us sing,
Our soldiers and sailors, our statesmen and king.

• • •

'Heart of Oak' was written during the Seven Years War and
quickly became popular, the wonderful year referring to victories
won in 1759. The words were by the actor William Garrick.

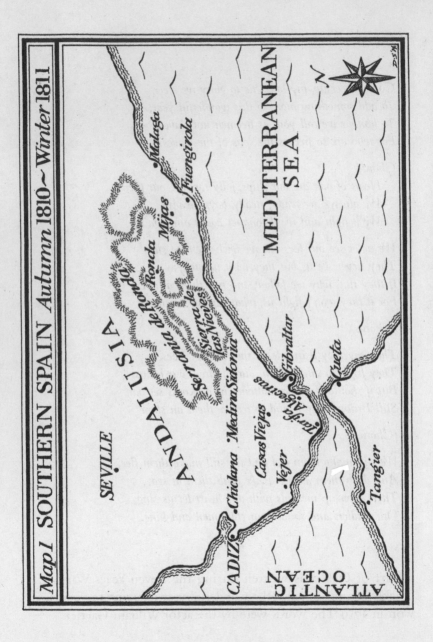

Map 1 SOUTHERN SPAIN *Autumn 1810~Winter 1811*

SEVILLE

ANDALUSIA

Serranía de Ronda

Ronda

Mijas

Sierra de las Nieves

Malaga

Fuengirola

MEDITERRANEAN SEA

Medina Sidonia

Chiclana

Casas Viejas

Vejer

Tarifa

Algeciras

Gibraltar

Cueta

CADIZ

ATLANTIC OCEAN

Tangier

N

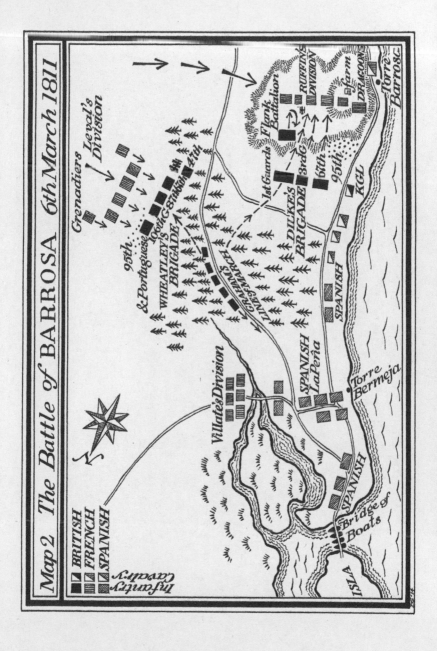

Map 2 The Battle of BARROSA 6th March 1811

I

The crest was close now, and the British officer allowed himself a moment of rest before he pushed on. He gulped a lungful of air and tried to ignore his aching thighs and calves. Lieutenant Williams felt exhausted; his back was a sheet of sweat, especially where his heavy pack pressed against his woollen coat. At least he had been right to wear his old jacket, bought two years before at an auction of a dead man's property after Vimeiro, and since then scarred by a lot of campaigning. No longer scarlet, it had faded to a deep brick-red colour so dark as to be almost brown, but that did not matter much on a moonlit night like this. His only other regimental coat was safely folded inside his valise, safe from the abuse likely from scrambling over steep sand dunes in the middle of the night.

There was the sound of scrabbling from behind and he did not need to look around to know that the others were catching up.

'Oh, bugger me,' sighed a faint voice amid laboured breathing. That was Sergeant Dobson, and it was reassuring that even the veteran was finding the climb heavy going. Although past forty, the sergeant had spent most of his life in the army and never seemed to tire, even on the longest of marches on the very worst of roads.

The breeze was picking up, rippling through the dry grass dotted all over the side of the dune, but if anything making the already close night even more stifling. It was a hot wind from the south-west – an African wind – and Williams had been told that after a storm it sometimes left a film of fine desert sand covering the rooftops and lanes here on the coast of Granada.

Tonight it simply whistled along the little valley, stirring up the dust in swirls. Williams had no doubt that it was local Spanish sand that kept driving into his eyes, the tiny grains feeling like vast boulders.

That same sand also kept slipping underfoot as they climbed. Three steps upwards usually meant one or two sliding back down, and after a while they found it easier to progress crab-like, going along the dune as much as they went up it.

'Leeway,' muttered Williams to himself, and failed to stifle a laugh as the thought struck him that their progress was much like that of a ship. Repeated explanations, some in the last few days, informed him that the wind drove a sailing ship simultaneously forward and to the side, so that a vessel moved diagonally rather than straight. Williams still did not understand why, but was willing to accept it as one more mystery of God's Creation.

'Sir?' hissed Dobson.

Williams looked back over his shoulder and saw the sergeant staring at him, face pale in the moonlight and the brass plate on the front of his shako gleaming. The veteran was using his musket like a staff to help him climb the slope, and Williams could not help wishing that he had done the same, instead of coming ashore with only his sword and a pistol.

'Sorry, Dob,' he said, and grinned. 'I was away with the fairies for a moment,' he added, using one of Sergeant Murphy's favourite expressions. The Irishman was down in the valley with the main party, spared the long climb because he had barely recovered from a leg wound taken in the summer.

'Ruddy officers.'

The sergeant's words were almost lost as a fresh gust of wind hissed across the dunes, but he could see Dobson shaking his head. An officer now, Williams had joined the army more than three years ago as a Gentleman Volunteer, too poor to buy a commission and without the connections to be granted one. Dobson had been his front rank man when Williams carried a musket and did the duties of an ordinary soldier, all the time living with the officers of the regiment and hoping to win promotion by performing some foolhardy act of valour and surviving to be rewarded. In spite of their differences – Williams was a shy, religious and somewhat earnest young man with a romantic view of life and honour, whereas the hard-drinking Dobson had been broken back to the ranks several times after going on sprees – the two men had taken to each other.

'You're my rear rank man, Pug,' the veteran had said, his hands on Williams' shoulders, and using the nickname the volunteer had picked up. 'If it comes to a fight then we keep each other alive, so I need you to know what you're at and not shoot me by mistake.' In the company formation the pair stood one behind the other and if they extended into loose order then they worked as a team.

'And if you must become a bloody officer,' he had added, his weather-beaten face serious, but his eyes twinkling with amusement, 'then you had better be a bloody good one, or you'll only get all of us bloody killed.' Williams had found himself returning Dobson's broad grin, and felt that he had truly joined the ranks of the Grenadier Company.

The veteran had taught him a lot about soldiering, and in more than three years of hard service in Portugal and Spain the two men had only grown closer. Williams had been commissioned after Vimeiro and the veteran had helped him win confidence as an officer. At the same time Dobson appeared a reformed character, no longing drinking and raised to sergeant once again. Such a remarkable change seemed entirely due to his new wife, the prim widow of another sergeant who had died on the grim road to Corunna, not long after Dobson's wife had been killed in an accident. It was an unlikely match, and yet clearly worked well for them both and for the wider good of the regiment, which thus gained a highly experienced and steady NCO.

Williams saw Dobson speak again, but lost the words in the sighing of the wind.

'Are we going, then?' the sergeant repeated more loudly, just as the breeze dropped away so that he seemed almost to be shouting.

3

Instinctively they dropped to the ground, the sailor behind Dobson a little slower than the two soldiers. Williams felt himself slipping down the slope and so grabbed two handfuls of grass and clung on. They waited, listening, hearing nothing save the gentle whisper of the wind, the still fainter sigh of the surf on the beach, and then, louder than both, the unnatural rattles, bumps and muffled curses as the main party carried their heavy loads up the track at the bottom of the valley.

Williams looked up, but could not see past the crest. He did not sense any danger, did not feel the slightest trace of that discomfort, nearly a physical itch all over his skin, that came so often when an unseen enemy was near. Dobson had long ago taught him to trust his instincts as much as his head, and always to suspect a threat even when one should not be there. 'Never trust any bugger who tells you it's safe,' had been the precise words, but now he sensed that even the veteran was relaxed. Williams wondered whether a fortnight on board ship had taken the sharp edge off their instincts, just as it seemed to have softened their muscles so that climbing this slope left them spent.

It took a concerted effort for Williams to keep reminding himself that they were in Spain, away from the main armies, it was true, but still in a region overrun by the French invaders since the start of the year. All Andalusia was now in the hands of Bonaparte's men, and his brother Joseph, puppet king of Spain, had been welcomed by cheering crowds when he toured the southern cities some months ago. As 1810 came to a close, there was not much of the country the enemy did not hold, and Massena's invasion force was also deep inside Portugal, as Lord Wellington retired closer and closer to Lisbon. Williams had seen some of the fortifications built along the heights of Torres Vedras to halt the French. They had looked strong, but so many people were convinced that the war was lost that it took a good deal of stubborn faith to believe that the invaders would be stopped.

This was enemy territory, and although bands of guerrilleros still resisted, most of them were in the hills and mountains further inland where it was easier to evade French patrols than here in the open country near the coast. Andalusia was big, and Napoleon's soldiers spread thinly as they struggled to control all the many towns and villages. There was no French garrison of any size for more than ten miles, and the few outposts too small for the soldiers to risk leaving their shelter at night when the partisans were most likely to roam. The beach below them was a good place to land, but then so were most of the beaches along this coast. There was simply no reason for enemy soldiers to be at this out-of-the-way spot on this night, and thus there should be no danger. Perhaps that was why Williams kept telling himself that he ought to be worried.

'Come on, then,' he said, gripping the clumps of grass and half pulling, half pushing with his feet to clamber up the last few yards of slope. His mind conjured up images of a line of French soldiers waiting just over the crest, bayonets sharp and muskets primed and loaded, having watched with amusement as the damned fool redcoats toiled up the side of the dune. He tapped the butt of the pistol thrust into his sash to check that it was still there, but needed both hands to climb the last four or five feet, which were almost vertical.

Williams eased his head over the top. Eyes gleamed as startled faces watched him, and then the pair of coneys bounded off through the grass. Otherwise the ridge was open and empty, stretching for ten yards or so before gently sloping down again. He pulled himself over and knelt to look around. The grass was thicker up here and the ground more solid underfoot. Ahead it dipped down a little towards the road, the bright moonlight showing that this stretch was paved and well maintained. On the far side the land rose again, and a few miles away he could see it climbing steeply towards the mountains of the Sierra de Ronda, darker shapes in the general blackness beyond. To his left the road wound down through several little valleys as it went further inland, but still followed the general shape of the shore. He could see it as a lighter thread running steadily on over the plains a good mile away. Williams looked to the right and could not see so far because the land rose a little before falling sharply back down towards the sea. Yet it was as they had expected, a neat round knoll on the far side of the road at the top of the valley they had climbed, and perched on its crest was the tower of a little church. It was all just as they had been told.

Dobson scrambled over the edge and knelt beside him. He was still breathing hard, but immediately brought up his musket, brushing sand from its mechanism and checking that the powder had not shaken out from the pan. A grunt of satisfaction showed that all was in order, and there was a loud click as he drew back the hammer to cock it. Prompted, Williams pulled the pistol from his sash.

'Looks clear,' he whispered.

'Aye,' Dobson replied.

The sailor came up to join them, but when he began to stand the sergeant reached up and gestured for him to crouch. There was no sense in offering too high a silhouette, just in case the land was less empty than it seemed.

'There's the old church,' Williams said, and pointed.

'God bless the Navy for landing us in the right place,' muttered Dobson, and winked at the young topman who had accompanied them. The lad unslung his musket. His movements were looser, less formal than those of a soldier or a marine, but he looked as if he knew how to handle the firelock. Thomas Clegg was rated Able Seaman and was seen as trustworthy by his officers, otherwise he would not have been included in this landing party, let alone chosen for this detached duty when there were bound to be plenty of opportunities to run off into the darkness.

'Cannot see the signal, though,' Williams added. The sign was to be a lantern shining from one of the windows in the tower, showing that the guides were waiting with the mules needed to carry the muskets, cartridges and other supplies brought by the main party. All were destined for the serranos, the partisans fighting in the mountains, but to reach these elusive bands of patriots the British needed to be shown the way. Waiting with

6

the guides was supposed to be a Major Sinclair, the man who had requested this aid.

Williams did not know much about the major, except that he had been on his own helping the guerrilleros for a long time. There were quite a few officers like that around, especially here in the south, some sent from Gibraltar, others from Cadiz, and still more from Sicily or any of the other Mediterranean Islands in Britain's hands. Many had a reputation for being unorthodox, and the little Williams had learned did not inspire a great deal of confidence in Sinclair. His friend Billy Pringle had gloomily told him that the major was not from a line regiment, but held rank in some 'tag, rag and bobtail corps' recruited from German, Italian and even French deserters from Napoleon's legions.

Captain Pringle commanded the Grenadier Company of the 106th Foot, in which Williams, Dobson and Murphy all served, and he was also at least nominally in charge of this mission to aid the serranos. In truth Pringle would be guided by Hanley, another friend and yet another grenadier. No, that was no longer true, thought Williams, for just a few weeks ago Lieutenant Hanley was gazetted as captain, and so would be transferred to command one of the other companies. His elevation left Williams as the only lieutenant in their little group of friends, but seemed to mean little to Hanley, whose three years as a soldier had scarcely altered his lack of interest in rank or the other formalities of military discipline.

'They're nearly at the top, sir,' whispered Dobson, his burring West Country accent still strong after a lifetime with the army.

Williams looked back and saw that the main party was coming to the head of the valley. The shapes of the sailors carrying their heavy burdens were vague, but the marines marching in front of them were clearer, their white cross-belts marking them out. He could not see either Pringle or Hanley distinctly, but guessed that they would be a little way in advance, looking for signs of their guides.

The wind freshened again and his nostrils filled with that salt smell, subtly different and yet still so clearly akin to the one he had known while growing up beside the Bristol Channel that it took him back to his childhood. That was surely another reason why he felt so safe when he should really be wary and alert. As he looked out to sea, the not quite full moon was bright in the sky, with a long reflection on the water outlining His Majesty's Ship *Sparrowhawk* and its two masts so perfectly that it looked like a painting. It was a peaceful, even beautiful, scene, and he was tempted to sit and simply stare out from the hilltop because it was so lovely.

'Look, sir, the light.' Dobson sounded relieved, and Williams had to admit that everything was going smoothly. Soon they would go down to join the main party, and then he and the other soldiers would take the supplies inland to the serranos while the sailors and marines rowed back to their ship. The redcoats were to spend a week with the Spanish, before going to another beach to be picked up by the Navy. It all seemed very simple.

Yet Williams did not trust it. Hanley was a splendid fellow in many ways, witty, educated and travelled – all things Williams admired because his own education had been severely limited by his family's straitened circumstances. His friend was very clever, and his sharp mind and fluency in Spanish more often than not took him away from the regiment and sent him off to gather information about the enemy. Much of the time Hanley was deep in French-held territory and he did not always wear uniform. Williams hesitated to employ so unbecoming and dishonourable a word as spy, but knew that that was the truth of it.

Hanley revelled in outwitting the enemy and often showed a ruthless streak in his willingness to gamble with the lives of others as if the higher the stakes the more satisfying the game. Williams sometimes doubted his friend's judgement, and had even less faith in the men who gave Hanley his orders, sure that they would have no qualms about sending them all to their deaths for the sake of some grand deception. They were clearly behind all this, plucking them all away when they were travelling back to join the battalion and sending them off to make contact with the guerrilleros. Before that they had all formed part of a training mission attached to the Spanish armies further north, and that posting had seen them stranded inside the besieged town of Ciudad Rodrigo as a token gesture made by the British to their allies. They had helped Hanley hunt an enemy spy and then been hunted in turn by a determined and ruthless French officer. Only through sheer luck had they managed to escape, and now they were once again dispatched into enemy-held country.

Williams suspected that there was far more behind their current orders than first met the eye. *Sparrowhawk*'s captain was one of Billy Pringle's older brothers, and what should have been a happy coincidence only made him more suspicious that this was no chance, but an element of some subtle scheme which he could not yet discern. Williams hoped and prayed that understanding would not come at too high a price, and felt himself being drawn ever further into the murky world in which Hanley took such evident delight. Still, at the moment it all seemed to be progressing most satisfactorily.

'Something moving, sir! Mile away to larboard!' Clegg had not quite shouted, but his report was given with a power no doubt intended to carry over the noise of weather and a working ship.

Williams saw that the young sailor was pointing to the left, down along the coast road. He stared, but could see nothing, and so pulled his cocked hat down more tightly and held it there in the hope of shading his eyes from the moon.

'Can you see what it is?' he asked.

'No, sir. Just a shade at this distance.'

There was something, but Williams was staring so hard that he blinked and lost it. He scanned the thread-like line of the road and saw nothing.

'See anything, Dob?'

'No, but my eyes aren't what they used to be.'

'It's there, sir,' Clegg repeated in a tone of mild offence. 'On the road.' The lad gestured again.

'If you would be kind enough to get my glass, Sergeant.' Williams carried his long telescope strapped to the side of his backpack and it was easier for Dobson to slide it out than for him to reach it. Then it did not matter because he saw it. The moonlight glinted on something metal and then there was an obvious dark patch moving along the road. It was coming towards them.

'You have fine eyesight, Clegg, fine eyesight indeed.'

Now that he had spotted the movement, Williams found it easy to trace, and so waited before using his glass in the hope of seeing more detail.

'Horsemen, sir?' suggested the sailor.

'I believe so. From the speed if nothing else, and coming this way.'

'Ours or theirs?' asked Dobson, although his tone contained little doubt that they were enemy. 'Though I can't say I can see them yet.'

'Must be French,' Williams said. 'And there is no reason for them to stop, so if they keep coming they will be here in fifteen or twenty minutes and if we can see them at this distance they must be in some strength.

'Well then,' he continued, trying to think clearly as the ideas took shape in his mind. 'Dob, I need you to go back to Mr Pringle and tell him I need the marines up here. Suggest that he hastens loading the mules as much as possible and then pushes on with them. Ask Mr Cassidy to take the *Sparrowhawks* back down to the beach and to wait for the marines there.' Cassidy was acting lieutenant on the brig and in charge of the landing party. 'Got all that?'

'Yes, sir,' Dobson replied formally, and stood up. 'You should go, though, and I'll stay.'

Williams smiled. 'They will obey you. If I go we will only have a discussion.' He was junior to all the others, but was more worried because he did not know what sort of man Sinclair was.

'Aye, you may be right, Pug.'

'When you come back,' Williams continued, 'split the marines into two parties. Leave Corporal Milne with one lot here and take the other half up to that rise.' Williams showed where he meant. 'Clegg and I will take a look further down.' He patted the sailor on the shoulder. 'I need those eyes of yours.

'We'll try to remain out of sight, but we will distract them if they are coming on too fast. You wait, and give them a volley when they get close. They'll only be expecting irregulars so will probably charge straight at you, so after that one shot take the men down the side of the dunes to the boats. If I don't see you I will be back here with Milne and we will give them another surprise before we bolt down to join you.' A thought struck him. 'You had better give Mr Pringle our apologies and say that we are unlikely to be joining them and so they must proceed without us, so tell them not to wait around, but press on. We can maybe give them half an hour's lead and that will have to be enough.'

Dobson nodded.

'Good luck, Dob,' Williams added, and watched the sergeant jog down on to the road and head towards the chapel. 'Come on, young Clegg, let us go and make some mischief.'

Williams ran along the top of the ridge as fast as the tussocks of grass allowed. He had his pistol in his right hand and the heavy telescope in the other. The straps on his pack had worked loose again, so it banged against his back as he ran, but although the night was no cooler and the wind stronger than ever the officer no longer noticed it. Tiredness had gone along with the uncertainty and that strange sense of peace, for now he knew what he had to do. That did not mean that it would be easy to do it.

He stopped on the rise where Dobson was to bring his men, lay down and propped his glass between two rocks.

'There they are, sir,' Clegg said, spotting them several moments before the officer.

Williams pressed his eye to the lens and tried to move the telescope as gently as possible while he hunted for the enemy.

It was a shame he did not have one of the night glasses he had seen on board the brig, but the moon was still strong and he soon found them. They were certainly cavalry, and were moving quicker than he had judged, so that when he pulled away from the glass to gauge the distance he guessed that they were now barely half a mile away. The French – they must be French for they were moving in better order than any partisans – were coming on at a steady trot, which suggested a clear purpose, whether or not it had anything to do with them. It was hard to know whether the enemy would be able to see the *Sparrowhawk* off-shore, but they certainly would by the time the road climbed up on to this ridge. Numbers were hard to determine in the darkness, but he doubted it was less than a company and probably a full squadron of more than a hundred riders.

'Come on.' Williams set off down the slope as the ground dipped into another little valley and then rose sharply to a round hillock, the highest point on the dunes. From the top Williams could see the road curving around its foot and then running in the gentlest of meanders down towards the coast. There was nowhere more promising down there, and so this was where they would wait, trusting to the steep sides of the hill to delay any mounted pursuit.

The officer pointed back towards the rise they had come from. 'Keep an eye out, Clegg, and tell me when Sergeant Dobson and the marines arrive.'

They waited, and it was hard to know how much time was passing. Williams promised himself once again that as soon as he had the money he would purchase a good watch, although even that would do nothing to hurry the sergeant along and perhaps it would only make him nervous to see the hands moving. He shook off his pack and strapped the telescope in place before slipping it back on. It was awkward, but they were going to have to move in a hurry and he did not want to risk losing it. Then he checked his pistol, flicking open the pan and feeling the priming. There was very little left and he was afraid some of the grains he touched would be sand instead of powder.

'May I trouble you for the loan of a cartridge,' he said.

Clegg looked surprised. 'Aye, aye, sir,' he responded through habit, and fished into his pouch to hand one over.

Williams bit off the end, spitting out the ball, which would be too large for the barrel even if his pistol was unloaded, and sprinkled some of the loose powder into the pan before closing it. Following his example, the sailor made sure of his firelock.

There was no sign of Dobson, and the French were getting closer. Now and again the wind carried the sounds of hoofbeats on the road and the bump and rattle of men and equipment. They waited, and still the rise behind and a little below them was empty. The cavalry came on, individual horsemen distinct now from the darker mass. The next strong gust carried with it a hint of old leather and horse sweat.

The French were close, the advance piquet of four riders no more than three hundred yards away, turning the bend which led towards the hillock. Williams glanced back. The rise remained bare and he wondered whether his message had been ignored or overruled. It was too late now, and so he must try to gain any time he could.

'Clegg,' he whispered. 'We will take a shot at the French in the hope of confusing them and slowing them down. I want you to wait until I fire before you pull the trigger. After that, we both run like rabbits. Keep to the slopes of the dunes.' Williams hoped that the sand would be too soft for the horses to follow. 'You understand?'

The sailor nodded. He was pale, but that could easily have been just the moonlight, and he looked to be a steady fellow.

Williams pulled the hammer of his pistol back to cock it and Clegg did the same. The French were close now, and he was surprised that they kept at a trot and simply rode along, apparently unconcerned that the road went between hills and offered so many good places for an ambush. Perhaps they did not expect any trouble from the serranos so close to the sea, and then Williams wondered whether the cavalry simply preferred to rush through ground where it was difficult for them to fight. If

13

that was so, then he might be doing precisely the wrong thing and would only force them to hurry even faster towards his friends. Doubting his judgement and not knowing whether or not the marines were coming to support him, Williams considered whether it was better simply to slip away and hope that the main party had got clear.

The piquet kept coming, little more than a hundred yards away and the main body a musket shot beyond that. If they kept at this pace then they would still probably catch the others, and so he had to try the only thing that might stop them. Williams decided and closed his eyes.

'Now!' he said, and pulled the trigger. It was an absurd range for a pistol at any time, let alone in the dark, but he still saw the burst of flame as a yellow blur through his eyelids and then Clegg's musket went off with a deeper boom and an even bigger flare. 'Run!' he shouted, without bothering to see whether either shot had struck home. There were shouts from the road, and the crack of carbines as the piquet replied.

The two men sprang up and fled, running as best they could through the thick clumps of grass and then skidding, almost falling, down the soft sand of the slope. There were more shouts and the sound of hoofs pounding on the paving stones. Another carbine fired and Williams heard the ball snap through the air only a foot or so over his head.

'Come on,' he called, swerving to run along the side of the ridge. The barefoot Clegg took no urging and sped ahead of him, his shoeless feet gripping better than the smooth leather soles of the officer's boots. Williams felt himself slipping, and his left side dropped down on to the ground. He was sliding, rolling on to his back, until one foot hit a rock and, dropping his pistol, he managed to take hold of some grass. Looking back he saw several French horsemen on the road at the top of the little ravine. The night was shattered by another sharp crack as a carbine flared, and a ball twitched the grass he was holding. Williams instinctively let go and started sliding again, free of the rock until one boot caught in a loop of grass and held him. He struggled free and managed to get to his knees.

One of the cavalrymen was walking his horse into the mouth of the little ravine. The others were behind, loading their carbines. Beyond them a clatter of hoofs announced the arrival of the head of the column. Someone was shouting orders in a clear voice.

Williams pushed himself up and managed to stand, right leg half bent to balance on the slope. The horseman was coming closer, calming his horse when one of its feet slipped for a moment. He was a hussar with his round-topped shako at a jaunty angle, and his fur-lined pelisse draped over his left shoulder. The man had clipped his carbine back on his belt and now drew his curved sabre, the blade glinting in the moonlight.

'Hey, *coquin*,' he said, urging his horse on. The animal slipped a little, dropping one shoulder, but again the hussar calmed it and came on.

Williams drew his sword and took guard, nearly losing his own balance before he recovered. The Frenchman stopped for a moment and smiled. Then he raised his sabre in salute, kissing the blade and at the same moment kicking his mare into a trot.

A volley of musketry split the night air as the hilltop above them erupted in flame and noise. There were cries and the scream of a horse from the road, and either this or the shots made the mare flick up its head. It stumbled, sand slipping away from under its hoofs, and then animal and rider were both falling, rolling down the slope.

Williams turned and ran, trying to bound on before his boots really sank down and started to slide. It did not quite work and he zigzagged along the side of the ridge, but at least Dobson had arrived in time to confuse the enemy. He saw Clegg waiting for him.

'Back to the boats, lad!' he shouted. 'Tell them we are coming!'

A second volley came, a little more ragged than the first, and Williams could not understand how the marines could possibly have reloaded so quickly. He ran on and now men were spilling down from the hilltop, marines in white cross-belts and with the tall brimmed hats worn by these maritime soldiers.

'Well done, Dob!' Williams yelled, and then used all his strength to go faster and get past the deluge of redcoats before they swept him away. He did not see his sergeant and had no time to look for him, but could trust him to get the men back down to the boats.

'Halt!' came the challenge as he struggled back up to the top of the ridge.

'*Sparrowhawk!*' he called, cursing himself for not thinking of a password, but hoping that the name of the ship would prove that he was not French.

'Here, sir!' A man in a marine's uniform beckoned to him, and when he got closer Williams saw the two white chevrons on his right sleeve.

'Ah, Corporal Milne.'

The corporal saluted. 'Good to see you, sir.' If anything Williams had the impression that the Royal Marines were more formal than soldiers from a line regiment. Milne's six men were kneeling or lying flat, muskets aimed at the road below them. Each had another firelock beside him.

'Mr Pringle's idea, sir,' Milne explained. 'They didn't have enough mules to carry all the guns.'

Good old Billy, Williams thought, and now understood the second volley from Dobson's men.

'Any minute now,' he said, watching the road. If the French dismounted and skirmished along the slope then he would be in trouble, and he was glad that these were hussars rather than dragoons, who carried longer muskets and were trained to fight on foot.

Loud and rapid hoofbeats echoed up the roadway as a score of cavalrymen charged in a dense knot along the road, led by an officer on a pale horse a good two or three hands taller than those of his men. Williams smiled. You could always rely on hussars – especially French hussars – to be bold.

'Wait for the order,' he said, trying to keep his tone matter of fact. Milne said nothing, but dropped down on one knee and brought his own musket up to his shoulder,

The hussars pounded along the road, fifty, now thirty yards away.

'Aim low, lads.' The corporal's voice was steady. 'We're not at sea now.'

The French were close, and Williams blinked for a moment and licked his lips, for they felt as dry as sandpaper.

'Fire!' he yelled, and the seven muskets banged, smoke instantly blotting the French from sight. Williams ran to the side so that he could see what was happening. Two horses were down, their riders tumbled, and another hussar was clutching at his stomach. The officer was unscathed and pointing towards the marines.

'Change muskets!' Milne gave the order that Williams had forgotten, but the men were already lifting their second firelock.

The hussar officer spurred his horse off the road, and here the slope was gentle and the ground firm. Half a dozen cavalrymen followed him, while the others were still disentangling themselves from the chaos on the road.

'Fire!' Williams shouted, and the muskets flamed again. 'Down the hill!' he screamed at the marines, for the French were so close that any survivors would be on them in seconds. 'Run! Run!' Milne was bellowing at them, pushing at any who were slow. A musket in each hand, the marines set off down the valley side, the corporal following. Williams saw the French officer still coming through the smoke, but the chest of the pale horse was dark so he guessed that it was wounded. Not quite sure why, he raised his own sword to salute the hussar, then flicked the blade down and slid it back into his scabbard. Other hussars were coming on, and one was levelling a stubby pistol. Williams turned and ran. He heard a bang and almost immediately there was a hot stinging along his right thigh.

It was easier to go down than up, and Williams slipped and fell as much as he ran down the slope. More shots came from the top of the ridge, but none came close. His thigh felt wet, but his leg still worked and he hoped it was just a nasty scratch. If the French were shooting then that was good, because carbines were notoriously inaccurate and at night the danger from them was small. What he feared more was the French charging down along the main track to the bottom of the valley, for they might easily reach the beach before his men.

He passed a musket dropped by one of the marines, but could not blame the man because it must be difficult to carry two of the heavy weapons down the side of a dune. He scooped it up and went on. The slope was gentler now and Williams saw a line of half a dozen men formed on the beach itself. Behind them was the cutter and gig, and men were busying themselves to get them ready.

'*Sparrowhawk*!' he called out.

Cassidy was chivvying the men aboard, the cutter much less full than when it had come ashore.

'Hurry up, lads,' he called. 'Mr Williams, if you please.'

Williams hurried, merely nodding back when Dobson grinned at him from the darkness. Sailors pushed at the heavy boats, helped by the rising tide, and then climbed aboard as they came free. In the prow of the gig, Williams sat beside Dobson and let himself relax. The sergeant looked quickly at his thigh and then grinned.

'Could have been an inch or two higher and a lot worse, sir,' he suggested.

'Thank you for that kind sentiment.'

'It's nothing, Pug. How did you get it?'

Williams shrugged and as usual found it hard not to confess everything to the sergeant. 'I lingered to salute a brave enemy,' he said, trying and failing to make it sound sensible.

'Ruddy officers.' Dobson shook his head.

The steady rhythm of the oars had already taken them some way out in spite of the tide. Williams smelled the salt air and felt at ease, but also guilty because he was leaving his friends as they went further into danger. Pringle and the others had been given a good head start and should get away. Yet the arrival of the hussars was one more coincidence and he liked the whole business less and less the more that he thought about it. Williams worried that he would never see his friends again.

2

'Fortune shines brightly upon us,' Major Sinclair declared as they came out of the shelter of a knot of pines and into the sunlight. The mist had burned away and Billy Pringle was glad of the warmth. They were high up now, having ridden throughout the night, most of the time climbing, and morning had come with a damp and chilly fog. No doubt it would soon be oppressively hot, but for the moment it was pleasant to feel the sun on his face. Pringle ordered ten minutes of rest before they continued the ascent into the mountains. Their mules did not have saddles and he suspected that Hanley and Murphy were as sore as he was. Billy took off his hat and looked up into the sky, breathing in the rich scent of resin from the trees. It was nice to enjoy a few moments of peace.

'No doubt many of my countrymen would say that it was all the luck of the Irish,' Sinclair continued. 'Is that not right, Sergeant Murphy?'

'Yes, sir,' the sergeant said dutifully, and then waited for a moment before smiling. 'All of us, just born lucky. Hush! Calm yourself, you donkey,' he added, turning to soothe one of their mules as it brayed and tried to shake off its heavy load. His own beast lashed out with its hind legs at the one behind, nearly unseating the Irishman. 'The problem with a mule,' he said once he regained his balance, 'is that the beast will serve you well for ten years just so that it can get the chance to bite you.'

Pringle was weary after a hard night, and suspected that Murphy was not only tired, but troubled by his barely healed wound. The left side of his own face was sore from the rubbing of his glasses. Pringle's good pair had been broken during that desperate fight at the River Côa a month ago – not by the French, but by the clumsy boot of Lieutenant Williams – and he had failed to find a replacement during their brief stay in Lisbon. These were his old ones, the lenses still good, but the arms bent badly from heavy use and always pressing too hard on his skin.

'Hush now, me darhling.' Murphy had thickened his accent and started to play the part of a stage Irishman. For those who knew him, this was a clear indication of his contempt for the strange officer. The sergeant soothed the mule, stroking its muzzle, and then began to whisper into one of its long ears. 'Calm now, me dear, there's no sense in going on so much and saying so little.'

Sinclair gave no sign of spotting the barb in that comment. 'That is us to be sure, blessed with luck and the goodwill of all God's creatures, especially the stubborn, contrary ones which so mirror our own characters.' The major had barely stopped talking throughout the long night's march into the Sierra, untroubled by the lack of response from his companions. It was clear that he enjoyed talking and, after so long a time with the partisans, most especially speaking in English. Nor was he short of opinions, and it was just as well that the three Spaniards with them did not understand the language, for the major had offered plenty of disdainful opinions of Catholics. Sinclair was Presbyterian – 'No damned candles, confessions or popery for me,' he had informed them early on, as if in answer to a question no one had asked, 'just poor old Eustace Sinclair doing the best he can for God, King and Country.'

Pringle had often wondered why so many Irishmen felt obliged on the slightest acquaintance to inform strangers of their faith and allegiance. It was not universal, there were several Irish officers in the 106th, and plenty in the army as a whole, many of whom lacked this belligerent urge to declare themselves. Nearly all were Anglos, some more English than the English, but he had met men like Sinclair before, although at least the major was not so crass as to proclaim that he was a gentleman. Yet there was still an inherent challenge in his words, aimed partly at the world in general, though most, it seemed, at his fellow countrymen.

The scars of the past ran deep, and the great rebellion of '98 was not really so long ago. Pringle had been fourteen then, and could remember that nearly every day a fresh story of massacre was being reported in Liverpool. His father and brothers away, only he and his uncle had been there to comfort his mother as she worried about the Irish population of the town running amok and slaughtering women and children. Twelve years on, that all seemed a distant memory, even if, he would guess, the wounds remained fresh for those caught up in it all.

Pringle had never been to Ireland, although he guessed at some stage there was a fair chance that the regiment would be sent there, and he would be the first to admit that he knew little, and thought less, of its troubles. Things seemed peaceful now, and '98 had had as much to do with the contagion of revolutionary plots as religion, so that it seemed unlikely to be repeated. The dream of joining Napoleon's empire was far less intoxicating than the cry of liberty, equality and fraternity. Men like Murphy were common in the army, and provided many of its best soldiers. Plenty of the officers were also good, the rest no better or worse than anyone else, and Pringle was convinced that more than a few were discreetly Catholic. Every year Parliament passed an Indemnifying Act, so that the law requiring proof of allegiance to monarch and the Church of England was quietly ignored. There were plenty of nonconformists like Williams who were equally glad of this provision. Pringle rather liked belonging to a country whose government routinely chose to deceive itself.

'One might incline to the view that genuine good luck would have caused us not to bump into the French patrol in the first place.' Hanley's voice snapped Pringle from his thoughts. His friend was never at his best in the early mornings and now sounded distinctly ill-humoured. In fact it had surprised Billy that Sinclair's near-continuous monologue had not prompted him to argue. Hanley had a near-insatiable appetite for disputation, eloquently arguing for the joy of it even when he did not believe a word he was saying.

'I beg your pardon, Hanley.' Sinclair stood no more than five foot five inches tall, dwarfed by the other redcoats, none of them much less than six foot, for the grenadiers were chosen from the biggest men in the battalion. Yet the major cut a neat, athletic figure and possessed the confidence of a giant. His eyes were the palest Pringle had ever seen, so faintly grey as to be almost transparent. His face was impishly handsome and constantly amused, which was the all the more surprising given the militancy of so many of his statements. 'I do not quite follow, my dear fellow.'

'I merely wondered whether we might boast a better claim to luck had we landed and not met French cavalry?'

'Ah, a philosopher, I see. Then I am all the more glad to make your acquaintance, Captain Hanley, and look forward to exploring many deep questions with you.' Sinclair's smile was so broad that he was almost beaming. 'But for the moment I will simply say that I believe you have mistaken the nature of Irish luck. We need constant difficulties and scrapes otherwise we would never know how lucky we are to come through them! An Irishman free of problems would be a very dull Irishman indeed. Isn't that so, Sergeant?'

Murphy laughed this time, a genuine roar of laughter. 'Your Honour's talking sense,' he said. 'And with that sort of wisdom, you can see why we need all the luck we can get.'

Sinclair bowed to honour the sentiment, and even Hanley was smiling.

'Well, at least we got away,' Pringle said. 'And now that we are a little rested, we should get away again and keep moving. With your leave, of course, Major?'

'Certainly, my dear fellow, certainly.' Sinclair had insisted that he was there to assist and not to take command. 'Just here to pave the way, old boy, and I shall be off into the shadows again once I have seen you to our destination.' He spoke in the rapid Spanish of the south to the two muleteers he had brought with him, telling them to check the loads before they went on. Hanley said something more quietly to the guide, who kept himself apart from the other Spaniards as well as the British. Sinclair had somehow arranged for the man to meet them, but confessed that he knew neither him nor the band he came from. 'We need to meet them,' he had said, 'and learn how best we can aid each other against the common foe. But the reputation of Don Antonio Velasco and his band is truly splendid. I suspect that I have heard more songs sung of him that any of the other chiefs.'

The guide was small, blind in one eye, and said no more than was absolutely essential, but had led them along tracks which they would never have found in broad daylight, let alone at night. What little he said, he said to Hanley, and this did not include his own name, or that of the leader.

'Ya veremos,' he said, and nothing more. 'We shall see.'

So they went on, the major chattering away, the bell on the collar of the lead mule ringing as it toiled up the steep paths, the other five pack mules following and now and then baying in protest or whatever it was that prompted mules to give voice. The riding mules were as awkward and contrary as most of their kind. Hanley fell more than once, and Pringle only stayed on by copying Murphy and keeping one hand entwined in his beast's mane.

'Sadly the spirit of patriotism seems undeveloped in the mules of Iberia,' Sinclair said as he watched Hanley climbing back on to his mount after another fall. 'A sorry state of affairs, and one that surely reminds us how brightly that spirit burns in the human inhabitants of these lands. They hate with a passion. And at least the mules have given no welcome to the invaders. According to the best reports they are as inimical to the French as they are to the rest of humanity!'

Pringle smiled at that. The other men said little, the guide nothing at all unless prompted, and then just, 'You will see.' He indicated the route solely by gestures.

'You ride well, Sergeant,' Sinclair said a mile or so on. 'You remind me a lot of a man named Murphy who used to deliver the coal in Ballymena. The resemblance is striking.'

24

'Probably my uncle. He was just like me except that he was small, fat and with red hair.'

'That sounds like the same man,' the major said happily. 'I am sure of it. And how is your good uncle?'

'Well, as far as we know. Apart from being dead.'

They went on for hours, and saw no one, but since they were led through pine forests, little valleys and dells, that was not so surprising. These were paths taken by those who did not wish to be seen. That was good, and showed that the man knew his business, but as they went on Pringle's worries only grew. From the start he had not cared for his orders. It was good to be busy, for he knew his own nature well enough to know that he needed to be kept busy. When he was not then he all too easily slipped back into old habits of drinking far more than was prudent. It was a fault that had seen him fight a duel last year from a mixture of wine-driven anger and frustration at the drabness of day-to-day life. Pringle liked the army, but liked even more the clear purpose of campaigning. Sometimes he feared that meant that he actually enjoyed war, but if so then there was probably little he could do to change, and if he kept busy there was scant time for such melancholy thoughts. War brought him friendships closer than any he had ever known and the all-encompassing, though essentially simple, problems of overcoming the enemy and remaining alive.

Pringle wanted to be back with the battalion, now that the 106th were returning to the war, although no one seemed quite sure whether they were heading for Cadiz or Gibraltar. Either way it would be good to be back in the family of the regiment, surrounded by men he knew, and with most of the great decisions made for him. Plenty of people said the war was lost, with Marshal Massena's great army poised to eject Lord Wellington from his toehold in Portugal. Pringle was not so sure, but, even if the war was lost, he reckoned it still had enough life in it to offer amusement for some time to come. He would prefer to make the most of it back with the regiment rather than stuck out here in the middle of nowhere with only the vaguest sense that he might be doing anything useful.

'How much further?' Hanley asked the guide.

The man shrugged. '*Ya veremos.*'

Hanley was behind it all, of course. While the party of the 106th returning from detached duty had been waiting for a ship at Lisbon, Lieutenant Hanley was summoned. He returned to them a captain, and with the news that he had new orders, sending him off to the guerrilleros here in the south. Pringle, Williams and the two sergeants were to go with him for protection, to help manage the supplies he was to take, and so that they could help judge the military prowess of the bands they encountered. Billy was unsure whether Hanley had volunteered their services, or whether the man giving the orders had chosen them. Mr Ezekial Baynes was a civilian, a trader in wines and spirits, and one of the most important masters of spies working for the British in the whole Iberian peninsula. He was a portly, red-faced, bluff and jovial old fellow with a razor-sharp and ruthless mind. Even Hanley was sometimes shocked by the merchant's willingness to play games with the lives of men, and admitted to trusting no more than Baynes' commitment to the cause and his shrewd intelligence.

Billy wondered whether he was fretting unnecessarily. Plenty of officers were sent out to meet with the partisans. Sinclair was one, but there were dozens of others in Granada and the neighbouring provinces – indeed, so many, and often sent by different commanders without consulting each other, that there was real danger that this would only foster the lack of coordination between the different bands. Hanley said that part of the aim of their mission was to see how best to unite the various leaders and their British and Spanish liaison officers so that a greater sense of purpose could be brought to the *guerrilla*, the 'little war' fought by the irregulars. That made good sense, and were it not for too many little things, he might have been content.

It had been unlikely, to say the least, that they should have been brought on his brother's ship. It had been good to see

Edward again, even if the circumstances were sad for it was the first time they had met since his brother's wife had died giving birth to a son who lasted only a few days more than his poor mother. Meeting the French hussars so soon after they landed was a greater worry. Williams, Dobson and the landing party had done a fine job of letting them get away, for they had seen no trace of pursuit as they began the long climb into the hills. He hoped that the others had not paid too high a price, and it was frustrating that they would not know what had happened until they were picked up in a week's time. If they were picked up.

Sergeant Murphy had dismounted and let the rest of the party pass until Pringle reached him.

'We are being followed, sir,' the Irishman whispered.

'Have you seen them?' Pringle asked.

Murphy shrugged. 'Not quite, sir.'

'Keep looking. It may be the partisans.'

'There is that, sir.'

Pringle wondered whether this was how the French felt wherever they marched in Spain or Portugal, always looking over their shoulders, never sure whether one or two – or hundreds or even thousands of – irregulars were lurking in the shadows, waiting to pounce on stragglers or anyone else who looked vulnerable. He shuddered, and for a moment felt very sorry for his enemies. Pringle did not hate the French. It was natural to see them as enemies, for the war had begun when he was very young, and was just another war between Britain and France in over a century of conflict. John Bull fought Johnny Crapaud on sea and on land and that was simply how it was. Pringle's allegiance to his country was so deep rooted that he rarely called it to mind, let alone felt any need to speak of it. When he thought at all, it was more of his regiment and friends, but even there the loyalty was instinctive. He fought for them, and because he was a soldier, moderately ambitious for distinction, and because he would have thought less of himself if he failed. Some of the French fought to impose their way of life or their power on others, but Pringle guessed most thought as he did, at least most of their officers.

Napoleon's men fought bravely and skilfully – too skilfully sometimes – and Pringle respected them. He could remember the British and French mingling as they filled canteens from the stream between the rival armies during that long lull at Talavera.

That would not happen in the 'little war'. The guerrilleros hated and were hated in return by the French. When either side bothered to take prisoners at all it was often only to execute them at a later time. This war was bitter and brutal, and was fought in any little place at any time when there was a chance to kill. Pringle could understand the hatred of the Spanish for the invader, and wondered whether he might act as the French had done, hanging and shooting indiscriminately, if he had seen some of his own men tortured and mutilated by angry peasants. He simply prayed that he would never face such implacable and elusive foes.

For the next hour Pringle did his best to look for any sign of trouble. Once or twice he thought he glimpsed darker shadows amid the trees, but could not swear to it, and it may have been imagination. After a while the woods thinned to isolated trees, until these too failed and all that was left was low scrub. The guide led them into a maze of tight little valleys, until finally they came to a small lake filled with dark water, sitting at the bottom of a circle of high crests. Big boulders and clumps of bushes dotted the grass around them. Little ravines led off on several sides, and the guide led them up one of them. When they came closer they saw a gap between two rocky slopes, the entrance barely wide enough for a man or a mule to pass through. The guide for once gave more detailed instructions, telling them to wait as he walked warily up to the gap.

'I think we might have arrived,' said Hanley.

'*Ya veremos*,' Sinclair replied, giving them all a stage wink.

The one-eyed guide produced a whistle and blew three short blasts and one long, echoes taking up the sound and repeating it from all sides.

'Would it not be a terrible shame if no one was at home,' Pringle said.

'Well, we could always leave our cards,' the major suggested.

'Begging your pardon, sir, but you won't have to,' Sergeant Murphy moved slowly, and slipped his musket from his shoulder.

Pringle looked around the great theatre-like bowl of hills and saw nothing. Then the guerrillas appeared. Men in brown stepped out from behind rocks or bushes, saying nothing. Horsemen rode out from the mouths of valleys probably little wider than the one they were near and just as hard to spot from a distance. There were at least thirty, with more appearing, and a good half were mounted. Pringle wondered whether Murphy had spotted them or simply guessed.

'No need for your musket, Sergeant,' Sinclair said softly. 'These are friends.'

'Glad to hear that, Your Honour. Glad indeed.'

Pringle hoped that the major was right.

3

Pringle spluttered, turning away as the jet of liquid sprayed all over his face. The laughter was loud, and once he had stopped choking he joined in, although he would have needed far more drink inside him to find the joke as hilarious as his hosts did.

'Waste of good wine,' he said, wiping his glasses clean with the tip of his long sash. The grinning partisan adjusted the tube coming from the wineskin and, once the officer had opened his mouth, squirted it with less force and more accuracy so that the Englishman could drink. Hanley was next, and was allowed to take a long sip before the Spaniard flicked the nozzle and sent the spray down his neck. This time the laughter was a great roar. When it was Murphy's turn, the sergeant was ready and jerked his head to follow the jet, swallowing more than went over him, prompting cheers from the guerrilleros.

After this initiation, the visitors were each provided with a simple mug, filled to the brim with more of the rough wine. Pringle stood and raised his drink.

'To Spain, and to the brave guerrilleros!'

The partisans cheered and drank and soon there were more toasts. 'Long live Spain! For Liberty! Death to the French!'

No one seemed at all concerned about the noise of their celebrations. They sat on the mossy grass, enclosed on all sides by high bluffs. The place, like a natural roofless house, was at the end of the narrow cutting where their guide had whistled to summon the partisans. It had taken some effort to get the mules to follow the path, and even more when for some ten yards or so it went through a cave, and only a good deal of cursing and plenty of blows forced the animals through. Finally they emerged into this glade, and were greeted by the rich aroma of wood smoke and a kid cooking over the fire.

There was no welcome for the muleteers brought by Sinclair.

'*Contrabandistas.*' Pringle had heard the leader of the guerrilleros mutter the word in obvious contempt, and then say a good deal more he did not quite catch. It did not surprise him to learn that the men were smugglers. There were always plenty of them, especially near the coast, where goods came ashore from Africa or Gibraltar and further afield and then were carried through the darkness to avoid tolls and tax alike. Such men knew the country well, but many saw no reason to give up their occupation simply because the French had invaded. All it meant was that they now avoided or bribed King Joseph's men instead of those serving the old king.

'It is best if I go with them,' Sinclair had said. 'Not sure I can find my way back to my fellows on my own,' he added, his expression making clear that this modesty was feigned. 'But these two are useful to me and know the country like the back of their hand. And if I have done all that I can here ...'

The leader of the partisans said nothing to restrain him, even though the major spoke in Spanish.

'Thank you, sir,' Hanley said after a long and increasingly awkward pause. 'You have been a great aid to us. I am sure that if all goes well, we may foster closer alliances between the bands and make life very difficult for the French.'

'That's the spirit. I dare say our paths will cross, perhaps even in the next few days?' He looked enquiringly at the guerrilla leader, but the Spaniard said nothing, until Sinclair went on. 'Which other bands do you plan on meeting?'

'That is up to El Blanco,' the man said. Don Antonio was not with the others at the moment, although expected some time during the night. It was the first time that they had heard his nickname, but then almost all the chiefs had nicknames. For the moment his cousin Carlos was in charge. He was a slim man with the mild face of a student and the cold eyes of a killer. Two pistols were tucked into his leather belt, along with a long clasp knife, and slung from his shoulder was a musket. Like most of the men he wore a red-brown jacket and tight-fitting breeches, with big silver buttons on the lapels and running down the seams. His hair was long and tied back in a pigtail – a few of his followers sported colourful ribbons in their hair. All wore broad-brimmed hats, and had either simple leather shoes or sandals. Their weapons were numerous, many of them captured from the enemy, and carried with a confidence suggesting skill in their use.

Carlos Velasco's expression was stern, showing no warmth even though he had spoken words of welcome and shown a brief eagerness when he saw the heavily laden mules.

'Well, I suppose I must make do with a "you will see" once again.' Sinclair still looked cheerful, but then switched to English. 'I cannot really blame these fighting devils for being cautious of strangers. One day I must get myself a red coat as that seems to help.' The major wore a pale grey braided jacket in vaguely military style along with a plain cocked hat. 'Had it made for me in Port Mahon before they sent me out here,' he had told them during the long journey. 'Am still not sure what uniform the Chasseurs are supposed to wear – could be bright pink for all I know as I have never seen my damned regiment and they have never seen me!

'Well, good luck to you all! Good luck to you too, Sergeant, although as an Irishman you have it already.' The muleteers looked for a moment as if they would demand to take the pack mules with them, but Sinclair bustled them away and the three rode off, escorted by the same guide who had brought them here. Pringle noticed that several other partisans left soon afterwards and wondered whether they were sent to shadow the little party on its way. He was now sure that Murphy had been right and they had been watched for some time.

The mood changed quickly. He heard several of the Spanish refer to the major as *Sinclair el malo* – Sinclair the bad. 'It seems they do not care for him much,' said Hanley as they sat and rested after arriving in the glade. 'I believe there is a Captain Sinclair active in the mountains farther east, so do not know whether he is "the good".'

'He is at least not so bad,' Carlos Velasco interrupted, speaking in strangely accented but good English. 'I do not get much practice these days, but spent a long time in your country,' he said in response to their looks of surprise. 'It was not through choice, but courtesy of your Lord Nelson.'

'I am very sorry.' Pringle realised the imbecility of the words even as he spoke them.

'And you are very English to say so.' Carlos chuckled. 'It is,' he hesitated for a moment, frowning, 'water under the bridge.' He snapped his fingers when they nodded, and then laughed in delight, his whole face softened. 'Good, I remember, and as always when the subject arises, I will remind you Englishmen that it was the Spanish who took your Nelson's arm. Splinters, I would guess. I used to be a surgeon,' he added. 'Well, still am, if we are unlucky enough to have wounded. I have sawn limbs off Spanish and English sailors, and on the whole was not treated too badly. Now the French are here in my country and there is not enough hate in the world to balance what they have done, so I am happy enough to be friends with the English.'

'Thank you,' Pringle said. 'We are most glad to hear it.'

Carlos sighed. 'The "good" Sinclair never comes out of Murcia so I have not met him,' he explained. 'Your friend Sinclair is a strange man. My cousin does not trust him.'

'He is a British officer,' Hanley said.

'He is, but he has poor choice in the men he helps. Smugglers like those he had with him, and even worse, bandits and murderers like Pedro the Wolf.'

'I have not heard of him,' Hanley said.

'Then you are fortunate. He likes to call himself El Lobo, and I do not know his real name, but he has plagued this country for years. Before the war he robbed and murdered, killing for sport and to make his name feared. Now he does the same, and sometimes he probably kills Frenchmen, but more often Spanish.

33

There are plenty of bandits like that around, and your friend Sinclair gives them guns and powder.' He spat angrily. 'Scum. The pigs should all be strung up from the nearest trees.'

'Although Major Sinclair belongs to the same army, neither of us had met him before we landed, and I must emphasise that our orders come from Lord Wellington and have nothing to do with the major.'

'Good,' the guerrilla said, 'then we may well get on and do each other some good. Now, let us eat and drink.' His face had hardened once again, but changed as they watched him. Carlos laughed and cheered with the others as they took food and wine, and then came truly alive when a couple of the men began to play guitars. Others danced, and then after many pleas the leader began to play and sing. He had a good voice, and, although Pringle could understand little of the verses, which seemed to be in a dialect or were simply too fast for him to follow, even so he found it deeply moving.

'They are love songs, I am guessing,' he said quietly to Hanley, 'but what do they say?'

His friend did not answer for a while, but looked more deeply moved than he had seen him for a long time. Hanley had black hair and a dark complexion, and after the years he had spent in Spain before the invasion and since then the rigours of campaigning, he looked more Spanish than English. Pringle could not help thinking that he seemed more comfortable here, surrounded by these lean, unmilitary and yet dangerous-looking fighters.

'They are love songs,' he said eventually. 'Beautiful and sad.' His voice sounded wistful, and although it may just have been the firelight, his eyes looked moist. That seemed to be it, until he added so quietly that he may not have realised that he spoke, 'I do love these people, and I do so love this country.' Pringle expected his friend to break into a smile and look embarrassed, but instead Hanley just kept staring into the fire. Well, his friend was always something of an odd fish.

Carlos finished and then embarked on another song, which was clearly more comic than sentimental. Billy Pringle found his mind wandering and began thinking about women, a wonderful, all-encompassing and familiar preoccupation which seemed simpler than concern for countries and causes. He began to smile to himself but did not care, and quickly the image of Miss Williams came to his mind. Anne was the oldest of Williams' three sisters, and, like his comrade, she was tall, fair haired and blue eyed. There was something of Williams' primness about her, certainly much of his earnest nature, and yet also that same surprisingly practical – at times even earthy – ability to confront life. Apart from the colouring, there was little resemblance between the pair, and he guessed Williams' face and build owed more to his Welsh father than his finely featured Scottish mother.

Pringle had met Anne Williams nearly a year earlier, on a brief visit to the family home in Bristol, and now they engaged in an occasional correspondence. Sometimes he wondered whether if this was no more than her natural interest in a close friend of her brother, reinforced when Billy had helped hunt a younger sister, Kitty, left with child and abandoned by her lover. Pringle had called the man out, wounded him in a duel, and convinced him to marry the silly girl – he still struggled to understand the whole affair and the decisions made by the pair. The husband was a light dragoon, and had since died, but at least Mrs Garland was a respectable widow rather than a ruined woman.

He knew Anne was grateful, for she had thanked him several times, always with considerable grace. Yet there seemed more than that, some affinity stronger than any obligation, something both felt. Billy Pringle did not fully understand it, even to the extent of knowing what it was he hoped for. That did not make it any less real. She came to his mind often these days, with thoughts of the little things, her movements, gestures, the look of fixed concentration as she laboured at her needlework, the tip of her tongue pressed between pursed lips, or the slight frown when she struggled to follow a conversation, and the sheer joy in her laughter. He found himself thinking of her more than other women, even those he had known with far greater intimacy. There was one image stronger than all the others, a memory of the afternoon when at her mother's insistence she had played and sung for them on the old pianoforte Mrs Williams had bought at the auction of property when a neighbour died. Never of the best quality, the instrument was barely in tune, and Miss Williams and her sisters had received only the little tutoring their mother could afford. Pringle had heard plenty of other, far more accomplished young ladies, and yet such simple songs had never moved him so deeply. There was something very natural about her performance for all its lack of polish, and he had watched entranced her hands on the keys, her face, and her chest rising and falling as she took breaths that were surely too tight for perfection.

Pringle had not noticed that the music had stopped, the dancing and merriment stilled.

'Gentlemen, you are welcome.' The voice was deep, the tone those of a well-educated Spanish gentleman. Pringle and Hanley both sprang to their feet, returning the bow of Don Antonio Velasco. The source of his nickname was obvious, for his thick hair was white – not grey or mottled, but pure white. As the Spaniard straightened up, Pringle looked closely and saw that the chieftain could not have been more than thirty. He was a slim man, of no more than average height, but his every movement was controlled and precise. Dressed in a finer version of the garb of his band, he had a French dragoon's musket over his shoulder and wore from his belt a sword, its hilt and scabbard lavishly decorated with gold inlay. It was a sword of honour awarded for bravery by Napoleon in the years before he had become emperor. That surely meant that El Blanco had met and killed such a veteran, and that in itself said a lot.

There were four partisans with him, two much like the others in the glade, if more heavily laden with weapons. Each had a blunderbuss slung from one shoulder and a carbine from the other, with a couple of pistols and a knife in their belt. The other two were smaller and younger, their hair cut short. Each was swathed in a long black cloak, had black trousers and polished Hessian boots of the type worn by officers. Their faces were smooth, neither old enough to shave, but each had a musket and sword. Pringle wondered whether they were more relatives of the leader, since they seemed unlikely bodyguards.

Hanley launched into a suitable speech, praising the leader and expressing the hope that as allies they might work together more closely in future. Then he led them all to the piles of equipment lying stacked beside the tethered mules. Lifting one of the muskets, he passed it to Don Antonio.

The guerrilla chief took it, felt the heft, examined the lock, and then in a fluid motion swept it up, aiming at an imaginary enemy on the bluffs. He pulled it back to full cock, then squeezed the trigger, letting it slam down and spark. Pringle wondered what the reaction would have been had the piece been loaded.

Don Antonio nodded as he brought the musket back down. 'English made,' he said. 'Tower pattern.' He looked at Pringle and Hanley in turn. 'What do you expect me to do with this?'

One of the boys giggled at their confusion, until Don Antonio silenced him with a glance. Pringle was annoyed. The lad had such smooth features, an almost effeminate air, and he did not liked being mocked by such a creature. It was hard to understand what two children were doing carrying arms. The other boy looked a little older, and his expression was wooden.

'I say again, what do you expect me to do with this musket?' The chieftain's expression was stern and proud, but did not seem hostile.

'Shoot Frenchmen,' Hanley suggested.

'But for how long?' Don Antonio said. He gave a thin smile, like a teacher disappointed in a pupil. He looked at a bale of cartridges that Murphy held up for inspection. 'Your muskets fire a bigger ball than our own, or those of the French. So we cannot fire your ammunition from our guns. We can put our cartridges in your muskets, but the ball will be loose and will not fire so well.'

'We could bring you enough new muskets for everyone, and more ammunition.' Hanley responded quickly, while Pringle was

37

too busy thinking how obvious this was and was depressed that no one had thought of it in planning their mission.

'You could, but could you also assure me that there would always be enough, wherever and whenever I needed them? I cannot amass great stores or magazines and leave them in a safe place, because there are no safe places. I must always be able to move. Do you see?'

'Yes,' Hanley said, and Pringle nodded in agreement.

'Good, then next time bring me loose powder, lead for balls, good flints – you English make the best – and shoes. Sometimes they are more important than guns. If you want to bring muskets, pistols and ammunition then bring me Spanish or French ones. You understand?'

'Yes, I believe we can help you in that way.' Hanley looked pleased by El Blanco's confidence in receiving aid from the British in future.

'Good. Now come with me and I will show you what we do.' Pringle was surprised at the prospect of moving so suddenly. He was even more surprised when Don Antonio spun around and kissed the boy who had giggled.

'Good God,' Billy said before he could stop himself, but it was a long embrace and a good minute before the couple parted. Don Antonio's lover smiled and then spoke in a light voice so obviously female that at last he understood.

'Good God,' he said more softly this time, baffled that he had not seen the two 'boys' for what they were from the very beginning. In spite of the short hair they were obviously young women, and pretty women at that, even if the silent one had no softness about her gaze.

'May I present my wife, Paula, and her sister Guadalupe.' The British officers bowed again. The sister gave the slightest acknowledgement, while Don Antonio's wife presented her hand to be kissed.

'They fight with you?' Pringle could not help asking after the pleasantries had been exchanged.

'With me sometimes,' the chieftain said lightly, 'but I am

pleased to say that usually they fight for me. Now, gather your things and we shall go.'

Dawn was still a few hours away when the whole troop filed out of the dell by a different, even narrower and more difficult path than the one they had used to come in. Guerrillas who knew the way led the riding mules for the three redcoats. More mules and a number of horses were waiting in a little valley outside, as were more fighters. Altogether there must have been some fifty men in the band, half of them mounted. Don Antonio had a beautiful Andalusian, and stopped to talk to the animal and caress its face before he mounted. The two girls rode smaller ponies, and both sat easily in the saddle, riding astride like men, their booted feet in the big stirrups favoured in the south.

Pringle had ridden with guerrilleros before, and so the quiet efficiency of the group did not surprise him. There were no shouted orders, no formality, but the whole band moved with a sense of purpose. Carlos Velasco rode with the two British officers and explained that when they arrived his cousin had been out scouting after reports that a French column was making for a pass a few leagues away. Now he had returned, assured by the leaders in the nearest villages that men were gathering to mount an ambush. El Blanco would help them, and hoped that two or three other bands would join him – he mentioned a number of names, all of which were new to both Pringle and Hanley.

'It would be good to meet with them,' Hanley said.

'If they come. I think they will, but you can never be sure,' Carlos explained. That was the big difference with the north. There many partisan leaders led bands numbering hundreds, sometimes even thousands, formed as the little groups coalesced into ever bigger commands. Here in the south that had not happened. Pringle did not know whether this was a reflection of the rugged landscape in Andalusia or the independent temperament of its inhabitants.

'Are the serranos coming out in great numbers from the mountain villages?'

'Serranos?' Carlos looked puzzled for a moment. 'Ah, I

39

understand, you mean the mountain folk. They call themselves crusaders. After all, this is where the last Moors were chased from the soil of Spain.'

Pringle wondered whether all of them had gone. Some of the locals were much darker complexioned than other Spaniards. Still, the little they had seen of the land had an exotic look, which he thought might resemble North Africa, and perhaps the impression was simply the natural consequence of similar climate. He had enough sense to realise that proposing either idea was scarcely tactful and so kept silent.

There was no mist this morning, and they rode, winding through valleys and over some gentler hills, until the sky grew ever more pink, and the sun rose magnificently over the crests ahead of them. Soon afterwards Pringle spotted something white in the grass beside the path they were following. Closer up he saw it was the naked body of a man, birds pecking at his eyes and the marks of wounds all over his chest. A few scraps of torn uniform were scattered near by, enough to show that he was a French officer.

'They caught him last night. Must have thought he had a better chance of sneaking past without an escort.'

One of the guerrilleros spat at the corpse as he rode past. Another jabbed with his lance.

'Not fit to be dung on the soil of Spain,' the man said.

Carlos looked down at the body with no sign of emotion when they passed.

'He was carrying orders confirming that the convoy is on its way, coming from Ronda and going to the coast. They wanted the garrisons there to send out a force to meet them.' He gave a wicked grin. 'I fear they will be disappointed. But it is their own fault. Sending no more than two hundred men to escort a convoy!'

'What is the convoy carrying?' Pringle asked, suddenly curious.

'Who can say? Supplies perhaps, or men from the hospital?' The guerrilla was matter-of-fact, but Pringle felt a chill at the thought of ambushing sick and wounded men. Please God, let it be supplies, he wished.

Soon afterwards they saw the first 'crusaders', a dozen or so men in broad sombreros and green velvet jackets, gaudy with silver buttons and colourful lace. Several had fine white stockings under the cross-lacing of their sandals.

'They like to put on their finest clothes to kill the French,' Carlos said. The men carried all sorts of weapons from captured muskets to ancient fowling pieces. More and more villagers were gathering, some groups numbering robed friars and monks among them, with a cluster of fifty or so all following a banner depicting the Virgin. A few carried nothing more than a pitchfork or scythe as a weapon, a couple merely bags full of heavy stones, but most had some form of firearm. Soon there were hundreds of them, swarming across the hillsides. There were women and children among them, most unarmed, but a few with muskets, and all in all it was unlike any army Pringle had ever seen, including the guerrilla bands of the north.

The mounted partisans soon split off under the leadership of El Blanco. Pringle was sorry to see the two girls go with him, although as they trotted away the motion was certainly a pleasing one, their hips and thighs rising and falling. It was strange to see women's legs as they rode, at once unnerving and arousing.

Carlos Velasco led the men on foot and took the redcoats with him. He left them up on a high crest, with a fine view down to where a deep valley opened into a wider plain.

'You are here to watch,' he said firmly. 'So wait until we return.' Then he took his men down the slopes and left them. Knots of crusaders moved past them, following the guerrilleros down the hillside. A few of the priests, some older men and most of the women and children settled down to sit as spectators on the slope, creating a strange air of festival.

Nothing happened for some time, and Pringle felt the lack of sleep catching up with him. Sergeant Murphy looked as fresh as always, and Hanley was keyed up with the excitement he sensed

41

around them, but Billy was weary and they raised no objection when he wrapped himself in his cloak and went to sleep.

Murphy shook him awake. 'I think you will want to see this, sir.'

The sun was a good deal higher and so he must have been asleep for more than an hour. Pringle took a sip of water from his canteen, and splashed some more over his face. He rubbed his chin, regretting that it was raw with stubble and that there was no time to shave, and went up to where Hanley sat on a rock, nibbling at a pastry.

'There are some more in the basket,' he said.

Pringle did not feel hungry and simply sat down beside his friend. 'It seems an odd way to witness a battle.'

'Though with much to recommend it,' Hanley said cheerfully.

To their left the valley curved towards them, for several hundred yards running through a steep gully. Above it were rocky slopes, often rising to little crests and peaks and filled with the dark shapes of the crusaders. After that the path weaved around between low hillocks, coming towards them, until it abruptly went down into the bottom of the much wider valley heading towards the sea. From this distance the Mediterranean looking a barely deeper blue than the sky. Pringle followed a big bird of prey as it cruised high, climbing on the hot air currents and scanning the land beneath for prey.

'There they are!' Murphy was standing behind them, pointing at the approaching French column. Pringle took out his telescope, pushed his spectacles up on to his forehead and peered through the lens. It was a shame Williams was not here, since his glass was more powerful, but even with the limited magnification, he could see a group of French cavalrymen coming along the narrow valley towards the gully. They wore black shakos, brown jackets and sky-blue trousers, and even though he could not see the details of their uniform he knew that they were hussars. Ahead of them a few men walked on foot, infantry skirmishers to protect the column.

Puffs of smoke appeared all along the hillside, the dull reports following on a few moments later as the sound reached them. The crusaders, eager to punish the hated enemy, had opened fire at absurdly long range. Pringle did not see any Frenchmen fall, but it did not really matter at this stage. El Blanco and the other partisans planned to attack the French from the rear. Unable to retreat, the little column would have to push ever deeper into the valley.

It did not happen quickly. The French skirmishers fanned out and popped back at the serranos as they hid behind rocks, while the Spanish replied. A dozen or so of the infantrymen charged at the nearest hillock. All but a few of its occupants fled, and the handful who stayed were shot down or stabbed by the angry attackers. Then the Frenchmen on the little hilltop were deluged with fire, unable to move higher up. In the meantime the column pushed forward. Pringle counted around fifty hussars in the lead.

'They are the Second Regiment, the Chamborant Hussars,' Hanley said. 'I remember them from Medellín,' he added, recalling that ghastly day when the Spanish cavalry broke and the French horsemen rode down the unprotected infantry, slaughtering thousands.

This was bad cavalry country, and as the hussars rode into the gully it became impossible for them to fight back. The crusaders were able to get close, firing again and again, and in spite of all their attempts no rider could make his horse climb its steep sides. Some of the hussars squibbed back with pistols or carbines, but they could see no more than the heads and shoulders of their tormentors. Pringle saw the first horses and riders fall. Some infantrymen were also down. He watched one man writhing in agony, saw another run out to his aid, but then the second man was down as well, lying unmoving like a sack of old clothes in the middle of the path.

The main part of the column was visible now, a dozen or so wagons. A score of infantry marched in formation ahead of them, wearing the sandy-coloured light coats so beloved of the French line regiments. Twice as many brought up the rear and a few dozen were scattered protectively on either side of the wagons.

As they came towards the gully the firing redoubled. More and more men dropped, the tails of their long coats flapping. The men at the front had broken up, spreading out to seek what little cover there was.

'Poor bastards,' Murphy said softly. Pringle nodded. Like the sergeant he found himself instinctively siding with the beleaguered infantry.

'Well, they should not have come, should they.' Hanley spoke with surprising brutality.

Pringle focused his glass on one of the wagons. Something moved in it and he saw a man raise himself up. Dear God, it is wounded, he thought.

That moment a bugle sounded. The hussars spurred their mounts and shot forward, galloping down the length of the gully towards the more open valley. Crusaders screamed in rage at them and fired. One horse dropped, its rider cartwheeling high before slamming with sickening force against a boulder. Another rode on, saddle empty, and its rider staggered dazed along the path until a handful of Spaniards jumped down and clubbed him to death.

'Bloody cavalry.' Murphy's tone was scathing. The horsemen left the infantry behind, and if Pringle could see that the hussars were doing no good where they were he could still imagine the despair of their comrades on foot as they saw the gaudily dressed cavalrymen escaping.

That escape was far from certain. As they came through the gully and the valley widened, first dozens and then hundreds of serranos spilled off the slopes and surged towards the fleeing horsemen.

'Look, there is Don Antonio!' Hanley had spotted the guerrilla leader leading a file of horsemen over one of the lower rises behind the French column and down into the valley. He halted some one hundred and fifty yards behind the convoy's rearguard, and more and more horsemen formed around him. Pringle thought that there were at least sixty, with more coming all the time, and that must mean that other guerrilla leaders had joined him as he had planned. Although scarcely regular cavalry – no two were armed identically and their horses were of all sizes – the mounted partisans threatened to ride down the French infantry, making the rearguard cluster together in a tight circle, bayonets ready to fend off the horsemen. So they stood and so they died, offering a target that even the wild crusaders would gradually whittle down. More and more of these risked jumping into the gully, pouncing on any isolated Frenchmen and shooting or knifing them.

'Like watching a bird die,' Murphy said softly.

Pringle glanced back at the sergeant, moved by the sadness in his voice. This was not the war that the officer knew, and he could not say that he liked to see it.

The trumpet sounded again, its notes urgent. Out in the wider valley, pursued by a loose crowd of serranos, the French hussars suddenly wheeled round and charged. The villagers stopped in their tracks, the cries dying in their throats. A few had loaded muskets and fired, but no horse or man fell. Pringle could imagine the drumming of hoofs, the hussars standing tall in their stirrups, cheering as they brought their curved sabres forward ready to lunge.

'They won't stand.'

Pringle saw that Murphy was right, and had the guilty sense that he was pleased to see the enemy soldiers gain their revenge. Already the serranos were turning to flee, but for many it was too late, and now the hussars were among them. They were too far away to hear the screams, but saw the curved sabres glittering as they chopped down. Bodies littered the valley floor behind the ragged lines of charging hussars.

The French chased the crusaders back to the mouth of the valley. Even then, a few enraged hussars tried to ride after them, only to be shot or cut from their saddles by the crowds that clustered in the broken ground. On the plain the hussars were masters, but they could not fight amid the rock-strewn hillocks and slopes. Again the trumpet sounded, and the forty or so hussars re-formed out of range of the peasants. They waited for a while, heard the fire slackening from back down the valley and must have known what that meant. Their infantry had died or was dying and there was nothing they could do. Eventually the hussars wheeled again, and set off down the road towards the coast. They left more than twice their number of bodies dotted across the valley floor.

Pringle could see that it was nearly over. The circle of soldiers was now a pile of bodies, the few survivors being hunted out from their hiding places. He focused his glass on Don Antonio, and watched him lead his riders along the row of abandoned wagons. Behind the chief was one of the young women, her black cloak and clothes clear. He watched as a man stirred in the back of one of the wagons, pulling himself up with his arms clutching the wooden side. The girl produced a pistol, pressed it against the man's chest and shot him.

On the slopes below them many of the women and other spectators were heading down towards the scene of victory. Most had long knives in their hands.

Billy Pringle snapped his glass shut. He did not want to see any more.

4

An hour or so later, some seventy miles further east along the coast and about five miles out to sea, Lieutenant Williams sat once again in the black-painted gig and enjoyed the momentary calm now that they were in the lee of the other ship. Up close the frigate looked immense, and at one hundred and forty-six feet seven inches it was almost half as long again as the *Sparrowhawk*. It towered above them, its three great masts so high that the men in the tops looked liked dolls. Williams wondered how they managed on a calm day, let alone in any sort of blow.

'Lively now, show them how it's done,' hissed the coxswain to the gig's crew as they worked the oars. 'Keep it steady.' Although it was not obvious, all of them knew that they were being watched, every action examined and dissected in the eager hope of seeing an imperfection, anything to confirm this ship's company's belief in its own superiority.

Captain Edward Pringle seemed oblivious, but once again everyone knew that he was missing nothing. Formally his rank was Master and Commander of the eighteen-gun *Sparrowhawk*, but convention dictated that he be called captain. The frigate's captain was a true captain, a post captain, confident that, so long as he remained alive and avoided disgrace, he would one day hoist his pennant as an admiral. Both sorts of captain wielded far more power than their namesakes in the army, and even a commander like Billy Pringle's older brother ranked as a major. On board their own ship, a captain's will was law in a way unimaginable in the army.

'She is a handsome craft and a sweet sailor,' Edward Pringle said, breaking the silence he had maintained as they rowed over in answer to the signal 'Officers to repair on board'. Williams still did not know why he was included in the party, his only guide a gruff 'You may be of some use' from *Sparrowhawk*'s captain.

The gig lurched as they once again felt the swell, but Williams made himself look up at the stern gallery of the ship. It was painted black, decorated in white and gold, and with the name *TOPAZE* painted in immaculately even and perfectly rounded golden letters above the row of seven windows.

'Say what you like about the French, but they build damned fine ships.' The captain smiled at Williams' evident surprise, almost the first trace of humour he had shown in their brief acquaintance. 'We had her from them back in ninety-three. Have even built some thirty-twos following her lines, but they never quite look the same. Too cramped, of course, far too cramped for comfort on a long voyage, but truly beautiful.'

Williams was unsure that he would employ the word, and yet could see the elegance of the *Topaze*'s lines and appreciate the training, ritual and taut discipline which kept a working and fighting ship in such a state of neatness and order. He could also, even though they were now windward of her, still catch a trace of the smells of fresh paint, tar and all the odours inevitable on even the cleanest of ships when more than two hundred men lived so close together.

Born in Cardiff, a few years later Williams' widowed mother had taken the family to Bristol, with its far bigger port, and had run a boarding house, mostly for the masters and mates of merchantmen who had no family. Later still, he became an apprentice clerk in a shipping office, and so the world of cordage, canvas, spars and chandlers' supplies was one he knew well. Although being on the coast was familiar and reassuring, Williams did not especially like the sea – or perhaps it was better to say that it seemed not to care for him – for he felt queasy at the gentlest motion and had suffered greatly on the transport ships which had carried the regiment to war and home again. It was far better aboard the *Sparrowhawk*, and he guessed that men-of-war were generally better handled and more stable than the old tubs hired to move soldiers. The milder waters of the Mediterranean no doubt also played a part, for, apart from one squall, the winds had been light. Williams could not yet claim to have embraced life at sea, but had to admit that this recent voyage was at least tolerable, rather than a prolonged test of endurance which he wished only to end.

'Gently now.' Without another order, the coxswain brought the boat alongside. The crew shipped oars, and after the softest of bumps the man in the bow fastened a long boathook into a ring on the frigate's side. Captain Pringle was already on his feet and went up the steps cut in the side of the *Topaze* with practised ease. He was a small man, thin of face and narrow of lip, so unlike his big, plump younger brother that Williams struggled to see any similarity. When he mentioned this to his friend, Billy had joked that 'Yes, it was a puzzle, but they do say I have a quite startling resemblance to the old baker's boy!' It was hard to imagine the older brother making any joke, let alone one with such vulgar implications. At twenty-eight, Edward Pringle looked older, although some of this was the air of stern omniscience he assumed as captain of his own ship. He also looked capable, and in this regard at least the brothers were alike.

Williams could not actually see the captain climb on to the deck, but heard the pipe whistling. Lieutenant Reynolds, *Sparrowhawk*'s only other officer, went next, just a little more slowly, even though the stocky, red-faced man must have been at least forty, his dark hair streaked with grey. Things were better than in the past, but even so unlucky and poorly connected officers in His Majesty's Navy could find promotion painfully slow, even in comparison to the army. The coxswain gestured for Williams to go next, just in case the soldier had forgotten the proper order of things. He had come clumsily down into the boat, foot slipping on one of the steps, and was determined not to make a similar mistake. Deliberation was likely to make things worse, and so he tried not to think, bounding from the boat and trusting to instinct.

His left knee struck hard against the timbers of *Topaze* and bounced out, his other foot was waving in empty space, while both hands clawed at the same step. Somehow one boot and then the other found toeholds and then he began to climb.

'Ruddy lobsters,' a voice whispered faintly from among the gig's crew.

'Hush, damn your eyes,' the coxswain said almost as quietly.

Williams ignored them and climbed. As he came nearer the top the side of the ship curved steeply inwards, another feature of French design which came as a great relief to the redcoat officer. Finally on deck, he found himself marvelling at the sheer bulk of the mainmast just ahead of him and the sense of being almost enclosed in endless webs of rigging and ropes. They were led aft towards the quarterdeck, where presentations were made to Captain Hope, his two lieutenants and a very young lieutenant of marines. Williams was glad that he had had time to don his good jacket, white breeches and boots, for this was a smart gathering. It was widely believed that the Royal Marines were always especially keen to outshine any redcoats from the army, and at least today he was able to give a good account of himself.

With introductions made, they processed down a companionway on to the gun deck. Williams had already passed several of the stubby carronades, the barrel half the length of a cannon, but far thicker and throwing two or three times the weight of shot. At close range these heavy smashers were devastating, but on the gun deck *Topaze* had conventional twelve-pounders, as big as the biggest cannon ever used by the army in battle. There were thirteen on either side, and these could throw their shot a mile or more. It was a humbling thought that even this fifth-rate ship, too small to serve in the line-of-battle of a great fleet action, could still fire a greater weight of shot than all the field guns of Lord Wellington's army lined up wheel to wheel.

Topaze's guns were silent at the moment, barrels black and carriages red-brown with recent paint, and it was not really the heavy armament which made a man-of-war so different from a merchant ship or transport. For Williams it was partly the Navy's dedication to – even obsession with – cleanliness. As they came down from the quarterdeck he saw dozens of sailors crouching, pulling at ropes to drag holystones – heavy blocks of Portland stone several feet in length – to grind the sand sprinkled on the planking of the lower deck, rubbing it smooth. *Sparrowhawk* holystoned the deck only on Sundays and Thursdays – the noise and sacred respect given to the work made it impossible even for passengers to ignore – and so he guessed Captain Hope must have a different routine on his ship. Everything was neatly stowed, where possible scrubbed, painted or polished until it shone, and there was also an abundance of everything. The ropes on a merchantman almost always looked old, their owners even less keen than their Lords of the Admiralty to spend money keeping their ships in trim. There was an abundance too of people, and in the end this for Williams was the key distinction. Men-of-war were crowded, bustling places in a near-constant state of activity – indeed, of many distinct activities carried on side by side. A merchant ship never had a big enough crew to attend to so many different things.

It was a world of its own, Williams decided, and one in which he remained a stranger, with a constant sense that he was in the way. No one said anything to him as they went through the doors, in his case instinctively ducking for he had more than once hit his head on the low doorways of *Sparrowhawk*. He was relieved to find that the frigate offered far more space, and when they came to the captain's day cabin, it seemed spacious indeed, bright sunlight coming through the stern windows he had seen from outside as they had rowed across.

Captain Hope came swiftly to the matter in hand, assembling them around the long table on which a number of charts were spread and weighted down.

'Gentlemen, as you know, tonight I intend to raid the harbour at Las Arenas.'

Williams had not known, but since he was supposed to be on shore with the others there was no reason for anyone to have told him. No one else gave the slightest hint of surprise. Instead they had the same predatory eagerness of the young captain. All of the officers, save for the marine – a gap-toothed fellow named Jones, whose mouth hung permanently open – had spent the greater part of their lives at sea. Captain Hope was twenty-three and had been made post more than two years ago. Reynolds had told him this, in a tone mingling admiration with the bitter disappointment of a man who had been a lieutenant for more than a decade. A post captain would rise steadily in seniority, but the prospects of a lieutenant put on shore on half-pay were a good deal less rosy.

'I had hoped the *Rambler* would have reached us, but there is no sign of her, and we must seize this opportunity while it is offered.' Williams had heard mention of the other brig, and understood that she and *Topaze* frequently cruised together.

'We cannot wait. At dawn this morning I stood off and took a look at the place and the harbour was busy. There are usually half a dozen or so privateers there, but today there are twice as many masts as usual. Some may be prizes, some merchantmen supplying Bonaparte's army, but there is a schooner and a couple of xebecs I am sure belong to Bavastro.'

That caused a stir, and Hope let them smile and chatter.

'He is an Italian rogue,' Reynolds said to Williams. 'Keeps a squadron with letters of marque and preys on shipping all along the coast of Spain. They do say Napoleon has given him medal after medal.'

'Yes, we all know that rascal, and it seems the report that some of his men have come farther west than usual is true. I have seen the schooner before, although have never been close enough to catch her. She is pierced for twelve guns, although who knows how many she actually mounts.'

'Can we be sure they are still there?' Edward Pringle asked.

'A good question, and as you would guess I cannot give a certain answer. Most must be, or we would have seen them leave. *Rambler* should be coming from east-nor-east down the coast, so there is always a chance that she will catch any of them trying to slip out that way. But if we wait longer then the odds are that more of them will get away, and so many fast, small craft will be the devil of a job to catch.

'Therefore we shall go in tonight in boats, cut out as many as we can and burn the rest. We shall need both your boats, Captain Pringle, as well as our own. There are two batteries guarding the harbour, and we must deal with them. Now you have all done this sort of thing before, so I do not need to tell you that we must move fast and everyone must know the tasks they are to perform.' The young captain paused for a moment, smiling. 'My apologies, Mr Williams, I am speaking out of turn and forgetting that you are not a mariner. It is perhaps unfair to ask you this in company, but from what Captain Pringle has told me, it appeared safe to anticipate your answer. With *Rambler* still absent and several prize crews not yet returned, we have fewer officers than I would like, and it is leaders we need on a night like this. Would you do us the honour of joining our little enterprise?'

It was a courteous enough request, but the unfairness was also obvious as the others all turned to look at him. Sergeant Dobson had strong opinions about volunteering and would no doubt stretch the boundaries of discipline to their limit in expressing them. The veteran had an equally strong sense of pride and a decidedly tribal attachment to the reputation of the company, the battalion and the army as a whole. Expecting and sympathising with the complaints, Williams knew that there was no real choice, both because of their duty and his confidence that a request could surely become an order if required. All that remained was to accede with grace.

Williams straightened up, coming to attention. 'It will be an honour to serve under your command, sir,' he said, and then bowed.

'Excellent.' Captain Hope looked genuinely pleased. 'I trust we shall provide you with a diverting evening. Even if boarding ships is new to you, much of the fighting will be on shore and I doubt very much that you have much to learn on that score.'

Williams bowed again, but could think of nothing to say that would not sound a little pompous.

'Good, then that is settled.' The young captain looked down at the table. Presumably his command of the small flotilla granted him commodore's rank, if only fleetingly, but no one mentioned the title and the redcoat had not spotted a pennant as he came aboard.

'Now if you would care to look at this plan of the harbour,' Hope said, and Williams craned his neck to see better. Las Arenas itself lay half a mile back from the mouth of a river, a place which before the war had thrived from fishing and the coastal trade. Its name came from the sandy beaches on either side, and the sandbanks which made the channel narrower than it seemed, and closed the port off to any really big ship. An old sea wall and jetty formed a harbour just in front of the village, but the estuary opened into a partly enclosed bay that was a natural anchorage. Most of the ships were anchored in the bay, although several were usually along or near the jetty. The batteries were both marked, one on the southern headland enclosing the anchorage and the other guarding the jetty itself.

'It's a tough little nut,' Captain Hope declared, 'and this is how we shall crack it.' He slammed his palm down on the table and began to explain.

They went in early, before the moon rose. Williams was in the leftmost division, formed from *Sparrowhawk*'s cutter and gig, a rope linking them so that they kept together during the long row in. Captain Pringle, Cassidy, a coxswain and sixteen sailors were crammed into the cutter. Williams, Dobson, a Midshipman Treadwell and *Sparrowhawk*'s gunner were in the gig, along with Corporal Milne, seven marines and six sailors. All of the sailors wore dark blue shirts or jackets. If they saw anyone this night who was not in blue or the scarlet and white of a marine then they were an enemy. To starboard, Captain Hope in his pinnace led the red and the black cutters from *Topaze*, some seventy officers and men divided between the boats. Williams could see Hope standing in the prow, searching ahead with the aid of a night glass. He could just see the outlines of the right division, with *Topaze*'s launch, gig and little jolly-boat filled with another fifty-five men. All the boats had just changed the men rowing. Half would now rest, and these men were to be the first to board or land on shore. Once they were nearer, the lines linking all the boats would be cast off as each went about its task.

Williams found the soft rhythmic slashing of the oar blades through the water restful, blending naturally with the gentle slap of the tide against the boats. It was still coming in, although he could sense the flow of the river emptying into the sea. They had already passed one of the sandbanks, a darker shape in the water, surprisingly small and low compared to the ones he had grown up seeing in the Bristol Channel. The tide was also far less formidable, and he had to concentrate as he tried to gauge whether or not it had started to turn. They wanted it to be going out so that it was easier for them to float out the captured vessels. Not that those were his first concern. When the signal came, the gig would cast off and his party was to secure the battery near the jetty. Once there, they were to spike or otherwise render the cannon useless – Mr Prentice the Gunner had tinderbox, fuses and a small keg of powder as well as hammer and nails. After that, they were either to retire in the gig, join Captain Pringle on one of the prizes, or take or burn any other vessel which had not been otherwise dealt with.

'We must not be too prescriptive,' Captain Hope had said. 'Night actions are always confused, and it is better to have the freedom to seize any opportunity.' Williams suspected that Edward Pringle was less convinced and fonder of greater rigidity, but he said nothing and deferred to the senior officer.

There was such an assurance about the naval officers' manner that it was readily infectious. Given that a few men must stay with the gig, there were fifteen of them to overpower the guards and gunners in the battery and hold it against any reinforcement until it was destroyed. Williams had asked Reynolds about the likely number of crews on board the ships and other defenders near by and was amazed, even appalled, at the reply. At the very least, the attacking parties would face three or four times their own numbers.

'Privateers tend to have large complements,' the lieutenant explained. 'Their business is to capture ships, so they rely on boarding and swamping their opponents with numbers. No sense pounding a little brig to pieces if you intend to make it your own property.' There might well be regular troops as well. 'Bonaparte has sent contingents of naval gunners to man the coastal batteries, and there are usually a few soldiers about.'

Reynolds had sounded gloomy, but only because he was to be left to command the *Sparrowhawk*. The brig was to come closer to the estuary, ready to meet any enemy who tried to slip out. *Topaze* was to engage the battery on the headland if it opened fire, so that the enemy might suspect they were under a full assault by ships and not parties in boats.

The plan was bold, and Williams could not help feeling that anyone proposing a similar attack on land would be dismissed as a reckless fool. Yet the sailors spoke with perfect confidence. They had all done such things before, of course, and belonged to a service which had been doing such things for decades, more often than not – indeed, far more often – with great success. As yet the army could not match such complacent expectation of victory, but then nor could it boast so many successful actions. It was just a few days since they had sailed past Cape Trafalgar, Williams and the other soldiers almost as deeply moved as the sailors to be so near such a hallowed place – if the ever-moving waters could be called a place. It was not quite five years since Nelson had fallen at the moment of triumph, and since then no French fleet had dared to challenge the King's Navy in battle. It was not the same on land, and Napoleon's legions crushed enemy after enemy. Under Lord Wellington the army had won a few battles, but somehow it always seemed to end with retreat.

'It's not really about numbers,' Reynolds had assured him. 'We will catch them by surprise.'

When Williams suggested that *Topaze*'s early morning reconnaissance of the port may have put the enemy on their guard, the naval lieutenant was dismissive. 'Oh, we are always cruising along these coasts and peering into harbours. It makes them nervous, I am sure, but is no sign that we are actually coming for them. No, my dear fellow, I only wish I was going with you,' he had finished, eager to be about his duties. 'Good luck!'

The eight boats rowed on, the lines between them hanging limply because it was never intended for the leading boats to tow. A big moon began to rise, and at first its brightness seemed to dim the stars. Williams knew that it was an illusion. He could still see the silhouettes of the other boats clearly. Captain Hope was still standing in the prow of the pinnace, staring through his glass, and in the nearer boats he could recognise other faces – there was Jones of the marines, mouth open. Ahead and to the right Williams began to make out the masts of some of the vessels moored in the bay. It was hard to believe that the raiders were not clearly visible to even the drowsiest sentry on board ship or guarding the batteries. He tried not to imagine gun commanders blowing softly on the match held in their portfires, the rods which allowed them to fire off a cannon at arm's length, avoiding the recoil savage enough to shatter flesh and bone. If the batteries opened now, then it would be at long range, but it was also a very long way for them to row back.

The boats rowed on, the push of the river growing stronger, and he guessed the tide had turned. The moon climbed higher, its distorted reflection long on the smooth water, and the whole world became tinted with silver. Williams could hear the little noises of men shifting in their seats, adjusting equipment or trying to get comfortable, and all the while the steady sound of the oars.

The familiar excitement was growing now, as was the equally familiar fear. Williams had seen shot and shell mutilate horribly, turning a healthy man in the blink of an eye into a tortured remnant, dying, or doomed to long years of helplessness and suffering. He dreaded the thought of losing his eyes, almost as much as losing his manhood. Suddenly an even more immediate fear of drowning seized him. There would be the thrum of a cannonball, the shattering of timbers as the gig was holed, and then the darkness of the cold water dragging down and down, lungs bursting as he tried not to breathe in.

Waiting was always worse, and this slow progress towards danger was unnerving. On land, he would have duties to perform, and would know the men he commanded, which somehow made it easier to remain calm, for their esteem mattered to him. Most of the men in the boat were still strangers. It was tempting to whisper encouragement, but that would too easily sound nervous, and nervousness was contagious. The same was true of obsessive checking of his weapons. He knew that the pistol tucked in his sash was loaded, and that his sword was ready to slide free of the scabbard. Its blade, and that of the boarding axe resting on his lap, was honed to a wickedly sharp edge. The axe was short and heavy, and some sailors liked to call them tomahawks because they were much like the weapons used by the savage tribes of America. Its job was to cut rope and tackle as much as to fight, but he suspected it would be a brutal and effective weapon if the need came.

'Prepare to cast off.' The voice came low from ahead of them. They were getting close.

'Cast off.'

The first gun fired.

58

5

The flash came from the top of the headland, the crack of the shot following a little later, and Williams thought he saw a flicker of movement in the air some way behind them. He did not hear the ball tearing through the air, which meant that it was not close.

There was an instant of hesitation, a collective drawing of breath. 'Row! Row!' Captain Hope's voice was clear, but the spell was already broken and men bent their backs, pulling harder at the oars. The pinnace led the central division towards the vessels anchored in the bay. These were close now, especially a big shape which was most likely the schooner. Beyond them, the rightmost division split, some making for the battery, others the privateers. Captain Pringle kept on towards the harbour, but Treadwell shifted the tiller so that the gig veered towards the beach further to the left. Williams could see a white, almost glowing line where the surf washed against the shore, and above it the pale line of sand.

A cannon flamed again, quickly followed by another. He heard the thrumming as one of the balls punched above their heads, but the shots were still going high and long. Perhaps it was hard for the gunners to see down from the hill, and the sea looked darker than it seemed to him.

'Come on, put your backs into it,' Treadwell said, keeping his voice steady. Men grunted as they pulled at the long oars, rowing faster, but keeping the practised rhythm.

Another gun thundered, much louder than the others, and Williams turned to look ahead and saw two more flashes as the battery by the jetty joined in. Captain Hope had told them that each battery mounted three cannon and it was reassuring to see that his information was correct.

A ball skimmed the wave, throwing up two spurts of foam fifty yards behind them before it vanished. The headland battery fired again.

'Lively now! Keep going!' Treadwell's voice cracked for a moment. He was twenty-three, no longer a boy, and so dark was the hair on his chin that he looked permanently unshaven, but for a moment he sounded shrill. He coughed, clearing his throat. 'Come on, lads!' he called more evenly.

Williams pointed. 'Take us more to the left – I mean larboard.' There was no sense in landing right under the battery. Treadwell either saw the sense or obeyed the tone through habit. As the boat turned the low waves rolled into it with greater force, but Williams scarcely noticed and his stomach did not complain. Fine spray washed over them and he tasted the salt on his lips.

The jetty battery fired again, the noise even louder, and one of the guns rang as it went off, as if a bell chimed at the same instant. The balls ripped the air over their heads, and they felt the draught wash over them before plumes of water marked their strikes more than a hundred yards past them.

'Why are they firing so wide?' Williams asked Mr Prentice. The gunner cupped his hand to hear better. The headland battery fired again. 'Why they all shooting so high?' Williams asked.

'Can't see us properly, and don't want to hit their own ships!' Prentice shouted back.

There were shouts now, more cannon and also the sharper reports of muskets. Williams looked to see flashes and movement around the outline of the schooner.

'That's the captain,' Prentice yelled in the Welshman's ear. Williams suspected that years with the guns had not helped the man's hearing. A long, low rumble like distant thunder rolled over the bay. 'That'll be *Topaze*,' the gunner shouted, attuned at least to that noise. 'That'll give the buggers something to think about!'

The keel grated on sand as the gig ran ashore. Williams had

not realised they were so close. He turned, pushing himself up, and saw that they were in the surf.

'Follow me!' he called, and sprang over the side, splashing into two feet of surprisingly cold water, and heading towards the sand. His legs felt sluggish as they fought their way through the weight of the water. The beach was a narrow strip of whitish sand, empty apart from themselves and three small fishing boats drawn up on to the land. Williams' sword rattled as it rocked against his leg, and then the sound was drowned by the battery firing again. It was two hundred yards away, the shape clear against the sky. He could see an earthwork about six feet high, the rampart gently sloped and shaped like a half-circle. Another gun fired and its flame showed the deep-cut embrasure. The wall looked thick, intended to deflect or resist shot hurled at it from the sea and not face an opponent on land. Williams could not see whether there was a ditch in front of the rampart, but guessed that there was since it had surely provided most of the spoil for the wall. Even so, it did not look too difficult to climb.

The officer led the party along the beach, keeping below the fort. There was no challenge. Every couple of minutes the three guns slammed shot out into the empty bay, but no one seemed to be watching them. Williams halted his men when they were fifty yards from the battery. Dobson and one of the marines knelt, muskets ready, watching the earthwork, while he divided the others into two groups. Treadwell, with the stolid gunner and the reliable Corporal Milne to back him up, would take the marines and work round to the left, looking for the entrance.

'There must be one at the back. Even if it is closed off then a pound to a penny the rampart will be lower there,' he explained. Midshipman Treadwell and the gunner simply nodded and did not question his right to give orders. 'Once you find it, then go straight in.'

At the same time Williams would take Dobson and five sailors and go over the walls, scrambling through an embrasure if it proved too difficult to climb elsewhere. If discovered then each party was to cheer, and that was the signal for the others to press their own attack as soon as they could. That was it, with a simplicity even the Navy might appreciate.

'Good, now let's let those gunners see their worst nightmare!' He grinned. Treadwell smiled in response, but the other men's faces showed nothing apart from the tautness of anticipation.

He gave the other party a minute before he stood and gestured for his own men to come on. Williams had his pistol in his right hand and his axe in the left. Dobson had his musket, the long, slim bayonet already slotted around into place on the muzzle. Two of the sailors also had muskets, two pistols and the other man one of the short pikes designed for boarding actions. All had cutlasses in their belts.

They walked forward. A big gun fired from the nearest embrasure, and for an instant the red light was almost as bright as day and the line of men cast long shadows behind them. His eyes adjusted slowly back to the night, but Williams was sure he could see something moving above the rampart.

'Come on,' he said, and jogged forward, boots crunching in the sand. Flecks of sand were stuck to his soaked trousers, and he hoped none had got into the lock of the pistol. There was definitely something there, a man kneeling on top of the rampart, and surely he must see them. The dark figure seemed to be waving his arms.

'Charge, boys! Charge!' Williams bellowed the order and then turned the shout into a yell of anger. He ran, flailing his axe with the left hand. The men were beside him, screaming out a challenge to the enemy. The man on the rampart fired, a sudden flash before the puff of smoke blotted him from view. There was a thin mist of dark, stinking smoke from the big guns drifting slowly towards them and they ran through it.

Williams did not know whether anyone had been hit, but had heard no cry. He ran on, reached the ditch and jumped down. It was shallow, flat-bottomed, and not well maintained because there were grass and brambles growing in it. The man on the rampart was gone, so he must have dropped back inside, and Williams' momentum took him up the sloping side of the main earthwork. The top was flat and four or five feet wide. One of the big guns fired and in a flash he saw the teams of seven or eight men toiling to serve each of the three big cannons. They were in uniforms which looked black, but most wore shakos and had epaulettes on their shoulders, which meant that they were regular gunners and no privateers. Men with bayonets glinting were coming towards him. A man just a few feet away stared up in horror, his ramrod thrust down into the barrel of a musket. Beside him another pulled the hammer back to cock his own firelock and raised it.

Without thinking Williams straightened his right arm and fired his pistol, the flame so close that it touched the Frenchman's face just as the ball punched a neat hole in his forehead and flung the soldier backwards. Men were rushing up on to the rampart either side of him, Dobson closest, and Williams leapt down, knocking the other soldier off his feet as both of them fell into the dust.

'Shoot the buggers!' Dobson's voice was loud over the chaos. 'Fire!' The sergeant's musket went off, and sailors on either side fired muskets or pistols. One of the Frenchmen charging towards them dropped forward, another cried out in pain and let his musket fall as he clutched at his shoulder.

Williams rolled on top of the sentry on the ground, and then slammed the heavy pistol down on to the man's head, feeling his nose break. Blood gushed over the Frenchman's face, as Williams spun the pistol to reverse it and hit the man with the brass of the butt. The soldier went still. Men were leaping down and around them, but the French were still charging, and Williams saw the point of a bayonet jabbing at his face. He rolled sideways, turning on the ground near the man's legs, and swung the axe to slice through the top of his boot. The soldier was screaming, and Williams jerked the axe head free and chopped at the man's other leg, slicing deeply into the back of his knee. He pushed himself up as the man fell, shrieking.

A sailor was down, clubbed by the butt of a French musket, but another of the tars chopped down, slicing across the soldier's

63

face and destroying one of his eyes. A third *Sparrowhawk* appeared, the man with the boarding pike, and he stood over his mate, jabbing with the spear and driving the enemy away. A sailor with gold earrings and tattoos all over his bare forearms was fighting wildly, his blows not connecting, but driving the enemy away. The gunners were leaving their pieces now to repel the attackers. Dobson twisted his bayonet free of the soldier's stomach, letting the man slump down moaning, and then parried the cut of a short sword and stabbed the gunner in the throat. Williams was up, and sprang back as another gunner scythed a heavy trail-spike at him. The man was big, not wearing his jacket so that his white shirt was very bright in the darkness. His party were no longer cheering, each absorbed in the space a few feet around him, and the only sounds they made were grunts of effort or pain.

Williams wanted to switch the axe to his stronger hand, but, for a big man with a heavy iron bar in his hands, the gunner moved quickly. He swung the pistol as a club, brushing the man's arm, but with no real force, and the gunner managed to avoid the slice of the axe. The Frenchman raised the trail-spike, and Williams flung the heavy pistol into his face, forcing the man back a pace, and giving him time to shift the axe to his right hand. Another gunner came from his left, jabbing the butt-end of a carbine into the officer's face, and Williams leaned out of the way, grabbed hold of the firelock with his left hand and then swung the axe into the soldier's head. The blade sank in with a ghastly thunk, the resistance less than in a block of wood. It was stuck fast, and Williams hefted the dying soldier, pushing him hard into the big gunner.

There were cheers from the edge of the battery, shouts of victory which snapped the will of the French to fight on. They stepped back from the fighting and the British came on after them. Gunners screamed as Dobson and the sailors stabbed and sliced at them. Half a dozen of them fell in as many instants, the man with the tattoos almost slicing a gunner's head from his neck in a clumsy and brutal stroke of his cutlass. Midshipman Treadwell stared on appalled as the marines bayoneted as many more. Then the French were gone, jumping out of the embrasures and fleeing into the night, leaving behind a stillness that felt unreal and was broken only by the sad moans of the wounded.

'Dobson, Milne!' Williams called. 'Two sentries on the entrance and another three on the walls. Make sure they keep a good watch.'

The two NCOs went about the business.

'Mr Prentice?' Williams shouted for the benefit of the gunner. 'How many men do you need to spike the guns?'

'Two will be adequate, thank you, Lieutenant Williams. You, Dickinson, and you, McClean, come with me.'

Williams looked around. The noise of the other battles all round the bay was growing again, or perhaps he was simply noticing it. There seemed to be fighting on several of the vessels. He looked out through one the embrasures, careful in case any enemies were watching, but no shots came from the night. Just to the left of the last gun position was the wide mouth of the harbour and the sea wall and jetty beyond that. Shots flashed out from on board the nearest of the craft moored there, and there were shouts and the clash of steel on steel. With an effort he put his foot on the corpse and worked the boarding axe free.

'The captain will handle them all right,' Treadwell said, appearing beside him. The midshipman was still struggling for breath, and paled when he saw what Williams was doing. 'Hot work,' he gasped.

Williams finished and straightened up, looking back into the battery. The remaining sailors and marines had carefully lifted the wounded French. The tar who had been knocked down had a growing bruise, but seemed otherwise unscathed. He did a quick headcount, did not believe the result, and so went through it again.

'Truly remarkable,' he said at last, unable to resist the evidence of his eyes. 'We have no one badly hurt.' He looked out again. The sound of fighting coming from the craft moored alongside the jetty was slackening. Out in the bay, there was movement up in the shrouds of several ships. Then a jet of flame erupted from the top of the headland, a big explosion that could only be the powder magazine of the battery up there.

'Bravo,' Treadwell said, tiredness gone in his enthusiasm for destruction.

'Waste of good powder,' Prentice declared with clear disapproval, having come up behind them. 'Old Jonas, the gunner on *Topaze*, never can resist making a din.' Behind him one sailor drove a long nail down the touch-hole of the cannon, hitting it again and again until it would go no further. Then he hit it from the side bending the nail, before his mate sawed quickly through the weakened metal. 'All done, sir,' the gunner reported.

'Excellent, Mr Prentice,' Williams said. 'Now, I believe we can be going. Mr Treadwell, if you would be so good ...'

The midshipman was not paying attention.

'They're moving, look, they are moving!'

Several vessels were moving out, including the big schooner, topsails already set as they began to tack so that they could make for the mouth of the bay. Treadwell was far more excited to see two big, barge-like vessels pushing off from the jetty, both rigged fore and aft. Behind them, a red glow sprang up on the deck of another vessel, licked against the rigging, and spread rapidly.

'The captain's done it! He's done it!'

Flames appeared on yet another lugger further down the jetty. The two captured prizes edged out, coming slowly, the lead one towed by *Sparrowhawk*'s cutter and the other, smaller one lagging behind under sweeps. A volley rippled from a dozen muskets on the sea wall on this side of the river, aiming at the hindmost prize. Another, bigger volley came a few moments later, and Williams saw a good fifty or so soldiers standing in passable formation on this side of the sea wall, firing out at the captured craft.

He glanced ruefully at the spiked cannon. Not that it mattered – even if they could still use them, none of the embrasures pointed in the right direction. There was shouting and more soldiers appeared running along to join the others. It was unlikely to be very long before they remembered the battery.

'Time to go,' Williams said. 'Mr Treadwell, Mr Prentice, if you would lead the sailors back to the gig, the marines will form a rearguard. Move smartly, gentlemen, we do not have much time.' He took one look back and was relieved to see the captured vessels moving a little faster, carried on the current of the river and the gently ebbing tide. The waters here changed so little compared to the seas he had grown up beside, but even so the shift in the current was clear.

He shouted to summon Dobson, Milne and the others, watched them scramble over the walls and drop down into the ditch. Before he followed, Williams took one last look out at the entrance to the harbour. The leading prize was already through, the other making good headway, but then he saw shapes in the darkness behind them, breaking up the moonlight glittering on the water. One, no, two rowing boats were following where none of the British boats should have been.

He jumped from the rampart into the ditch, saw Dobson and Milne kneeling at the far side, waiting to cover him, and yelled at them to get moving. The sailors were a good way ahead, and it seemed so much quicker jogging across the sand than when they had advanced. Before they got aboard, Williams ordered them to reload all the muskets and pistols. There was muttering at this, provoking curses from Milne, but they were all still too buoyed up with what they had done to resent such fussiness with any spirit. It was more than a minute after they had pushed out that Williams could see past the curve of the coast around the battery. The first prize had set sail now and its lead was growing every minute even in these light airs. Before long it would pass a cable's length ahead of them, making for the main channel. Canvas appeared on the second one and it too began to go a little faster. Williams squinted as he peered into the shadows behind it and then spotted the sweep of oars in the water.

'There are French boats closing on the second ship,' he said, for the moment not caring that the craft almost surely did not warrant the name. 'Two of them, I think, and they must mean to board and take her back. Only they haven't reckoned on us.' He grinned, and this time was pleased to see several marines and sailors return the smile. 'Mr Treadwell, steer for the second ship, if you please.'

The midshipman hesitated for a moment, his face taut, and Williams suspected that he felt they had already done enough for one night. Yet it was only for a moment.

'Shipmates need our help,' Mr Prentice said firmly, pressing the midshipman's arm, 'so of course we must all bear a hand.'

Treadwell shifted the tiller and he now smiled as well. 'Pull hard, lads.'

The leading prize was already past them, well into the channel, and the other barely one hundred yards away. A large French boat rowed alongside, within a pistol shot.

'That's a gunboat,' said Mr Prentice in one of his loudest whispers. 'Be something big in the prow.'

The other Frenchman rowed astern, steadily gaining.

'They'll fire grape to clear the deck and then board from the other one.' Treadwell was surely right. Prentice nodded in agreement.

'Then we must take the gunboat and then deal with the others,' Williams said, half wondering whether they would be less likely to follow him on water, but seeing no sign of it. Treadwell had already steered so as to cut off the gunboat.

Williams worried that he did not know what he was doing, wondering whether the prize would simply accelerate and leave them far behind to deal with two boats full of angry Frenchmen. It did seem to surge forward, running with the current as they turned and felt it driving against their side. The gunboat was coming on quickly as well, more quickly than he had expected, until the Frenchman turned to bring its bow gun to bear.

A musket ball struck splinters off the plank of the gig just beside his hand. Another hit an oar, the force throwing the sailor off his stroke so that he caught a crab. For a moment the gig foundered, twisting against the waves and rocking. Men on shore were firing at them. The range was long and they probably had more hope of warning the gunboat than doing real damage. So far the Frenchmen seemed oblivious as they concentrated on bringing their cannon to bear.

'Get the stroke, damn your eyes.' Treadwell spat the words at the sailors, who quickly recovered and pulled hard towards the gunboat. More shots came from the shore, one snatching Mr Prentice's battered round hat off and knocking it into the sea.

'Bloody sauce!' he shouted. 'That cost ten shillings.' The gunner was grinning.

'You were robbed, sir,' Dobson said.

They were close now, but Williams could see that the French boats were even closer to the prize. Men appeared at the rail, and muskets banged as they fired down into the boat, which had bumped alongside, waiting to board.

'Come on, lads!' Treadwell shouted. Faces turned on the gunboat and saw them coming, mouths opening in shock. Dobson twisted where he sat and aimed quickly. The musket banged and one of the French rowers was flung back. Confusion followed and the gig slammed into the side of the gunboat just as someone pulled the lanyard on the cannon. The flint slammed down, set off the powder in the tube and then the main charge. An instant later, the twenty-four-pounder went off with a great roar, bathing the side of the prize in a flash of red light and then a cloud of smoke. Williams heard the whining rattle of grapeshot peppering the high side of the captured ship. The French gun captain had aimed a little to the side to avoid hitting their boarding party, and the sudden impact of the gig near its stern had twisted the gunboat. Someone on the prize was screaming, but then that was lost in shouts and shots as the French boarded.

Williams was in the prow of the gig and was crouching ready when they struck. The shock almost knocked him back, but he steadied himself, took a breath and raised his pistol, aiming at the face of the startled French coxswain just a few feet away. He pulled the trigger, felt it jerk in his hand as the charge went off and through the smoke saw the man pitched overboard. Behind him, marines raised their muskets and two fired, the muzzles inches away from his ears. The flames scorched his hair, and the sound exploded so close to his ears that he could no longer hear as smoke billowed around him and his nostrils filled with the rotten-egg odour of gunpowder. He leapt into the chaos, everything happening so fast that there was no time for thought or fear. One of the French rowers was dying, blood jetting from his throat, and another was clutching at his arm. Williams swung the pistol into the wounded man's face and let it go. His foot caught on a rowing bench and he tripped, falling forward, the axe sinking into a man's leg instead of his face.

Marines trampled him as they surged on to the gunboat. He had forgotten to give the orders to fix bayonets, so they clubbed and swung with the heavy firelocks as Williams struggled to get up. He had lost the axe. Someone trod on his fingers, but he was half up and punched a Frenchman in the chest since he had no weapon. The gunboat was still turning, and with so little space the fight was clumsy and brutal. More marines boarded, one barged Williams and the Frenchmen he was grappling hard against the side, and the Frenchman fell overboard, splashing into the water. He clung on to Williams' coat, dragging him down, until the officer managed to free his own arms and hit the man's elbows hard. On the second blow the grip loosened, and the man slipped away into the darkness. Williams saw his mouth open in a scream, but could still hear no noise.

More of the gunboat's crew, some living, some wounded or dead, were flung into the sea. Williams managed to get up, saw the axe and no sign of the man he had struck, and grabbed it. Mr Prentice – the hard-of-hearing, grey-haired Mr Prentice – had somehow forced his way on to the gunboat and was near the great cannon, clubbing again and again at a man who cowered beside its barrel. A marine lifted another French sailor and flung him bodily into the sea. Three more raised their hands until another wild-eyed marine slammed the butt of his musket into the head of one of them, knocking him over the side. The other two jumped.

Williams looked around. His ears were filled with a strange roaring sound. One of the marines was hurt in the arm, bones perhaps broken for he could not move it, and Mr Prentice had a slash across his cheek, but those were the only injuries. They had caught the gunboat by surprise and its crew had not had time to recover. Two sailors had secured the gig to the other boat, and Treadwell and the remaining rowers kept both under some control as they drifted with the current. The prize was past them now, the other French boat beside it and a fight raging on its deck.

'Back to the gig!' Williams could not really hear his own voice and tried to shout even louder to make sure that it carried. 'We need to help them on board!' A marine pulled away from him, looking surprised, and the officer guessed that he was yelling. The roaring was fading, and he dimly caught something about '… the whole bleedin' world can hear you …' as the men started to move. Mr Prentice was at the stern with one of the sailors, and Williams realised that they were unshipping the tiller bar so that they could throw it into the water.

Williams climbed back into the gig, and crouched behind Dobson and Corporal Milne, waiting with loaded muskets in the prow. He faintly heard the veteran sergeant make some crack about not having volunteered for this and then his hearing came back.

'Nice change for you to see some proper fighting,' Milne said, and then looked puzzled because the officer seemed so pleased.

Mr Prentice was the last to clamber back aboard and then they cast the gunboat off.

'Lively now,' Treadwell called to the rowers as they settled back into rhythm. Tired men somehow found new strength as they pulled on the oars. The prize still had no sails set and was drifting with the current. As they watched, the last few Frenchmen clambered up the side, letting their own boat drift free. Dobson raised his musket to aim, but then lowered it, shaking his head.

'Come on, catch the rascals.' Treadwell urged the sailors on. 'It's a prize full of gold and jewels!'

One of the marines laughed. 'How about a boat full of doxies!'

'Them too, if you like,' Treadwell agreed. 'Pull, lads, pull!'

'Bring us to the far side,' Williams called to the midshipman, saw confusion on the man's face and managed to remember the right term. 'Larboard side, Mr Treadwell, larboard side,' he said, and was rewarded with a nod. It would take a little longer, but there was a chance they might gain some surprise and they would just have to hope that the *Sparrowhawks* on board the ship could hold out. There were still shouts from the deck, but he had not seen the flash of a shot for a minute or two.

They came alongside, and Williams saw the steps on the side of the hull and readied himself to jump. A head appeared over the rail, looking down at them, and the head was wearing a flat-topped shako. Dobson's musket boomed and the head vanished.

Williams jumped on to the side of the ship and began to climb.

6

' *En avant!* ' Williams caught the words distinctly, the second one dragged out and turning into a scream of rage. Feet pounded across the deck above him. The shape of a man loomed over the rail, and another musket fired, flinging the soldier's head back. He tottered, and Williams pressed himself against the side of the ship, feet as deeply into the steps as he could manage, afraid that the man would fall on to him. Instead he staggered backwards and the officer dragged himself up, feeling someone climbing up behind, urging him on. Two soldiers lay on the planking and he slipped in a pool of blood as he came on board. There were more bodies scattered around the deck, and shouts and screams, and he could see a bitter struggle towards the bows. A knot of men were surrounded and he guessed these must be the *Sparrowhawks*.

A soldier stamped on his front foot as he jabbed a bayonet at the red-coated officer. Williams used his free hand to ward off the attack, grabbing the muzzle of the man's musket, glad that he was wearing gloves because it was hot from firing. He twisted towards the man, trying to push him off balance, and swung the boarding axe to chop into the soldier's arm near his shoulder. The man screamed, dropping his musket, and Williams pushed him aside. Someone raised a pistol at his face and fired, but the flint sparked on the pan and nothing happened. Williams flung the axe at him and it spun in the air as it went so that the blunt haft hit the French sailor in the face. Drawing his sword, he pressed on, slashed twice at the man, brutal, unskilled blows because there was no time for anything more, and then he was down.

Milne was beside him, bayonet fixed, Dobson and the marines spilling on to the deck. Frenchmen were all around them, recovering from the initial shock and now stepping forward with determination. A pistol fired, the flame vivid in the darkness, and a marine grunted as he was hit in the chest. The French sailor sprang forward to step into his place, then screamed as Dobson's bayonet caught him low in the belly, to be twisted and dragged free by the veteran. A man with epaulettes on his shoulders came at Williams, sword point moving quickly in carefully judged thrusts. He blocked the first, but the man was so quick that he was immediately lunging again, and the tip of his sword slashed open his sleeve, drawing blood. Williams stepped forward, hoping to surprise the man, but the Frenchman's blade was already back up, fending off his own jab. The sailor with the boarding pike stabbed it forward over the officer's shoulders and forced the Frenchman back a pace.

One of the marines must still have been loaded because he drove his bayonet into a French soldier's stomach so far that its point came out of his back, then fired the musket, ripping a ghastly hole in the soldier's body. The marine seemed shocked, and then a cutlass slashed down across his face and he screamed, letting go of the firelock, its blade still in his victim, and went down on his knees, hands pressed over his eyes. The cutlass came down again, half cutting through his wrist, and the man sank to the ground, curling up protectively. Corporal Milne swung up his musket and slammed the butt into the French sailor's chin. Williams just managed to parry another lunge by the man with epaulettes, and only the sailor's boarding pike kept the Frenchman from closing while his guard was down. There were half a dozen of them on deck, still in a tight half-circle, and they were making no headway.

Treadwell saved them. The midshipman had let the gig fall back and then led the remaining sailors in a scramble up the prize's stern, coming over the rail behind the Frenchmen pressing around Williams' little group.

'*Sparrowhawk!*' Treadwell yelled, and then shot a French sailor through the body, cutting at another with his dirk. More shots followed as the sailors with him fired pistols or muskets into the press. Another Frenchman was down, the rest recoiling, and Williams' men surged forward without any need for an order. Milne clubbed another man down, Dobson jabbed with his bayonet, and Williams sliced hard to cut through the arm of a soldier about to aim a blow at the veteran, acting on instinct. Then the sailor with the pike pushed him to one side and used the staff of his spear to catch a great downward hack from the French officer, who for the moment had abandoned his scientific swordsmanship.

The French were going back, but the officer with epaulettes yelled out to rally them and for the moment they obeyed. Treadwell came up beside him, slicing with his short dirk, but his blow was easily beaten aside and the Frenchman thrust once, the tip driving through his left eye. The midshipman slumped, his dead weight dragging the sword down before it came free, and Williams hacked at the man's outstretched arm, cutting through sleeve and flesh. A hiss of pain and the Frenchman let go of his sword. Williams raised his own sword and cut, a glancing blow across the man's body and driving him back.

'Bastard!' the sailor screamed behind him and drove the pike into the man's side. Williams was about to finish him off when a French soldier jabbed at the sailor, slicing into his leg. The officer punched the man in the face, driving him back, and the sailor managed to limp to shelter behind the little line of men. More of the enemy were down, and the French seemed to be fighting less hard, giving way and almost letting themselves be cut down.

Williams pressed on, hacking at a man just above the collar, carving into his neck so that the blood sprayed and the soldier collapsed, choking as he bled his life out on to the deck. Milne's boot skidded in the pool, but the luck was with him, because his sudden lurch meant that a sword-cut missed him, and the marine beside him put the man down with a well-timed lunge. Prentice appeared, his jacket slashed open, another graze on his forehead, but the blade of his cutlass dark with blood. Dobson had lost one sleeve, and everyone seemed to have cuts or scratches of one sort or another. Williams slashed at another man, a fair blow across his body, but it seemed only to knock him backwards, and he realised that the finely honed edge must already have been blunted. He had never known a fight as long and as hard as this.

The French parted and they reached the ragged band of *Sparrowhawks*. Captain Pringle was with them, sword in his left hand, his right pressed to staunch the blood from a wound in his side. Half a dozen other sailors were still standing around him and most had wounds.

'Good to see you,' Pringle gasped, but had no breath to say any more. The enemy were just as weary, but they were still determined and there were at least two dozen of them clustered around the starboard side, panting as they prepared to renew the fight. Numbers were about even, or slightly in the enemy's favour, but before Williams could call on them to surrender, the French raised a shout and came forward.

No one still had a loaded weapon, and the fight was a question of blades and clubbed muskets, of exhausted men clawing at each other with their last strength. Afterwards Williams could remember almost nothing of those last minutes, other than weariness and clumsy blows. He thrust with his sword, aiming at the face and eyes to drive his opponents back, and sometimes all he could do was bludgeon them with the blunted edge, or punch with the hilt. On land the side that felt itself losing always ran. On board a ship there was nowhere to go, and so they kept fighting, quarter neither asked for nor given, grunting because they were too tired and parched to shout, and slowly the French were pushed back. Only when there were three still standing did they drop their weapons.

Williams saw the men surrender and struggled to understand what it meant. The world had become a few feet of deck, of fighting, killing and moving on, with the stench of blood and death all around. Puzzled, he stared at the Frenchmen, and it was only the flood of utter exhaustion that stopped him from stepping forward and thrusting his blade into them one by one. Looking to either side, the officer could see that the others were in a similar state. As if lifting a great weight he pointed his sword down and rested the tip against the planking.

'Prisoners,' he said. The Frenchmen were wide eyed and it was a while before they nodded. 'Prisoners,' he repeated. He turned round and looked for someone to take charge. Captain Pringle was sitting on a grating, his back against the mast as an elderly sailor with deep black skin and grey hair peeled back his shirt. His blue jacket was already folded beside him, and the sailor worked with care. Even so the captain winced as his shirt was removed. The sailor stopped, his face concerned, but Pringle gave a weak smile and urged him on.

For the moment the captain was occupied. Williams spotted Corporal Milne, and then noticed that two fingers were missing from his left hand and another marine was bandaging the wound. Then he saw Dobson, tapping his clay pipe free of ashes, and looking weary.

'Sergeant,' he said. 'Secure the prisoners. Make sure they are disarmed and then we can see to their wounded.'

Dobson looked surprised. Then he sighed, put his pipe away and looked around. 'You! And you,' he shouted at two marines in the voice of the eternal sergeant, 'come with me.'

Williams made his way aft, stepping carefully to avoid the bodies strewn everywhere, most of them still moaning. He would need to get men to help them as soon as he could, but wanted to make sure that the ship was secure. To his relief a sailor was at the wheel, with Mr Prentice leaning against the capstan in front of him as a marine tightened a belt around his thigh to stop the blood flowing from a deep wound. Fewer than thirty British had boarded, including Captain Pringle's party, and a quick count suggested a dozen had no serious injuries, while eight or nine more ought to be capable of some work. Treadwell was dead, along with one of the marines and a sailor who had come on board with the captain. The remainder were badly hurt and their chances would depend on getting them quickly to a surgeon.

A rough count suggested that there were about fifty French, nine or ten dead, and three times that number badly wounded. Most of them must have been the crew of the vessel, presumably released from below when the soldiers boarded. Adding in the men from the gunboat, Williams could not understand how they had succeeded against those odds. The rules just seemed different at sea.

Milne reported, hand bandaged, and assured him that he was fit to work, so Williams set him and a couple of marines to caring for the wounded. After that he headed back to see Captain Pringle, who was still sitting as the sailor wound a clean piece of cloth around his waist, pulling it tight. Williams blinked as the sun came up on the horizon and that made no sense for surely it could not be dawn. Yet there the sun was, a great red ball in the east, and somehow the hours must have passed. He could not account for them. Battles were always strange in that way, and time could pass in a flash or crawl by at a snail's pace, each moment crammed with activity, fear and exhilaration, but he had never known anything like this. Now they were past the headland, he could see that the sun was well above the waters and the light of day was obvious. In his memory the fight occurred wholly in darkness. He was too tired to solve the mystery.

'Ah, Mr Williams,' the captain said. 'I have not yet thanked you sufficiently for your arrival. Things were becoming difficult.'

'Happy to be of service, sir.'

'Now,' Pringle continued, getting to the matter in hand. 'I see my coxswain is at the wheel. Good, Bennett is a splendid fellow. With the wind off the sea we must rely on the current to take us out of the channel. Once we are out, get Treadwell to hoist sail. It will take some effort, but we should be able to work her out into the bay and rejoin *Topaze*, *Sparrowhawk* and the other prizes.'

'I regret to say that Mr Treadwell is dead.'

'Ah.' The captain seemed to have no more to say, so Williams gave him the full list of casualties.

'Nasty business, but as far as I can tell we have taken half a dozen prizes and burned three or four more. That will give them something to think about.'

Williams nodded, too tired to think of anything to say. Men died and were maimed, and that was all there was to it. It did not help to brood, to twist argument in justification, or to wonder whether you might soon follow them. Such thoughts would come often enough unbidden, most of all in the small hours of sleepless nights to come, and there was no sense in dwelling on them now.

'Treadwell did well, damned well,' the captain said. 'As did you, Mr Williams, damned well indeed.' He drank from a flask proffered by the sailor. 'Will you take some brandy?'

'No thank you, sir,' Williams said. 'I do not really drink,' he explained, not wanting to be thought ungrateful.

'Really? William did say you were an extraordinary fellow.' It was strange hearing Billy Pringle referred to in that way. 'I dare say you will take a nip, won't you, you rascal.' This was to the sailor, who seemed a solemn man, but took the flask gratefully. 'This is Caesar,' Pringle continued, pleased to see Williams' surprise. 'John Julius Caesar to be precise, able seaman, and one of my best topmen.' The sailor gave the flask back and raised a knuckle to his forehead. 'Doesn't say a lot, but there is no one I would prefer by my side in storm or battle.'

Williams was intrigued. The name was a curious one, and it was a pleasing thought for a man fascinated by the ancient past to know that he had just fought alongside 'Julius Caesar'. He longed to hear the man's story, wondering whether he had once been a slave. Williams' mother was fond of abolitionist tracts and he had read many stories of escape from servitude, but it would have been a greater thrill to hear such a tale from a man's own experience. The sailor stared blankly at the army officer, and concern for good manners restrained him from asking so personal a question.

Then there was a grinding sound and Williams was flung forward. A big man, he landed heavily against the wounded captain, so that Pringle hissed in pain and let out a string of blasphemies. The prize lurched to a halt, and Williams managed to get up. Pringle mastered himself, waved Caesar away when he tried to help and then looked around. For just a moment, Williams could see a lot of his younger brother in the older Edward.

'Bugger,' said Captain Pringle. 'We're aground.'

They were on the sandbank where it widened slightly just before it came to an end. Last night the shallow draught of the boats had meant that none were troubled. The prizes ahead of them must either have seen the danger or simply had the luck to steer past.

Carried by Caesar to the stern rail, Pringle looked closely for some time.

'We're nearly over. Just the keel caught.' He looked up at the sky. 'Tide is nearly out – once it turns back we should float off in three or four hours, at least if we are lucky. That is assuming that the French let us wait around.'

'Cavalry on shore, sir!' Dobson shouted.

'Least of our worries,' Captain Pringle muttered. Williams joined the sergeant on the starboard rail and looked at the shore to their north. The beach was less than three hundred yards away. A few infantry skirmishers had been there for some time, popping away with the muskets even though no ball had yet hit anyone on board the ship. Behind them a half-squadron of hussars rode along the sand, the men gaudy in brown jackets and sky-blue trousers. At their head was an officer on a white horse. His uniform looked more that of an infantryman, save that the jacket was a rich green rather than the normal French blue. Williams wondered whether he was a German from one of the many states controlled by Napoleon.

'Try a shot, sir?' Mr Prentice suggested in his usual loud tones. The prize had gunports for five guns on each side, as well as two apiece at the bow and stern, but actually carried only half that number. The gunner was standing next to one of the two little four-pounders of the starboard broadside.

Williams looked at Pringle, who shook his head.

'No time for that, at present,' he said. 'Mr Williams, would you be so good as to secure all the French prisoners below. Put them all forrard. Mr Prentice, get some men and move all of those four-pounders to the bow and secure them. We need to shift the weight forrard.'

It took ten minutes to move the prisoners below, the wounded carried by the others. A marine guard was placed at the hatchway. As Williams went back to see Pringle he paused for a moment to look at the French on shore. The green-coated officer had dismounted and was staring at them through his glass. Skirmishers still fired now and then, and he heard a ball pluck the shrouds above his head.

Pringle was sitting when he reached him, and looked very pale. Caesar and another tar were rigging up a block and tackle and fixing a sling under the muzzle and breech of one of the long six-pounders placed to fire to the rear.

'It's all about weight,' the captain explained as Williams came up. 'If we can ditch these stern chasers and shift the other guns forrard then that might just lift the keel off the sand.' He watched approvingly as, with the help of four marines, the sailors hauled the black-painted barrel off its carriage. 'That's a good twenty-two hundredweight there.

'There is no room for us all in the gig, let alone for the prisoners, so we cannot set fire to her and escape. Which means that we must get her off, or ...' He left the thought unfinished.

A sailor appeared, knuckled his forehead in salute, and Williams recognised young Clegg. He had not noticed the young topman was with them until now, but was pleased to see him. Pringle was less pleased by the sailor's report.

'No anchor on board, sir.'

'Blast, that's typical of the ruddy Frogs. Liberty to be bloody awful sailors if you ask me.' The name *Liberté* was painted in peeling gold paint on the stern. Pringle had the master's papers, but had not had any time to look through them. 'Well done, Clegg. Now, lad, take a look at the mainsheets and check that they are sound. We need to be ready if the wind changes.' Williams nodded to the sailor as he departed.

'I wondered about putting out a kedge anchor and trying to warp her off,' Pringle said to the redcoat officer. Williams understood the vague principle. If the anchor was towed by a small boat and then sunk further back, the cable could be attached and turned by the capstan so that the ship was pulled back towards the anchor. 'But the useless bloody French aren't bloody well carrying a spare bloody anchor,' he added bitterly. 'And of course we cut her cables when we brought her out. Don't know why they had the anchors down when they were tied up in harbour, but the ways of godless revolutionaries are ever mysteries to good Christian folk.'

Williams failed to detect the irony so familiar from Billy Pringle in his older brother. Edward Pringle simply seemed angry.

'Artillery, sir!' It was Dobson once again who called the warning. Williams helped the captain over to look at the shore. This was far more serious. A team of eight horses – twice the number usual for so small a gun as a four-pounder – was being whipped along the beach. The hussars were further back, the men dismounted and holding their horses, and several of the latter stirred with interest as the drivers slewed round in a spray of sand. Gunners rode behind the green-painted gun carriage and limber. They were in dark blue, with tall red plumes and red epaulettes visible even at this distance. Williams guessed that these horse artillerymen had been summoned from some way away, and so had harnessed a double team to get there with a single gun as soon as possible. Springing from their horses with well-practised ease, the six gunners lifted the trails of the gun from the limber, ran it into position, hefted the barrel from the travelling to firing position, and began to load.

Prentice joined them, limping heavily and wincing if ever he let weight fall on his injured leg.

'Guns stowed forrard, sir,' he reported. 'But I could get one ready and make their life difficult.'

Pringle shook his head. 'We need to get her off.' There was

a splash from behind them as the barrel of the stern chaser was hoisted over the side and dropped. 'Well done, lads,' the captain called out.

'Mr Prentice, how long would it take you to unspike a gun?' Williams asked the gunner.

'You are thinking of the ones in the battery?'

He nodded in answer. The battery they had attacked the previous night was around half a mile away, and they were well within range of its heavy guns.

'Well, I did a decent job for the time,' Prentice continued, 'but nothing like sawing off the trunnions. With the right tools and a fair wind I could get one of them clear in an hour. Be two hours if I had to drill it and you never quite trust a gun after that, but the nails probably weren't in hard enough for them to need to drill.'

'So they should have them working again by now?' Williams asked, for he was confident that the gunner's guesses were sound.

'Aye, if they've any idea at all of what they are doing.'

'Which means they could be pounding us by now.' Pringle clearly understood. 'In an hour or two they could reduce us to so much matchwood, or burn us to the waterline if they are able to heat shot.'

'And since they have not,' Williams continued the thought, 'they must want to take us back and be confident of doing so.' As they spoke the gunners on shore had prepared the little cannon and now stepped back. The gun captain lowered his portfire to touch the slim tube of fine powder in the touch-hole – flintlocks and lanyards were too fragile for service with guns on land – and then gun and crew were all lost behind a cloud of dirty smoke. A ball hummed through the air, going high and wide.

'We shall know if they fire only for our mast and rigging,' Pringle said. 'Well, that means we must hurry,' he added, and then passed out. Williams caught him before he hit the deck.

'Lay him down,' he called to a couple of marines. 'Keep him in the shade.' The sun was becoming hot now. He saw a look of concern on Caesar's face. 'Keep at it. Get that other gun over the side. Clegg, you take five more men and tip the carriage after it.' He pointed at the gap in the rail above the stairway. It looked to be wide enough for the gun carriage and as it was on wheels they could push it rather than hoist the thing over the side.

'It's made some difference,' Prentice said, looking at the line of the deck, but his tone was doubtful. 'Battery or no,' he added, 'if they have another gunboat they can stand off and kill or sink us as they please.'

'I know,' Williams said. 'Is there any way we can protect the mast from their shot?' The four-pounder fired again from the beach, and this time the ball struck the rail a few yards from them, flicked up long and horribly sharp splinters, and then skimmed at head height across the deck.

Prentice shook his head. 'But it is hard to be so accurate at that range. It's a small gun, so even a direct strike will not necessarily bring it down.'

'Sir.' Dobson stamped to attention. 'Corporal Milne tells me there are bales of cotton in the aft hold. It won't stop a shot, but better than nothing.'

Williams looked around and could see that most of the fit men were busy. 'Good. Take Milne and two others – I have no more to spare – and start bringing them up. Stack them, lash them if you can, along this side.

'Mr Prentice, the sailors in your party are to be ready to hoist sail. Do you have a good man to lead them?'

'Clegg is good, sir, I'd like to take him.'

'He's young, isn't he?'

'All the best sailors are. You never really take to the life if you go to sea after you are twenty. He's been afloat since he was a boy.'

'Good, Clegg, then. Put him in charge. I'll be able to give you more when the other gun has gone over the stern.'

'Aye-aye, sir. And sir?'

'Yes, Mr Prentice.'

'The tide has turned. If only the wind shifts as well.'

'Yes, Mr Prentice, I know.'

The four-pounder fired every two or three minutes. That was a slow rate of fire, and Williams guessed they were taking great care to lay each shot. The fifth one took the arm off a marine, and the ninth sent a shower of splinters into the face of a sailor. The twelfth was even more worrying, for it chipped the mast. Others went through the rigging, but only occasionally did any harm.

'Lucky they haven't any bar-shot,' Mr Prentice shouted in Williams' ear. Designed to slash through the ropework and spars of a ship, such ammunition was rarely carried by artillery on land. After a while they had thick cotton bales protecting the base of the mast and all along the starboard rail. When shot struck them it threw up a great puff of white dust and debris. The bale was either knocked down or punched through, but it helped to reduce the number of splinters.

'Boats, sir! Boats astern. Three of them. No, five!' Clegg was up in the rigging and was pointing back towards the harbour. The boats were rowing towards them. They were small and brightly painted, and Williams recognised some of the fishing boats they had seen drawn up on the beach. None appeared to be the gun-boat Mr Prentice dreaded, but even from this distance he could tell that they were crowded.

With a great splash and fountain of water the barrel of the remaining stern chaser was dropped into the sea. Leaving the tackle where it was, Caesar and his party rolled the carriage to the rail and pushed it overboard.

Liberté began to move. First it was slight, then the gentlest of pressures from the tide carrying them forward. The *Sparrowhawks* cheered, yelling from parched throats even as another shot slammed into one of the bales and sent up a shower of white cotton.

'Keep her steady, Bennett,' Williams shouted, remembering the coxswain's name just in time, and hoping that the order was clear enough even with his hazy understanding of nautical language.

'Aye-aye, sir.' The man seemed happy enough, and surely had no need of firm instructions to steer clear of any more sandbanks.

Caesar cried out, blood bright on the side of his head, and then there was the sound of a musket shot.

'Bloody Frogs!' the able seaman yelled in a voice that spoke more of London than anywhere more exotic. 'Bloody, bastard, bloody Frogs!' The top of his left ear was a ragged mess.

Another musket ball smacked into the stern rail beside him, making the sailor duck down. Williams ran to the stern and crouched to see over before another ball flicked past an inch from his hair and he too dropped back. The leading fishing boat was barely one hundred yards away, the next fifty yards behind that and the other three trailing.

'Marines!' he called. 'Dobson, Milne. Get half a dozen men loading muskets and you two fire back at them. Show them they can't have it all their own way.' As soon as he had spoken he remembered Milne's injured hand, but then saw that the corporal was still holding his musket and had begun to load. It looked as if the man would manage, and it was better to have steady men firing regularly than looser volleys from the less experienced.

Liberté was gathering way and he was trying to decide whether they should work the sweeps or set sail. The wind had almost gone, but then he felt a faint breeze.

Caesar grinned, showing discoloured teeth and several gaps between them, but it was a smile of pure joy.

'Wind has shifted, sir. It's nor-nor-east. From the land, sir,' he added, in case the soldier was as dim as many of their kind.

Williams smiled and stood up. 'Clegg, get some canvas up,' he shouted. Dobson and Milne fired the first shots at the fishing boat and then took cover as a spattering of musket balls smacked into the wooden rail. The four-pounder on shore barked out, the ball tearing through the air and missing the mast by a finger's breadth.

Then another heavy gun went off, from the other side this time, and Williams looked to see two cutters rowing towards them, each with a gun mounted on the bow. The first – *Topaze's* red cutter – had fired at the fishing boats. The range was long, and he saw the sea short of the leading French boat convulsed as the burst of grape landed, but it was enough to warn. Help had arrived, the only help that could be sent so close inshore in such still airs.

It was not quite over. The battery opened up from near the harbour, firing at the cutters rather than *Liberté*, but these were small, low marks at such a range and the shot did no more than soak the sailors with spray. On the beach, the four-pounder's crew redoubled their efforts and sent a succession of shots, two of which punched holes in the raised sail. Too late the battery commander decided that the *Liberté* was lost and began to fire at it. One shot went home, shattering part of the stern rail and taking the foot off a marine. Another hit lower, making the hull shudder, but it was above the waterline and the *Liberté* kept moving, going faster as she was able to turn and run before the wind. The French kept firing for another ten minutes, but each shot fell a little further behind.

Mr Prentice stumped up.

'Well, we appear to have made it,' he shouted. 'You know, I do believe we could make a sailor of you, Mr Williams.'

John Julius Caesar, his back to the gunner, and a bandage round his head, winked at the officer. 'Begging your pardon, sir, but the gentleman looks like he might be better learning to be a tailor.'

Williams looked down at himself. His breeches were filthy, torn at the knees and stained with blood and tar. His jacket – his good jacket, he realised, for he had not remembered to change after the conference with Captain Hope – was in even worse condition, covered in filth and ripped so badly that most of one sleeve was gone.

'Get Clegg to see to it, sir,' Caesar suggested. 'He's a dab hand with a needle.'

Williams smiled then began to laugh. It was probably relief, but at the time he could think of nothing more amusing than the thought of being given sartorial advice by Julius Caesar.

7

'There are opportunities, definite opportunities.' Hanley concluded his long report, fleshing out his written account of their mission to Granada. 'We saw everywhere indications of considerable enthusiasm.'

'But perhaps a want of organisation?' Rear Admiral Sir Richard Keats' tone was blunt, but his round face had a ready smile and his eyes were perceptive.

Hanley considered his answer for a while. 'Certainly. However, I doubt that much organisation would be practical with the serranos. They are peasants, angry at the invader and ferocious, but wholly without discipline.' He remembered the wild pursuit of the French hussars and the massacre as the cavalry had turned and charged. 'Short of conscripting them into regular units and moving them elsewhere, I cannot see any prospect of changing this, sir.'

There was a sudden lurch of the deck beneath them, the big ship stirring even though it was at anchor. The swell of Cadiz's outer harbour was often considerable, but the calmer, inner harbour was too dominated by French batteries to be altogether safe.

Daniel Mudge, confidential clerk to the governor of Gibraltar, looked positively green as the ship rolled again. The stern cabin of HMS *Milford* was vast compared to the cramped little brig-sloops which had taken Hanley, Pringle and the others down the coast and then brought them back. The ship was a 'Seventy-Four', the mainstays of the line-of-battle warships of the fleet, crewed by some six hundred men, and with two gun decks mounting heavy thirty-two- and eighteen-pounders.

'My apologies, Mr Mudge,' Sir Richard said generously. 'I fear we are at the mercy of one of Monsieur Barrallier's bright ideas.'

'A Frenchman?' Major General Lord Turney's voice dripped with contempt. 'I did not know this was a captured ship.'

'Indeed it is not. Barrallier was a royalist and made ships for us.'

'No wonder it is a tub,' the general declared, although Hanley was unsure whether his scorn was directed at royalist refugees or Frenchmen in general. It would not have been at the suggestion of aristocracy, even foreign aristocracy. Lord Turney must have been fifty or more, but this was clear only when he was seen from up close. No more than average height, he was broad shouldered and trim waisted, and active in his movements. His face showed the darkening of long service in India and Egypt, but the wrinkles were few – at least the visible ones, for there was a hint of make-up about the man. The general cultivated an odd mixture of elegant and genteel complacency and vigorous military masculinity. When they had looked at the maps earlier on, Hanley had noticed that Lord Turney leaned back and twisted to odd angles when he concentrated – eyesight going, almost certainly, but too vain to wear spectacles, at least in public.

'My lord, the French have built many beautiful and fine sailing ships,' the admiral replied, concealing any distaste felt at the soldier's scorn of this ship. 'Sadly the old *Milford* is not one of them, and rolls like a dog in the lightest winds. Therefore we should press on and come to our purpose for the sake of Mr Mudge as well as our own pressing duties.' Sir Richard delivered a series of precise, pertinent questions as if they were a rolling broadside, and Hanley did his best to reply in the same style.

Yes, the serranos would resent any attempts to make them more regular. No, the bands of guerrilleros were not united. No leader seemed to have more than two or three score followers. Yes, the chiefs sometimes were willing to work together, but no, it seemed unlikely that the bands would unite more permanently.

'Their proud and independent spirit is their great strength, and if it hinders concerted effort it is the reason why they fight, and will continue to fight,' he said.

'And what of the enemy?' Sir Richard asked. 'Major Sinclair insists they are weak and dispirited. Is that not right, Wharton?'

Joseph Wharton, the admiral's chaplain and it seemed a good deal more, stepped forward. The man had an uncanny knack of blending into the surroundings, as well as a jovial character when he chose to draw attention to himself. Hanley liked him, and suspected that most men would, particularly clever, sensitive men.

'Sinclair states that the French garrisons are spread very thinly across the south. Marshal Victor's corps is entirely devoted to the siege here at Cadiz. Marshal Mortier's and General Sebastiani's are either in garrison or forming columns to chase the partisans. They must always be ready to meet any attack from General Blake's Spanish in Murcia.'

'Yes, but if they catch him, they'll have him for breakfast,' Lord Turney cut in, more scornful now of the Spanish than the French. Hanley found his dislike of the general growing ever stronger, as did his despair at the folly of selecting such a man for a campaign which would rely heavily on working with Britain's allies. Yet in truth this opinion was not uncommon. Blake survived in Murcia, at least for the moment, and there were other Spanish armies further east in Catalonia, but elsewhere they had been swept from the field. There were forces here in Cadiz, others sheltered under the guns of Gibraltar and a handful of other coastal fortresses, and the Marquis de Romana kept his army together in southern Portugal. None had the discipline, training and numbers to match the French in the field and so they raided and fled, surviving only because the enemy could not be everywhere at once.

'If you will forgive me, my lord.' Wharton sounded like a country parson gently chiding an old friend among his parishioners for some minor misjudgement. 'The essential point is that they have not caught him, and show no signs of doing so.' Blake was not a gifted general, was jealous of rivals and showed as much sensitivity as Lord Turney in expressing his opinion of his allies, but he did seem to have a talent for survival.

'The French certainly have more problems with which to deal

than they have soldiers available. Sinclair makes a good case for their being dangerously scattered and exposed, especially along the coast.' If the Allied armies were few and weak, the British controlled the seas. 'Furthermore, the major claims that most of the garrisons consist of Germans, Poles, Italians and other foreign corps, and that these men feel little commitment to Bonaparte's cause. Unless the circumstances are very favourable, he does not believe that they will fight well.'

'The major expressed much the same opinion to me,' Hanley commented.

'And do you believe him to be right?' Sir Richard fired another question.

'In truth I cannot say, sir. We were there so briefly and had no time to observe any of the garrisons. However, I should say that the guerrilleros seemed to hold most of Bonaparte's troops in wary respect.'

Lord Turney was dismissive. 'Don't signify. They are irregulars and will never stand against drilled troops in the open field. With us, it is a different matter.' The general and Mr Mudge had come up from Gibraltar to urge the mounting of a raid on the coast, to be led by Lord Turney and consist of British troops and ideally some Spanish as well. Gibraltar's governor was keen, but nothing could be attempted without the active assistance of the Navy, which only Admiral Keats could provide.

'Gentlemen,' Sir Richard said, attempting to draw them back to the main issue. 'All in all it is reasonable to assume that the enemy is vulnerable, especially along the coast. The more that we can do to keep them spread out the better, for it will help us here at Cadiz, as well as the partisans in the country and Blake in Murcia.'

'And Wellingon outside Lisbon,' Lord Turney cut in.

'Indeed. He would not want any troops here in the south free to march north and aid Marshal Massena's invasion of Portugal.' He paused for breath. 'Our purpose is a sound one, the opportunity is offered, but that does not in itself help us to decide where to strike.'

'Malaga,' Mudge said, struggling with another wave of nausea. Hanley suspected that the choice of one of the bigger ports was intended to lure the admiral into accepting the enterprise. Like all the harbours it was a nest of the privateers who plagued the sea lanes and tied the Navy down in the dull necessity of escorting convoys. There was also the prospect of prize money, for if enemy vessels were taken and auctioned then naval officers benefited and the admiral most of all.

'What do we know of its defences?' The admiral looked once again at Wharton.

'The walls are poorly maintained and large in extent. If there is only a battalion as garrison then they will be unable to man them adequately. The people are said to be restless under occupation, and ready to rise against the French.'

'Sea defences?'

'Sinclair maintains that they are weak, with only a few small batteries.'

'And I wonder, is he fit to judge such things?' Sir Richard pondered.

'He says that he has been there in the last few months, and that the "French" in the garrison are really Poles and of poor quality.'

Sir Richard grunted, and Hanley was unsure what that signified. 'We had better find out as much more as we can. Is there anyone else in the area?'

'Captain Miller of the Ninety-Fifth is with the partisans a little further along the coast,' Mudge said, his face pale and his eyes glassy. Hanley felt truly sorry for the man, but then the sympathy began to extend to his own innards and he tried to ignore the gently moving deck beneath them. He wanted to stand, but the admiral had sat them all around the table and it would be impolite to move.

Sir Richard nodded. 'Good,' he said, 'have him write with all he knows of the current situation in Malaga and the surrounding country.'

'Perhaps somewhere else first, and then Malaga?' Lord Turney suggested. Hanley guessed that the man did not really care where the expedition was going so long as he was given the command.

'Perhaps,' the admiral agreed. 'Yes, I believe the chance is there and we should seize it. Anything to keep the French too preoccupied to notice that they are close to trapping us on a lee-shore.

'Well, gentlemen, I believe that is all for today. My barge is waiting to take you ashore.'

They stood, and Hanley was about to leave when Sir Richard gestured for him to stay. The general was almost at the door, telling poor Mudge how eagerly he was anticipating the dinner waiting for him, with plenty of good fat mutton. When Lord Turney gave the clerk a hearty slap on the back, Hanley worried for a moment that the spotlessly clean deck of the great cabin was about to be defiled. It was close, but Mudge recovered and then shot through the door with the desperate look of a thirsty man heading for a cool spring. The general looked back, the briefest flash of irritation revealing his annoyance that the young captain was to be privy to secrets denied to him. Sir Richard was looking away, and after Lord Turney tried and failed to catch his eye, the soldier decided not to make a point of it.

'Silly fellow,' the general said, and swaggered out. They heard the marine sentry outside the cabin stamp to attention, and then the door was closed.

'Now, Hanley,' Wharton began, 'we would like a few more words with you. I suspect it is necessary for you to go back, but in the meantime, what is your honest opinion of Sinclair and his reports?'

'The major took us to our meeting with Velasco's band, sir. We saw him again the day after the ambush of the convoy, by which time we had been taken on to meet another leader. The major arrived in the company of a leader who styled himself El Lobo. I do not think the others cared much for him as the man was a bandit before the war.' That was putting it mildly. There was great discomfort among the other leaders, but no one wanted to challenge El Lobo to his face. Hanley did not blame them, for the man looked as murderous a rogue as any he had ever seen. One of his followers had brandished a bag of ears, fingers and he had little doubt other things, cut from the bodies of his victims. 'Sinclair was full of praise for El Lobo, and said that the French did not dare set foot in his territory unless they had a whole regiment.'

'What did the other Spaniards say about him, Mr Hanley?' Wharton asked. He was not a heavyset man, and had a thin face, but the features within it seemed bigger than they should be. His brow was heavy, his nose broad, and his chin prominent. It made him stand out and, combined with his kindly manner, made the man attractive rather than ugly. A failed artist, Hanley could not quite work out why this was so, but he wondered whether the attraction would prove stronger to a certain sort of man. Wharton displayed no sign of such an inclination, but then their acquaintance had been brief. However, even that short time had confirmed Baynes' description of the man's considerable talent.

'They were grudging. They said that it was true that the French rarely went to El Lobo's territory in the mountains, and then quietly added that like most wolves he preyed mainly on the weak.'

'And what do they think of Sinclair the bad?' Wharton smiled at Hanley's surprise at the use of the nickname. 'We hear things, my dear Hanley, even here at Cadiz.'

'Most of them do not care for him,' Hanley conceded, 'and I suspect that the ones who do not like him are some of the best of the chiefs.'

'Well, at times like these sometimes we need rogues and wolves as much as *optimates* and good men we would more readily trust,' Sir Richard said. 'The question is whether or not the other chiefs will work with him.'

Wharton took over. 'Major Sinclair has written to us – and also to Gibraltar and no doubt Lisbon as well – asking for promotion and for more supplies to come through him. He promises great things. I believe to "set all Andalusia alight in a new crusade" was the expression. The major has a way with words, I'll grant him that. He seems a clever fellow, and he has been active for a year or more in a region that has now become important. There are plenty of other officers out there among the irregulars, all reporting to different authorities, but none have been there so long or have such grand plans. Yet no one seems to know him, not well, anyway.'

'The chiefs do not like him,' Hanley said, 'and do not really trust him, although I cannot entirely say why. I doubt that this will change. Yet I have no doubt they will take supplies they need from him or anyone else able to reach them. So to that extent they will work with him, and probably join any enterprise if the prospects seem good and they are not forced to admit him too closely into their own plans.'

Sir Richard nodded. 'As we thought. There is nothing to be gained by throwing all our aid behind this one man.'

'Yet if I may make a suggestion, sir,' Hanley began.

Wharton gave an encouraging smile – the errant parishioner was about to redeem himself. 'Please do.'

'Then there might be something to gain by giving the major a little of what he wants. That would place the burden of justifying this and future support firmly on his shoulders. Better a man kept in eager hope than one already disappointed.'

The admiral and his chaplain exchanged glances. 'Then we are of one mind,' Wharton said. 'And I am most pleased to see that the recommendation of a certain gentleman in Lisbon on your behalf appears to be most sound.

'Good,' the chaplain concluded. 'We keep Sinclair going and see what he does. A better prospect may still appear and we may as well get the most out of the resources we have. And we will also keep you fully occupied.'

'This raid will go ahead. It makes sense, but such affairs are never straightforward and there is always an element of risk where wind and tide are involved – something you soldiers never seem to realise,' Sir Richard admonished gently. 'Lord Turney will command, for this will principally be mounted by the forces at Gibraltar and he is the senior major general there. Well, he is an experienced officer with a long record of distinguished service.' There was a trace of doubt in his voice, but the admiral did not choose to explain, and laughed instead. 'Well then, he will command, and I trust him more than I trust Sinclair, although perhaps that is because I have no wife or daughter with me on station.'

'Lord Turney has something of a reputation,' Wharton said, and added when Hanley showed mild surprise, 'as I said, we hear things, my dear Hanley, even here at Cadiz. And at the moment his morals do not concern us.'

'Indeed not, and I am glad for it,' the admiral said, before turning back to Hanley. 'More than likely your regiment will form part of the expedition, so you may be seeing them soon.' When they arrived at Cadiz, Hanley and the others had learnt that the 106th was in Gibraltar, save for a few stragglers here in the city.

'My fellow officers are eager to rejoin the battalion.'

'Yes, well, in time, but for the moment, we may need some of them as much as we need you.' Sir Richard smiled. 'You trust them, do you not?'

'Most certainly, sir.'

'Good, they do seem capable, especially that young fellow Williams. I have named him in my report on the attack on Las Arenas.'

'That is most kind, sir, I am sure he will be honoured.'

'There may be even better news than that for him,' the admiral began, but was interrupted when Wharton coughed. 'Indeed, that is a subject about which we must be discreet. I may be able to tell you more when we understand things a little better.'

97

8

'Are you sure that this is wise, Ned?' Billy Pringle asked his older brother.

'For the last time, William, don't fuss,' came the distinctly querulous reply. 'You sound like Mother.'

'I do not, for I have not once bid you wrap a muffler more tightly around your neck against the chill.'

The sun baked down on them and sparkled on the blue water of Cadiz Bay. They were walking along the city walls overlooking the outer harbour and every now and then the soft breeze picked up and gusted over the ramparts, swirling up dust and making Williams and the others cling on to their hats for dear life. The two officers had gone to visit Pringle's brother in the hospital, and he had then insisted on taking a promenade. 'I want to see my ship, and make sure that damned fool Reynolds has not run her to ruin in the last week.'

The *Sparrowhawk* was in the outer harbour under the temporary command of its lieutenant, since Edward Pringle loudly insisted that he would return to duty in a few days and so there was no need to find a replacement for him. 'I need to be seen up and about,' he had said, and so with reluctance they had agreed, but only if they accompanied him. In the last half-hour he had bid good morning to several naval officers, whose duties or desire for exercise took them near the harbour. Williams noticed that the wounded commander always straightened up and brimmed with bonhomie whenever they saw another sailor. For the moment there were only soldiers and Spaniards in sight, and the show of rude health was relaxed a little.

'It is a slight scratch to the stomach, William, a mere trifle. You will realise when you have seen more service and taken a wound yourself.' Edward Pringle peered up at his taller brother, brushing away the arm proffered for support.

'I was shot in the stomach at Talavera, Ned. I am sure the family will have mentioned it to you.'

'Not surprised, you are a damned big mark for them to aim at.' Billy Pringle ate moderately, was an active man who had held up well to the rigours and privations of campaign and yet somehow always remained bulky, indeed plump, around the waist.

'They had no trouble hitting you either, Ned, and you are still just skin and bones, for all that you throw yourself at food like a starving man.'

'Yes, but my fellow had to get close, is that not right, Mr Williams? With you he could stand off a cable's length and still be sure of his aim.'

The change in Edward Pringle was remarkable, as the ship's captain receded. It did not vanish, but on shore and in the company of his brother he was a different man; a far more emotional one, willing to laugh and much inclined to snap and mock.

'Damn it, William, do not stand so close, I need no support. Dear God, even Clara never pressed so close.' It was the first mention of Edward's late wife, and it seemed to shock him. Williams had been wondering whether it would be proper to express his sympathy, or whether that would be the unkind opening of a deeper wound than the cut to his side.

'I believe she knew your peppery disposition,' Billy Pringle said with a gentle smile. 'And yet still persisted in her affections.'

'Aye, she did, poor thing.' Edward turned away, leaning on the parapet of yellow stone and gazing out at the water. 'It's a terrible and lonely thing to be a sailor's wife. There was added joy when I heard that she was with child, more than simple pleasure, for I hoped it would give her company of a sort.' Billy moved to stand beside his brother, and gave him a gentle pat on the shoulder. Williams dithered, unsure whether he should step away and give them some privacy.

99

'She was a sweet girl, but had the strangest of notions. Did I tell you that if it were a boy she wanted us to name the poor devil Lemuel? She was fond of the name, it seems, remembering a kindly uncle.' Edward's tone was incredulous.

'My parents called me Hamish,' Williams said. 'And yet were in every other way devoted to all their children.'

Edward Pringle's shoulders began to shake. No sound came, but Williams feared that emotion had overcome him. He had grown up with three sisters who cried often, and in the last few years had seen plenty of strong, brave men reduced to tears at the deaths of friends. There was always the wave of sympathy and the desire to offer comfort, but it troubled him because at the same time his instincts were repelled. A man looked so unlike a man when he cried, more like some animal or less than an animal, and it was hard not to turn away in disgust, unwilling for them ever to know that he had witnessed their collapse.

'Hamish Williams! You poor, poor bugger!' Edward Pringle was laughing, and though tears streamed from his eyes they came as a flood of near-hysterical amusement. The naval officer threw back his head and guffawed. 'No wonder you have such a talent for violence!'

Williams bowed, grinning, and Edward laughed all the more.

'I regret to say that my sisters are fond of calling me Ham,' the Welshman continued, pitching the sailor into fresh hysterics.

A finely dressed party of Spanish gentlemen, several in the powdered wigs and velvet jackets still popular at court, stared at them in disapproval.

'It's fine, my dear fellows,' Edward said to them, his face bright scarlet and stumbling over his words as he laughed. 'We are busy consoling a pickled ham!' Williams did not really understand the joke, but Billy was at the mercy of the slightest pun and was now as helplessly convulsed as his brother.

'It is the pickle, do you see ...' he said before he became incapable of further speech.

Williams apologised in Spanish, bowing to them, but saw only scorn on the gentlemen's faces. They did not acknowledge him in any other way, and simply moved on.

It was some time before the brothers recovered, and Williams let them laugh it out, wondering what it must be like to have a brother. A few redcoat officers passed them by, but he recognised none of them. Two were guardsmen, as disdainful as the Spanish gentlemen of his two companions' display. Most of the British troops were several miles away, further south on the Isla, the long peninsula connecting Cadiz to the mainland. Only part of one battalion was actually in the city itself, along with various unattached officers like themselves, and men serving on the staff. The commander, General Graham, spent as little time here as possible, and in spite of his advancing years, rode out each day inspecting the defence works being dug on the Isla. Williams had met the general when he was still a colonel and serving with Sir John Moore, and had found him not only an affable soul, but a splendid soldier. The prospect of serving under him again was most appealing, although it seemed unlikely since the 106th was in Gibraltar, and presumably they would soon be sent to join them.

'Oh, dear me, dear me.' Edward Pringle had laid his hat down on the parapet and was dabbing his forehead with a handkerchief. 'You could always make me smile, young William,' he said to his brother.

'And you could always terrify me, you great tyrant. Do you recall the time you strapped my wrists to the bedposts and told me it was a grating and that you would give me twenty-four lashes with the cat for stealing your top?'

'Well, you had stolen my top – and theft from a shipmate is a serious matter.'

'You had just broken my whirligig!'

'Entirely accidental.'

'I was only seven!'

'You must stamp on the impulse to crime before it grows,' Edward Pringle said, and smiled at the memory. 'But it did not matter, since Father was drawn by the noise and beat us both.' He thought for a moment. 'He ran a taut ship, did Father. I imagine his men feared him more than the Devil himself. He certainly scared poor Clara, but since Mother adored her it probably did not matter. After all, Father was so rarely at home.

'Forgive us, Mr Williams, but reunions are a rare thing in our family. Did your father frighten you when you were a boy? It is hard to imagine such a thing, meeting you as a formidable soldier.' Edward did not notice the expression of his brother.

'My father died when I was very young,' Williams explained.

'I am so sorry – for both my clumsy question and to awaken an unhappy memory. This can be a sad and sorrowful world, but do not let my ill fortune deter you or my rogue of a brother here. You should marry, both of you.' This time Edward noticed Billy's expression and realised that he must have touched on another sensitive topic. 'That is my opinion at least – the joys far outweigh even the worst sorrow. Come, let us resume our walk, I have not yet seen my ship.'

The ramparts were more crowded as they approached the main anchorages. Most of the time they had a hand to their hats, either to raise them in greeting or stop them from being plucked away by the wind. Cadiz was home to Spain's Regency Council, the successor to the junta which had collapsed when the French swept through Andalusia at the start of the year. The city was full to the brim, packed with tens of thousands of people who were part or wanted to be part of the free government, or who simply wanted to live in the last great city of free Spain. Prices rose atrociously, finding accommodation was an expensive nightmare, but Cadiz thrived and ate food brought in by sea. Protected as it was by the grand bays of the harbours to the east and the Isla to the south, as yet the French siege did not press tightly on the city itself. Free of this threat, the ambitious schemed for power or reform and the clever or greedy made money. In the morning people promenaded, and in the evening they dined and danced. Cadiz lived as if in a constant festival.

Few smiles greeted the three British officers, save when they met others of their own kind. Their uniforms were faded and drab against the bright gallery of colours worn by the wealthy civilians and the gaudily uniformed officers and volunteers of the Spanish army. The fighting regiments were outside the city, manning the defences, and here they encountered solely the men less keen to be near a likely battlefield. There were also the women, as richly garbed as their escorts, although invariably wearing a dress of heavy black material. This was more than compensated for by the bright gloves, sashes and parasols. They walked with grace, dresses stirring in the wind, and Williams knew his friend well enough to be sure that Billy Pringle was subjecting them to detailed scrutiny. It was soon clear that Edward was doing the same.

'You should marry.' The bitter words kept going through his head, mocking a dream which had surely become unattainable. Since he had met her more than two years ago, Williams had loved the only daughter of Major MacAndrews, the second-in-command of the 106th. Beautiful and high spirited, Jane MacAndrews was just twenty, but the child of this elderly major had lately received a substantial inheritance from her mother's American family. Williams loved her, the emotion all the more deep from coming to know her as more than a mere vision of loveliness. When the army retreated through the mountains to Corunna she had been left behind, and Williams had found her and brought her back to the regiment and her family, rallying stragglers and fighting off the French on the way. Seeing the girl tramping through the snow, helping along a child, or crouching on the floor of that cold barn, cleaning and comforting filthy soldiers dying of wounds and disease, had caused an esteem that had seemed already boundless to grow far greater.

Jane was fond of him. During those days there had a been an instant, all too brief before it was interrupted, when she had fallen into his arms and they had embraced, lips pressed together. He cherished that memory, but it had never been repeated. At Corunna, after it was all over, he had proposed, clumsily using the worst possible words in his nervousness, and had been rejected with vehemence. Then they had parted, and save for a single encounter when he had returned to England after Talavera he had not seen her. That meeting was another pleasant memory, with encouragement of renewed friendship and perhaps of more. They had corresponded a little since then, her letters brief and formal, but still so precious. Yet there was no promise of any sort, and thus it was too late. His funds were modest, his income now solely from his pay. He hoped for promotion, but needed another year of service even to be eligible for a captaincy, assuming one came vacant, and that would yield no more than a salary of one hundred and ninety-one pounds, twelve shillings and sixpence a year before deductions. Though more than he had ever earned in his life, it was scarcely wealth, and for a man of such comparative poverty to propose to a wealthy heiress ... No, that could not be borne. If there had been some understanding between them then it would be different, but there was not. Honour dictated that it must be over.

'She is quite lovely, is she not?' Edward Pringle said with great pride and even greater force, wanting to gain Williams' attention.

'Perfect,' he said, mind still far away.

'I should not go that far.' The naval captain was surprised at the reaction. 'Indeed I should not, for I have always felt the rake of her masts is not quite as it should be. But then they will never let a sloop rest in the yard for long enough to make such an experiment.'

Williams realised that he was talking about the *Sparrowhawk*, and after a moment found her twin masts, beside a big third rate. The outer harbour was crammed with ships, at least nearer to this shore. There were French guns on the other side of the bay, and so the ships sat at anchor out of range. Williams had never seen so many warships in one place, not even when the army had first sailed to Portugal, for then they had mainly been carried in transports and merchantmen.

Thoughts of the past again rushed his mind back to Jane Mac-Andrews. She and her mother were here, somewhere in Cadiz. The major had been here for some weeks, promised command of a temporary formation being put together for the defence of the Isla. Then news had come that Lieutenant Colonel Fitz-William was so seriously ill as to necessitate a return to England. MacAndrews was summoned to take command of the 106th at Gibraltar and had left a day before his family arrived here to join him. Sergeant Dobson had seen them and been invited to call at their rooms, for the major and his wife were fostering his grandson, abandoned by its mother to the care of Williams and Jane before Corunna. The veteran's wild daughter, Jenny, was somewhere with the French army, mistress to an officer, and selling information about their forces to men like Hanley.

Edward Pringle launched into a long and enthusiastic description of each vessel in turn, and Williams found that he was drawn from his gloomy preoccupation. He wished that he had brought his telescope with him, but the passion of the naval officer for his subject was infectious. First he pointed out the King's ships, eleven great ships of the line, two frigates and several smaller vessels including the curiously shaped bomb-ships, each of which carried a huge mortar set low in its deck. The sailor spoke of a ship as some of the wealthier army officers spoke of horses, their shape, their character, virtues and vices, and then with as much assurance of many of their captains.

There were a dozen Spanish ships of the line, and Edward named them as well, although he knew less of their captains or the handling of the ships. A couple were huge three-deckers with more than a hundred guns.

'The Dons have always liked to build 'em huge, not that it has done them any good. They handle badly in any sort of blow.'

Williams noticed the frowns of nearby Spaniards. They might not understand the words, but the tone, and the dismissive mention of 'the Dons', was bound to cause offence. He wondered whether he would have been so sensitive a few years ago, but these days some of his countrymen seemed boorish in their manner. They also tended to speak too loudly in public.

'Shocking state she is in now. All of them, really, rotten and worm-eaten from end to end, the men on board as decayed as the ships. Do you know we have had to provide gunners so that we can use some of them as floating batteries? Scarcely one of them has even a quarter of its proper complement.'

Billy Pringle was also clearly aware of his brother's tactlessness. Perhaps sailors spent too long at sea and in the society of others of their ilk. To be fair many soldiers were as lacking in good manners, but why must their companion be so loud?

'What about the French ships?' Billy asked, eager to distract his brother from his theme of the inadequacies of the Spanish navy. 'I believe that is one,' he added, pointing out a hulk moored without spars and with only the lowest section of its three masts sticking up.

'Yes, there are three or four prison hulks left, although I believe all are to be emptied soon. Look, there on the far shore, near the headland.' Williams spotted a darker shape among the white breakers. 'That is one of the ones which got away. We thought they had gone adrift in the storm, but it turned out the prisoners had overpowered the guards and then cut the cables. The tide took them back to the far shore and their own army. Another one did it a few days later. We chased them and fired into the hulk, so fewer made it that time, but it was a close business and we lost quite a few men in the exchange of fire. Unpleasant, though. Shells set the ship on fire and some of the men must have burned.'

'Was it necessary to fire on them at all?' Williams asked. He had heard of these escapes by several hundred French prisoners of war. They had surrendered to the Spanish back in '08, but instead of the promised return to France the men were cooped up on overcrowded hulks, poorly fed and left prey to cold, damp and disease.

Edward Pringle looked surprised by the question. 'They are enemies, going back to fight against us one day, and they were breaking their parole as prisoners.'

'As the Spanish had first broken their word.' Williams noticed Billy rolling his eyes, and realised that now he was the one voicing loud criticism of their allies. It seemed best to move on, and they began to go down a long flight of stone steps on to a lower promenade right by the sea. Wind trapped by a corner of the great stone walls buffeted against them here with considerable force, and they hunched into it, clinging tightly to their hats. A good half-hour after noon, the crowds had thinned considerably. Edward Pringle had spent time in the city before, and took them to eat in a tavern a little further along. It was cool inside away from the sun, and the Pringles drank wine while Williams had sweetened lemon juice, before sharing a table of bread, ham, fish cooked in olive oil, fruit and pastries.

Edward Pringle told them of long months spent blockading this very port when Britain and Spain were still at war. The half-dozen other people in the room were all British officers of one service or another, so that neither his brother nor Williams felt this to be too sensitive a subject. Billy said that he was sure the owner of the place had heard a lot worse and guessed that he had long since ceased to listen. 'If he does not care for it, he can always spit in our food,' Edward added cheerfully.

Trafalgar had been fought almost within sight, and after the battle the surviving French and Spanish warships had taken refuge here at Cadiz. 'And there we kept them, all bottled up, but it is dull work, and harder here than at Brest or Toulon.' For most of the war the Navy had kept close outside the main enemy ports, waiting in sufficient strength to smash all but the biggest fleets if the French or their allies should come out. There had been no big battles since Trafalgar. 'They know they cannot match us for seamanship or gunnery,' Edward boasted, and hearing him two other sailors sitting near by raised their glasses in honour of the sentiment.

'Hear, hear!'

'Blockade work takes its toll on men and ships,' Edward Pringle continued after a moment. 'Here you can spend hours or days of labour just to stay in position. There are never enough ships so all stay on station longer than they should. All Boney has to do is wait, sit inside his harbour and build ships. Do you know he builds five or six more line-of-battle ships than us every year? Well, he can afford to, can't he, controlling nearly all the timber of Europe. His navy keeps getting bigger and one day might be so big that even seamanship and gunnery will not be enough.'

Williams was surprised. For the last few years he had assumed that Britannia truly did rule the waves, unchallenged and unlikely ever to be challenged again after Trafalgar.

'Is the threat so great?'

'Not soon,' Edward Pringle said after a moment. 'It will take a long while, but then it looks as if Boney will have a long while, won't he? But you can see how dire the consequences might be if Spain goes under, and the French get their hands on the Spanish fleet. Can you imagine it? A dozen or more line-of-battle ships just here and at Gibraltar, and more elsewhere, all handed over to him. Two or more years' advantage gifted to them just like that.' He snapped his fingers.

'You do not seem to think much of the quality of those ships,' Billy said.

'Aye, and we must take the chief blame for that. Cadiz is a safe anchorage, but has little in the way of yards or docks. Spain's fleet has never been based here, but they had to sit at anchor, riding out each big storm with no prospect of supplies to repair any damage. Their own government took over, starving them of men and money – why pay for idle ships, they thought. And this is the result, half of them barely fit to float, let alone sail. Not that they could not be repaired in time. No, Boney would love to get his grubby hands on them, so that must not happen. I hear that several will be convoyed away in the next few days. One or two may have to be towed, they are in such a state, and we are loaning them hundreds of sailors. Glad I'm not one of them. If the weather turns half of them will go to the bottom.'

Edward Pringle sat opposite them at the table, the other two with their backs to the door, and now the sailor was looking with great interest in that direction. 'Now there is something I would sail for ever and for ever,' he said.

Williams turned, and then sprang to his feet, banging his knee painfully against the table leg.

'Mr Williams,' said a voice he had not heard for over a year save in memory and dream. 'And Captain Pringle too, what a pleasure to see old friends.'

Miss MacAndrews stood in the doorway, struggling to balance a basket on one arm as she folded her parasol. She wore a long-sleeved dress of pale pink muslin, white gloves and a deep bonnet. With the dazzlingly bright sunlight coming through the open door behind her, the dark outline of her legs and body was precisely traced against the pale, almost translucent dress.

Williams struggled to speak, swamped by emotion made worse by the granting of a sight generally reserved for his dreams. The irrelevant thought came to mind that perhaps this was why the local ladies favoured black dresses rather than the pale colours fashionable in England.

'It is good to see you, Miss MacAndrews,' Billy Pringle said, as the two redcoat officers tried to ignore a soft 'Quite wonderful to see you' from his brother.

Williams managed to step forward, moving so close that his view was less dramatic and the brothers' perspective masked altogether. He thought he caught a muttered 'Damn' from behind him. 'May I be of assistance?' he asked.

She smiled, the wide mouth parting to reveal neat white teeth. He could see her better now, and her looks overpowered him again as they always did, but now it was more the sparkle in her eyes than the smooth skin, delicate features and the never quite tamed locks of red hair escaping from beneath the bonnet. At the moment, whatever the future held, he was filled with joy to see a friend. The love was always there, however hopeless, but so was the simple delight in her company.

'Thank you, but I believe I can manage. I was looking for my mother. She wanted to meet with a Mr Henegan of the Commissariat in the hope of securing passage to Gibraltar on one of the convoys. She was not at the other place where she thought he might be, so I came here. It does not matter, I was merely hoping to walk home with her.'

A cough, and a presence close by his arm, prompted him. Williams presented Edward Pringle to the major's daughter, and saw something of his younger brother's charming ways for the first time. Edward bowed, kissing the fingers proffered to shake.

Miss MacAndrews dazzled him with a smile and a compliment about the Navy. She and her mother had travelled out in a cutter carrying dispatches. 'We were treated with great courtesy, even in so confined a ship.'

'I am sure they must have been honoured to carry such precious packages, Miss MacAndrews,' Edward Pringle said with a smoothness Williams felt unbecoming in a man so recently bereaved.

'Forgive me, gentlemen, but I must go,' the girl replied. 'Happy reunion though this is – and an honour to make your acquaintance, Captain Pringle. You must all call on us,' she added, and Williams hoped he saw a particular emphasis and look in his direction as she spoke. Then he remembered the changed circumstances and for a moment despised himself as a fortune hunter. It would not do.

He followed her into the street, noting the speed with which the very fair-skinned girl popped her parasol back up. The hot wind caught it, and she struggled to hold it steady until it slackened.

'It comes from Africa,' he said for want of anything better.

'I beg your pardon, Mr Williams?'

'The wind, it blows across the sea from Africa.'

'Ah.' She nodded, understanding him. 'It is remarkable to see that continent from the other side of the city.'

'I am continually surprised by the snow on the peaks of the mountains,' Williams said, merely for the sake of being with her, 'for I had always associated Africa with great heat.'

' 'Tis a shame it disappoints you.' Jane smiled again. 'For my part I regret that it is so close and yet still so far away. I should like to see a camel, Mr Williams,' she added, looking wistful, until the humour surfaced again. 'It is the first time I have seen the African coast – or at least the first time I can remember. We were at Gibraltar for a while when I was little.' Over the years her mother had accompanied her father to garrison after garrison throughout the world. 'But I do not remember seeing it then. I do remember being chased by an ape and being unable to sleep lest it followed me home!'

'And here you are in Cadiz being followed by another great ape,' he said quickly.

Miss MacAndrews gave a little laugh as genuinely amused as it was proper. 'Well, at least you are a friendly one – and a good deal more becoming in appearance than that horrible beast!' She gave him an arch look. 'Though scarcely better dressed!'

Clegg had done a remarkable job of repairing his jacket, and from a distance all looked well, but it was unfit for close scrutiny. Williams decided that he must have a new one made, even if it took the bulk of his remaining savings, already largely devoured because he had not been paid for six months. The army struggled to cope with detached service when it came to such things.

'The ape apologises,' he said, and bowed.

Miss MacAndrews smiled again. 'But I really must go, for there is Mama.' Williams saw the tall, straight figure of Mrs Mac-Andrews standing on the wide rampart above them. She was an imperious, somewhat terrifying lady, and he had come to like her a good deal. 'I do not think she has spied me,' Jane said, 'but I must go. It is good to see you. You must call as soon as your duties permit. Tomorrow afternoon if not before. You will be astounded to see how much young Jacob has grown. Sergeant Dobson looks so proud of him. Goodbye, Mr Williams.'

The girl walked away. Her mother had been engaged with her maid, but now noticed her daughter and waved, extending the wave to Williams. He had deliberately stood just in front of the door to the tavern, blocking the route and forcing the Pringles to beg his pardon if they wanted to join them. Billy had sensed his mood and not done so, restraining his brother's obvious enthusiasm for the company of the young lady.

Williams stepped back, letting the brothers come out, but making sure that he was able to watch the girl as she went to meet her mother. The others had their backs to her and Edward looked disappointed.

Jane struggled as the wind caught her parasol once more, and then she began the long climb up the stone steps to the top of the rampart. He watched her go, and even the dark despair of knowing she was unattainable was something precious to him, somehow bringing her closer before she was lost.

'Delightful girl,' Edward Pringle said. 'Most charming indeed.'

Miss MacAndrews was halfway up the steps when the wind, which had slackened, blew with redoubled force and was funnelled by the shape of the high walls. The parasol shook and then folded inside out. The girl's high-waisted dress swelled like a balloon, the skirt rising. Even at fifty yards' distance Williams saw Jane gasp in surprise, mouth opened wide at this sudden assault by nature. Though she was a small girl, her legs were shapely and sheathed in white silk stockings, held up by pink garters just above her knees.

'You appear deep in thought, young Williams,' Edward Pringle said, oblivious to all this. 'Would you care to share the rich fruits of your wisdom?'

The parasol was either let go or plucked from the girl's hand, which at least gave her more opportunity to fight against the wildly thrashing material of her dress. Miss MacAndrews managed to push the skirt down as the wind dropped, but a few steps further on it struck again. Dress and petticoats flew in spite of all attempts to control them, exposing stockings, garters, bare skin above them and something white.

'The thought appears a happy one, as well as profound,' Edward continued.

Williams licked his lips, which felt so very dry.

'Behold, the oracle is about to give forth.'

'I was thinking of Socrates,' he said at last, and managed to glance at the two Pringles in turn. Miss MacAndrews was nearly at the top of the stairs, her dress held firmly down in front as far as her knees, but billowing more generously at the back. Jane looked around, searching to see whether there were witnesses to this immodest display, and so it was easier for him to look at the other men in the hope of concealing his recent attention.

'Very admirable, I am sure,' Edward said. 'You are an extraordinary fellow, Williams.'

'In particular, I was thinking of Socrates and his wife, and how they met.'

The naval officer frowned. 'Something of a shrew, as I recall.'

Yet Billy may have caught the reference, for he turned slightly, and just saw Miss MacAndrews as she reached the top of the rampart. Her skirts twitched one last time, revealing several inches of stockings.

'Damn,' Billy Pringle said softly. 'Kept that to yourself, didn't you, Mr Williams.'

Edward did not understand, and by the time they continued their own walk, mother and daughter had vanished.

'Delightful girl,' Edward said again. 'Truly delightful.' Neither of the others could be drawn into conversation for some time, and so the sailor talked again of ships and the sea.

9

Jane MacAndrews could not sleep, and so stared up at the ceiling. A streak of silvery light crossed it because the shutters resolutely refused to close that last inch, and there was the hubbub and occasional shouts of revellers still walking the street below. It was not the noise that kept her awake, nor was it the smell of burning oil from the men selling fried sardines to passers-by. She was used to both by now. Long years of following her father meant that she and her mother were seasoned travellers, and so they had brought all their own linen, and even their own mattresses now filled with fresh straw. If not ideally soft, they were well used to them by now, and at least it was reassuring to know that you were not sharing your bed with all the local vermin – and indeed those imported by previous occupants.

Young Jacob was asleep once again after waking in a nightmare. She had listened to the nurse calming him, and then heard her mother arriving to complete the task. Esther MacAndrews had not done that for some time, and it was this and other strange behaviour on her mother's part which left her confused, her mind too active to rest.

It had begun yesterday, after meeting Williams, Pringle and his brother the navy captain, and just after that horrible climb up those windy stairs. Jane felt herself blushing even at the memory. Such things happened, and did not much matter unless one had an audience. She hoped that no one had noticed, for the promenades were almost empty, but she could not quite convince herself. Williams had seen, she suspected, and perhaps his companions, although none of them had looked at her any differently today. Most men looked at her, and had done so for years now. It could be uncomfortable, tiresome, flattering or a mixture of them all, but she was used to it, and it merely made it all the more important to be in control of herself and her appearance. The loss of her good parasol was to be regretted. Red of hair and pale of skin, she did not cope well with the sun, and for the walk home had had to rely on her long sleeves, gloves and the shadow of her bonnet for protection. A close inspection in the mirror had revealed no trace of the freckles always ready to invade her face and arms at a moment's notice.

'Really, Jane, there are less obvious ways of drawing a gentleman's attention,' her mother had drawled when she reached her on top of the wall. Esther MacAndrews' South Carolina accent tended to become more pronounced in proportion to the irony in her words. 'Many would say that even showing an ankle is over-bold.' If Jane was blushing now, at the time her face must have been bright scarlet.

'And how is Mr Williams?' her mother continued, and the pause was significant and quite deliberate. 'And Captain Pringle as well, of course.' Jane's father had commanded the Grenadier Company of the 106th when Williams joined as a volunteer and Pringle and Hanley were subalterns. Both her parents liked the young men, and Mrs MacAndrews showed a particular benevolent amusement towards Williams, and was aware of much – if not quite all – of the volatile friendship between the Welshman and her daughter.

Jane's mind wandered a little to this different cause for concern, but considerable uncertainty had always formed part of her feelings towards Williams and only rarely did that keep her from sleep. Her mother worried her far more at the moment.

Yesterday Mrs MacAndrews' heart did not seem to be in the teasing, something in which she generally took such delight, and her manner as they walked was distant. Several times she repeated herself or answered a question different from the one her daughter had asked. It took concerted pressure to prise any explanation from her at all.

'It is nothing, my dear, nothing at all. I had a shock, that is all.' Very little in life ever disturbed Esther MacAndrews' poise, and Jane could not remember anything shocking her mother.

'Do not fret, Jane. It really is nothing,' she said after further questioning. 'I thought I saw someone I have not seen for many years.' From the tone it was clearly not someone who evoked fond memories. 'I was mistaken.'

Jane got no more, and by the evening her mother's manner was closer to her usual ebullient self. Today she seemed fully recovered, and when Williams and Pringle called on them in the afternoon she joked with them and at their expense. Mrs MacAndrews was adept at baiting young men, and especially young officers, mixing boldness with pretended offence, always surprising them and keeping them off balance while narrowly remaining within the confines of polite society. Often incorrigible, she was also imperious.

'We have invitations to a ball this evening and need escorts,' she had announced suddenly. 'As members of the regiment I shall expect you to fulfil the roles – and to do us proud.' She subjected them to close scrutiny, even though Jane doubted she had missed anything about their appearance. Esther MacAndrews took a keen interest in clothes, without letting that interest rule her life, and Jane hoped that her own instincts were similar. 'Sometimes the best of men can be derelict in the matter of applying polish to their boots.'

Both men had looked down, although in each case their Hessians were gleaming.

'Not that that is a concern, since I trust you have shoes. However, Mr Williams, that jacket simply will not do. Do you have another?'

'I regret to say no. At least none in better condition.'

'You need a wife to look after you,' Mrs MacAndrews said mischievously, darting a look at her daughter. 'Well, that simply will not do if I am to be seen with you. You must borrow one of the major's coats we have here in his trunk. What do you think, Jane, the blue one with the braid?'

Resistance was doomed, although the lieutenant made noises about not wanting to impose.

'Nonsense, I shall not be disgraced.' She eyed them both again. 'Yes, I think you shall be my escort, Mr Williams. You are the taller of the two and I plan to wear my feathers.'

That had surprised Jane, which made her suspect that it was intended to do so. She was never quite sure whether her mother encouraged her to view Williams' attempts to court her with kindness.

'Good, that is settled,' Esther said, not waiting for anyone to express a view. 'Yes, and if memory serves, you dance as ill as the major, Mr Williams, so that will be all the more fitting. Unless you have had time for some lessons?'

'I regret not.'

'Hmm, as I suspected. MacAndrews has consistently found excuses. You soldiers are all alike.'

The gentlemen returned at seven, Williams obediently wearing the blue jacket produced earlier by their maid. Jane's father was a tall, lanky man, less big about the shoulders and chest than the lieutenant. Williams had managed to fasten the top two brass buttons on the jacket, but given up all attempts at the remaining seven. Instead he had borrowed a respectable grey waistcoat from Hanley.

'You will do, I suppose,' Mrs MacAndrews decided, 'and at least I shall not loom over you.' Jane's mother was five foot ten inches tall, and even in her forty-fifth year was a strikingly handsome woman, her hair still raven black, nature requiring only the slightest assistance to maintain the shade. Her gown was green, a deeper shade than the gloves and the turban topped with tall peacock feathers. Mrs MacAndrews would most certainly have loomed over a man even of average height.

It was something of a mystery how two such tall parents had produced their diminutive daughter. Jane sometimes wondered whether her siblings would have been more like her parents in stature, but neither of the brothers nor her sister had survived infancy. It was a sorrow which she knew hung over her parents' lives, and yet they had never let it burden her, nor did she feel that they had indulged her. A life of following the drum gave little scope for indulgence.

This evening Jane had decided to adopt some of the local fashions. It began with shoes, higher heeled than would be fashionable in England and just made for her a few days ago. She hoped that the leather was as soft as it appeared and that they would not prove too stiff over the course of the evening. Her gown was from London, short sleeved and made from turquoise silk. It had a high waist, something that did not seem to be common here, and a generous, even daring neckline. The sun had nearly gone down, and she relied on gloves reaching above her elbow for protection from its last rays. She had spent some time practising with a newly bought black mantilla, trying to perfect the graceful gestures of the women of Cadiz as they adjusted this combination of head covering and shawl. Unlike her mother, she had taken the unusual step of wearing her hair down, since this again seemed the Spanish preference. The maid they had hired in the city had proved a great help.

'You see that we have among us the perfect Iberian contessa,' her mother said. 'There, is our 'Juanita MacAndrews' not magnificent? Or is that too stiff a question for you gentlemen?'

Pringle looked surprised, and Williams guilty at that, while Jane struggled not to show that she thought she understood her mother's meaning. She worried that some witticism would follow concerning her embarrassing misfortune yesterday, so that it was a great relief that instead Esther hurried them out.

'I do not care to be later than politeness demands,' she said.

The ball was a grand affair given by a member of the Regency Council, and the hundreds of guests were packed into a great hall and surrounding rooms. It quickly became stuffy in the extreme, and they all drank a good deal of the iced lime juice proffered by the liveried servants. The hall was a blaze of colour, lit by thousands of candles in heavy chandeliers hanging from the ceiling. Whites, reds, blues, yellows and greens all stood out, almost in highlight from the black of the ladies' dresses. Within minutes of arriving Jane counted eight Spanish generals resplendent in gold-laced blue uniforms, two bishops in black and red, and a good few splendidly dressed fellows surrounded by such obvious deference to mark them out as some of the Regency Council or other men aspiring to power.

Lieutenant General Graham was there, and came to pay his respects as soon as he was free. It was he who had provided Jane's mother with the invitations.

'I first met this lady when she rode with General Moore's staff in Spain,' the general explained to one of his ADCs as the introductions were made. 'You would not have believed it, cool as anything, elegant as anything, calming her horse as French shot ploughed up the ground. I tell you this, if the world knew that such beauty could be seen in battle, then we would no longer struggle to recruit for the army!'

The general had a long face and a forceful nose. At sixty-one he remained full of vigour, and only hair more grey than brown, some slight thickening around the neck and chin, and an increased prominence of his ears betrayed any signs of age.

'And Miss MacAndrews, this is truly a great delight. Scottish father,' he confided to the staff officer, 'do you see, and so such radiance is understandable. To meet such ladies makes me regret that I am not a good deal younger.'

'I am sure that if you were, then both our hearts would be in peril, General,' Mrs MacAndrews said. 'Is that not so, Jane?'

'Indeed, Mama.' Jane curtsied, prompting Graham to bow. The general showed obvious pleasure at the compliment, and the flirtation continued for a while, before he recognised Williams.

'I believe we have met before, Mr ...?' Unable to discern rank since there were no insignia on the blue jacket, the general turned the statement into a question.

'Lieutenant Williams, sir. One Hundred and Sixth. And may I present Captain Pringle.'

Lieutenant General Graham broke into a smile. 'Of course, of course. Though I believe you were Ensign Williams when we met.'

'Yes, sir.'

'Yes, indeed. That was back with Moore as well,' Graham explained to his staff. 'This young fellow gathered a few dozen stragglers and stopped the French from taking the one bridge leading around our flank. That was fine soldiering, sir, fine soldiering indeed. Moore thought so, and you cannot give higher praise than that. Aye,' he added, the memories returning. 'Of course, you were with him when he fell.' It may have been the flickering candlelight, but Jane thought the general's eyes were moist.

'Are you officers on your way to join your regiment at Gibraltar?'

'Yes, sir,' Pringle said. 'Although we have lately been sent to Granada.'

'Oh.' Graham nodded. 'Keats has got his claws into you, has he? Well then, we shall have to see what we can do. And you too, madam? Have you had any more luck in finding passage to Gibraltar and your husband?'

'Regretfully not, General.'

General Graham's gaze flicked past the ladies. 'Ah, then I believe here is someone who may be able to help. May I present to you Major General Lord Turney, who is soon to return to Gibraltar. Lord Turney, may I name ...' Graham began his introduction with the ladies.

Jane turned to see the dignified if distant smile of the major general grow swiftly into something far warmer. Lord Turney was finely dressed, his red coat and white breeches exquisitely cut to flatter his graceful frame. His back could have been no straighter without danger of snapping, his stride was determined and manly, and yet still with a delicacy appropriate for the ballroom.

'An honour, my dear ladies, a great honour indeed. Such fine English beauty shines out all the more in this company.'

Jane thought that a strange compliment, offensive surely to the Spanish ladies, several of whom and their escorts were within earshot even over the hubbub of conversation. It also carried an implication that she and her mother would be less conspicuous in London.

'I believe that Lord Turney and I have met before.' Jane was surprised at her mother's tone. This was not banter or flirtation, but had a genuine hard edge.

'Surely not, ma'am,' Turney said, offering another slight bow. 'It is impossible that I could ever forget so fair a lady.'

'Only a fool could do that,' General Graham agreed. 'Still, are you a fool, Lord Turney?' His tone was light, though a little forced. Jane wondered whether the older man had any high opinion of the other. The difference in age between the two was less than she had thought. Turney must at least be as old as her own father. That made his close inspection of her somewhat less flattering. He did not cross the bounds of convention, but Lord Turney's steady consideration of her face and figure was not so discreet that she – or indeed any woman of sense – would not be aware of it. That was surely deliberate, but then the thought was driven from her head.

Mrs MacAndrews was biting her lip. It was a gesture Jane had worked hard to stop herself from doing when worried, and she had never before seen her mother do it. Williams looked uncomfortable, and she noticed that his arm was being squeezed with considerable ferocity.

'Indeed, sir.' Esther spoke with a hard edge to her voice. 'Indeed, and I recollect that it is not the first time your memory has failed.' She took a deep breath. Jane watched Lord Turney closely, baffled by the scene and her mother's cold anger. Did his eyes flicker, recognition and perhaps something else betrayed for an instant before the elegant calm was restored?

'If so, then you have my sincere apologies.' Lord Turney bowed very low this time, and reached out his hand to confirm the apology.

Esther MacAndrews did not even glance at it. 'Jane, I am not feeling well. It is the heat. We must retire to somewhere cooler and more open. Will you excuse us, General,' she made a slight knee to Graham, 'gentlemen?'

'Of course, of course.' The general sounded a little confused, but more concerned for their health. 'Of course, you must go. Goodnight, Mrs MacAndrews, Miss MacAndrews.'

Her mother led the way, Williams' arm still held in a vice-like grip, half dragging the big man through the crowd. They went through a long side room and out into one of the gardens, where lanterns hung from the branches of trees to light the tables and pavilions. There were plenty of people there, but the press was less close, even though no breeze stirred the night air. The gentlemen were sent to fetch drinks. 'I need something stronger than juice,' her mother said. 'So let Pringle choose it as I believe he is the better judge.'

Jane tried without success to draw her mother into discussion of the hanging baskets of flowers. The matter of the silk drapes on the pavilions similarly failed to excite her interest.

'Damn him, damn him for making me angry.' The words were whispered so softly that Jane barely heard them. She doubted her mother was aware that she had spoken aloud.

Hoping to lighten the mood she instead considered the passers-by. 'That is an uncommonly tall lady over there with the scarlet gloves,' she said, 'and especially since her escort is so small.' The gentleman wore a yellow velvet coat and high powdered wig, but still was dwarfed by his companion.

'The one in the dress is a man, Jane,' her mother said flatly. 'It is the lady in the wig.'

'Lady seems over-generous,' she replied, and now could not understand how she had missed the signs.

'Festivals here are a curious affair.' Esther MacAndrews did not sound interested, and when the gentlemen returned she emptied the glass quickly and then announced that Pringle must escort her home. The latter was flustered before this, and Jane had the malicious thought that the captain may have begun to attend a 'lady' only to discover that it was in fact a man. Billy Pringle was very ready in his affections towards the fair sex, and Jane did not think less of him for that.

'We should all leave,' Jane declared.

'No, we should not. I do not feel well, but you should enjoy yourself, my dear, and take the chance to dance.' Her mother was adamant and not to be shifted. The deft exchange of escorts was equally irresistible. 'Williams will take good care of you. If he does not, then I shall have him shot!' The joke was weak and not delivered with any enthusiasm.

Williams and she wandered, heading towards the sounds of music. Nowhere could they find any sets being danced, and the boleros and fandangos were certainly beyond Williams' capacities. Jane wanted to learn these dances, but had only had the chance for some basic tuition, and at present was more eager to practise her singing and playing. Both had come on considerably during the year they had spent in England.

In one of the bigger pavilions they found an orchestra playing waltzes. There were considerably more British and other foreigners there, and although many Spanish ladies were drawn on to the floor, over time Jane noticed that few returned more than once. A dance where the partners held each other so closely was no doubt scandalous to those unused to such innovations. She danced twice with Williams, who had declared that he knew the steps. This was true, at least of the essentials, and he seemed less awkward than when they had first stepped out together two years before. Yet there was also a reserve about him, not she felt from shyness, but something else that was new. Both his conversation and his manner stopped a little short of the intimacy she had come to expect.

Jane also danced with a captain of the Foot Guards who had travelled out with them on the same vessel, and through him two of his fellow officers. They were all competent and charming, although none showed any unusual wit. Williams said something about that being only to be expected when she mentioned this to him.

'If you are not already engaged, then may I crave the honour of a dance, Miss MacAndrews.' Lord Turney appeared from nowhere, his manner so courteous that she had accepted before realising who it was. It was still an honour to be asked by such a senior guest, but she could not help wishing that it had been General Graham instead.

Yet Turney was a fine dancer, as vigorous as he was agile, and soon the floor cleared as the couple drew admiring gazes. The general held her firmly, and very close, leading with a bold step.

'That fine lady, your mother, is from the Americas, I would think?' His voice was clipped and precise.

'Yes, my lord, from Charleston originally.'

'A loyalist family, I presume, although she is clearly not old enough to recollect the Rebellion. But then I can scarcely believe that she has the years to be mother to a daughter who must be at least eighteen.'

Unsure whether or not that was a compliment reflecting badly on her, Jane did not reply for a moment. 'I am twenty, my lord, and my mother is still young.' She could not think of anything better to say, for this questioning surely concealed a deeper purpose.

'Of course, though in your case you combine the freshness of a spring bloom with a sophistication far beyond your years.'

The general seemed satisfied and said no more than a few formal pleasantries for the remainder of the dance. His hold became tighter still, pressing her to him in a manner so intimate that it surely deserved the disapproving stares of some of the watching locals. It was done with skill, and Jane found no way to loosen the grip. The general was dangerous, and also very gallant. At the end of the piece he bowed, thanked her, pressing her hand firmly, and then vanished back into the crowd.

She saw no more of him and soon they ventured back into the gardens. It was getting late and Jane suggested that they leave. Her shoes had begun to press during the dancing and she longed to bathe her feet. As they threaded their way between the pavilions they passed more women dressed in breeches and men's coats and men in dresses. It seemed odd for folk given to such habits to be offended by a waltz, but then these were the fringes of a great ball and granted far more licence than elsewhere. Several times Jane saw ladies startled by something and felt that licence might be too slight a term.

'Lieutenant Williams, as I live and breathe. Oh, and the very lovely Miss MacAndrews.' The voice was heavily slurred with drink, and belonged to a slim fellow with a badly scarred face. There was something familiar about him apart from his manner, but Jane realised who he was only when Williams replied.

'Hatch,' he said. 'I did not know that you were still in Cadiz.'

'Oh, still here, Williams, waiting for the call to duty and glory. Though it is Lieutenant Hatch now, if you please.'

'My apologies. I have not yet had a chance to offer congratulations. You have transferred to a foreign corps, I recollect.'

Hatch was a small man, wounded badly in the head at Talavera. Jane remembered him as a vulgar fellow, who never seemed to be altogether sober. He wore a blue jacket with green cuffs and collar, and wings on the shoulders. Those were the mark of a flank company, which suggested it was the uniform of his new regiment and not simply one of the fashionable undress coats, like the one Williams had borrowed.

'Yes, I am with the light bobs – the rifle company of the Chasseurs.' Hatch bowed, looked nauseous, and slowly straightened up. As he did so he leered very obviously at the front of Jane's dress. She did not remember seeing him quite as drunk as this. Not long ago her mother had hinted that the transfer to the foreign regiment had not been voluntary, but imposed by Colonel FitzWilliam as a punishment. Apparently there were unpaid gambling debts and other misdemeanours, and so it was felt better to have the fellow away from the regiment, at least for a while. By the sound of things her father had acted on the colonel's behalf and helped to arrange the matter.

'Well, congratulations indeed.' She could feel Williams' utter distaste for the man as he held her arm. 'But we must bid you goodnight.'

Hatch ignored the hint and fell into step beside them. Jane managed to avoid a loose attempt made to take her free arm.

'Good to be with friends,' Hatch said. Williams glared, but

said no more. The press of the crowd was thicker down one of the aisles and they had to work their way through, jostled on all sides. Some of the touches felt more deliberate than accidental. Then Jane was pinched – undoubtedly pinched – through the silk of her dress. She jerked up straight, and Williams must have felt the motion for he looked down at her, face concerned. Jane shook her head to signify that it was nothing. Used to gentlemen whose hands were inclined to wander too freely during a dance, she had not before encountered anything so gross. The sight of other ladies being startled suggested that she was not singled out.

'I need friends, you see,' Hatch explained, ignoring the silence of the other two. Jane wondered whether the officer was responsible, but his hands were clasped together in front of him. It seemed better to avoid a scene.

'There are enemies out there,' the scarred officer continued. 'A father and his ruffians out for my blood. That is if they can find me.' Hatch touched his nose, inviting them to join his little conspiracy. 'I have taken precautions to evade pursuit.'

'Really,' Williams said without the slightest trace of interest. Jane felt another touch, this time different, more like the pressure of something being pushed against her. She tried to peer back over her shoulder, but having her hair down made it more difficult. Williams leaned back and his face filled with anger.

'Oh yes, from the beginning I threw them off the scent by telling them that my name was Williams.' Hatch chuckled, and did not seem quite so drunk.

Williams' arm slipped free from Jane and he squared up to the other officer.

'You did what, sir!' His voice was loud and made several people turn. Jane took the opportunity to twist and saw that someone had stuck a sweet pastry on to her dress in the middle of her bottom. She reddened in a mixture of outrage and shame.

'Well, Williams is a good name for a rogue,' Hatch said in a level voice. He was slouching, his whole manner avoiding any challenge.

'For goodness' sake,' Williams began, and then Jane interrupted him with a yelp. A man in a gold-laced white coat and plumed tricorne hat had walked past her, and as he did his arm flicked over, brushing against her chest and dropping something sticky down the front of her dress.

The civilian grinned, and Williams swung into a punch that knocked the man off his feet and sent him crashing back to overturn a table. Jane was wriggling, trying to pluck whatever it was back out, but her fingers were clumsy in her gloves. There was cream on them and she guessed it must be another pastry.

Another civilian shouted something at Williams, and the Welshman punched him as well, sending him staggering backwards. Hatch had gone.

'We should leave,' Jane said, trying to copy something of her mother's usual firmness. Williams looked belligerent, ready to slam his fist into the world at large, and several men appeared willing to confront him. 'Take me home, sir,' she said, and the appeal to duty and her protection did the trick.

Neither spoke, but they hurried on their way as fast as Jane's tight shoes would allow. They were near the corner of the last street before their lodgings when two men in long cloaks and wide hats blocked their path.

'Señor Williams?' one said, struggling to pronounce the name.

'Yes, damn it, what do you want?' her companion said gruffly, then realising that he had sworn. 'My apologies, Miss Mac-Andrews.'

Steel glinted as the men produced slim knives from beneath their cloaks.

Jane screamed, felt foolish immediately, but did not stop. Williams pushed her back, stepping forward to place himself between the girl and their assailants. He jabbed a punch, but the men stepped back easily. They moved a little apart so that they could threaten him from two sides at once.

Shouts came from behind them and the sound of running feet. The two cloaked men exchanged glances and then fled.

'Are you all right, Jane?' Williams said, so concerned that he used her Christian name. 'Are you hurt?'

'I am fine,' she said, but there was no time for more because the Guards captain and his friends appeared – it was they who had given chase and frightened off their assailants.

Thanks were offered, solicitous enquiries made about her health, and she had four escorts to take her the last short distance to her door. She was too tired to speak beyond the necessary courtesies. It had been a long and unnerving night.

Fatigue had not produced sleep, even once she was bathed and could feel clean again – she feared it would not be so easy to clean her gown and other clothes. So much had happened, so quickly that Jane could not find rest.

The assailants were probably seeking that drunken fool Hatch. That seemed most likely, and their interest had been in Williams and not her. People spoke of stabbings in the streets almost as a commonplace now that Cadiz was crowded with so many ambitious, jealous and greedy men. She hoped that her friend's life would not be endangered again so soon, although from a few things Pringle had said the Welshman had once more been flinging himself into danger in the last few weeks. Jane resolved to ask Dobson about what had happened when the sergeant next called to see his grandson. She feared a recklessness about Williams, and wondered about his odd reserve. Her feelings towards him had grown stronger in the last year, far stronger, even though they still fell just short of certainty. It would be hard indeed to lose him now – or was that better than to commit at last only to lose him in a few months' time when his boldness exhausted his store of luck?

Yet it was her mother who concerned her most, and then suddenly, as the clocks struck four in cruel reminder of how much sleep she was losing, Jane understood. The thought was clear and somehow she knew it must be true. Her parents had married in 1783, not long before Britain and the new United States of America concluded a peace treaty. Her father had been a prisoner of war, a young lieutenant, and he had escaped his captors alongside another officer. That man had brought with him her mother, then a little shy of her eighteenth birthday, and daughter of a wealthy family, nearly all of whom were patriots fervent for the cause of independence. With the militia on their trail, the other officer had fled, and after several narrow escapes, her parents had managed to reach the British lines outside New York. By that time they were in love and had married as soon as a parson could be secured.

That was the bones of the story, as it had been told to her. In the last few years she had begun to question some of the details. Mrs MacAndrews had given birth to a son before the year was out, suspiciously soon after they had married. Her parents were always vague as to why she had chosen to leave with two escaping prisoners of war, talking airily of her taste for adventure. Eventually her mother admitted that she had fallen in love with the other British officer, but not to say anything about it to the major. Her father knew everything, and they had long ago ceased to worry about such things. Jane kept her promise and found that the changed story did not alter her attitude towards her parents, whose happiness was so obvious. Yet she wondered whether that first baby had been a half-brother.

Lord Turney must be the other officer, her mother's lover and perhaps the father of the child. Jane felt that it must be true, and it explained so much. The title was clearly an Irish one, and no doubt inherited since then, so that she would not have recognised the name. Memories of dancing with the man rushed up and were disturbing. Not only was the man old enough to be her father, if things had been different he might have *been* her father. The closeness of his touch as he had pulled her hips towards him in the waltz now seemed uncomfortable indeed. She almost wished for another bath.

Jane must have fallen asleep in the end, for she woke to a bright strip of sunlight running across the ceiling.

'You look quite unwell, Jane,' her mother said as they took breakfast. 'I fear some of the food last night was not of the best. However, I have news. I have decided not to follow your father to Gibraltar. It is likely the regiment will move, so we might only reach there to find him gone, and this is a more comfortable place to stay than the Rock. Here you should not be frightened by apes,' she added with a smile. 'Do you remember that when you were a little girl?'

'Yes, Mama. Of course, if you think it best, then we must stay,' Jane said – and avoid further encounters with Lord Turney, let alone the prospect of being cooped up in a ship with him on the journey down.

Jane was sure that she had got to the heart of the mystery.

10

This time it all went smoothly. With Edward Pringle back
on board, the *Sparrowhawk* took them again through the
Straits of Gibraltar and landed them at night along the coast
from Malaga. The winds were ideal, and when they went ashore
no French cavalry stumbled across their path. Hanley, Williams,
Dobson and Murphy were the only British soldiers. Pringle
was not with them, having been sent to Gibraltar. By now he
would be back with the battalion, at the head of the Grenadier
Company, and no doubt drinking too much of the Gibraltar
black-strap, wine infamous for being both cheap and very strong.
Hanley knew Williams would have liked to be with him – not
for the drink, of course, but to be back with the battalion –
and that puzzled him a little since he knew that Mrs and Miss
MacAndrews were still in Cadiz. Probably his friend's sense of
honour was screwing him up inside and making him feel noble
for being away from the woman he loved. Hanley pitied Williams
for the constant battle the man fought to match his own ideals,
and rather envied him because he had fallen so deeply in love
with one woman. Such closeness was not something he had ever
felt.

With the British came a Spanish lieutenant, two soldiers, fifty
muskets – this time Spanish models begged from the army at
Cadiz – two thousand cartridges to go with them, thirty short
swords, and six barrels of powder. Lieutenant Vega was from the
area, and had arranged everything. Mules and guides were waiting, and they moved inland swiftly. El Blanco's band was one of
the first they visited, giving him half of their supplies.

'Better,' the chieftain said, smiling this time when he looked at one of the muskets. 'Much better.'

Their welcome was warm from the start, probably because they did not have Sinclair with them, and the next morning they all rode to a high peak and looked down towards the coast.

'The French hold their forts,' Don Antonio Velasco told them. About a mile away they saw a group of high-walled buildings on top of a lower crest. 'That was the Convent of Santa Clara. Now it holds one hundred soldiers – Germans who serve the French.'

Don Antonio's wife rode beside him, dressed all in black – boots, trousers, shirt, cloak and even her broad-brimmed hat. Hanley had told Williams about the women who rode in the band, but the Welshman had still made the same mistake as he and Pringle, at first taking them for boys.

'You were right not to let Lupe come,' the leader said to his wife, who made no reply. 'She used to live there, like many girls when they come of age, waiting for marriage.'

'An unhappy memory?' Hanley asked.

'There was a French column going along the valley,' El Blanco said. 'This would be back in January. Shots were fired, who knows from where, and so the French stormed Santa Clara.'

'Poor child,' Williams said in his slow Spanish. 'Was she hurt?'

'She was violated.' It was Paula Velasco who spoke, and her voice was surprisingly deep. 'Again and again. So were the nuns, and many were killed. And so she is seventeen and no longer a child. She says little and only hates and kills.'

Hanley had heard many such stories in the past years, so much so that the mind became hardened, but the young woman's tone was so brutal that he felt again the terrible sorrow of this war. When he thought of such things it sickened him to remember how he had once admired Napoleon as a bringer of enlightenment. Yet French officers seemed so affable when he met them, brave and chivalrous. Were there others, some different breed he had not met, capable of such appalling savagery?

'We all hate.' El Blanco's voice was harsh. 'We have good reason to hate. I would slit the throat of all one hundred men up there as soon as I would clean dirt off a boot, and with less feeling. But ...' He waved his hand at the distant convent and his voice trailed off.

'But,' he continued after a while, 'we cannot get at them in their forts. If I led my men to attack Santa Clara then they would be shot down. If I raised a thousand crusaders from the mountains and took them with me then most of them would die in the attack and still we would achieve nothing. Without cannon we cannot pierce their walls and so they are safe. I cannot starve them out because in time a column will come and no matter how many we are we cannot stand against a French regiment in open country. We can harry them in the passes, hold them for a while, but they will get through and then we must run or die.

'I cannot stop them from going wherever they will and I cannot take their forts. Not even if I led all the guerrilleros for a hundred miles and all the peasants could I do these things.' He sounded bleak now. 'I can hurt them a little, kill a few and make the rest nervous in the night, but I cannot beat them. For that we need an army, a proper Spanish army, with guns and cavalry.'

'If a force comes, will you help it?' Lieutenant Vega asked.

'Of course. We will do everything we can. The people will rise if they have a chance.'

'And do you think the other bands of guerrilleros will do the same?' Hanley said.

'All the ones worth having will come. We have not seen Spanish soldiers for a long time.' Don Antonio gave a wry smile. 'Even a few of you heathen English would be welcome.'

'Good, then for the moment you must show us more of the country and tell us all you know about the enemy's dispositions.'

They rode on, and saw more French outposts, a mixture of converted buildings such as churches and monasteries, and freshly dug earth and timber structures, usually with a high central tower surrounded by a rectangle of wooden walls. None of the garrisons was very big.

'Their main forces stay in the towns,' Don Antonio told them. 'They move around a lot. We can at least make them do that by threatening their outposts and making them march to the rescue. If nothing else, at least we shall wear out their boots!'

Other guerrilla chiefs said much the same thing. The French were kept busy and were spread out in garrisons or mobile columns. Everything Hanley saw confirmed Major Sinclair's reports, save that the partisans did not seem to think the foreign allies stationed in the area were of such low quality. Malaga's defences were certainly weak.

'Of course they are, man,' Sinclair assured him when they encountered the major around the campfire of another band, a few days later. 'It's a plum ready to fall.' The Irishman was pleased when Hanley told him to write a list of the aid he needed and where he would like it delivered, and even more excited to hear that there was a serious prospect of an expedition in the next few weeks.

He was also still convinced of the low quality of most of the troops in the area. 'Look, the irregulars are brave fellows, but to them all soldiers look the same. These Germans and Poles hate it here. They're stuck in garrisons and murdered if they stray alone outside, and all this for an emperor who doesn't give a damn about them and shows it. Why, a good quarter of El Lobo's band are deserters – Swiss, Italians, Germans, Poles, and God knows what else. There are some with nearly every leader.'

Hanley had to admit that was true. El Blanco and a few others led only Spaniards, but in several bands he had seen such men, usually silent and often grim. They had fled from their regiments, and tended to fight with the desperation you would expect from men whose only alternative was the firing squad.

On the last day they looked at one more French outpost.

'Moorish work, I do believe,' Williams said, as he studied the sand-coloured fort overlooking the sea.

'Undoubtedly,' Hanley said after he had taken a turn with his friend's telescope. 'Three guns by the look of it.'

'That is Sohail Castle,' Vega informed them, and smiled. 'I was born in the village near it. It is called Fuengirola.'

Two hours after sunset they showed a lantern from the beach, and *Sparrowhawk*'s gig pulled through the surf to take them off. Hanley was well pleased by the success of the mission, encouraged by the spirit of the guerrilleros and the quality of the information they had supplied. Yet most of all it was the ease of it. For five days they had ridden almost at will through land occupied by the enemy. They had seen plenty of little French outposts, but only twice had they seen cavalry patrols, and in each case only from a distance. El Blanco had teased one group of dragoons, running away, and then appearing again in plain sight, always just out of reach. For two hours the horsemen in their brass helmets and green jackets had followed. No shots were fired, for the enemy never came within range, but it was a fine display of cunning and easy familiarity with the ground. Don Antonio's Andalusian horse had not even broken into a sweat.

This coast was vulnerable, Hanley was sure of it, and said as much to Williams as the boat pulled them across to the brig.

'Very well,' he said with an air of exasperation, after his friend did no more than grunt and rub a deep gouge on the side of the boat. 'You tell me what I have missed?'

'I am not privy to the councils of the mighty, so I may be the one who does not see clearly.'

Hanley pressed him. 'Come on, Bills. Something is worrying that fat head of yours and I would like to know what it is.'

'I do not believe that the enemy are demoralised,' Williams said. 'From what I have seen of them, Napoleon's allies fight as hard as the French.'

'Well, others have similar doubts, but that does not alter the fact that their garrisons are widely dispersed. They are vulnerable,' Hanley insisted.

'Yes, the enemy is not prepared to meet an attack from the sea. The opportunity you speak of exists. Yet from the little you have said, I am puzzled as to what such an attack is meant to achieve. Are we to hit for the sake of it or with clear purpose?'

It was a question Hanley dared to ask a few days later when he was back in the stateroom of the *Milford* in conference with the admiral and his chaplain.

135

'The wisdom of a lieutenant.' Sir Richard Keats chuckled to himself. 'Ah yes, Williams of your regiment. Do you know General Graham himself mentioned the fellow to me quite specifically? Think of that. It seems this subaltern has caught his eye and so he asks me "not to steal promising officers from the army without good reason". The impudence of the man.' The admiral chuckled again. 'Yet your lieutenant has asked a most pertinent question.'

Sir Richard paced over to stare out of the stern window. There were distant pops from near the French-held shore as some of his gunboats engaged their French counterparts. 'They're damned lively today,' he said. Hanley and Wharton waited in silence.

'Malaga,' Sir Richard said at last, still staring from the windows. 'If we can take Malaga and hold it then not only will we deny the privateers a base, but it will be a thorn in the French side. They will have to concentrate troops to mask it and keep them there, and even then will not be able to stop us raiding and supplying the irregulars. If thousands of their soldiers are tied down watching Malaga, then it will make it harder for them to bring their full force against Cadiz, and harder too for them to support the assault on Portugal.'

The admiral nodded. 'Yes, if we can do that then it will be well worthwhile.'

'You do not sound sanguine, Sir Richard,' Wharton ventured.

'Well, it may work. But the truth is that Campbell dreamed up this idea, the Spanish want it, and there are times when it is better simply to try anything than to do nothing.' General Campbell was the governor of Gibraltar. 'I would prefer Graham to be in charge, but he has plenty to keep him busy securing Cadiz. The Regency Council had done next to nothing to prepare for the siege. Indeed, had it not been for the initiative of one Spanish general who came here against his orders, then the place would have fallen to the French and the war in this part of the world would be over – maybe the war in the whole country.'

'The Duke of Alburquerque,' Wharton explained.

'Yes, I have had the honour of meeting him. He impressed me greatly,' Hanley said. 'But I did not know he was in Cadiz.'

The admiral snorted in disgust. 'He's not, not any more. The fellow saves Spain, saves her government anyway, and then gets torn to shreds in the newspapers. Always plenty of rivals for a successful man, and they weren't going to let him show judgement as good as that and take the credit for it. He is now ambassador in London, if you'll believe it! While we have to deal with bloody-minded clowns like Blake and old women like La Peña! It is enough to make a man weep.'

'Lord Turney will lead the expedition itself,' Wharton said.

'He may be up to it. I cannot say I care for the man, but he has a good deal of experience.' Sir Richard glanced sharply at Hanley, no doubt with regret at expressing his opinion before so junior an officer.

'Yes, he may do well, and this could prove a great stroke. Malaga would be a prize.' Sir Richard came back from the window. 'Now then, what does that remind me of?'

'The *Liberté*, Sir Richard,' Wharton said.

'Of course, of course. I think it important you know, although you must not speak of it. That boat your friend Williams helped cut out – here is the damn fellow again intruding everywhere. Well, she was more important than she looked, for she was carrying more than bales of cotton.'

'Gold, Hanley.' Wharton enjoyed revealing the secret. 'Six chests full of gold coin. And a senior French officer, although sadly your friend and the other boarders cut him about so much that he has been in no position to talk.'

'Pay for the army?' Hanley suggested.

Wharton looked dubious. 'Maybe, maybe not. It would seem odd to risk sending that by sea. No, that suggests they needed the money quickly – perhaps to buy support?'

'The Frogs are up to something,' Sir Richard cut in, 'so we must cut across their bows and rake them before they can do it. We can start by taking Malaga, and you can help Lord Turney do it – you and that friend of yours. Promising officer indeed!

I am sure General Graham would be happier if the two of you do not get killed in the process.'

'That is kind of the general,' Hanley said.

Sir Richard grinned. 'Well, he is a sentimental old fellow. I should also like you back, because you seem to have your uses. Good luck, Hanley, good luck to all of us.'

'Amen,' the chaplain added.

II

'So you bring me to watch a battle, Mr Williams,' Jane Mac-Andrews said, slim eyebrows raised. 'Some might consider that a strange choice of sights likely to amuse a young lady. Or did you perhaps bring me here so that we could quiz the crowd assembled to witness the slaughter from afar? There are plenty of ladies among them. Do you see the one with the red scarf – mantilla, I believe it is called in case you do not know. She is on the arm of that elderly gentleman in the frock coat and tall hat. Now, do you believe her to be his daughter, or the young wife sold in marriage by a cruel stepfather to an ancient and wicked old miser? Or is there something worse in her tale?'

Williams knew that he was not being very good company this morning, and struggled for something to say. The ramparts were thronged with civilians and some soldiers staring north at the headland curving round at the far end of the bay. There was a French fort at Santa Catalina, and today the British and Spanish gunboats were to attack it at ten thirty. The whole town appeared to know all about it, and so the crowd had gathered. Williams doubted that the French would not have seen the boats and other vessels assembling for the assault, but even so was worried that there was so little secrecy. Rumours spread in Cadiz even faster than the yellow fever raging in some of the poorer areas.

'Your thoughts suggest a changed taste in novels, Miss Mac-Andrews, running more to the macabre and Gothic than the humorous,' he said at last. There was so much he needed to say, unpleasant though it was, but he did not know how to say it. The girl overwhelmed him. There were plenty of other attractive, even beautiful, ladies, a good number of whom were lively, witty, accomplished, and some even brave, but none thrilled and daunted him as she did. Being in her company – especially like this, alone in her company in spite of the crowd – brought him a joy he had never otherwise experienced, even now when it was laced with the bitter knowledge that he could no longer in decency hope to win her heart.

'A response,' Jane said. 'One might even say a gentle riposte. So in turn may I suggest that your own fondness for the dramatic and the grim has also grown. Last week it was an attempted assassination by ruffians, and now a battle. If I let you escort me next week then what am I to expect? A grand gladiatorial combat perhaps?' The girl leaned her head forward so that she could peer up at him, trying to look like a tutor reproving a child. 'Or perhaps pirates will descend to plunder and burn, and I shall be carried off to the harem of a Barbary sultan? Do you think I should be flattered by the gauzy garments that heroines in stories are forced to wear in such circumstances? I believe I might carry off a veil.' She pulled loose the long ribbon tying her bonnet and stretched it across her face. 'But would you come and rescue me, Mr Williams, climbing the castle walls and carrying me back to the bosom of my family with virtue still intact?'

That was no real question. Williams had fought to protect this girl before, and would not hesitate to do it again. He would die for her without hesitation, and would certainly kill for her.

'Well,' he said, and spread his hands in apology, 'I do have many duties keeping me busy.'

Miss MacAndrews tapped him lightly on the arm in reproof, and the crowd gasped and then cheered because a long object had shot into the sky. It sparked with flame and trailed a long streak of smoke, and a moment later a high-pitched screaming sound reached them. The missile arched high and then looped back to fall in the sea a hundred yards short of the French battery.

'A rocket,' Williams said. 'A Congreve rocket. I have never seen one before.'

A dozen gunboats fired, flashes, puffs of smoke and then dull booms as the sound wafted back to the shore. In reply the fort blossomed clouds of smoke. One of the Navy's bomb vessels joined in, and Williams was amazed to see its hull shudder when the great mortar fired. The flight of the shell was clear to the naked eye, and reminded him of the bombardment at Ciudad Rodrigo earlier in the year. From this distance it all seemed harmless, a display less impressive that the fireworks in Vauxhall Gardens, but he had plenty of memories of the carnage wrought by jagged fragments of shells, or the ease with which heavy shot ripped men into fragments.

The crowd applauded, and then cheered when another rocket shrieked into the sky.

'I should say that the carnage appears to be a popular success,' Miss MacAndrews said.

'Surely you did not think that I would bring you to an inferior engagement? No, no, I gave strict instructions to the admiral to ensure satisfaction. What would best entertain a young lady, I said to Sir Richard – failing a descent by Barbary corsairs, which he was unable to lay on. I must have nothing but the best, I said.'

'Perhaps next time the admiral might instead suggest that we attend a race day. I understand that several are planned by the regiments on the Isla for later in the month.'

'There will be fewer explosions,' he explained, breaking the news to her gently. 'And certainly no rockets.' Another Congreve whizzed into the air, going lower this time and diving into the cloud of smoke surrounding the French position. The sound of firing was now a steady rumble.

'Nevertheless, a race meeting has considerable advantages. For one thing it is far easier to know what is appropriate to wear. I do not know whether this is suitable for today's occasion.' Miss MacAndrews had on a dress in Indian muslin, white with a faint pattern of fine flowers. A deep blue jacket protected arms and neck, gloves covered her hands, while the broad-brimmed straw hat worn tied as a bonnet shaded her face. She once again wore her hair down, the thick mass of curls falling around her shoulders. Further shelter was provided by a new parasol, and the absence of any but the faintest breeze made this easy to manage. 'I feel safe from the sun, but is it all appropriate for watching mortal combat?'

'You look magnificent.' He wondered whether he should mention that such fashionable gowns were sometimes a little revealing when bright light met shadow. Presumably that was occasionally true in England – he had certainly seen a cartoon on that very theme, with fat gentlemen leering at the silhouettes of young ladies in the latest fashions.

'You truly look magnificent,' he repeated. 'I do not believe there could ever be any sight more lovely.' He meant every word, but cursed himself for he should no longer say such things. There was no hope.

Miss MacAndrews smiled. 'There now, was that so difficult? It is merely courtesy for a gentleman to pay some compliment to a lady when he escorts her out. Some admiration of a bright ribbon or a new fabric will usually suffice. But I shall take "magnificent".' Her eyes flicked down for a moment, a practised gesture although one he knew also marked real emotion. Then she looked up and the mischief was back. 'However, I am left unsure whether this is suitable for a battle at sea.'

'You can never be too well dressed to be a corpse,' Williams said under his breath, his harsh thoughts bringing the saying to mind.

'I beg your pardon?'

'It is something French officers say. They like to dress well for a battle in case it is their last.'

The girl frowned and was silent for a long time. More rockets flew high, and the bomb ship fired again. Williams thought that it must take a long time for them to load so cumbersome a weapon. One of the gunboats rowed back towards them, withdrawing from the fight, but the others continued to pound the fort. Now and then plumes of water were flung up by the French return fire.

'Do you wish to die, Hamish?' It was rare for Miss Mac-Andrews to use his Christian name and always a sign of intimacy

142

and her seriousness. With her soft voice, touched with no more than the merest hints of Caledonia and the Carolinas, she managed to bring him close to caring for the name.

'My soul is secure,' he said. 'The saved sinner does not need to fear death or what follows.' For all his fervent belief, Williams rarely spoke about his faith, fearing to boast. He hoped he lived in a worthy manner. Miss MacAndrews' faith was not the same, but he felt it to be real and differing only in detail.

'That is not what I asked.' She lightly bit her lip, and he recognised another sign of deep consideration and earnest purpose.

'I hope to live to a ripe and active old age,' he said. 'And I am prudent enough to wish for a peaceful end. Not fearing for what follows does not mean I do not care for this world – or some who are in it.' Damn, he should not have said that, but the words rushed out before thought took control.

Another dip of the eyes showed an appreciation of the compliment. When first he had met her, Jane had done such things with art, changing her manner to win over whoever she was with. She was still well able to flirt with the best of them, but was more natural with her true friends. That only made her manner all the more overpowering – and her anger terrible.

'Then why do you fling yourself into danger so recklessly?' Miss MacAndrews flushed with a deep rage, only just under control. Her eyes were moist. 'Why do you seek death as if nothing in life could matter?'

Williams reeled at the unexpected onslaught. A bigger explosion came from the French battery at La Catalina. There were shouts of joy from the crowd. The girl took his hand, pressing it tightly. 'I am a soldier,' he managed to say. 'My duty takes me into danger.'

'Was it duty that had you volunteering to join the Navy and raid an enemy port! Was it duty had you climbing on to a ship filled with enemies!'

'You have been talking to Dobson, Miss MacAndrews.'

She nodded. 'It took some time to worm it out of him – and then more about the summer and battles and sieges. In the end he enjoyed himself telling stories about you. He laughed and said that it was amazing that you came through it all with scarcely a scratch, and that you acted as if you were afraid of nothing.' She frowned, struggling to understand. 'Do you believe you cannot be hurt, or does life hold so little worth to you?'

'I know that I can be hurt. There are so many things I have seen – worse than anything I could ever have imagined before I enlisted. If they can happen to others they can happen to me.' This hurt now, in a different way, for the girl's concern was surely stronger than that for a friend. 'Your father is a soldier,' he went on. 'I should have thought that you would understand the perils incumbent on any officer. If I am to be a soldier then I would wish to be a good one, to prove myself, and for advancement.' He wondered whether Dobson had told the lady of how her father had led a desperate charge just a few months ago, riding up a hill at the head of a mix of men from several corps, somehow driving the French back. Men had fallen all around him and yet the major rode unscathed.

'Advancement.' She spoke with obvious disappointment and more than a little scorn. 'Is that all it is for, Hamish? Vanity and gain!'

'No. There is no choice, for I am a poor man and I must do my best to rise. Otherwise I could never offer comfort and security.' How could he explain? If he rose and kept rising in the army, became colonel of his own battalion, then he would be a man of some means. Not equal to the girl, but not so much poorer. Then, but only then, might it be honourable to seek her hand. Yet how long would that take – ten years if he enjoyed the greatest good fortune ever a man could, but twenty more likely, or never at all. MacAndrews had served for thirty-five years and was one of the finest soldiers he had ever known and was still a major. He could not ask the girl to wait, even if she were so inclined.

'I am no longer so very poor.' She spoke slowly, and once again her eyes flicked down from his gaze and did not look up. 'Comfort is pleasant enough, but far from everything.'

'Honour.' He gasped the word, clinging to it although the taste was so bitter. 'It would not be right. Not equal,' he tried to explain. He wanted to hold her, to press her tight, but this was agony for it was the closest she had ever come to hinting at feelings matching his own and now it was too late.

She looked up, eyes moist, but with fire in them again. 'If it were unequal the other way, would you hesitate?'

Williams wanted to tell her, to repeat all he had said before of his utter devotion, and to say it all as finely as he had so many times in his dreams.

'It is not the other way around,' he said.

Jane straightened up, slipped her hand free and looked out to sea. 'I believe we have been neglecting the battle.' Her voice cracked as she spoke.

They said no more for a while, but several civilians looked in their direction. Williams wondered whether their emotion had been so very obvious, and then caught traces of the conversations and laughed.

'You sound cheerful.' Miss MacAndrews sounded displeased. 'And what are they all saying about us?'

He laughed again. 'They are talking about your eyes. "Blue eyes", they keep saying. I should have thought your hair was just as remarkable, but it seems to be the eyes that fascinate.'

'You have blue eyes,' Miss MacAndrews said. 'Indeed, bluer than mine, for my own are more grey than blue.'

'It is not the same,' he said.

Out in the bay the gunboats were withdrawing, rowing back out of range. A high plume of black smoke coiled up from the French fort, so some damage had been done, although Williams doubted that it was more than could be swiftly repaired. At least one gun was still firing and he saw a strike in the water smash through the oars of a gunboat. Sieges happened slowly. Today's battle might delay the enemy for a few days, but fortifications would be repaired and new guns placed in the embrasures. For that delay, much powder had been spent and men had no doubt died or been maimed on both sides.

'Shall we go?' he asked, offering his arm.

Miss MacAndrews nodded, and they made their way down from the wall and into the street.

'When we met in England last year,' she said after a while, 'do you remember what happened?'

'Every moment,' Williams said. 'We were awkward and then agreed to be friends, who would not rush, but grow to know each other slowly. Then I made you angry again when I told you that I was soon to depart for Spain. Oh yes, and then you hit me.'

'That rather suggests an unprovoked assault. Is your memory truly so false?' The girl's arm pressed against his far more tightly than was usual.

Williams stopped to raise his hat to a Spanish general and his staff riding along the busy street. Resplendent in gold lace, his cocked hat lavishly plumed, the general had a soft, uninspiring expression. He gave a curt nod to acknowledge the salute, but then touched his hat to the young lady.

When they had passed, Williams looked at his companion. Jane stared back with her usual ram-you, damn-you confidence, but also with something else. It was an expression he had seen only once before.

'If I recollect,' he began, and wondered how he could pretend that the memory was not burned into his heart, 'then I must confess that there was provocation and that the fault was mine. Yet I shall not beg your pardon, for the act was deliberately done and I stand by it.' It had happened after she had begun to storm off, and he had chased, pulled her close into a long embrace and kissed her.

'Any suggestion of contrition would also be spoiled by the silly grin you now have on your face,' Miss MacAndrews said.

'For that at least, I shall apologise,' he said, the smile spreading.

'It was not so terrible a thing that I should never care to have it repeated.' Jane spoke quietly, scarcely louder than a whisper, and then she matched his smile.

The street was packed, and they walked quickly to turn off into the lesser lanes taking them towards her home. Their arms were still looped tightly around each other, and to Williams the girl beside him felt different, tense and excited at the same moment, and guessed that he was the same. They were both like children lost altogether in an exciting game. His mind yelled out to him that this was wrong, that he should not lead her on because he could offer her nothing at all.

As they walked, they kept looking at each other, smiling and laughing even though nothing was said. They cut through a narrow lane, but a fruit seller appeared at the moment they thought they were alone, and so they pushed on into a wider way, Jane tripping along so that he did not have to slow his longer stride.

'Lieutenant Williams!' a voice shouted. 'Lieutenant Williams!'

Silently he cursed, swearing with a fluency he would never have employed out loud. It was a surprise how easily the thoughts came to him.

'Ah, Lieutenant Williams, this is fortunate.' It was Edward Pringle in his best uniform, with white breeches, stockings and the shoes with the gold buckles. Beside him was Cassidy in less splendid attire, though no doubt his finest. The poor man had failed his lieutenant's examination and was thus back to master's mate instead of acting lieutenant. 'Our orders have come to leave on the afternoon tide. Hanley knows, for we sent to your billet, but he could not find you and has sent the two sergeants to look for you.' The naval officer bowed. 'I regret to take your escort from you, Miss MacAndrews. By the way, may I present Mr Cassidy.'

'Sir,' Jane said, formal once again, even if her skin was a little red.

'I thought we were not to go until tomorrow, sir.' Williams tried to keep the despondency from his voice.

'The convoy is ready, so we are to go now. They are eager. I have just come from Admiral Keats and have my orders. Cassidy will take you to your billet and once you have your things will take all you redcoats down to the harbour. You have forty-five minutes before the gig will take us aboard *Sparrowhawk*, so we must hurry.'

'I ought to escort Miss MacAndrews to her door.' He was sure the argument was doomed, but made the attempt. Part of him wondered whether it was for the best, which did not reduce his regret even slightly.

'No time, no time.' Pringle bowed again, wincing a little since his wound was still not quite healed. 'I know it is small consolation to the company of a very old friend, but I would be honoured to escort the lady. My business is done, so I shall still be able to meet you all in the harbour.'

'It is not necessary, sir, I am quite capable,' Jane said.

'Nonsense, nonsense. You are a friend to my brother and to my good friends from his regiment. I will not hear of anything else.' Edward Pringle was ebullient. 'Indeed, I shall accept no contradiction.'

'Give my compliments to my father.' Jane had already asked him to perform this service and given him a letter to carry from her mother. 'You are to serve with Lord Turney, I believe?'

'Best not to speak of such things in the street,' Pringle whispered in mild rebuke, but Williams nodded.

'Goodbye, Miss MacAndrews,' he said, and kissed her hand, holding it for one long moment. His whole body thrilled to the touch, and he thought he felt a tremor from her. Miss Mac-Andrews leaned forward a little and spoke so that only he could hear. 'I know nothing of Lord Turney as a soldier, but I suspect it is unwise to trust him as a man,' she said, and then straightened up. 'Good luck, Mr Williams.'

It looked as if she wanted to say more, but the company held her back. She glared at Edward Pringle, who did not appear to notice.

'You must hurry, Mr Williams,' Edward said, very much the master and commander of his own ship.

Williams wanted to ask the girl more, but then he did not want to leave her at all.

'Duty,' he said, and led Cassidy away.

'Splendid fellow that,' he heard Pringle saying to the girl as he left. 'Just like a hound straining at the leash, and not even so fair a damsel as yourself can hold him back when there is a whiff of powder in the air. And only a few weeks ago he was carving his way through a host of foes ...'

'Damn,' Williams said.

'I beg your pardon.'

'Nothing, Mr Cassidy, nothing at all.'

12

Africa did not look so very different after all. There were no camels or sand dunes, and Williams searched in vain for new smells or sights. Some of the crowd were dressed differently, with men in robes and a few – a very few – veiled women walking abroad, and the beggars clustered around Ceuta's main gate looked older, more wrinkled and even filthier than those in Spain, but these days limbless men were common enough everywhere. Houses and walls alike resembled those of Granada and the rest of Andalusia. It was hard to decide whether this province of Spain looked more Spanish or southern Spain looked more African, for a thousand years of intertwined history blurred such distinctions. The oddest thing was to look back north and see Gibraltar and the coast of Spain – indeed of Europe – across the narrow Straits. It did not quite seem real to him.

There was plenty of time for such reflections, for after a promising start, everything was taking far longer than it should. *Sparrowhawk* had carried him to Gibraltar, where he had transferred to the *Topaze*, for Lord Turney was using the frigate as his headquarters and Williams was temporarily attached to his staff.

'Good to have someone who has seen something of the country,' Lord Turney had said in greeting, before going ashore on urgent business. He had not explained his intentions in any detail, nor paused to ask Williams any questions about the coastline or the irregulars on shore. The lieutenant had to assume that the general had already seen the reports he and Hanley had prepared.

Hanley had gone, taken by Edward Pringle in his brig to carry a fresh stock of arms and ammunition to the bands of guerrilleros, encouraging them to raise the country when the expedition arrived. Dobson and Murphy had both rejoined the battalion, and Williams had given the letter to Major MacAndrews to them since he was not permitted to leave the ship. Captain Hope gave him a very warm welcome, shaking him by the hand and praising his actions at Las Arenas.

'You did well, sir, very well, especially for a man unused to the sea,' the captain said. 'Though if you will believe it, the prize agent appointed by the admiral was a greedy fellow, and wanted to rate you as a ship's cook when it comes to your share. Can you believe it? I have no wish to cause offence, but I suspect that, like me, you could scarcely boil an egg if required!'

Edward Pringle had made some comment about prize money, and Billy had ribbed him for turning pirate and fighting only for plunder, but he had not taken them seriously.

'Do not worry. Captain Pringle and I insisted that you be rated as one of our officers. I believe it is your sergeant who will become the cook! Ha, ha! Now, sir, I must be about my business.' That business was organising the convoy, and soon the captain and the naval officers were all hard at work writing out orders and signals for the ships they were to take to Ceuta and then towards Malaga. With nine transport ships, some British, most Spanish – several of which were in a shocking state – and all run by 'bloody-minded swabs of masters unable to keep station or follow the simplest signal', Captain Hope had his hands full.

Only Lieutenant Jones of the Royal Marines was unoccupied, and he too spoke with enthusiasm about prize money. 'Not wealth, Mr Williams, not to speak of anyway, but even so we can all expect a sum amounting to several years' pay.' Jones liked talking about money, and as the two of them sat in the semi-darkness of the gunroom, Williams' attention soon wandered. His lack of reaction did nothing to daunt the marine, who continued to talk.

An hour later Williams went on deck to get a breath of fresh air, for it was stifling below decks in the cramped frigate. Apart from in the main cabins he could not stand up straight anywhere – there looked to be barely more than five foot of height on the lower deck. With care he managed to avoid banging his head on the timbers, although the prospect of moving about in the dark and during a storm was not one he cared to contemplate.

On deck there was no sign of bad weather, indeed the air scarcely moved, making the heat oppressive as the sun began to set. The tense mood of Captain Hope and his officers was not one to invite conversation, and so he stayed on the windward side of the quarterdeck. After a while he was joined by a captain in the blue coat and black facings of the Royal Engineers. Both of them watched while a contingent of gunners came aboard the frigate.

'One Hundred and Sixth?' the man asked on seeing the red facings on Williams' jacket.

'Yes, sir. Lieutenant Williams of the Grenadier Company.' Silently he wondered whether that was still true. Away from the battalion for more than a year, he wondered whether other officers had been posted to the senior flank company in his, Pringle's and Hanley's absence. The latter was certainly now on the books of another company.

'I am Harding,' the engineer said, taking off his hat to wipe his bald head. Like most members of a corps where promotion was by strict seniority, Captain Harding was not a young man. 'Not with your regiment?'

Williams explained his attachment to the staff.

'Well, it appears that you will arrive far sooner than the rest of your battalion,' Harding said. 'The so-called "Conqueror" looks more like a wreck than a ship.' The 106th were to be carried in the Spanish ship of the line *El Vencedor* of seventy-four guns. 'Looks a death trap to me.'

Williams accepted the offer of the engineer's glass and studied the ageing Spanish warship. She was jury-rigged, with temporary spars fitted to the low stubs of her masts – the topmasts having been removed several years ago.

'The yards here are doing their best to plug the holes in her and keep her afloat,' Harding said. It seemed that he had been in Gibraltar for several years and knew the place well. 'Hard to know how she managed to limp here from Cadiz, but it will take days before she will be ready to move again And I hear the *Rodney* will stay to escort her. That's what they say, at least, but I heard a whisper that she will end up towing her all the way.'

'Are we to wait?' Williams asked.

'The rest of us leave on the morning tide, so I am told,' Harding said. 'We will miss your fellows, I do not doubt. Aye, and the *Rodney*'s guns.'

Williams shifted the glass to look at the big British seventy-four and the contrast was stark, for she was a new ship, launched just a few years ago and kept in fine trim. On her lower deck she mounted thirty-two-pounders, bigger than the heaviest siege guns used on land. He suspected the engineer was right and that they would miss both his battalion and the weight of shot of the warship. However, he was relieved to hear that the 106th would not be left on their own in the dilapidated *El Vencedor*.

Lord Turney came back, but he and his brigade major spent the evening drafting orders and proclamations to be distributed to the Spanish when they arrived, encouraging them to take up arms. Williams, Harding and the other officers were not invited and had still only a vague idea of their purpose.

'The general does not want our enterprise spoken of too freely,' one of his staff explained. 'This place is bound to be riddled with spies.'

On the morning of 11th October *Topaze* had weighed anchor and led the flotilla south. The fourteen-gun brig *Rambler* went with her, as did eight transport ships. Captain Hope ordered the slow merchantmen to crowd on as much sail as they could safely bear, but even so the convoy inched forward, fighting the current with the help of only the lightest of breezes. The sun was setting by the time they reached the harbour at Ceuta, and it was too late to embark the Spanish infantry regiment which was to join the expedition.

At first light on the 12th, boats began ferrying the six hundred and forty men of the Imperial Toledo Regiment to the waiting transports. Williams had gone ashore with Lord Turney's staff the night before, and slept in rooms provided by the small British garrison in the town's citadel. Their mess was most welcoming, but it soon became clear that there was little love lost between the Allies in Ceuta.

'They don't trust us, you see,' a major from the 2/4th Foot told them. 'And if you want proof of that take a stroll with me along the walls.' Williams did, and quickly realised that all the embrasures of the citadel were empty. 'That happened the week before we arrived. Must have taken them ages, but they moved every cannon out just in case we had any ideas of outstaying our welcome.'

Yet his first impressions of the Toledo Regiment were good. The soldiers were neatly turned out in blue jackets cut rather in the French style, with a white front and yellow collars, cuffs and turnbacks. Officers still wore cocked hats, but the rank and file had replaced the bicorne of the pre-war Spanish army and adopted a broad-topped shako, which again looked distinctly French. A few months ago the regiment had taken part in a raid which had marched deep into enemy-held territory, fighting a few skirmishes, but wisely retreating as soon as a strong force came against them. It was already in a better state of training than many of the Spanish regiments Williams had seen. Given more time, and the confidence which came with a few early victories, he suspected that these would prove very fine troops.

Lord Turney certainly liked the look of the blue-coated soldiers, and visited several of the transports to ensure that they were properly accommodated. To Williams' surprise the general spoke Spanish well, albeit with a somewhat Italian accent, and so was able to ask the officers whether they were satisfied. Several were not, complaining that the rations they were given by the British masters of the ships included meat even though it was a Friday.

'Damned fellows don't have the sense to realise that they are dealing with Catholics,' the general said to his staff after a pointed discussion with one of the merchant captains, who had insisted that he had nothing else to give them and had done everything according to regulations. 'Damn the authorities for not thinking of this either.'

On the last transport Lord Turney greeted the Spanish colonel with considerable warmth, apologising for the provisions, praising the condition of his regiment and asking whether there was anything they lacked.

Pleased with the compliments, the colonel said that he needed nothing.

Lord Turney frowned with concern. 'It seemed to me that not all the men carried firelocks as they embarked?'

The colonel was embarrassed, and Williams guessed that the failure of his own commanders was something he had hoped to conceal from his foreign allies. Lord Turney persisted, and with considerable reluctance the colonel admitted that his battalion lacked no fewer than one hundred and forty-eight muskets.

'You have cartridges for the remainder, I presume?' Lord Turney asked, a hard edge growing in his voice.

'None,' the colonel said.

'What are our own reserves?' he asked his brigade major, Captain Mullins.

'If you recollect, my lord,' Williams interrupted, remembering what Hanley and Pringle had told him, 'the balls from our own firelocks will not fit the Spanish ones.'

Lord Turney gave a curt nod. 'Ah yes, I remember. Thank you, Mr Williams. Captain Mullins, see that the Toledo Regiment is issued with the muskets needed to make up the deficit from our supplies, and ensure that they have a hundred English cartridges for each one.' He explained the arrangement to the colonel. 'It is not ideal, sir, not ideal, but if you take care it will be possible to supply each soldier with the correct ammunition. Now I must go to your governor to supply the want of cartridges for your own firelocks.'

'You would not believe such neglect,' he added, switching to English. 'Such damned dirty neglect that would send soldiers to fight without giving them powder and ball – without even giving some of them a musket. Some fat old bugger hoarding his stores to flatter his own sense of importance, no doubt. Or selling them off at a profit and denying the brave men under his authority the slightest chance of doing their duty.'

Williams hoped that the Spanish colonel did not speak English, for this was delivered within earshot. No doubt the man knew and deplored the failures of his superiors, but no proud man – and a good soldier was inevitably a proud one – would care to hear them exposed so openly by a foreigner. Yet Williams had to admit that Lord Turney appeared to know his business. He had sensed that all was not quite right with the Toledo Regiment, and worked hard until it was remedied. He immediately wrote to the Spanish governor of Ceuta, using language of considerable tact, and late at night a healthy store of cartridges came on board.

'At least he has moved promptly, but why the bloody man didn't do his job in the first place escapes me. Too many rogues promoted to high office, that is the problem,' Lord Turney declared. 'Do you know, in Gibraltar there is a fellow who used to play in an orchestra who is paid considerable sums and given charge of substantial stores, and charged with their distribution to help the partisans. He is a rich man, and as far as I could see spends most of his time playing the guitar to serenade young ladies – and some not so young. Don't blame the rogue for that, but there is a war to be fought or he will back to playing the fiddle in some orchestra instead of living in a great house.'

For the moment, the war was not to be fought quickly whether they willed it or not. On the 13th they left Ceuta, but the wind had shifted against them, and, although it was still light, it took hours for the clumsy transports to beat their way back to the Spanish coast. Williams spent much of the day on deck, finding that he was far less inclined to feel ill in the open air than below decks in the crowded frigate. The convoy crawled along, while Lord Turney grew impatient and Captain Hope grasped the rail so tightly that his knuckles went white as he hoisted signal after signal to keep the convoy together.

Night had fallen, with a slim crescent moon hardly challenging the bright starlight by the time they neared the Spanish coast and made the rendezvous with the gun-brig HMS *Encounter* and five gunboats from Cadiz under the overall command of Captain Hall, who soon reported on board the *Topaze* as Lord Turney summoned his officers to receive orders.

Captain Hope's day cabin was a good deal more crowded than when Williams had heard him explain the plan for the raid on Las Arenas. This time his role was secondary, and Lord Turney was at the heart of things.

'Well, gentlemen,' he began, nothing but enthusiasm rippling the surface of his calm confidence. 'Many of you will have heard something of our enterprise, but until now its true nature had to be kept secret.' The general spoke in English, and Williams found it strange that the colonel of the Toledo Regiment was absent, and a captain – presumably able to understand the language – was present in his stead.

'We have two objectives,' Lord Turney continued. 'The first is to relieve the pressure on Cadiz. Although the city enjoys a formidable position it is far from impregnable, and so we must draw some of the besiegers away, reducing their numbers and thus their capacity to prosecute the siege with vigour. At the moment their batteries threaten almost all of the inner harbour and a good deal of the bay. We need to slow them down and press on with the strengthening of our own works.

'The second intention is to foster the fighting spirit of the brave Spanish irregulars. We must keep alive the animosity of the peasants, by showing them that the war is not yet lost. If they do not despair and capitulate, then the irregulars, especially those in the mountains, are well placed and well able to harass the French as they bring supplies through the mountains to their forces outside Cadiz and along the coast.

'Therefore our commanders have resolved to attack. Ours is the major part, but as we speak General Blake with the Spanish Army of the Centre is mounting an advance from Murcia. At the very least this threat will keep General Sebastiani and many of his troops too far away to respond to our descent upon the coast. The prize is Malaga, but we cannot strike directly, and so instead we will land here,' he pointed at the map spread out in front of him, 'and take the castle near Fuengirola.'

Williams had to stand on his toes so that his head brushed the deck above in order to see over the press of officers. He and Hanley had traversed much of that country, but he found it hard to relate his memories to the map. Distances and the relationship of places appeared badly skewed. He doubted that there were good maps of the area, but could not help wondering why they had not asked Hanley to make one, for his friend was a talented artist.

'Once we have that post in our hands, the French are bound to march against us with all their force, drawing off men from the garrisons throughout the region. Depending on circumstances, we may then re-embark, and perhaps even make a strike at Malaga. However, I do not propose definite plans for we cannot predict every contingency. Much depends on the enthusiasm of the peasantry. We are assured that they are ready to rise up, but I have heard such reports in the past and found many to be unfounded.' He turned to one of the naval officers. 'Captain Hall, will you be good enough to tell us of the most recent letters you carry from General Campbell at Gibraltar?'

'A pleasure, my lord.' Williams thought the sailor held differing views to the general. 'We are assured of the weakness of the French garrisons along this coast and the patriotism of the peasants. They are ready to take up arms against the invader given the slightest encouragement. In addition, the batteries protecting the mole at Malaga itself have been stripped of guns – perhaps they want them for one of their outposts or even to besiege Cadiz.' He paused, looking at the general for guidance.

'Pray tell them of General Campbell's suggestion,' Lord Turney said, giving an easy smile. 'It is better that everyone should know.'

'Very good, my lord. General Campbell is convinced that this intelligence changes our understanding. There is a great opportunity for a *coup de main*, a sudden assault directly on Malaga without first mounting a diversion. With the mole stripped of its armament we can bombard the eastern side of the town, while all of our boats carry marines and sailors to the mole and seize it. Such a success will surely spur the townsfolk to rise, and then the rest of the force can be landed to reinforce the town. That is the general's plan, and I do believe it could work.'

'If the guns have been removed from the mole and if the peasants rise.' Lord Turney's scepticism was obvious, even scornful. 'And if I land my regiments outside the town I shall not only have to ford this river,' the general tapped his finger on the map, 'but march through this wide plain. We have no cavalry, gentlemen, not a single trooper, and that is cavalry country if ever I saw it.

'I honour your confidence, Captain Hall, indeed I do, but the risk of a severe repulse is too great. These latest reports come from Major Sinclair, do they not? Yes, I understood it to be so. You have met the man, have you not, Williams? What is your opinion of his judgement?'

Surprised to be singled out, Williams felt uncomfortable as all eyes turned to him. 'I have met Major Sinclair only briefly. He appeared a highly committed officer, but I do not feel that I can pass judgement on his abilities on so short an acquaintance.'

Lord Turney gave a wry smile. 'That is scarcely a ringing endorsement. I have heard that the major is a great enthusiast. Is that not right?'

Williams' discomfort increased. He had not cared much for the garrulous major, but did not want to blackguard a man behind his back without strong reason. However, no one could doubt the Irishman's enthusiasm. 'He is, my lord.'

'Indeed, I suspect an enthusiast led astray by other enthusiasts, all reporting what they long to believe is true, rather than what their eyes tell them. Such things are understandable, but no basis for sound decisions.'

Hall glared at Williams. Clearly the naval officer was unconvinced, and the Welshman wondered whether he might not be right. The boldness of the raid on Las Arenas defied military logic and yet had succeeded.

Having swept the governor's plan aside, Lord Turney resumed.

'So, our first objective remains Fuengirola and its castle. It should not prove too formidable, but we will all benefit from an engineer's assessment, if Captain Harding would be so good.'

'Sohail Castle is a medieval fort, shaped like a distorted rectangle and high walled.' The engineer looked at his notes. On the previous day he had asked Williams quite a few questions to add to the little information he possessed. 'Possibly some cannon, although one of our sources claims the guns are more than two hundred years old so they may or may not still be sound. Garrison of less than a company. It is overlooked by higher ground some three to four hundred yards away, and if necessary a battery established there would be well placed to batter the wall.'

Lord Turney rubbed his hands, a curious gesture for a man who was so consciously elegant. 'That should not prove at all formidable. Captain Harding did not mention that the garrison are from the Fourth Polish Regiment. Mercenaries, no less, so little reason for them to risk their lives.' The captain in charge of the Chasseurs recruited from deserters and prisoners shifted uneasily, but Lord Turney either did not notice or did not care. 'I doubt that they will fight, but if they do, then we can knock down those old walls and go in with the bayonet. We will have a brace of twelve-pounders, as well as a howitzer, and also the even heavier guns of the Navy.'

Williams doubted it would be so easy. From what he had seen, the castle was in good repair, and its walls were high. It would not withstand a formal siege, but then he doubted they would have time or leisure to mount one. It was hard to tell whether Harding was also concerned by the general's dismissal of the obstacle presented by the castle, but the engineer said nothing.

He listened as Captain Mullins read out a list of the French troops in the wider area, and was baffled because he gave much lower estimates than the ones he and Hanley had received from the guerrilleros. Some of his confusion must have shown in his face.

Lord Turney waited for the brigade major to finish. 'You have concerns, Mr Williams?'

Again the eyes turned on him. Some were sympathetic, while others resented the attention given to the most junior officer in the cabin.

'Forgive me, my lord, but barely ten days ago Don Antonio Velasco and other partisan leaders supplied us with somewhat larger figures for the soldiers in these garrisons.'

'More enthusiasts,' the general said, 'and no doubt equally well meaning, but not experienced soldiers. In most cases we can safely halve the numbers they report. And of course, nearly all of these troops are more foreign mercenaries.'

It was not his place, and no doubt ill mannered, but Williams found himself persisting. 'I also believe the castle may prove more formidable. Its walls are high and would be difficult to escalade. In addition, I believe ...'

'I think we can leave such matters to the engineers,' the general said in his best avuncular manner. Williams thought Hall looked pleased at his discomfort, and could not help wishing Major MacAndrews was here to raise further objections to such cavalier predictions of easy victory. Still, even if he were, the Scotsman was a major and Lord Turney a major general. His lordship was in command, and until now had shown talent for organisation.

'Well, gentlemen, with Mr Williams' permission' – that was an unnecessary and ungraceful remark – 'I believe we have concluded our business. We are running up the coast and will land tomorrow. For the moment, all I can add is good luck to you all, and good hunting!'

13

The trumpet sounded, the call insistent as the five notes were repeated.

'Forward march!' Officers repeated the orders all along the beach.

It was half past ten in the morning on Sunday, 14th October and Major General Lord Turney's little army began its march on the castle. Williams was impressed by how smoothly the landing had gone, confirming his admiration for the Navy's discipline and organisation. The Cala del Moral was a pretty inlet with a pretty name – the cove of the mulberry tree. *Topaze* and the transports were all anchored close inshore, *Rambler, Encounter* and the returned *Sparrowhawk* a little further out to sea, but their boats employed ferrying the cannon and gunners ashore. The naval gunboats were stationed all along the beach, their flat bottoms allowing them to go close in and cover the shore with their eighteen-pounders. If Frenchmen – or Poles – had appeared to oppose the landing, then they were ready to sweep the beach with canister or the heavier grapeshot.

No enemy appeared, so the boats went back and forth and the troops landed, forming up by company and regiment on the beach. In the lead were the 2/89th Foot, black facings on their red coats. They had spent much of the last year serving as additional marines to the Mediterranean fleet, and when Williams went with one of the first boats he saw that the soldiers looked more comfortable than most redcoats who found themselves afloat. A lot of the men were Irish, and they gave off the same cheerful confidence as men like Sergeant Murphy. One or two of the older men even said they remembered when Lord Turney served in the regiment many years before. As the boats ran on to the sand, they sprang out and splashed ashore with a good deal of spirit.

The 89th were a good regiment, but there were few of them. This was the second battalion, depleted by constant drafts to the first battalion stationed far away in India, and only four weak companies had somehow ended up in Gibraltar and so been chosen for this expedition. A Major Grant was in charge, a thickset man with a face tanned to the colour of old leather from long service in the Indies.

Williams was less impressed with the Chasseurs – or the Foreign Recruits Battalion as they were called officially, though almost never in practice. He watched as the boats returned and brought the blue-uniformed foreign regiment ashore. They looked capable enough, moving with the confidence of old soldiers, but he could see no sign of animation. The men did a job and no more. With them came Lieutenant Hatch, his face pale, though that was more likely the consequence of drink than fear. The man disliked him, and if Williams could never quite fathom why, it had been hard over the years not to let his own distaste for the fellow grow in return.

'Not murdered, Williams,' Hatch drawled as he passed on the beach. 'Those Spaniards should hire some of my rogues. Brandt here would kill anyone or anything for a couple of dollars, wouldn't you, Brandt?'

A corporal with the innocent eyes of a child and the face of a brigand nodded. 'One dollar, if it is a friend,' he grunted in a thick accent. Williams could not tell whether he was German or Swiss – nor indeed whether the offer was to kill a friend or show generosity to one.

'Take your riflemen and extend as pickets to the left of the Eighty-ninth,' Williams said, not bothering to engage for there was so much to do. 'Major Grant is up there, and will show you where to take post.'

As Hatch and his riflemen strolled away – there was no

impression of urgency about their movements – Williams wondered whether the scarred lieutenant had really hoped that he would come to harm, or had simply thought that assuming his name was amusing. Hatch noticed him watching, said something to the corporal, who spun round and dropped to one knee. Brandt raised his rifle, aiming at Williams, and held it there for a moment until Hatch patted him on the back. Half a dozen other chasseurs had stopped to watch, but all now moved off up the beach, laughing.

'Cheerful rogues, though I cannot say I am easy around them. They look ready for any mischief.' Harding had arrived to join him. 'Any sign of the French?'

'Not a whisker,' Williams said, and that seemed strange. Sohail Castle was only a couple of miles away on the far side of a line of low, sandy hills. Yet they had seen no one – no civilian, and certainly no enemy soldier. He had been surprised at how easily the guerrilleros had moved across the country without detection, but it was hard to believe that the arrival of some one and a half thousand infantry could go unnoticed. 'But that does not mean much save that they are half-decent soldiers. I suspect riders are carrying the news to Malaga and the other bigger posts even as we speak.'

By ten o'clock the three infantry regiments were formed up on the beach and Lord Turney issued a simple system of orders by bugle call – advance, halt, re-form and charge. Williams was again impressed by the general's talent for getting things done. Issuing orders directly in English, Spanish, German, Polish, Italian and goodness knows what else was bound to be cumbersome. The general took the brigade through some simple manoeuvres along the sand using the trumpet calls and just a few basic orders. It worked well, at least as well as could be expected at such short notice, and even Hanley was impressed.

'Seems so much simpler than our usual system,' his friend said.

'Quite, although I dare say it might be more difficult if you wanted one battalion to charge and another to re-form.'

Hanley took this in as if it were a great piece of wisdom. He had arrived soon after the landing, bringing with him a number of partisans, none of whom Williams recognised.

'No, you have not met any of these. El Blanco has promised to come and so have several other leaders.' Hanley had not shaved for a day, perhaps two, and his always thick hair had sprouted into a heavy stubble. Lord Turney was not impressed.

'You look like a damned gypsy,' he said. 'And who are these gentlemen?'

Hanley made introductions and passed on pledges of support from other leaders.

'Not here, then?' Lord Turney did not sound surprised, but he did bother to switch to Spanish and praise the men Hanley had with him. 'Courage such as yours will drive the French for ever from your homeland,' he said, and was greeted with a cheer.

When they finally moved off, two companies of the chasseurs formed a skirmish line, supported by the rest of the five hundred men from their corps acting as supports. Lord Turney rode at the head of the 2/89th, although most of his staff walked. There were a few dozen mules with powder and provisions and then the Toledo Regiment as rearguard. A quick inspection of the coast road along this stretch had revealed that it was unfit for the cannon.

'Won't do, my lord,' Harding said after looking at the heavily rutted dirt track. 'Might be fine if we had them on field carriages, but we could strain all day with these and not move them half a mile.' The two twelve-pounders were on naval carriages, low off the ground and with four small wheels, while the howitzer was on a low base like a mortar, and needed a cart to move it.

With nothing else for it, the guns were re-embarked and would be carried round the headland and brought ashore again if necessary once the landing place was secure.

'Won't matter,' Lord Turney announced, flicking his whip to knock a fly off the side of his bay's head. 'I doubt that we'll need them at all, but even if we do we can bring them ashore easily enough. Get them back on board *Topaze* and ask Captain Hope to bring the squadron up the coast as soon as he is able. Gunboats to lead, as arranged, so that they can support us.'

So they advanced, Williams walking with the general's staff until he was needed, while Hanley took the partisans forward as scouts. The road was narrow, in truth little different from the sandy ground on either side, and as the sun rose to its height men sweated as they toiled up and down the rolling hills, the wind blowing sand into their eyes. The chasseurs straggled, and when Lord Turney saw parties of them leaving formation to rove inland he sent Mullins and Williams to chase them back.

'Lord Turney wants every man with his company at all times,' Williams told Hatch.

'There are calls of nature,' the lieutenant said, looking at Williams as if he were fussing over nothing. 'Would you have us defecate in the path of the brigade? I expect some of these lads would if it gives you pleasure.'

'Do that and you can clean it up, Lieutenant,' Mullins shouted, having jogged up beside them. 'Keep them together.' He raised his voice. 'Stay together, d'you hear! No stragglers and no one off foraging. You're wearing blue and the locals won't know you're not with the French any more! Understand?'

The nearest chasseurs nodded, faces blank.

'Doubt it will do much good,' Mullins said to Williams as they walked back. 'But we must do our best to stop them molesting the peasants. Don't trust the buggers not to desert, but we have them with us and need them, so must make the best of it.'

At two o'clock in the afternoon they passed the tower of the old windmill and came over the last rise. Sohail Castle was beneath them, and there were men in blue jackets on its walls. For the first time they saw the enemy. The squadron were following, but none of the big ships had yet come round the headland. Only the gunboats were nearing the shore, and for the moment they waited out of range of any guns in the castle. Williams saw that each of the heavy boats – their shape was much like a cutter – had taken down its mast, ready to close in under oars. They were small vessels, low in the water and, apart from a sloped 'dog-house' where the officer could rest, there was no shelter and little space for provisions. He did not envy the men who had sailed them along the coast from Cadiz. Edward Pringle had told him that all sailors hated serving on such small craft unless they could go ashore at the end of each day.

Ten minutes later Williams, Mullins and a captain from the Toledo Regiment crossed the valley and walked up the rise towards the south wall of the castle. A private from the 89th carried a white flag. On the hill behind them, the brigade had spread out to show their numbers. If reports were right and there was no more than a company in the castle, then the Polish infantry were outnumbered ten to one.

Mullins made a long speech in French, but Williams paid little attention to the platitudes, intended to flatter the enemy so that they would not feel it dishonourable to surrender. Putting himself in their position, he could see no reason to give in. From up close the walls were dauntingly high and looked in very good condition. Near the corners he saw the barrels of two tiny cannon – two- or three-pounders perhaps, but still nasty little brutes to have firing canister at men running into the attack. From where they stood he could not see the heavier pieces, mounted in a shallow bastion projecting from the east wall and looking out to sea. For all their numbers the attackers had no ladders, nor any material to make some, which meant that they must knock a hole in the wall, and at the moment their only guns were afloat, facing the wall hardest to reach for attacking infantry.

Mullins finished with a flourish. 'Therefore, in the hope of avoiding needless waste of life, we call upon you, as brave men to other brave men, to yield this fort and surrender. What is your answer?'

Several men looked down on them from the battlements. One, an officer from his cocked hat and epaulettes, had thick black side whiskers and a moustache drooping down past his chin. He had listened with evident impatience to the long appeal.

'*Venez le prendre*,' he called down in gruff dismissal and then turned away. The other defenders remained in sight, watching.

Mullins sighed. 'He said "Come and take it."'

'I know,' Williams said, and it was obvious that the Spanish officer had also understood and showed no sign of surprise. 'We might as well go, then, before we outstay our welcome.'

'Yes, that would never do,' Mullins replied. 'It would be so terribly ill bred.'

When they climbed back up the hill the general did not display the slightest trace of disappointment. Nor did he appear to be in any great hurry. Officers were summoned from each of the three battalions, but it was a good half-hour before they arrived and Lord Turney was ready to issue orders. In the meantime he had shared a light lunch with his staff, and was dabbing his lips with a napkin as he spoke to Major Grant, and the commanders of the other corps.

'Well, those fellows think they can hold us off. It will still be an hour or more before the bigger ships arrive and can bombard the castle, but the gunboats are ready and will surely suffice.

'Tell the chasseurs to advance and engage the enemy on the wall. The Eighty-ninth to remain in line and support from the hillside. Toledo Regiment to wait in reserve. If the enemy waver, then we will press harder until they crack.'

Williams was unsure how men could press harder against high walls, but his thoughts were interrupted when an oddly high-pitched boom rumbled across the valley, followed an instant later by another. There was smoke shrouding the bastion on the east wall, and Williams just glimpsed the second ball throw up a fountain of water very near one of the gunboats. The boats must have begun to row inshore when they saw the flag of truce returning, and were now in clear sight of the castle.

'Impudent fellows,' Lord Turney said. 'We must ensure they soon regret what they have started.'

As if in answer one of the gunboats disappeared from sight as the big eighteen-pounder in its bow belched fire and smoke. Williams wondered whether Captain Hall was in that boat because it acted as a signal and the other gunboats all fired. Balls ploughed up earth near the foot of the castle wall and he saw one strike against the stone.

The general wanted to supervise the action from close by, not least because this was a situation stretching his four simple signals. In spite of his enthusiasm he kept his horse at a walk, leaning back in the saddle as he let it find its own best path down the slope. His staff followed behind.

The fort's heavy guns did not fire again, and as they went down the slope there was a steady thumping as the gunboats flung ball after ball at the east wall. Yet compared to artillery on land, their firing was slow. Then Williams remembered the cramped fight on the French gunboat at Las Arenas, and realised that it must be difficult to ram and load a gun in such a craft, even with the rails allowing it to slide back when it recoiled. Nor was the boat so steady a platform as land. When they did fire, he again saw only one hit on the wall itself, though another ball skimmed across the rampart and caused several of the defenders to throw themselves down behind the parapet.

'Do you think this will work, Bills?' Hanley asked, ever ready to rely on his friend's military judgement over his own.

'If we're lucky, or the French are fools.'

They hurried on, and watched as the chasseurs extended in skirmish line and moved up the slope towards the castle. Half of each company remained in two ranks some fifty yards back as supports, and the 89th were a long musket shot behind them. Lord Turney rode boldly some distance in advance of the redcoats. The blue-coated chasseurs worked in pairs, as good skirmishers should, and in Williams' opinion they did it well, not bunching up, and making as much use of the scrubby cover as they could. They closed to around one hundred yards and began to fire at the defenders behind the parapet.

Only then did the Poles reply. The two little cannon barked out first, and one burst of canister peppered the sand around a bush and left a chasseur screaming because his kneecap was smashed. Then a ragged volley of musketry hammered down from the wall, flicking up more lumps of earth and making the chasseurs dive for cover. Williams did not see anyone fall.

'Poor devil,' Hanley muttered.

The general mistook the voice. 'One cannot make an omelette, Mr Williams,' he said in quick reproof, not bothering to finish the quotation. 'You will understand that if you see a bit more service.'

Was that insult or ignorance of his record? Unlike the general, Williams had not served for decades, it was true, but Vimeiro, Corunna and Talavera were surely enough to count as considerable experience. He could scarcely act the schoolboy and plead that it was not he who had spoken.

Mullins darted him a sympathetic glance, and Hanley patted him on the arm apologetically.

After the first ordered shots, firing became more general, both sides firing as they loaded. The light cannon on the wall were well served and flung bursts of canister not only into the skirmish line, but also the supports. As the general and his staff watched one of the half-companies was struck, the two deep line rippling like a flag in the breeze. By the time NCOs had shouted and pushed the men back into place, two of the chasseurs were crawling back through the long grass and another lay unmoving. Men broke ranks to help the wounded men.

Lord Turney's tanned face darkened in anger, and he turned back to his staff. 'You, Mr Williams, stop skulking at the back!' The general's voice was harsh. 'Tell those blackguards that only one man is to help a wounded comrade. The rest stay in the firing line or I'll have the hides off their backs!' He was pointing to the men in front and over to the right where half a dozen chasseurs were using a blanket to carry the soldier hit in the knee in the first volley. Another blue-coated soldier followed carrying his own and the man's firelock.

Williams ran forward, wondering what language the men spoke. It was never pleasant to tell men to leave a comrade, but helping the wounded was an old dodge allowing men to retire to safety – and as often as not not return until the action was over. At this rate half a dozen hits would deplete a company so that it became useless. In the 106th the bandsmen were used to carry back the wounded to the surgeons, but he doubted the regulation of the recently formed chasseurs had advanced so far.

'Stop!' he shouted as he ran up to them. 'You!' He pointed at one of the men at the head of the party. 'Just you take him back! The rest of you go back to your company. Understand!'

A cluster of heavy grapeshot struck the ground just beside him, flinging sand high, along with a clump of grass ripped up by the roots. Half the chasseurs let go and flung themselves to the ground. Somehow Williams stopped himself from flinching and simply watched them. The man he had ordered to carry the wounded soldier did not move and for a moment watched the officer, until a sergeant arrived and shouted at them in a guttural language. Williams thought that it might be German, but the dialects often sounded so different that he could not be sure. The soldiers turned and began walking back to the firing line. As they went they unslung their muskets – the one carrying the injured man's weapon laying it down beside him before he left. The officer helped the remaining chasseur to lift the wounded man and watched as he started off with him.

The sergeant gave the officer a curt nod.

'Your name?' Williams asked, trying to make the word sound how he thought it should in German.

'Mueller,' came the reply, so bland that he wondered whether it was assumed. There were streaks of grey in the chasseur's brown hair, and a lined face which spoke of long years lived in the open. He had the air of a veteran about him, and Williams wondered how many armies the man had served in.

'Thank you,' Williams said, and went forward to the nearest formed support.

'One man only to help a wounded comrade,' he called to the officer in charge. 'General's orders.'

'Jolly good,' the captain replied in a voice not suggesting great intelligence. He was taller than Williams, but as thin as a character from a cartoon, with a great bulging Adam's apple and an unnaturally long neck. 'Hear that, Sergeant?'

Mueller was there and bellowed at the men.

Lord Turney had not ordered him to do so, but his implied slights stung so bitterly that Williams felt obliged to take his message forward to the skirmish line. He jogged over the tussocks of grass, forcing himself to stay upright, even when he felt the wind of a ball slicing through the air just inches from his face. Here and there a corpse lay in the grass. One of the light guns barked, so close that the noise came almost at the same instant one of the skirmishers was flung back like a rag doll from behind the cover of a low hummock. Half of the man's face was missing.

Closer to the fighting, Williams could hear the sharper cracks of rifles amid the near-constant crackling of musketry. He spotted an officer, standing in the shelter of a low bank topped by a wizened little tree, leaves and twigs continually plucked off by musket balls.

'Orders from the general,' Williams shouted as he came up. 'Only one man to aid a wounded comrade.'

'Really? What if he doesn't want to?' Hatch drawled, turning so that Williams saw his scarred face. The blue-coated officer stood looking to the side, forcing the other man to stand in front of him, all but his lower legs exposed to fire from the walls. Still smarting at the general's barbs, Williams could not ignore the challenge and so stood there. A moment later a ball snapped just above his head.

'Anything else?' Hatch asked.

'No, other than to keep the pressure on the enemy.'

The amusement in Hatch's eyes was obvious. More leaves were plucked from the little tree and tumbled down on to his hat, but he did not move. 'Oh, we are doing our best,' he said.

Something slammed into Williams' shoulder and he was flung to the ground. Hatch watched with interest, but no obvious emotion, as the other officer rolled on the sand. Reaching up, Williams felt his right shoulder. The gold-threaded wing which marked him out as an officer of a flank company was ripped open and gouged through by the line of a musket ball. Williams pressed with his fingers, but although the shoulder itself was sore the skin was not broken. Lying down he was sheltered from fire and the temptation to stay for a moment would have been irresistible if Hatch had not been there watching. He got up, brushing sand off his jacket. Out of the corner of his eye he could see a jagged piece of the ripped shoulder wing sticking up and waving each time he moved.

'Bloody awful shot,' Hatch remarked.

'It will break my tailor's heart,' Williams said, trying to push the torn wing back down because it was already irritating him.

Hatch was taking a long time to say anything, but his eyes never left the Welshman. Another ball flicked past his left thigh and slapped into the ground a yard away.

'Really dreadful practice. Not like my fellows,' Hatch said, and then raised his voice. 'How much do I owe you now, Brandt?'

The chasseur corporal was crouched in a little gully on the far side of the tree, a rifle in his hand. Three other soldiers squatted close by, each loading weapons to pass to the corporal.

'Six dollars,' the corporal shouted.

'Bloody liar,' Hatch replied. 'I'm sure it is only four.'

'No, six dollars. Number three in the head.'

'I'm paying him for the Frenchmen he kills,' Hatch explained, still speaking slowly and watching Williams as he stood under fire. Then a blast of grape sheered a couple of branches off the tree so that they tumbled on to the lieutenant and he dropped, hunching up into a ball.

Williams grinned. 'Good day to you, Hatch. I must tell the other companies.' He walked away, and thought back to the time a gunner told him that the Royal Artillery ran towards their guns, but always walked away. It had always struck him as an admirable nonchalance.

A chasseur running up to reinforce the skirmish line dropped, his whole body suddenly loose as he fell on his face. The comrade running beside him stopped to stare down, and then gasped as a musket ball drove into his leg. Blood spread rapidly, darkening his blue trousers as he slumped down. None of the other foreign soldiers was near by, and Williams ran to help the man. The wound was bleeding badly, and without anything else to use, he unrolled his sash and tied it higher up the thigh. A glance told him that the other chasseur was dead, and so he helped the wounded man up, and went back with him.

The formed supports of the chasseurs were by now mostly fed into the skirmish line, but the squat figure of Sergeant Mueller still had half a dozen men with him and sent one to relieve Williams of his burden. Lord Turney was no more than thirty yards away, leaning from his horse to speak to Major Grant of the 89th. The general flashed an angry look at Williams when he saw him aiding a wounded soldier, but then jerked back on the reins as the major shuddered, limbs shaking from the strike of two or three heavy balls of grapeshot. Lord Turney's bay reared away, until a firm hand and a smack of his whip brought the beast back round.

By the time Williams reached them Mullins and two soldiers with the black facings of their regiment were clustered around the major. Grant had lost part of his jaw, had an arm broken and mangled, and a deep wound just above the hip. A sergeant and two more soldiers from his regiment ran up, and soon transferred the softly moaning major on to a blanket. The rules for officers were seldom the same as those for men, and the elderly major was carried away, the men trying to keep the motion as gentle as they could.

Mullins saw the questioning look on Williams' face and shook his head.

'We must try an escalade,' Lord Turney said. Some of the major's blood had spattered across his leg and the general looked puzzled when he noticed it.

'There are no ladders, my lord,' Mullins said in a flat tone.

The general stared at him, and then seemed at last to recover himself. 'No, of course not. In that case, Williams, you will run back to the chasseurs and have their companies pull back to that line.' He waved his whip at a position some two hundred yards from the fort. 'You see? Good, now hurry, sir, hurry!'

As Williams ran off, he heard the general giving a string of orders.

'Mullins, come with me. We need to ensure the security of the flank. Where is Harding?'

Williams ran on into the smoke and noise.

14

Hanley watched the hull of the frigate disappear behind the smoke of her guns as the *Topaze* delivered a broadside, beginning at the bow and each cannon firing in turn. At around five o'clock she and the other larger ships had arrived and begun to take station. There was a slackening in the bombardment as the gunboats formed a new line and other boats rowed over to bring them fresh supplies of powder and shot. By half past the frigate was ready and the gunboats had formed line abreast and rowed in far nearer to the shore than they had come before. When the *Topaze* fired, so did the heavily armed brig *Encounter*. Neither could get close in, and although some shot struck the wall, he could see no sign of serious damage. Soon the frigate aimed higher, trying to strike the parapet and the men behind it. Hanley had focused on one of the Poles when he was smashed into a spray of red and pitched down into the courtyard.

The gunboats were closer and had heavier guns so were able to do more damage, and they seemed to be concentrating on the enemy battery. There were already several small holes in the low wall protecting the guns. For a while these fell silent, but later they opened up once more, and since then had fired steadily. Amid the rolling thunder poured in from the sea, Hanley could distinctly hear the curious, almost ringing discharge of the old guns in the castle. Time and again they struck the water close to one of the gunboats in the line. He chanced to be looking directly at one when its bow was struck squarely by a heavy shot, punching through the timbers and flinging fragments of wood, gun carriage and flesh in a ghastly and lethal explosion. As

Hanley watched through his glass the boat slid beneath the water, the weight of the gun unbalancing it as the sea flooded through the hole in its side. One moment there was a boat and some two dozen crew working oars and cannon, and then nothing apart from debris and a discoloured patch amid the waves. He thought he saw one man swimming away from the ruin, but that was it.

Beside him the partisans were restless. They had come in answer to the call, but apart from their polite welcome the British general had not asked them to perform any service. While it was entertaining enough to watch their allies bombard the enemy in the castle, all of them felt that they could be of far more use than this.

'Shall we go to the general?' It was the third time someone had asked the question.

Hanley sighed, disliking the answer as much as his audience. 'We were sent here and asked to wait. I am sure Lord Turney will be eager to send for you all, very soon.'

He folded his little glass and put it in his haversack. Another shot from the castle struck true, cutting a swathe through the crew of a gunboat, and Hanley was glad that he had not been watching it through his telescope. It was all too easy to imagine the carnage.

'Hanley!' A voice called – a voice which for all its huskiness seemed out of place in such surroundings. Paula Velasco and her sister were leading their horses across the sandy hill towards them. Both were clad in their usual black, from boots to the wide-brimmed hats, the only colour provided by the bright red scarf each had looped at her neck.

Hanley stood up, smiling in welcome.

'My husband sends his greetings,' Paula said. 'This morning we drove off the cattle kept outside the fort and killed a couple of their sentries.' One of the other partisans had said something about this, but had not known which band had done it. 'Most of the men are getting them away, and El Blanco has gone to scout the road between Mijas and Alhaurin. He says you will stir up a hornet's nest, my friend.' The young woman was clearly amused, and both she and her sister showed obvious delight at the pounding of the castle. Hanley had never seen Guadalupe so animated.

He thanked her and made a decision. 'We should go to the general.' Faint cheers came from the other partisans.

It took a while to find Lord Turney. Captain Hall was on the hilltop nearest to the castle marking out positions for the guns if they were ever brought ashore, so they went there first. He sent them further back to the Toledo Regiment and it was there that they caught up with the commander, waiting with a few of his staff as a huddle of Spanish officers held a debate.

'Damn them, do they expect the war to stop for a day because of the Sabbath?' Hanley heard the general speaking with considerable anger to Captain Mullins. 'They pulled the same superstitious nonsense at Talavera.'

Hanley had been at Talavera, which the general had not, and knew that the story was untrue, but he had heard plenty of British officers willing to repeat the lie that the Spanish army did not fight on Sundays.

'They regret the lack of opportunity for a divine service,' the captain said.

'As do I, but where the hell do they expect me to find a priest?' Lord Turney noticed Hanley and the guerrilleros coming towards him. Distaste and annoyance flashed across his face before he mastered himself.

'My lord, I have fresh reports from the partisans,' Hanley said in Spanish, aware that the general was fluent. 'Don Antonio Velasco sends important messengers to us and is even now leading a patrol along the road to Alhaurin.'

'Most useful, I am sure, and in due course I will attend to them. At the moment I am engaged in convincing our allies of the need to watch that road, and secure it against any French advance. That is if these …' Lord Turney stopped short, taken aback as he stared at the two figures in black, no doubt noticing that their shapes were not those of boys.

'Captain Hanley, you should introduce me.'

Hanley named the Spanish ladies to the general, who had dismounted and was extremely gallant, kissing their hands and paying compliments to their looks and courage, and the great reputation of Don Antonio himself.

'There are sixty French in Mijas, and some three hundred in Alhaurin, about one third of those dragoons,' Paula Velasco reported with assurance. 'That was yesterday, but I doubt that the numbers have changed much. Don Antonio rides to watch them, and will also send men to the Malaga road, where there were several thousand soldiers. He should join us some time tonight, or send word if it is better for him to stay where he is.'

Lord Turney beamed at the young women. 'You should be one of my officers, dear lady, for never have I heard a more suitable report. However, numbers of the enemy are always hard to judge.'

'You doubt my word.' There was anger in the voice.

The general's smile did not waver in the slightest. 'My dear lady, a thousand pardons. Not the slightest disrespect was intended. But a commander of an army must treat all news with a degree of caution, and not rush to change plans without need. You have my thanks as well as my undying admiration.' He reached for her hand again, caught it before the lady could withdraw, and bowed to kiss it once again. 'I look forward to meeting your husband, for it is obvious that he is the most fortunate of men.'

Even Paula Velasco smiled at that, but then the general excused himself and beckoned Hanley to follow him.

'Most charming, but this is scarcely the time or place for such things,' Lord Turney said. 'It might be more useful if the fellow had come himself with all his partisans.'

Hanley was at a loss to imagine what forty or fifty irregulars could add to the efforts of a brigade of infantry faced with a staunchly held castle. 'I believe it is a mark of faith, sir,' he suggested. 'Sending his wife to us as messenger.'

'Depends how much he likes his wife. Not sure sharing a bed with an amazon might not pale after a while!' The general snorted with laughter. 'But that is of no matter. We need to get these fellows moving.'

179

In fact Lord Turney was able to convince the officers of the Toledo Regiment without needing Hanley's assistance.

'Feel like a stroll, Mullins?' Lord Turney asked the brigade major once the Spanish colonel had agreed to send four of his six companies.

'Of course, my lord. Happy to oblige.' Hanley thought the man looked weary, but could hardly admit this to the general.

'Take Hanley with you,' the general added. 'He can make sure everyone understands what is happening. I'll give you two companies of the chasseurs as well. Take them a few miles up the road and find a good place to hold off any French column in case that young lady's husband is right and there are more of them about than we expected. Mijas is four or five miles away, but you should not need to go that far.'

'I think I know the spot, my lord,' Hanley said. 'Around half a mile before the village where two of the tracks meet. It is overlooked by a round hill.'

'Good man. That sounds perfect.'

'I suspect that some of the partisans know the land better.'

'Leave 'em here. They don't really understand soldiering. Besides,' the general added with a twinkle in his eye, 'you never know.'

It took half an hour to organise the little column before they moved off, the chasseurs extended as skirmishers to the front. Hanley noticed Lieutenant Hatch leading one group and returned the languid wave. Lord Turney had withdrawn all save one company from the attack on the castle and was leaving the Navy to batter it. The wind had picked up, and Hanley's last glance at the sea showed white waves rather than the glassy calm of earlier.

As they reached the road junction, the two sisters appeared. Nothing was said, but he presumed they had not cared for the general's company, or for the assumption that he could order them around. He was about to speak to them when he noticed Mullins arguing with the Spanish major in charge of the troops from the Toledo Regiment and hurried over.

'They want to take the village,' Mullins said with more than a hint of despair.

Hanley listened as the Spanish officer explained that it would be a better position to block the road, and that the houses would give them shelter for the approaching night. He translated for Mullins, who insisted that the general had not instructed them to go so far. They could see Mijas ahead of them, its whitewashed houses casting long shadows in the setting sun. There was a solid-looking wall surrounding it, and no sign of the enemy.

'There are French there,' Paula Velasco said, trotting up behind them. She spoke with absolute assurance, as if stating the obvious.

'Can you see them?' he asked.

The young woman pulled the brim of her hat down to shade herself against the dying sun. 'I do not need to. There are sixty or maybe a few more.'

The Spanish major was not impressed. 'We have five hundred. Your Germans can guard the flanks, but we are going straight across the plain and into that village.'

Mullins did not have the rank to order his ally, and lacked the energy to protest. 'Come on, Hanley, let us sort out the chasseurs to give best support.'

The sun was a red ball amid waves of pink and red cloud by the time the Toledo Regiment advanced against the village. They had formed line, six deep to give weight to the advance, and the major swept his sword down as he led them marching straight at the walled village. At one hundred yards the first few muskets popped from loopholes in the dry stone wall. A man in the front rank was hit, his head snapping back with the impact.

The major held his sword high and shouted out the order to charge. The regiment cheered and the men ran forward, bayonets coming down. A line of twenty or more men stood up from behind the wall. It was a small volley, but one of the Toledo Regiment was dead and three more stretched on the grass crying out in pain. The major shuddered as he was nicked in the arm, but kept on running. More muskets fired from loopholes and two more Spanish soldiers fell.

'Fire!' Mullins screamed at the nearest chasseurs. 'Fire and advance! Drive those rogues back behind their wall.'

Rifles cracked and the men ran forward to kneel again some ten yards ahead. Beside them a man waited until they had loaded before firing again.

The line of Poles behind the wall seemed to waver, but it was only to duck down so that a second rank could stand and present muskets. The volley punched at the charging Spaniards, and a few more fell and the rest stopped. The major yelled at them to come on, imploring and cursing. One man fired, his musket still thrust out towards the enemy. Several more raised them to their shoulders and pulled the trigger, and then all along the now scattered line men fired.

Hanley did not see any of the Poles fall, but it was hard to see most of them at all, especially now thick smoke blanketed the line of the wall. Chasseurs fired with musket or rifle, and the Toledo Regiment was reloading, ignoring the pleas of its major. The men would not move, and so they loaded and fired and loaded and fired into the smoke, sending bullet after bullet into the thickening cloud. Now and then one would fall, struck by a ball, but on both sides it was mainly chance whether a shot struck home.

'Charge!' Mullins shouted, and Hanley followed him, struggling to draw his sword, which wanted to stick in the scabbard. A dozen or more of the chasseurs followed them. The captain led them to the right of the Spanish line, heading towards a low building outside the wall of the village. One of the chasseurs cried out as he was hit in the leg, but managed to limp on.

Hanley was breathing hard when they reached the shelter of the building. Mullins gestured to a chasseur to be ready and then launched a kick at the door, making it fly open. He charged in, sword and pistol in hand, but the dark inside of the building was empty. Outside, Hanley peered around the corner, saw Polish infantry no more than twenty yards away and ducked back just in time to avoid the two bullets which smacked into the wall where his head had been. Mullins came out again, and in spite of his gestures pushed him aside and looked around the corner. Most of the Poles must have been reloading because it was a good twenty seconds before a ball pecked the stone just above his head and the captain sprang back. The closest chasseurs grinned and the officer could not help giving a wry smile.

The Toledo Regiment continued to fire as fast as they could. Now and then a man dropped, but for all the fury the return fire from the village did not slacken. As the sun vanished behind the hills it became dark quickly, so that each shot was a great flame in the night.

'We need to pull them back,' Mullins shouted, but by the time they reached the Spanish infantry the Toledo Regiment was already retiring. They did so calmly, more frustrated than daunted by the enemy, and so they marched in the gloom back to the hill that they were supposed to have occupied. The chasseurs covered the retreat. To Hanley the whole business seemed pointless, but no more pointless than infantry firing at castle walls for hours on end. Out to sea the sky was ripped by a wicked fork of lightning, so clear against the brooding clouds. Hanley had counted to fourteen before the thunder rolled in from the beach. The guns had fallen silent at the castle, but he could not remember when he had noticed them stop.

'Captain Hanley, is that you?' someone called out of the darkness. He saw the pale shade of a grey horse approaching through the night, the darker shapes of other riders behind. Peering into the darkness he saw that the rider wore a cocked hat. 'It is, is it not, my dear fellow?'

'Major Sinclair,' he said, recognising the voice at last.

'Ah, good, the very chap.' The Irishman came closer and gestured at the leader of the men escorting him. 'You remember El Lobo?'

'Señor,' Hanley said, and introduced them both to Captain Mullins.

'Where is the general? It is imperative that I see him at once.'

'Take them, Hanley, I had best stay here,' the captain said.

Lightning again stabbed down out to sea, and this time Hanley reached only twelve before the thunder roared.

'Such dramatic punctuation seems a little overdone,' Mullins said.

Major Sinclair laughed. 'Lead on, Hanley, lead on,' he said.

15

On board the *El Vencedor* Major Alastair MacAndrews heard the clap of thunder only a couple of moments after the lightning flashed through the stern windows of the great cabin. Rain hammered against the glass, the deck sank beneath him before surging up over the next wave, again and again, and he was glad that they were under tow. The Spanish captain looked to have spent most of his sixty-five years at sea and knew his trade, but the big seventy-four was in such appalling shape that experience was unlikely to be enough in this weather. Even before they left Gibraltar the pumps had been working without pause. With only one hundred of his own men and eighty sailors loaned by the Royal Navy, the captain had little more than a quarter of the proper establishment. *El Vencedor* was rotten and filthy from neglect, its crew now too overworked to do much about either.

The first battalion of the 106th, almost one thousand men if officers and NCOs were included in the count, had been on the ship for two days and at sea for one. None was happy, but he had told them all at every opportunity to keep their dislike of the ship to themselves. If all went well, they should land some time tomorrow afternoon to support Lord Turney's expedition.

'God willing,' the Spanish captain had added after making this prediction. None of them knew very much about the general's plans, and MacAndrews had got the impression that these were fluid. There was a chance they would remain on the ship and be kept for the descent on Malaga.

'As God wills,' the Spanish captain had said when he mentioned this, and the Scotsman suspected piety and prayer were their best hope in this hulk.

He still had not quite got used to Lord Turney being that rogue Jack Stevenson. The thought had never occurred to him, and he was glad to have received Esther's letter before he was summoned to meet the general. Turney was by then prepared, but the major had matched him for mock surprise and courtesy. The memory of saying 'Bit different from America' and the general's cough, look of discomfort and 'Yes, yes, to be sure' was something he would cherish for a long time. In truth he had not hated the man for long. Stevenson as he then was had cut and run, thinking only of himself and careless of both lover and comrade. Yet that had led to his journey with Esther, to falling in love and to a life together, where if there was sorrow mingled with the joy, that joy was more wonderful than anything else he had ever known.

Turney was no coward – not then and, given his reputation, not since then. He was vain, selfish and, if MacAndrews was any judge, a young rake had simply turned into an old rake with the added advantage of title, reputation and comfortable wealth. It was good that his wife and daughter were not with him in Gibraltar; Esther because she would be upset at the memories – or judging from her letter almost homicidally angry – and Jane because she was still young and might not have the sense to see the scoundrel for what he was. Whether Lord Turney was a general worth the name was harder to say, but it was not something he could alter. For the moment it was enough to hope that the pumps kept the water at bay, the storm did not get worse or – chilling thought – snap the towline. Half a battalion of the 2/4th Foot had run aground in a transport ship just a few months ago and not twenty miles from where they were. Five companies taken prisoner just like that, and if it was still better than a watery grave it was not a pleasant prospect. MacAndrews was for the moment in charge of a fine regiment, so just let them get to dry land with a decent chance of proving themselves and he would be happy.

'God willing,' he said, and raised his glass to the Spanish captain.

The storm reached Fuengirola around midnight as Hanley was still looking for Lord Turney. Lightning slashed across the night sky, the first low crack turning into a great peal of thunder which felt as if it was right over their heads. He was glad that Sinclair had left his horse with the guerrilla leader for no doubt the animals would be skittish in this weather, and there was enough happening on the beach to make them nervous. He led the major across the sand, weaving between the hundreds of soldiers and sailors working to bring the cannon ashore.

A heavy blob of rain hit him in the face. For a few moments he heard and felt the patter growing heavier until the drops started to slam into them, driving down to soak clothes and sting where they hit skin. The next flash of lightning showed the men toiling, the bare-backed sailors dripping with rain as well as sweat as they heaved on the lines to drag the two twelve-pounders across the sand. Hanley flinched as the thunder came, hunching down with his head between his shoulders. He saw an officer of the 89th and had to shout to be heard over the hissing of the rain.

'I'm looking for the general.'

'Try the hill.'

Hanley's eyes had adapted to see dimly in the black night when another fork of lightning seared into them. He saw men dragging the stumpy howitzer on its cart up the slope above them. The rain was turning the ground to mud, and he caught a cry of 'Heave, lads, heave!' before the roll of thunder drowned out everything else. He could see little apart from the slow fading glow of the lightning, and stumbled as he led Sinclair up the slope. The Irishman took his arm.

'Thanks,' he shouted.

Climbing the hill was a struggle, made worse by the gusts of wind making it hard to keep their cloaks drawn about them, and adding even more force to the rain. One small sailor with a barrel of powder on his back was blown over and rolled down the hill for a few yards. Soon he was back up, helped by his mates, who lifted the burden on to his back once more and resumed the climb.

At the top Captain Harding was bawling to be heard over the wind and rain, urging the men to dig faster. There was already a ditch some two feet deep and spoil piling behind it in spite of the rain which kept washing some of it away.

'I wondered about a side channel leading downhill to carry the water away!' Harding shouted when Hanley asked how the work went. 'Too much work, though. We need to be ready at dawn.'

'Is the general here?'

The engineer shook his head. 'Left ten minutes ago. Was going to see the Spanish colonel, and then heading back to the beach. That'll be the best place to look. No, damn it, man, keep those tarpaulins tightly over the barrels!' This to a group of marines working in the corner of the battery. 'Blast you, do you want it all spoiled?'

On their second visit to the beach they found Lord Turney. Williams was near by, hat pulled down and swathed in his boat cloak.

'You Welsh always bring your own weather, don't you!' Hanley said as he passed his friend.

The general was not happy, and not simply because of the rain. He was looking at a party of thirty sailors clustered around a gun.

'I thought the whole point of this new carriage was to make it mobile!' Lord Turney yelled at a naval lieutenant.

'More mobile than the standard pattern,' the man insisted resolutely. 'The wheels are too small for the sand, especially when it is so wet. And it's top heavy. The only way to get it up that hill would be to take the barrel off, rig up some ropes, and hoist it there.'

'And how long would that take?'

The lieutenant wore a round hat and plain blue jacket which looked quite black in the gloom. 'Fifteen hours? Maybe twenty.'

Lightning flashed and revealed the angry frustration in the general's face. For a moment Hanley saw the stubby gun more clearly. It was a carronade, its heavy barrel not resting on its carriage by the usual two trunnions set in grooves, but held in place by a heavy spike beneath the breach, which sat in a hole in the carriage. Normally such guns were fixed on a pivot by the gun port and had wheels only at the back allowing them to swivel and be aimed. This one had four wheels on the carriage more like a conventional cannon, but remained an unwieldy weapon to pull about on land.

'Can you get it to the top of the beach?' Lord Turney asked. 'Above high tide.'

'Yes, my lord. It'll take an hour, but we can do that.'

'Then take it to that low rise over there on the right. Dig a rampart to make a position and have it so that it can fire to cover anything we do on the beach. Understood?'

'Yes, my lord.'

'Good man. I'll send Captain Harding down to check that the position is sited properly.' The general looked around and saw the bulky shape of the tall Williams. 'Mr Williams, run to the battery on the hill and ask the captain to visit the beach when he has a free moment.'

'Sir.' The Welshman vanished into the gloom.

'Excuse me, my lord,' Hanley said, but saw that the general had not noticed and so raised his voice. 'My apologies, my lord, but Major Sinclair has arrived with new intelligence.'

'Ah, Hanley. Take him over there and wait with the others. Mullins will show you.' Lord Turney dismissed him with a wave of the hand. 'Captain Hope.' Hanley had not realised the naval officer was ashore. 'We must be careful that the ammunition goes to the correct batteries now that we have two.'

Mullins led them away to the feeble shelter of a canopy strung between four poles. Three officers were waiting there, all come in from working with the partisan bands. Two were lieutenant colonels and the other a captain. Hanley had not met them before, although he had heard the names. None was in much mood to talk – not even Sinclair – except to express their impatience at waiting so long, and so the five men waited in sullen silence, now and again soaked as rain blew in from the sides or a heavy drop gathered and fell through holes in the cover.

The thunder became distant, and half an hour later the rain slackened and then stopped. The clouds broke and a silvery light which seemed almost as bright as day after the blackness of the storm allowed them to watch as men toiled on the beach and headed up the hill. Williams came down the hill just as the general arrived to speak to them.

'You can come on out from your lair, gentlemen!' Lord Turney sounded more cheerful, but was still speaking very loudly after hours of yelling over the wind. In spite of his age, the general was striding along briskly, with the young Captain Hope taking three steps for his two to keep up.

The two lieutenant colonels reported first, recounting the efforts made to raise and arm the peasants. Each one assured him that the situation was promising, and might soon bear fruit.

'Excellent,' Lord Turney said with little enthusiasm. 'Though such things are less vital for our present needs.' He asked the captain to speak next, respecting the time of his arrival over seniority. His news was almost as vague, of raids by the partisans, and bands that might rally to join them in a few days, but one thing was more encouraging.

'General Blake has advanced with the Army of the Centre.'

'Blake is beaten!' It was Sinclair who interrupted. 'My apologies, my lord, and to you too, Captain Samson, but he was beaten and driven back at dawn this morning – well, yesterday now. That is why I have ridden here so hard. I feared that the news would not otherwise have reached you.'

'Beaten,' Lord Turney said. 'Are you sure?'

'I saw it, my lord, and have come fifty miles to get here. His cavalry fled precipitately and then the French hussars and Polish lancers swept in on the flanks of his infantry. Half a division was lost in twenty minutes, and he has gone back as fast as he can with the rest.'

The general clearly believed him, as did the others. Blake had no reputation as a commander even among his countrymen, and there had been so many similar disasters in the last few years.

'Are the French pursuing?' Captain Hope asked. 'We may still benefit if their main force is drawn off.'

'It took less than a division to beat him,' Sinclair said. 'Sebastiani has three and a half thousand men at Malaga, but by now they will surely be marching towards us.'

'How long to get here?' Lord Turney had at last realised that he no longer needed to shout.

'We should expect them before dusk tomorrow – perhaps earlier.' Hanley thought that Sinclair's guess was about right. It was a good twenty miles as the crow flew and the road wound a fair bit.

Captain Hope glanced around at the activity on the beach. 'My lord, if we act now then we could be at Malaga by tomorrow afternoon. With luck the *Rodney* and its tow will have joined us so that we will have a thousand fresh soldiers. How many men will Sebastiani leave in garrison, Major Sinclair?'

'He must have some idea of the numbers here, so he will not risk leaving too many behind. A few companies at the most. Enough to hold down the civilians, but only if they have no support. My spies confirm that the mole in the harbour is undefended, my lord.' Sinclair and the naval officer both sounded excited, and for Hanley's part he would be glad to see the back of this dismal beach.

'No, it will not do,' Lord Turney said.

Captain Hope broke the silence, although Hanley could sense that Sinclair was itching to speak.

'There is an opportunity, my lord,' the naval officer said. Still the general said no more. 'Malaga is the prize, my lord. This was always meant as a diversion, and the wind is now in our favour.'

'No, it will not do,' Lord Turney said once again. 'If we reembark they will have beaten us – a mere company outnumbered ten to one. What will the peasants think if the French then make us fly before they have even come in sight?'

Captain Hope persisted. 'We do not need to win here, my lord.'

'That may have been true yesterday, but our attack failed. If we go it will look as if we are beat. And then it will take hours and the *Rodney* may come with the One Hundred and Sixth, but it may not. And we may fail in Malaga, if the harbour is not quite so unprotected as we think, or if the luck runs against us.'

The general had begun to speak louder, but now calmed himself. 'It is too much of a gamble, Captain Hope, although I much admire your spirit. With the battery on the hill I am confident that we will take this castle before noon tomorrow. Either we can install a garrison or slight the place, and then re-embark without difficulty. I hear Sebastiani is a bold man, but if he is fool enough to risk his men on the shore and in range of your guns, Captain Hope, then we have an even better opportunity. Who knows, with the One Hundred and Sixth as reinforcement we may even put him to flight.

'No, gentlemen, we will stay and win this fight. And to do that we all have a great deal to do. Thank you for the intelligence and your advice, but we must all be about our business.'

'If you will excuse me, my lord, then I shall go with the partisans and look for Sebastiani.'

'Ah, Sinclair, that is good of you.' Lord Turney stared at the major for a while. 'Yes, very good. I cannot spare Hanley for I need him to carry a message to the Toledo Regiment.' He searched among his staff. 'Mr Williams will guide you to our outposts on the Mijas road and set you on your way. Then I want you to hurry back with the reports from our pickets, Williams. Goodnight to you, Sinclair.'

Hanley was not sure, but thought that he heard his friend sigh at being sent out again on a round trip of a good six or seven miles. Cloud came in from the sea, and the stars and slim moon were covered. Raindrops spattered on the sand, and lightning flashed out to sea.

Williams and Sinclair set off up the path inland, the Irishman striding off at a brisk pace and forcing the other officer to jog along reluctantly beside him.

Paula Velasco was lost and in pain, and cursing herself for a fool. Lupe had been restless, and both of them could see little point in waiting here where they were ignored. If the weather had not been so bad they would have slipped away to rejoin her husband, but instead they decided to seek shelter in one of the farmhouses on the road, or even in Fuengirola itself. Hanley had told her that the soldiers were forbidden from entering the little cluster of houses, but saw no reason why this should apply to them. They had money to pay if anyone was still in the houses, and if the sight of their weapons was not in itself sufficient to encourage the owners' hospitality.

They had headed towards the road, but before they got there Lupe's horse was terrified when lightning struck a tree and the animal bolted, carrying her sister off into the darkness. Paula's own little gelding stirred, ears twitching in its eagerness to follow, but she calmed it and walked it forward, waiting for Lupe to come back. She did not, and though it was hard to judge time in the hammering rain, she began to fear that something had happened. It could just be the foul weather, enough to confuse them both even after many nights spent out in the open, but still she worried, and began to press on faster, looking as best she could for any sign.

As they came along a bank her horse stumbled, its shoulder dropping and the animal crying out as it struggled for balance, until a great roll of thunder made it rear and Paula fell, boots free of the stirrups, hitting the ground hard and rolling down a steep bank.

She must have lost consciousness and did not know for how long, because her next memory was of lying awkwardly on her side, covered in mud and with a shallow stream flowing around her. Her head was sore, her hat and cloak both gone, and when she tried to push herself up a terrible pain stabbed at her right shoulder. She could move her arm, but only slightly, and the price was an agony which made her sob in misery. Her left arm was fine, and shifting her weight and using this she managed to sit up, and finally to stand. The rain had stopped and pale light bathed the slopes of the ravine above her. It looked too steep to climb, and so she followed the water as it flowed down. It was tempting to call out, but she was no longer so sure where she was, and perhaps there were enemies near by. Paula's slim sword must have come loose in the fall, because the scabbard was bent and empty. There was a pistol in her sash, and she uttered a silent prayer for a miracle that would have kept the powder dry.

The sky grew dark again and rain started to fall, washing some of the mud off her face. Her clothes were already soaked through, the shirt clinging and cold, the leather breeches uncomfortable. Her riding boots keep slipping on the grass, and she had to walk slowly to stop from falling.

'Lupe!' she called once, but doubted her voice carried far in the wind and rain. There was no real point calling for her sister, and prudence returned, telling her that silence was better. If only the pain were not so bad and she knew where she was. Paula Velasco walked on for what seemed like hours, wandering through a maze of rolling hills and little ravines. After a ferocious downpour during which she had to close her eyes and trust that she would not fall, the rain eased and she realised that she was on the main track. On the far side was a cottage, its whitewashed walls a dull gleam in the darkness, and a sliver of red light coming from a crack in a door or shutter. It was shelter if nothing else, and Paula went towards it.

She was not alone. A year spent with her husband's band had honed instincts which she had not known that she possessed, and even exhausted and in pain she knew that there was someone out there. Paula reached down, awkward with her left hand, and slid the pistol from her sash. Her fingers were cold and clumsy, but she managed to pull the hammer back.

'*Español?*' she said in challenge to the black night. '*Inglés?*'

A cruel laugh came from the darkness. Paula raised the pistol, searching the night for the threat. Someone ran at her, coming from the side, and she swung, wincing with pain as her shoulder throbbed in protest.

A man shouted in a language she did not know and then she pulled the trigger, the muzzle pointing squarely at his chest, and the flint sparked, but the rain had turned the powder into a useless sludge and nothing happened.

Arms grabbed her from behind, agony searing through her shoulder, and she screamed in fear and pain.

16

Ten minutes before and the rain would have drowned the sound. Instead Williams heard a high-pitched scream, an awful scream of torment, and he ran towards the noise. He was on his way back to the beach from the outposts carrying the report that the French did not seem to be up to anything – something he suspected was true given the weather, but doubted that the chasseur pickets had taken any real trouble to find out.

Another cry turned into a great sob and then there was silence. He was sure it was a woman and so he drove himself on, running down the muddy track. Pushing back his cloak, his hand gripped the hilt of his sword as he ran and slid the blade free.

The track turned past a rise crowned with bushes which waved in the wind and went down into a little dip. Williams saw a patch of light, bright light in the open door of a cottage, and then the door was slammed shut. He pelted along the path, muddy water splashing up on to his already filthy boots and cloak, and then was on the grass. Outside the door he stopped, took a breath and then launched himself at the door, kicking so hard that his foot snapped one of the planks as it slammed back. He blinked at the light of fire and candle which seemed dazzling after hours wandering the dark night.

There were men in the small single room of the cottage, all of them in the dark blue of the chasseurs, and two were crouching over something, while another cowered in the corner of the room. The fourth man came at him, the long sword bayonet of a rifle in his hand, lunging at the officer.

Williams parried the blow, flicking the blade aside and then jabbing to force the soldier back.

'Drop it!' he shouted. The man hesitated, but when no one came in after the officer, he suddenly lunged again. Shouts echoed around the room, and behind him the two soldiers sprang up, one grabbing a rifle.

Williams parried the blow and then swayed back as the chasseur swung his left fist in a punch which flicked his ruined shoulder wing.

'Damn it, you rogue, I'm an officer!' he called out, feeling foolish as he spoke, but the soldier hacked at his head this time. Williams was faster, whipping his curved blade down to cut through the man's elbow. The chasseur howled, arm almost severed, and the sword bayonet dropped from his lifeless hand. Behind him the man with the rifle was raising it, pulling back the hammer, so the officer barged the wounded man on to his comrade, knocking the barrel high as he fell. It went off, the noise appalling in the small room, and the flame singeing Williams' face and speckling it with powder. He stamped with his front foot and thrust the sword forward. A moment's resistance on his collar and the tip speared into the chasseur's neck. More blood gushed from the dying man's throat as he dropped on top of the soldier bleeding from the great gash in his arm.

The man curled up in the corner whimpered. The other had a corporal's stripes on his sleeve, but let his knife fall to the floor and held his hands up. His trousers were unbuttoned and hanging open.

'I surrender,' he said, and Williams saw that it was Brandt, the marksman so praised by Lieutenant Hatch.

A moaning came from behind and the officer aimed the sword at the chasseur corporal and gestured for him to go back. On a heap of straw behind the man a woman lay, and moaned through the red gag tied around her mouth, the skin around one of her eyes swelling into a bruise. Her right arm lay in an odd posture beside her, the fingers curled unnaturally. Her left was bound by a musket sling looped into an iron ring set into the wall – probably something the peasants used to tether an animal. Many a poor family would keep a goat or two in with them for safety.

The woman was almost naked. Her shirt had gone and her bare skin was pale in the light of the candle and little fire. Black rags lay in the straw, mingled with silver buttons from where they had sliced through the seam of one trouser leg and torn it away. Williams must have interrupted Brandt as he worked on the other one, for it was half cut and pulled back and when that was done the young woman would have been naked apart from her riding boots.

Williams brought his blade back up so that it no longer pointed at the corporal and saw the fear slip from Brandt's eyes. The officer stepped forward and put all his weight into the blow as he slammed the hilt into the man's face, flinging him back against the wall. Brandt slid down, blood gushing from his split lip, and Williams kicked him hard in the chest, knocking the breath out of him, so that he slumped to the ground.

That done, he went over to the wall, pulled the sling so that the hitch knot came free and unclipped his cloak, handing it down to the girl. It took a moment, but then the memory came back and he recognised the short-haired wife of the partisan leader El Blanco. She looked to be in great pain and still stunned by all that had happened, but it seemed that he had arrived in time to save her from the very worst.

Brandt was still lying on the floor, hands pressed against his chest, and Williams felt a strong urge to step over and thrust down, finishing the scoundrel off and saving the cost of the rope.

'No,' he said aloud. 'You'll hang.' He was about to untie the scarf gagging the young woman when someone came through the door, bayonet fitted to the rifle he held ready to cover the room. He was dressed in the blue jacket and trousers of the chasseurs, had a dark sash and sergeant's chevrons, and Williams felt a wave of relief when he saw that it was Mueller.

'What the devil is going on?' The voice was English, as slurred although not quite so disdainful as usual, and Lieutenant Hatch appeared behind the sergeant. 'Williams?' he said in surprise.

'What the bloody hell are you up to? We heard shouting and a shot and ...'

The lieutenant noticed the young woman and his eyes widened as he realised that she was nearly naked. Paula tried to pull the cloak to cover herself, but her left arm was stiff from being tied up. Williams helped her, brushing her soft skin as he brought the wet cloak up over her breasts. Then he took off the scarf. Paula licked blood from her lips, but did not speak.

'You old rogue,' Hatch said.

'Don't be a damned fool.' Williams' anger took the lieutenant aback. 'This is the wife of Don Antonio Velasco, the leader of the partisans. Your corporal and these men dragged her in here and attempted to ravish her. When I tried to stop them they attacked me.'

Mueller was staring at the corporal with utter contempt, and Williams was confident that the man was a serious soldier and no friend of Brandt. He used his boot to prod the man wounded in the throat.

'Dead.'

Hatch showed no regret at the death of one of his men. 'Well, looks like you've paid one of them out already, and made a start on the others.' His breath smelt strongly of alcohol.

'They'll hang, both of them,' Williams said. 'I do not think the other fellow helped them – but then he did not help her. The court martial can decide.'

'Yes, quite. Well, Brandt, I told you that you were born for the gallows and now you have proved me right. Sergeant, have two men drag the corpse outside, and get someone to bandage that swine. Place him and the other two under arrest. You and another two men will escort them back to the beach.' Williams could not remember Hatch behaving so correctly and wondered whether for once the man was sober in spite of the smell. Surely he could have had little chance to drink very heavily in the last hours.

'Mr Williams,' the scarred lieutenant asked, 'might it not be a good idea if you went with the sergeant and the prisoners? Make sure the charges are laid. Be too easy for things not to be done properly, as I dare say tomorrow will be even busier than today.'

He did not care for Hatch, did not care for him at all, but the fellow was a British officer and late of his own regiment, and in this case he was right. 'Yes, that is for the best. Will you take care of the señora?'

'My dear fellow, do you really need to ask that?' The lieutenant seemed genuinely offended. 'I do not think we are needed, but if we are called away I'll be sure to leave good reliable men to stand guard outside this hovel.'

'Of course, my apologies – it has been a trying night. I will try to find Hanley, who is most likely to know how to reach her husband and friends. We may also need someone to witness as she tells her story.'

When they left with the prisoners, Paula Velasco was drinking brandy from a flask, held to her lips by one of the chasseurs so that her own arm was free to keep the cloak tight around her. As far as Williams could see the other chasseurs were shocked by the attack, and behaving with great tenderness and consideration to the lady. Hatch was kind, efficient and not troubling her with gallantry. It had been a ghastly business, but could easily have been so much worse.

Williams led them through a steady drizzle, with one of the chasseurs following, then the prisoners and then Mueller and the other guard, both with sword bayonets fixed. The wounded man was dazed, and they kept at a pace he could match, if only with a great effort. Corporal Brandt said nothing at all, but the other man complained in a steady whine that he had done nothing. After a while Mueller hit him with the butt of the musket.

'He says he did nothing,' he explained to Williams. 'I say that is why I hit him.'

The officer was not listening. He held his hand up to stop them. 'Quiet,' he hissed. Williams dropped to one knee, looking at the low ridge a hundred yards or so to their left. He was sure something was moving, and then he made out a darker shape between the ground and the sky.

'Wait here,' he whispered. 'Not a sound.' Mueller grunted an acknowledgement.

Williams was convinced men were moving parallel with the road, he reckoned lots of men, and he did not know why any of their own brigade would be there. He went at an angle to cut ahead of them, hurrying to get off the road and then going more carefully, bent to keep low. The drizzle faded away and a break in the clouds gave a thin gleam of pale starlight. He stopped in the shelter of a boulder and looked. He was sure they were there, and as he waited he caught the muffled sound of men moving, their weapons and equipment rattling gently.

He went forward, crawling in the open and crouching as low as he could in any hollow. There was no sign of any flank guards, but that did not mean they were not there. The sky was clearing, the light growing a little brighter, and then he saw silhouettes on the crest a short way ahead. They were soldiers definitely, carrying muskets with their long bayonets fitted, and wearing long coats and flat-topped shakos. The hats were too wide to be either the 89th or the chasseurs. It could be the Toledo Regiment, but if so then what were they doing? There were several dozen at least out there, perhaps fifty or more, formed up in a little column starting to file down into a ravine. Someone gave an order, but he could not catch the words. He did not think they were Spanish.

A cry came from behind him, a loud cry, followed by an angry shout and the noise of a scuffle. The shapes of the men in the column quivered. He ducked back, and saw two figures running through the night from where he had left Mueller and the others. An order came from the direction of the column, a much louder shout this time. The noise of movement increased, and peering past the cover he saw that the column was hurrying away.

The two fugitives ran, another man some way behind them, and Williams took a snap decision and dived into the one on the right, taking him by the waist and knocking him down. It was the chasseur who had kept complaining. The other man was past him now, yelling out something, waving his hands as he fled towards the column.

Mueller came up, too late to catch him, and knelt down beside the officer. 'Bastard Brandt,' he said. 'Bastard Pole runs to more Poles.'

There was some loud talk, but to his relief the column did not stop and bring their bayonets looking to see who was watching them. Instead they went on at a run, vanishing over the crest. Fighting an unknown number of enemies in the darkness was evidently not part of their plan.

'Go to the fort, I think,' Mueller said. 'Bastard Poles are good soldiers.'

It seemed the likeliest thing. These were surely the men from Mijas or one of the other small garrisons, bravely trying to slip in to join the garrison in Sohail Castle.

'How is your powder?' Williams asked the sergeant, who was happily sitting on the chasseur they had caught.

'No good. No shot.' That was no surprise. A shot or two might have alerted sentries in enough time to come looking for the Poles, especially if they could provoke the column into shooting back at them, but after all the rain there was no chance of that. Four of them could not hope to stop fifty men, and shouts did not carry so far or convey the same sense of urgency.

'Then I had better follow them to make sure where they are going,' Williams whispered to the German sergeant. 'Take this one and the other prisoner as fast as you can to the beach and report to the most senior officer you can find. The general should know about this. I'll take one of your chasseurs and use him as a runner if I have news.'

Sergeant Mueller shook his head. 'No,' he said. 'Better I follow. If I go to officer he not believe me. You are officer and you are English. He believe you, so you go.'

Williams knew he was right. There was a chance, a slim chance to be sure, but still a chance that if he reached a senior officer, even a company commander, quickly, then they might still be able to catch the Poles. The sergeant was a foreigner with a strong accent, and there was bound to be a delay before someone acted on his news. He might even be dismissed.

'You are sure?'

The sergeant looked at him, and Williams suspected that the German felt the officer was wondering whether to trust him.

'I follow,' he said. 'And one day I kill bastard Brandt.'

Williams patted him on the back. 'Who do you want to go with you?'

Lieutenant Hatch made sure the woman had plenty of brandy, and insisted she take some of the bread and salted beef one of his men produced from a haversack. A little colour had returned to her pale cheeks, and when given more brandy she was able to fall asleep, still wrapped tightly in Williams' heavy cloak. The Welshman was quite the Sir Galahad, saving a damsel in distress.

It was a shame about Brandt. 'Still, saves me eight dollars,' he said aloud, making the two soldiers in the room stare at him. 'Talking of a wager.' The men went back to stirring up the embers of the fire, which gave off enough smoke to make his eyes itch. These peasants never seemed to bother with chimneys.

The corporal had claimed to hit another Frenchman during that nasty little fight at Mijas, hence the eight dollars. Hatch was inclined to believe him, for the man's marksmanship was uncanny and he had taken to the British rifle with great delight.

'I like Mr Baker,' Brandt kept saying, when told that the weapon was designed and made by Ezekiel Baker of London. The corporal was a killer, no doubt about it, and although Hatch had been happy to encourage him in his trade, he had also found the man a disturbing presence. It was clear that he would kill anyone with very little thought, and the lieutenant had allowed him a loose rein, fearing a shot in the back in the next skirmish. Well, the man was gone, and good riddance. He enjoyed a brief fantasy of the corporal breaking free and shooting Williams through the heart, but dismissed it. Sergeant Mueller was a good soldier, too good to let that happen. He had always kept the corporal in check, and he was sure no love was lost between the men.

It was not the first time Hatch had dreamed of killing Williams, or having him killed in revenge for the best friend he had ever had. Poor Redman was another officer from the 106th, and if not the brightest of fellows was a great sport. He and Hatch had been inseparable, two lively young ensigns making game of the world. Redman hated Williams from the moment he saw him, annoyed by his pious manner of living, his pompous ways, and most of all the ease with which he took to soldiering – too much like a tradesman or common soldier to be a real gentleman. Redman died in the battalion's first engagement, stabbed through the heart with a bayonet, and Hatch believed wrongly that Williams had killed him. As months and now years passed, the hatred grew, made worse because he feared to call him out, and so he had taken every chance to blacken the man's reputation. Little of it had stuck, and the hope that the French would end Williams' life and career had proved vain.

As he waited in the shelter of that smoke-filled hovel an idea took shape. It shocked him, at first, for he had never done anything like it before, but that made it all the more delicious. He would spite the Sir Galahad and the man would never know, unless one day he chose to tell him. Brandy played a part in his thoughts, for he had drunk even more than the sleeping woman.

'Out,' he said to the two chasseurs. 'We must let the señora sleep. Both of you stand guard on the road. I shall sit here to protect the lady. Go!'

The men were reluctant to leave the fire and roof over their heads, but sullen looks were the extent of their protest. Hatch barred the door behind them. Half of one board hung back from Williams' kick. He unbuckled his sword and laid it down on the folded cloak which doubled as a blanket.

The officer rubbed his eyes and moved to watch the sleeping woman. She had a nice face, even with the bruise and the short-cropped hair. Something in it reminded him of Jenny Dobson, that slut of a soldier's daughter whom both he and Redman had taken to their beds for a very modest price. Hatch did not know that Sergeant Dobson had murdered his friend in the chaos of battle at Roliça, but then by this time his loathing for Williams was a thing in itself, so much a part of him that it no longer needed a reason.

Paula Velasco slept soundly, sighing softly. Her left hand had slid from beneath the cloak and Hatch saw that the musket sling was still tied around it. Lifting it gently, he found that the other end was long enough for him to fasten it to the iron ring without pulling on the arm or disturbing her. The red scarf was on the ground, and he took it and pressed it against her mouth. Paula's eyes opened, dull surprise changing in a moment to fear. She struggled as he looped the scarf over her head to keep it in place, and as she shifted her angry curse turned into a bitter cry of pain, but both were muffled.

Hatch shushed her, but said nothing. Then he grabbed the cloak and whipped it aside.

17

The twelve-pounder slammed back as it fired, the little wheels of its naval carriage rolling across the planking the sailors had laid during the night. Beside it the captain of the second gun pulled the lanyard, snapping down the flint to ignite the fine powder in the tube and an instant later the main charge. Flame belched from its mouth, followed by smoke, and the gun jerked back like its mate. The short-barrelled howitzer gave a lighter cough and Hanley was sure he could see the dark shape of its shell as it was lobbed high to drop down on to the castle. Men were already swabbing out the twelve-pounders, and even though it was several hours to noon the Royal Artillerymen were sweating into their blue wool coats as they worked.

Lord Turney was beside the battery, standing with his staff and with Captain Harding, all trying to observe the fall of shot.

'They will not take much more of this,' the general declared, slapping his gloves against his leg. For a man who had spent the night being drenched by rain, Lord Turney cut a surprisingly elegant figure – no doubt thanks to the concerted labour of the two servants who had accompanied him on shore.

They were some three hundred and fifty yards from the castle, and somewhat higher, and the guns had now been firing for over three hours. Out in the bay, the four remaining gunboats were pounding the east wall, supported by the gun-brig *Encounter*. The other brigs with their short ranged carronades kept further out, and today the *Topaze*'s crew was too busy rowing back and forth with shot and powder for the little boats to work their own guns. Captain Hall's boats kept up a steady fire with their eighteen-pounders, working under the baking sun. There was only a light breeze and a gentle swell, and the practice was good. Undaunted, the Polish heavy guns replied, but whether through shortage of ammunition or exhaustion, the shots came less often and with less accuracy. Early on a sixteen-pound ball shattered the arm of a gunner in Boat Seventeen, and half an hour later two men died as another shot grazed at head height across the same gunboat. Each time it rowed back out of range, tipped the corpses over the side and passed the wounded on to one of *Topaze*'s boats, before moving forward again to resume its task.

At seven minutes to eight, Gunboat Seventeen had its revenge when it struck the bastion just to the left of the main battery on the east wall. Weakened by the steady pounding and the crumbling of ancient mortar, a good ten feet of the stonework collapsed, tumbling down to drop outside the wall. Men fell with the stone, and there were several blue-coated bodies in the mound of debris. None of them moved. A cloud of dust added to the dirty powder smoke around the wall.

'Bravo!' Lord Turney cheered the sailors. 'Keep at it, lads!'

From sea and land the bombardment continued. Between the heavy blasts of the British guns and the higher-pitched replies of the Poles, Hanley could hear the cracks of rifles as the chasseurs crept as close as they dared and sniped at the defenders. The twelve-pounders were too light to make a breach and so instead worked on the parapet of the south wall, slamming shot after shot as closely grouped as they could, and over time the battlements were chewed apart and holed. Every gap gave more chance for the riflemen to catch one of the Poles exposed.

'Beautiful! Quite beautiful!' The general was watching through his glass when a shrapnel shell from the howitzer exploded a few feet above one of the two-pounders mounted on the wall. The thin iron casing split apart, spraying two hundred and eight balls of the size used in cavalry carbines. Lighter than a musket ball, they still spread out to form a lethal cloud which cut down all three gunners manning the light piece. 'Well done!' Lord Turney took the telescope from his eye to praise the howitzer's crew. 'Keep at it, my lads, the place will crack soon!'

Hanley wondered whether he was right. Captain Hall did not appear quite so sanguine, and it was obvious that Williams was dubious.

'Do you remember how close the French guns had to come at Ciudad Rodrigo before they really started to tear up the wall?' the Welshman said in a low voice.

'The walls there were a lot bigger.'

'Aye, and so were their guns,' Williams said at the very moment there was a slackening of the noise.

'Come now, Lieutenant Williams, I'll have no croaking here.' Lord Turney glared at the young officer. It was obvious that the general had taken a pronounced dislike to the Welshman, and Hanley found it odd that he should bother. 'Reinforced or not, the inside of that place will be like a taste of hell for those Poles. They won't stand it much longer – not for Boney's sake.'

Lord Turney had responded angrily when Williams brought the news of a fresh company of Poles moving through the darkness.

'Damn it, man, why didn't you fetch support and stop them!'

Williams had not answered so absurd a question, and simply explained that he had sent two out of his three men to follow the enemy. Hanley had not been there when Sergeant Mueller arrived to confirm that some fifty or sixty Polish infantry had found their way to the north wall of the castle, beside the river, and been admitted through the main gate.

There was no one to stop them, for the general had not set outposts to encircle the castle, although Hanley confessed to himself that he had not thought of this until now. Williams obviously had, and Lord Turney seemed to sense this and took the implied criticism very hard.

'They should not have got through. If my officers were about their duty instead of gallivanting around rescuing bloody women who should not have been here in the first place.' Williams' report of the attack on Paula Velasco had outraged the general when he heard about it, but that was soon forgotten in his annoyance that the castle had been reinforced. 'A battlefield is no place for women, however brave, and her husband was a damned fool to send them. Asking for trouble.'

Captain Mullins was shocked at this, and Hanley could sense Williams' anger rising at this shifting of some blame to the victim. The brigade major's insistence on the seriousness of the crime helped mollify the Welshman. He insisted on hearing again all the details, and the general's temper snapped when he heard that the men had attacked an officer, and thus challenged military discipline.

'Goddamned rogues! If we had time I'd try them and shoot them now. Serve us right for enlisting bloody deserters in the first place. Have them sent on board the *Topaze* and ask Captain Hope to clap them in irons. Pity you let the leader go!' he added, renewing his open disappointment in Williams' actions.

Guadalupe rode up at this point, brought there by one of the other guerrilleros. As soon as she was told her face became savage and she slammed her big spurs into the side of her horse to hurry to her sister.

'Go with her, Hanley,' Mullins ordered before the general had reacted. 'Do what you can to make sure that they are helped and protected.'

A partisan gave the officer his horse, a strong and fresh Andalusian, and he was able to catch up with the young woman before long. She said nothing, and Hanley felt that silence was for the best. When they arrived two chasseurs stood guard some distance in front of the little building. Hatch was nowhere to be seen, which was odd since Williams had said that he had promised to stay. Paula sat hunched up in the heavy cloak, eyes staring blankly, and did not seem to recognise her sister.

'I found some soldiers from the Toledo Regiment and a solid-looking sergeant to help them,' he told Williams when he came back and they stood watching the bombardment with the rest of the general's staff. 'They are going to take her to a little convent a mile or so outside Fuengirola.' He tried to spot the building, which was on the crest of one of the hills, but could not. 'There are a few monks there skilled at caring for the sick. Her shoulder and arm look bad, and her sister worries that she is developing a fever.'

'The general is right,' Williams said, half to himself. 'I should not have let Brandt escape.'

'You cannot do everything. It was a miracle you came along in time to stop them.'

'Do you know I was on the verge of killing the man, even though he had given himself up.' Williams seemed ashamed of himself. 'All of them. It would have been easy.'

'I am sure you did the right thing,' Hanley said, although in truth he had far less strong convictions about such matters of morality than his friend. 'When I came in and saw the poor thing I was ready to slaughter the men to blame. Beaten, arm badly hurt, and left without a stitch of clothing apart from your cloak, and her sister with tears streaming down her face from her own terrible experiences. Who wouldn't kill after seeing that?'

Williams did not seem to hear, sunk in stern examination of his own soul.

'Don't worry, Bills.' Hanley tried to sound confident. 'We'll get the rogue when the castle surrenders – that is if a cannonball hasn't already knocked his head off!'

'Well said, Hanley. That's the spirit.' Lord Turney was brimming with confidence. 'Mullins, send someone to signal the Navy to cease fire. This battery is to do the same. Then you and Williams can carry over another summons to surrender. Pound to a penny they are ready to quit.'

Twenty minutes later the British guns went silent, followed soon afterwards by the Polish cannon. The gentle wind came in off the sea and made the thinning clouds of smoke drift away from the walls and the battery position. It took another five minutes for the emissaries to go down the hill, cross the valley and approach the castle, and five more to return.

'They refuse to surrender,' Mullins reported. Williams whispered to Hanley that the Polish officer had been considerably more blunt in his reply, but that did not change the essence of the answer.

'Well then, send to Captain Harding instructing him to resume the bombardment as soon as he has resupplied with powder.' The general nodded to the Royal Artillery lieutenant in charge of the battery. 'You may as well open fire straight away. Pound them, and keep pounding them and they will give in in the end. You and your men are doing excellent service.'

Lord Turney looked grave, for a partisan had brought a note from Major Sinclair. The rider was a burly rascal, one of El Lobo's men, who stared impassively at the scene of battle. Hanley recognised him from the night before, and similarly had no doubt about the authenticity of the message, or its seriousness.

Gen. Sebastiani with a division of six infantry battalions numbering 4,700, two field batteries with sixteen guns, and a regiment each of Dragoons and Lancers, in total 800 men, is approaching along the Malaga Road. Anticipate he will reach you by 3.30 to 4 o'clock in the afternoon.

yr obedient servant, James Sinclair

Before the gunboats began firing again, the general led all of his staff away from the battery.

'If they come, then we need to know where to hold them, Harding,' Lord Turney told the engineer. 'This is not good cavalry country, and that is something, but they have over three times our numbers, and until the fort's guns are silenced we cannot take our own artillery off in the daylight.'

The general went on foot, for there were not sufficient horses for the others, and he went with care, but even so they were fired at from the castle on several occasions. No shot came nearer than a ball which went over Williams' shoulder and plucked the cocked hat from the general's head.

'Blackguards,' he said cheerfully, and, picking it up, made an elaborate bow to the castle wall.

They climbed the hills again, and spent five minutes looking at the remains of a stone tower on the western slope.

'The walls are solid, my lord,' Harding confirmed. 'With a bit of work we could station fifty men here and they would be hard to dislodge.'

'Good, see to it when you have a moment.' As they headed back towards the battery, the general dictated a series of orders to Mullins. 'I shall go presently to consult with Harding and Hope. The Navy must be aware that we may need to be taken off and that the gunboats will be required to give us protective fire.

'The Eighty-ninth have been on duty all night and this morning. Stand them down, send them to the beach where the enemy's fire cannot reach and have food brought to them. In their place form all of the chasseurs save for the riflemen and station them on the flank of the battery to act as security. You take the order to the Chasseurs, Williams.

'Are the companies from the Toledo Regiment returned from before Mijas?'

'No, my lord,' Mullins said. Hanley had not heard the general issue that order, but conceded that he may have been absent when it was done.

'Send to them at once. Have them return here since we do not have the numbers to fight at such a distance and the position is not one to render it possible to resist for long. Bring them back to rejoin the rest of their regiment and ask the colonel to form up behind the Chasseurs as a reserve. You had better take that one, Hanley.'

'My lord!' It was Williams who interrupted with an excited shout. 'The *Rodney* is here!'

The general stopped and peered out to sea, squinting a little. Hanley was more than ever convinced that his eyesight was less than perfect, but it took him only a moment to see the dark shapes of the British and Spanish warships.

'Thank God.' Hanley was close and heard the softly spoken words. 'This is splendid, truly splendid,' he said out loud. 'Could not have happened at a more opportune moment. Be good to see your battalion no doubt, Hanley. You too, Williams.' The smile was warm, and for the moment his criticism of the Welshman forgotten.

Lord Turney gestured to his groom, who led the general's horse over. Neither a big man nor a young one, he swung himself into the saddle with practised ease. 'Well then, we all have plenty to do. To your duties, gentlemen.' The general gave a gentle tap of his heels and the horse willingly set off at a brisk walk down the side of the sandy hill. Behind him in the battery the twelve-pounders thundered out almost as one, and Hanley instinctively looked round and saw some more blocks of stone fall from the parapet.

'No mention of Malaga, I notice,' Williams said to him.

So much had happened that it was hard to remember that they had come to this place only to distract the enemy. Hanley shrugged. 'Well, it does sound as if we have drawn the French here. Perhaps we could still sail there faster than they could walk.'

Williams straightened his back to stand to attention. 'As Sergeant Dobson would say, "Yes, sir. Certainly, sir."' He thought for a moment. 'Dob would have killed them. Well, it is too late and we had better both be off. Good luck to you.'

Hanley watched his friend jogging away, unsure whether to envy or pity him for having such a serious nature.

There were corpses piled up in one of the storerooms of the castle. Corporal Brandt helped to carry yet another dead man to join the stack, laying him out like a piece of lumber. The soldier who was carrying the body with him had powder stains all over his face and a bandage around his forehead. He looked wild eyed and his jacket was dirty and torn, but he did not look beaten. The British were chipping away at the fort's garrison as they chipped away at its walls, men ripped in two by the heavy shot or more often cut by splinters of the walls and fragments of shells. The howitzer took a steady toll, and its small-calibre balls wounded many even if they rarely killed. Others fell to the riflemen, some by ill luck and others when a marksman spotted them moving past one of the gaps torn in the battlements. He noticed that two of the men near the bottom of the pile had neat holes in the forehead, and forced himself not to smile because he was sure he had claimed them on the first day.

The Poles of the 4th Regiment of the Grand Duchy of Warsaw were suffering and dying one by one, but there were still a good one hundred and sixty men able to carry a musket and on balance Brandt was happier inside than outside the walls. He was alive and that was the main thing, and even if he had lost his pack with most of his possessions, he did have half a dozen gold napoleons he had found on a corpse during the night. He and his comrade, the Dane Jorgesen, had slipped away in the darkness after the failed night attack at Mijas and gone to see what could be found. There were always pickings on a battlefield, if you knew where to look and took care. Seeing the woman had seemed a rare piece of luck, especially as it was not until she called out for someone that they realised it was a woman. He should have listened to Jorgesen and taken her then, out in the open, but it had been so long he wanted to enjoy it, and so they had dragged her to the house. He had scared one of the chasseurs there with his threats and easily persuaded the other to join in the fun. Then that bastard British officer Williams – the one his own lieutenant hated so much – had burst in before they had started, killed Jorgesen, and cut the other man through the arm.

There was no point fighting. Roll with the punches and ride your luck – that was the way to live, and it had steered Brandt through thirteen years as a soldier in the Austrian, Prussian, Russian, French and now British armies. These were good times for a soldier quick in his wits and who knew how to kill and take care of himself. The luck was still with him, for they stumbled across the enemy and they were countrymen of his and did not want to make noise, so they had not shot at him when he saw his chance and made a break for it. They might not have taken someone who could not speak Polish, but they took him, marching him between two guards, and so he crept with them as they reached the castle, waited through that farce when the garrison did not believe that they were Poles, until they were finally let in.

'Deserter, eh?' a big whiskered captain had said, peering at him by torchlight. The officer wore a square-topped *czapka*, that uniquely Polish headgear, instead of the French-style shakos sported by his men.

'Been waiting my chance, sir,' Brandt replied, playing the part of the good and patriotic soldier. 'I was ordered to surrender at Bailén, then given the choice of rotting in a prison hulk or enlisting with the British. Thought it was the best chance to get away. This is the first time they have brought us back to Spain. I could not believe my good fortune when I heard there was a Polish regiment here.'

'Yes, it is surely better to be shot by a firing squad from your homeland than by foreigners.' The captain looked him in the eyes, trying to judge his truthfulness.

'I'll admit I signed on with the enemy, but many a good Pole has been forced to do that before now. It wasn't the first time for me, but that was before we had a country of our own. I won't blame you if you don't believe me, but I'll willingly fight and die for that uniform,' he gestured at the captain's coat, 'and for the Grand Duchy.'

The captain stared at him for a long time. 'Lock him up,' he said in the end. 'Put him in the old barracks.' Brandt was taken to a small room and locked in. There were no windows, but a strip of light appeared under the door to show that it was daylight and almost immediately came the dull crumps of the bombardment. An hour later the door was wrenched open and a sergeant appeared.

'Put this on,' he growled, holding out a blue jacket with the red collar, cuffs and a yellow front. 'Captain Mlokosiewicz says you can do some work.'

Brandt took the jacket, noticing a hole and a dark stain on the back.

The sergeant grinned. 'Don't worry, that makes it lucky. No one gets shot in the same place twice.'

Brandt put it on and found that the work was carrying the wounded to the surgeon and taking the dead to the pile. He did it willingly and well, carrying wounded men as gently as he could, talking softly to soothe them, and never hesitating to go out to where a man lay sprawled and moaning behind a demolished section of battlements. When the bastion collapsed, it was Brandt who led the rescue party, working with their hands as they pulled out seven mangled corpses – the other two had fallen outside. He did it to win trust, because he intended to survive, and because there was genuinely something good about being with Poles, hearing their accents and laughing at their jokes. His cheek was grazed when one of the balls from a shrapnel shell scythed across it.

Then a lieutenant recognised him as from their home town, and he could feel the others accepting him. 'I remember, you're Dr Brandt's son. The little bugger who had to run off when there was that trouble with the maids.' The memory amused him. 'Heard you went off abroad. Ever been in the artillery?'

'Yes, sir, Austrian.'

'Good, take him to help Sergeant Zakrewski.'

Brandt found himself with the crews serving the two big guns on the eastern wall. They were old, very old, and clumsy pieces.

'I heard they dredged the bloody things out of the sea,' the sergeant said, as Brandt joined the men at the ropes pulling a gun back to the embrasure, 'but Kaminski there reckons they're from a museum. He and that ugly one used to be gunners in the Russian army, so they can't hit a damned thing.'

Kaminski was the captain in charge of the other gun, and was busy sliding a reed with fine powder down into the touch-hole. 'Don't listen to that bollocks. He's only jealous because I sank one of their boats yesterday.'

'Luck, just luck!'

An eighteen-pound ball struck the parapet, spraying them with dust and the other crew with heavy fragments of stone. They all dived for cover, but one had his jaw smashed by a lump of the wall, and was spitting flesh, blood and some of his teeth. He was led to the rear and bandaged, but returned within fifteen minutes. Sergeant Zakrewski clapped him on the back.

Brandt took over the job of ramming down charge and ball, and sponging out the barrel after each discharge. They had only five men at each of the clumsy sixteen-pounders and so he helped pull on the ropes as well to run the gun up. In the Austrian service he had been a driver, looking after the horses rather than serving the guns, but he had seen it done often enough and it was all fairly simple, much like loading a great musket or rifle. He knew enough to make damned sure that a man had his thumb over the touch-hole when he rammed or swabbed so that the rush of air did not set off any remaining powder and blow the ramrod back through him. He had seen that happen and it was not pretty.

They loaded and fired, loaded and fired, again and again. Only the sergeant and Kaminski laid the guns and saw whether or not they hit anything. The British shot kept coming, although sometimes they fired at other parts of the wall. Brandt did not think they were near to making a breach, but now and again a shot struck the mouth of an embrasure or skimmed over the parapet. One gunner's head vanished in a spray of blood and bone, but otherwise there were only wounds, and most of those were light. Another shot came lower and with a high-pitched screech left a groove in the thick barrel of one of the guns before it slammed past and drove into the back of the western wall of the castle.

'Do you reckon it's safe to fire it?' Brandt asked, his finger running along the scar in the metal.

'Probably not,' the sergeant said happily, 'so get out of the way.' Brandt quickly pulled his hand back and got clear of the wheel and then Zakrewski lowered the portfire and the cannon roared, slamming back on its trails for two yards. In a modern battery there would be a slope behind the guns, so that each time they fired they would roll back down, but this was a makeshift position and so it all had to be done by brute force.

Brandt had been there an hour, maybe more, when he was

sent for and led to the southern wall. 'We need someone to work that swivel gun,' Captain Mlokosiewicz told him. 'I've got two volunteers and you to tell them how it works.' A body lay behind the gun, one arm hanging down from the wall, and two wounded men were being carried away, all struck by casing or shot from the British shell.

As with the bullet hole in the back of his tunic, Brandt had to hope that lightning did not strike in the same place twice. The two-pounder swivel gun was easy to load, but a clumsy weapon, spraying canister or the larger balls of grape in a wide area. He doubted that they hit any of the elusive chasseurs as they dodged from cover to cover and sniped at the wall, but he certainly made a few of them duck. There were one or two former comrades that it would be a shame to hit, and once he did deliberately fire a fraction high – not that it made much difference with the crude gun. The rest of his company, let alone the rest of the battalion, could live or die without his caring one way or another.

When the British stopped firing the captain shouted at them to cease fire as well, and he watched as the flag of truce came up to demand surrender. One of the officers was Williams and it was so tempting to point the loaded swivel gun at the man and empty the charge of grape into that swine. It would not do, for he must be the obedient, dutiful soldier at last back with his own people, and so he obeyed the captain. Instead he turned so that his back was to the British, on the off-chance that they won and he had to assure them that he had never been more than a prisoner.

Captain Mlokosiewicz sent the British away. Brandt was not surprised that the envoys were not allowed too close, and certainly not permitted to come in and see the charnel house the castle had become. The garrison were brave soldiers, but no one really wants to die in a lost cause and some were bound to urge surrender.

Soon the firing resumed, and he went back to blasting at impossible targets with the swivel gun. A ricocheting rifle bullet spat up from the parapet and drove into the shoulder of one of his assistants, sending the man reeling back so that he nearly fell off the wall. Brandt kept firing the gun, and only stopped when he saw a group of officers creeping around down in the valley. One was Williams, and so he plucked up a musket dropped by one of the dead men, checked that it was loaded and primed, and then leaned forward beside one of the crenellations to take careful aim. A rifle bullet slapped into the wall inches from his head, but he ignored it, letting his breath half out and waiting for the right moment before he squeezed the trigger. The musket banged, smoke blotting out his view, and when he moved to the side all he could see was the British general bowing and sweeping with his hat, while Williams crouched near by. If only he still had his English rifle it would have been different.

'Well done. Nearly got that old bugger!' Captain Mlokosie-wicz said, patting him on the shoulder. A few yards along a shell exploded, peppering a man with dozens of the little carbine balls so that he shook like a puppet and then dropped to land with a dreadful thump on the earth of the courtyard.

Brandt noticed the captain's shoulders sagging. He was staring out to sea, and when he followed the gaze he saw two big warships, one towing the other, and a number of smaller vessels coming around the headland. 'More of the sods,' the officer said wearily. 'Well then, now or never.'

Ten minutes later Brandt was loading the musket again and waiting with ninety of the fittest remaining men behind the gate in the north wall. They were led by the lieutenant who had brought the reinforcements in last night and all were volunteers. In his case this was a generous description.

'You'll go, won't you?' Captain Mlokosiewicz had said, a wicked grin under his great whiskers. 'It's probably for the best, you know,' he added.

'Happy to help,' Brandt said, and tried to look brave and noble. There was nowhere else to go, and given that the alternative was probably prison or a firing squad, he had to ride his luck again and hope for the best.

The captain led the reserve of forty men, quite a few of whom were bandaged. The wounded unable to run were up on the walls to keep up some fire on the enemy.

'Men, we are going to attack and take that damned battery on the hill,' the captain announced. 'There are ten times as many of them as there are of us, so we know one thing – the enemy will certainly be surprised.'

Laughter echoed round the courtyard. 'Let only half of us go and surprise them even more,' a voice said.

Brandt thought that they were mad, and all drunk on courage, but he guessed he was still being judged so he laughed with the rest.

The gates swung open. They were in the north wall, overlooking the river and out of sight of the British, so the lieutenant led his party quietly round along the western wall, and still no one seemed to have noticed them. At the corner of the south and west walls he raised his sword and began to run. The men of the 4th Regiment cheered and followed him down into the valley.

18

There were skirmishers dotted along the slope ahead of the Poles, but when the chasseurs finally saw the oncoming infantry they ran. There were too few of them to fight, their rifles were slow to load, and it would take more than a few shots to stop the mass of infantry surging down the slope, so their officers and sergeants yelled at them to retreat. One man's foot caught in a loop of long grass and he fell forward. Before he could rise, a Polish infantryman jabbed down with his bayonet and the man screamed, arching his back away from the pain, until the soldier kicked him to free the blade and ran on. Two more chasseurs dropped their weapons and surrendered, to be pushed roughly to the rear by Poles who were not inclined to stop.

Williams saw the rifle company of the Chasseurs running back up the far side of the valley to the shelter of the rest of their battalion. Hatch was among them, as was the capable Mueller. The formed companies numbered some four hundred men, in line two ranks deep, running along the crest of the hill beside the battery position. At the moment they were at ease, muskets grounded, and he waited for their commander to take charge.

The skirmishers were coming up the hill, not retreating but running as fast as they could with no thought of glancing behind or stopping to fire and slow the enemy. They had outstripped the Poles by a good hundred yards, but the loose column of infantry with their blue coats and yellow fronts was already at the bottom of the valley. He guessed there were about a hundred of them. A smaller group was now following behind in support.

Someone bellowed an order and the line of chasseurs came

to attention. The first of the riflemen reached them, but instead of running to the flank the man barrelled straight into the line, pushing his way through. His face was blank, his mouth open, and he had dropped his rifle and his pack to run as fast as he could.

Hanley appeared beside Williams.

'What is happening?' he began, and then stared in shock at the little body of enemy surging up the hill towards them.

The fleeing skirmisher pushed his way through the formation, the nearest files spreading out like startled sheep. A sergeant standing in his place behind the company tried to grab the man by the collar, but he pulled free. More skirmishers ran up to the battalion, and the whole line shook as if it was in the wind.

'Canister,' Williams yelled at the Royal Artillery lieutenant. 'Load with canister!'

'We're already loaded,' the man replied.

'Then fire what you have got.' He turned to Hanley. 'Bring the Toledo Regiment. Tell them to come quickly or the battery is lost.' A lieutenant had given a captain an order, but Hanley cared little for military discipline and trusted his friend's instincts when it came to battle.

The crews of the twelve-pounders hauled on ropes to shift the aim of the guns, but these were naval carriages not designed for such big adjustments. Then the gun captains adjusted the turnscrews to point the muzzles down.

'Can't see 'em, sir,' a sergeant in charge of one of the crews shouted to his officer. The Poles were on the hillside beneath them, and no gun could shoot down at such a steep angle.

The chasseurs broke. They had not been formed long and did not know their officers well. If they had had time to prepare themselves, time to shoot at the enemy or to march forward steadily against them, then they may well have stood, but this was too sudden. The Poles should not have attacked, there were too few of them and no one expected such folly, and too many of the chasseurs and their officers could not accept that it was happening. Something must be wrong, and with their own riflemen pelting up the hill towards them they simply became more nervous. Another skirmisher forced his way into the ranks, and then two more. Sergeant Mueller was screaming at them to halt and to rally, but then the Poles cheered again, a great deep-throated cheer so different from the normal French chants. Men turned all along the line and began to run. It was like a pail filling with rainwater and suddenly pouring over the brim. The battalion collapsed, officers and sergeants resisting for only a moment before they too joined the flight. No one wanted to be last and to be caught by the dreadful enemy and so nearly all of them ran, and those who stayed raised the butts of their muskets in the air to surrender.

A Polish officer was leading the charge, swinging his sword around his head, and he found the energy to run even faster up the hill as the blue-coated defenders fled and his own men cheered again. The sergeant in charge of the left-hand twelve-pounder nervously jerked the lanyard too soon and the heavy cannonball slammed through the air several yards over the lieutenant's head and he roared in fear and relief, amazed to be still alive.

Mueller was level with the battery, three men still with him, and they turned, dropped to one knee and then fired. A Polish infantryman was flung back, tripping another man as he rolled down the slope. The sergeant in charge of the second twelve-pounder jerked the lanyard on his gun, but the flint failed to spark.

'Get back!' Williams yelled at the artillerymen. 'Get back!' Their own officer was staring blankly at the onrushing men and so the Welshman grabbed him and pulled him away. The crews dropped rammers, sponges and all the other heavy equipment and most started to run. One sergeant cut with a short sword at the Polish lieutenant as he sprang up on to the rampart. The officer parried the blow, but before he could cut down one of his soldiers was beside him and fired his musket, not bothering to bring it up to his shoulder. With a gasp the sergeant reeled backwards, dropping the sword and staring down at the blood spreading out over his stomach. Another Pole followed the lieutenant over the rampart and dodged the clumsy blow of a gunner wielding a trail-spike. The infantryman swung the butt of his musket into the man's jaw, knocking him to his knees, and then reversed the weapon, driving his long slim bayonet into the gunner's chest.

The Poles surged over the breastwork and into the battery and the remaining artillerymen fled. Williams went with them, but tried to break away in the direction in which Hanley had gone to fetch the Toledo Regiment. Behind him the Poles were cheering wildly at a triumph which had seemed so impossible and yet proved so easy. Williams went down into a little gully, using his hands to pull himself up the other side, and bounded over the little crest.

Ahead of him, the Toledo Regiment streamed down towards the beach, mingling with the fugitives from the foreign regiment. A small party of officers and NCOs had not fled and were clustered around the colours, but there were no more than a dozen of them.

'The chasseurs ran into them and they panicked!' Hanley shouted, as if he could not quite believe what he was saying. In just a few minutes the entire Allied defence had collapsed under the attack of a force a tenth of its size.

'Back to the beach,' Williams said, and the two men ran over the sandy slopes. The 89th were there, and if they were steady they still outnumbered the Poles by a large margin and should be able to take the battery back. Out to sea, boats were clustering around *El Vencedor* and before long their own 106th would begin landing, but that would take time and for the moment the four companies of the 2/89th were the only troops left.

The two hundred and eighty remaining men of the 2/89th were forming line on the mound of shingle at the top of the beach. Most of them had dark stains on their hands and faces, and Williams realised that the black dye of the facings must have run when their wool jackets were soaked in last night's storm. Sergeants shouted and pushed men into place with their half-pikes. The movements were slow and clumsy, and some of that was because these companies had spent little time drilling together, but more was the same sense of shock he had seen up on the hill. This should not be happening, and officers and men alike still struggled to accept that it was.

Then Lord Turney ran up from the beach. His horse was waiting for him, and he put a boot in the stirrup and almost bounded into the saddle, setting the animal in motion, and riding to the front of the 89th.

'Right, lads, those bloody foreigners have run like rabbits and it's up to you to save the day. You're the Eighty-ninth, you're Irish and English, and you're the stoutest fellows in the world, so we are going to go up that hill and we'll drive those rogues off with the bayonet.' He drew his curved sword from its heavily decorated scabbard and waved it high. The blade, heavy with gold inlay, flashed in the bright afternoon sunlight.

'Fix bayonets!' The senior captain bellowed the order. The long blades scraped out and then clicked into place as they slotted and locked around the muzzle of each firelock.

Up the hill one of the twelve-pounders blossomed smoke and a cannonball tore through the air over the line to land on the beach.

Lord Turney stood high in his stirrups. 'Eighty-ninth, follow me!' he shouted, and walked his horse up the hill.

'Forward march!' The senior captain of the 89th gave the order and stepped off behind the general. The drummers beat the rhythm and the line marched off, the dressing still a little ragged, but on ground like this that would soon have happened even if they had begun in immaculate order. Soldiers marched with the butt of their musket in their left hand, the weapon resting against their shoulder, the tips of the bayonets a line of steel higher than the plumes on their tall shakos. There were one hundred and twenty men in each of the two ranks, and behind them a thinner line of subalterns, sergeants and drummers.

Williams went to join the other staff officers marching on the right flank of the line nearest to the castle, although thankfully out of range of musket or the swivel guns on the wall. Another gun fired from the battery, aimed better this time, and the ball bounced a few feet in front of the line and then rose to rip off a man's leg beneath the knee and shatter the hip of the rear rank man behind him.

'Close up!' shouted a young sergeant who had felt the wind of the ball as it passed and gone pale. 'Quiet, my boy, remember you're Irish,' he said to the soldier who was screaming because he had lost his foot.

'It's not your bloody leg,' the man shouted angrily, but the rage seemed to drive away the pain, because he stopped screaming.

The line marched on, the men closing to the centre to fill the gap left by the wounded men. It was a gentle slope on this side of the hill, less sheltered than the one the Poles had assaulted, and the infantrymen turned gunners managed to fire each gun once more before they were masked. A discharge of canister mostly went high, making a weird rattling, ringing sound as the balls struck the row of bayonets. Three men had their shakos knocked off by balls going low, but the one in the middle was also hit by a bullet which punched through his forehead. He dropped like a sack of old clothes and his rear rank man stepped faster to take his place. The other gun fired a ball on almost the same line as before. One moment the two men of the next file to the right were marching forward with the rest. Then the front rank man was cut in two, his legs standing for a few seconds after his mangled torso was ripped off and flung against the soldier behind, whose ribs were splayed open and right arm torn off as the same shot gouged a bloody path through his side. The young sergeant was drenched in their blood and stared at the ruin of the two men, stopping as the line marched on.

'Cat got your tongue, Sergeant?' shouted the man who had lost his leg. The NCO recovered from his horror.

'Close up, lads, close up,' he managed to croak through a mouth which seemed drier than he could ever remember.

The 2/89th pressed on, keeping in step as well as men could on the sandy slope. Muskets began to fire as enemy skirmishers sniped at the line. Williams could see blue-coated voltigeurs bobbing up to fire from among the hummocks and waving long grass on either side of the battery.

Lord Turney's horse whinnied in pain and turned to the side, arching its long neck. Williams could see blood on its chest. Something was odd, but he could not place it. One of the staff officers beside him grunted as a musket ball struck his thigh.

'Go on, I am fine,' he said, pulling his sash loose to bind the wound.

The battery was less than a hundred yards away, and Williams began to wonder when the general would order the charge. It was still too far, for over that distance men would straggle and it would be so easy to stop and begin firing, but it was hard to walk in silence as the enemy fired into the line. Not far from him one of the redcoats was flung back, blood jetting in a great fountain from his neck.

The 89th marched on, faster now as they closed the distance, and none of their officers tried to keep them in check. Drummers pounded the skins on their drums, but no one was listening to the rhythm any more, and it was more a question of fighting back by making noise.

A second bullet struck the general's horse in the head, and Williams knew what had bothered him, for he was sure the sound was the sharper one of a rifle rather than the dull boom of a musket. The animal fell, but Lord Turney was already free of the stirrups and sprang off, landing on his feet. He staggered, then regained his balance, and walked on, sword resting against his shoulder as if nothing had happened and he did not have a care in the world. Another ball flicked the long grass beside his feet, but he did not acknowledge it and simply walked on.

Williams glanced back over his shoulder. Some two hundred of the chasseurs had re-formed and were advancing to the right and some way behind the 89th. There was a red-coated officer at their head and he realised that it was Mullins. Over on the left, but much further back, the Spanish officers and NCOs were restoring order to their own regiment. Down on the shore redcoats were splashing into the surf from two big longboats with more rowing behind them. It was too far to see any detail, but he could not help wondering who from among his battalion was here. It would not surprise him if Pringle, Dobson and the rest of the Grenadier Company were in the lead.

A familiar rattling sound brought his thoughts back to the task in hand, and he saw that some sixty or seventy Polish infantry were formed in a line three ranks deep and had just brought their muskets up to their shoulders. A third of the men were behind the flanking rampart of the battery, the rest standing in the grass. Standing tall on the rampart itself was an officer, and Williams heard him shout out the order and saw the sword sweep down before the line vanished behind smoke. A captain of the 89th walking on the extreme flank of the line let out a piercing shriek as a ball drove into his groin. Two men next to each other in the same company were pitched back at the same instant, one hit in the chest and the other with a gaping hole where his left eye had been. A dozen men dropped all along the line and the formation seemed to quiver.

'On, Eighty-ninth, charge, charge!' Lord Turney pointed his sword up the hill and ran at the enemy, drawing out the word into a cry of rage.

The redcoats cheered, and Williams found that he was shouting as well, and so were the other staff officers. He sprinted forward, realised that he had not drawn his sword and fumbled with the hilt as he ran. The Polish skirmishers were going back, and the line was wavering, for they were being charged by three times their own numbers, but the lieutenant yelled at them and they steadied, lowering their muskets to the charge.

Barely three yards away the redcoats hesitated, halting and staring at the men in their blue jackets with yellow fronts. Polish and British soldiers eyed each other nervously, not knowing what was going to happen, teetering between surging forward and running away. The redcoats were in a line much wider than the men in blue, and on the flanks it slowed to a walk, but kept going forward.

'On, lads!' Lord Turney shouted, his voice mingling with that of the Polish officer as he urged his men onwards, and then he rushed up the slope of the rampart.

'Come on!' Williams yelled, and other officers took up the shout and went with him to join the general, and then the whole line surged into a fresh charge. The line of men in blue wavered and some of them began to go back. The general was hacking at the Polish lieutenant, and his parry unbalanced the young officer so that he fell back into the battery. Williams was ahead of the others, and one of the enemy skirmishers suddenly stood up from behind a boulder and thrust with his bayonet at the officer, ripping his breeches as it broke the skin on his left leg. The Welshman jabbed at the man, forcing him back. His leg was painful even though it was little more than a scratch, and he followed up with a lunge which flicked over the man's musket and bayonet and drove into his side. He wrenched the weapon free, drawing back to make a fresh attack, but the man had dropped his firelock and was clutching at the blood welling from the wound.

Williams ran on. The Poles ahead of him were all in flight and so he headed left towards the battery where some of the enemy fought on. He could hear shouts, grunts of effort and the dull impact of blows with butt and bayonet as he ran towards the low rampart, and then flame ballooned up from inside and he was knocked over, the wind taken from him.

He stared at the sky for a moment, but did not think himself hurt and pushed himself back up. The remaining Poles were streaming back from the battery, leaving half a dozen wounded or dead from the fighting and another three moaning and badly burnt because the fuse which they had lit to blow up half the reserve powder proved shorter than expected.

'Well done, lads, well done,' Lord Turney called out to the men. 'That's the stuff to serve 'em! Captain, form the companies in line ahead of the battery.' The general pointed with his sword to where he wanted them to rally, at an angle so that they looked towards any French reinforcements coming down the main road towards these hills. Down the slope, the Polish company was reforming out of musket range, rallying on their supports.

'Ah, Williams, good man.' Lord Turney appeared genuinely pleased to see the Welshman. 'Go to the Spanish and ask the colonel to bring his regiment up on our left. They should occupy that hilltop.' He gestured at a height about a quarter of a mile to their flank. The ground in between was mostly lost in the folds of the rolling line of hills. 'It is the one with the two olive trees. They will see it clearly as they approach.'

As he set off, Williams heard another man being sent to bring the chasseurs up on the right, and yet another dispatched to fetch the artillerymen back, for the attackers had left some ammunition unscathed, though the neat piles of canister rounds and shot were strewn about where they had been kicked over. The Poles had either not carried spikes or preferred to keep the guns for their own use.

Hanley was with the Toledo Regiment, talking to the colonel and a couple of mounted guerrilleros. It made it easier to pass on the general's orders, and the Spanish officer readily agreed, and said he knew the spot the English lord wanted him to hold.

'You should tell the general of this, Bills,' Hanley said. 'These partisans report seeing a patrol of French dragoons on the outskirts of Fuengirola village, and a column of infantry on the main track crossing the hills.'

'Sebastiani?'

'They think not, and say they are the garrison of Alhaurin. A few hundred at most.'

'You had better come back with me,' Williams said, and started on yet another run up the steep little hills. As they got closer they saw that Lord Turney was on the right of the re-formed 2/89th, staring through his glass at the castle.

'Infantry, coming over the hills!' One of his staff pointed to the left, but Hanley and Williams were still a short way down the slope and could not see what he was looking at.

'They must be Spanish,' they heard the general say as they ran up. 'Ah, is the Toledo Regiment moving to cover our flank?' he asked as he saw them.

'Yes, my lord, but …'

The general did not let Hanley finish. 'Yes, that is right, then, they will be Spanish. Were they in blue?'

'Yes, my lord,' the ADC replied.

'Then they are the Toledo Regiment.'

'Excuse me, my lord,' Hanley said, 'but reports from the partisans say that several hundred French infantry and cavalry are advancing on our left. They have seen dragoons in the village.'

Lord Turney frowned and appeared puzzled. 'No, it is too early for Sebastiani to be here even if he has made the fastest of marches. They must be mistaken.' The general started walking along the front of the line of redcoats. 'Come, we had better make sure that our allies go to the right place and stay there.'

'The partisans believe that the men are the garrison of Alhaurin, my lord,' Hanley said as they followed.

'Nonsense, Sinclair's reports placed barely a company there. They must be seeing things. At most it is a patrol and nothing to concern us for the moment until their main force arrives in a few hours.'

'Look, there they are!' Williams had spotted a little column in dark blue jackets and trousers moving along the top of the hill with the two olive trees. The officers stopped, just a few yards beyond the left of the 89th's line.

'Yes, they are the Spanish, just where they should be – and a damned sight faster than I expected.' Lord Turney sounded pleased that the day was at last going as planned. He stared at the distant infantrymen, squinting in an effort to focus. 'Yes, blue and yellow, that is the Toledo Regiment. And the damned fellows aren't staying where they should be so they must be Spanish!' The general snorted with laughter as the little column kept marching off the top of the hill and down out of sight.

'They're Poles,' Williams said, with more certainty than he felt and forgetting the proper courtesies.

'Damn your impudence.' Lord Turney's tanned face went a darker shade. 'And damn your presumption.'

'My apologies, my lord, but I am sure that those men wear the same uniform as the ones who sallied out to take the battery. It is like that of the Toledo regiment, but not the same.'

'Don't be a fool, no one could make such a distinction at this range.' Lord Turney smiled at the captain of the left-hand company of the 89th and called to him, 'Hold your fire, we have Spanish coming in from the left.'

The head of the column breasted a hillock some eighty yards away. The men had round-topped shakos like the Spanish and bluecoats, but now that they were close Williams could distinctly see the yellow fronts.

'My lord.' Hanley's voice quavered. He was facing away, down the slope to where the head of the Toledo Regiment was beginning its climb up on to the high ground. 'The Spanish are over there.'

The general opened his mouth, his face flushed even darker, and then stopped as he saw the much bigger column ascending the hill. Williams was watching as the nearer men responded to an order and deployed into line.

'Eighty-ninth! Enemy on the left.' If the general had been wrong, still it was impressive how quickly he reacted. 'Captain, wheel your company and follow me.' The senior captain was in front of the line and now looked in this direction. 'The rest of the battalion is to conform!' the general called to the man.

Then a great shout came from over on the right. A few muskets banged from the distant chasseurs. Williams could not see their target, but guessed that the men who had sallied from the castle were advancing again.

'Williams, make sure the Eighty-ninth form to support Captain Keith's Company.' Williams noticed the general's care in using the name of the commander of the nearest company. 'Hanley, run back to the Toledo Regiment and implore them in God's name to hurry.'

The 89th's left-flank company had wheeled to face the Polish line. The other three were beginning to move as sergeants called out orders and jostled men into place. Lord Turney stood beside Keith.

'Forward march!' The general gave the order in an imperious voice, easily carrying over the surge of gunfire from the right. Once again the redcoats stepped out, although this time they were advancing on a larger force, at least until the other companies came up. The Poles had come on again, but now halted, some sixty yards away. In a ripple of movement which made it look as if they were turning to the right, the two hundred men brought their muskets up.

Lord Turney and the single company kept going, not checking for a moment, but then there was flame and smoke and a sound like thick fabric ripped by giant hands, and the two-deep line of redcoats jerked and shuddered as the volley slammed into them. Keith was down, wounds in both legs and his shoulder. Three of his men were dead, a dozen or more wounded and moaning.

'Charge, boys, charge!' Unscathed, Lord Turney sprinted at the enemy, his ornate sword held high. The two staff officers still with him and fifteen of the redcoats followed him, and Williams was amazed it was so many. Their cheer was thin, and the rest of the men looked around them, wondering what to do. The next company stopped in its tracks, frozen in mid-wheel.

'Get moving,' Williams shouted as their sergeants began to bark at them, but the men shuffled and some did not move at all. Beyond them, the line of blue-coated chasseurs was breaking apart as more and more men streamed in a mass back down the slopes towards the beach. One of the redcoats from the company, frozen in the act of wheeling, turned and tried to run, but a sergeant took him by the shoulder and shook the man.

Lord Turney and his little band had reached the Polish line, and the enemy stood, baffled at being attacked by so few. Lord Turney sliced with his sword, and around him several blue-coated soldiers reeled back, clutching at wounds. Some of the redcoats stabbed with their bayonets, and then the spell was broken and the Poles broke formation as they clustered around them. The rest of the line, a good one hundred and fifty men, charged forward, led by two mounted officers, and they roared as they came, bayonets reaching for the enemy.

'Present!' The captain of the next company of the 89th ordered his men to prepare to fire, even though only about a third of them were able to see the enemy properly. Men brought their muskets up and there was a series of clicks as hammers were pulled back to full cock.

'Fire!' he shouted, and muskets slammed back into shoulders as the men pulled triggers. It was a ragged volley, much of it going wide or high, and one of the balls by ill fortune struck one of Lord Turney's little group squarely in the back. Two Poles were down, but the rest streamed forward, the three-deep line spreading out as they came.

Most of the redcoats fled. Some were too slow and meekly dropped muskets or raised them upside down to surrender as the Poles reached them. A few fought, and one man yelled as he ran his bayonet into an enemy's chest and then screamed when the man's comrade knocked him to the ground and then took careful aim, waiting for a moment before thrusting through one of his eyes to kill him.

Williams ran with the others, hoping that they could restore order nearer to the beach. The last he had seen of Lord Turney, the general had been clubbed to the ground and so he was either dead or taken. For a moment he hoped the Toledo Regiment might survive the rout and drive the enemy back, but the deluge of red- and blue-coated men fleeing back to the beach swamped the Spanish and they too dissolved into flight. Nearly a thousand men flooded down the rolling hillsides towards the beach, chased by less than a third of their number. They ran in silence, and most of those in the lead had dropped weapons and heavy packs so that they could run faster. Men from all three regiments mingled together, and as he ran Williams saw no one he recognised.

It was not good cavalry country, and the small squadron of French dragoons did little more than watch. The Polish infantry followed at a distance, nervous in case the enemy realised just how few men had beaten them, but some were already back in the battery position and began turning the guns towards the beach.

Williams headed to the right, hoping to get clear of the crowd and have a better chance of doing something. A chasseur barged him out of the way, and he slipped in the sand and fell, landing awkwardly on the leg grazed by the bayonet. Feet trampled him, the men blank-faced as they rushed as fast as they could, but then the press thinned. He pushed himself up and scrambled on to the top of a low hillock on the edge of a deep gully.

He was near the back of the flood now, and the closest Poles were a line of skirmishers working in pairs and moving carefully down the hill some one hundred and fifty yards away. One pair stopped behind a low pile of boulders and a man fired down the hill, tumbling a fleeing redcoat into the dust. Down nearer the beach he saw some formed troops, and guessed they were the first of the 106th.

Then the breath was knocked from him and he staggered as something appallingly hot drove deep into his side. A hammer blow slammed against the side of his head and he fell, rolling off the grass and down the steep side of the gully.

19

The howitzer fired first, but the infantrymen turned gunners had not quite understood the shrapnel shell, so that its fuse was too short and it exploded high in the air barely a hundred yards from the barrel. On the beach Major MacAndrews heard the crump of the explosion and looked up to see the little cloud of dirty smoke in the air. Then he saw one of the long guns fire from the battery and watched as it cut a bloody swathe through some of the fugitives. The entire brigade looked to be in rout, the enemy pressing hard, and he had no more than the two flank companies of his own battalion and a detachment of Royal Marines to save them from utter disaster.

'Captain Hall,' he said to the naval officer who had accompanied him ashore, 'I should be most obliged if you will signal for all ships to send every boat they have to take men off the beach.'

'Of course. And I shall realign the gunboats so that they can best sweep the approaches to the beach.' Both men kept their voices calm.

'Major Wickham, Captain Pringle. Place your companies on either side of the carronade battery. The Light Company on the left and the Grenadier Company on the right. Ensure the men are loaded and wait for my order.' MacAndrews did not care for Wickham, but the man was making a rare appearance back with the regiment and was senior to Pringle. That was one more reason why he had wanted to get ashore with the first party, so that the fellow would not be in charge. The other was to consult with Lord Turney and find out what the regiment was required to do, but there was no sign of the general, and the only thing left was to bring off as many men as possible.

As the Grenadier Company marched past he noticed Sergeant Dobson in his proper station at the rear, as usual carrying a musket in place of the regulation half-pike. Ever since he had sobered up he was one of the finest NCOs in the battalion. Now the veteran winked as he passed, and spoke in a low voice.

'Biggest balls-up since Flanders, sir.'

MacAndrews smiled. His wife often accused him of enjoying chaos, and he suspected it was true. Perhaps it was a Scottish thing, a satisfaction that other people's mistakes led to confusion and ruin, but that he could prove his own worth by dealing with it.

'Lieutenant Jones, leave a sergeant and a dozen men to stop fugitives from swamping the boats, and take the rest of your marines and occupy the rocks at the edge of the beach looking towards the castle. I do not think they will come that way, but it is sensible to take the precaution.'

The first fugitives were arriving on the beach. One group scattered when a twelve-pounder ball hit the sand and flung up a great cloud of pebbles and dust, but then they were up again, all apparently unscathed. MacAndrews looked for officers and sergeants among the fleeing soldiers to start rallying their men. So far it was mainly the blue-uniformed chasseurs who were arriving, and he doubted that the men in the lead were likely to be the most reliable, but had to work with what he had got. He saw a captain among them looking calm, and went to the man.

'Stop them,' he commanded. 'There is nowhere much for them to go unless they want to swim, so it should be easy. I want the Chasseurs formed over there.' He pointed to the right of the beach. 'Send the Eighty-ninth to the centre and the Spanish beyond them.'

The captain stared at him, and MacAndrews wondered whether the fellow did not speak English, but suspected it was simply panic. He was covered in dried blood, evidently from someone else for there was no other trace of injury. He grabbed the man's collar, shook him, but still the eyes were vacant. Then a sergeant stamped to attention beside him.

'Mueller, sir!' he said.

'Good man,' MacAndrews replied, letting go of the captain. 'Start collecting as many chasseurs as you can and form your regiment over there.'

Two more cannon shot skimmed the rise above the beach, throwing up plumes of sand. One ran through the crowds of men without causing any damage, but the other struck the knee of a soldier from the Light Company, flinging him aside, with just a ragged stump left of his leg. Muskets popped from the castle, and one of the swivel guns opened fire. The range was long, but not so long that bad luck could not allow a few shots to strike home. One of the marines was dead, a tiny hole in the centre of his forehead.

Slowly, some of the fleeing men began to rally. More officers and NCOs emerged willing to shout over the chaos and call their soldiers to them. MacAndrews saw the scarred face of Hatch on the beach, looking excited, almost happy, and with a rifle slung over his shoulder, but the man was pushing and yelling at the chasseurs to form them up.

'The general is taken,' Hanley said, appearing from nowhere.

'Aye,' MacAndrews said. He felt no particular emotion and after so many disasters it probably did not matter any more. He listened as Hanley told him a little of what had happened. Biggest balls-up since Flanders, he thought to himself, and knew that he was smiling.

Up at the top of the beach the carronade belched a spray of heavy grapeshot at the first few Polish skirmishers to creep over the top of the lowest hills. The gunboats added their fire a few minutes later, two angling to send balls bouncing across the approach to the beach and the others sending shots at the castle in the hope of disturbing the men shooting from there.

All of the fleeing men who were going to escape were on the beach by now, and MacAndrews left their officers to deal with them. A naval lieutenant backed by his own sailors and the marine detachment was sent to supervise the loading of men into the boats. Now and then shot from the battery landed on the beach and men were mangled and killed. A shell from the howitzer exploded above the re-forming 89th and the carbine balls scythed round in a wide arc to cut down half a dozen of the redcoats.

The major walked back up to the flank companies of the 106th.

'They're getting a bit lively,' Billy Pringle said. As usual Wickham looked detached, no more than an observer who was not really involved.

'Deploy a skirmish line only if they start to be a real nuisance.' As long as the enemy were willing to stay back then MacAndrews did not wish to provoke them. There was a danger that dispersed men would get cut off and left behind, or even worse hit by some of the fire coming from the boats. At the moment the Poles seemed content to keep their distance and snipe only at long range, but that might change when they realised that the enemy was re-embarking.

A long peal of thunder rolled and drummed in from the sea, as the air above them was ripped and dozens of very heavy shot flew over to slam into the slopes of the hill. The *Rodney* had anchored and unleashed a broadside of its great guns. A few minutes later they fired again, and this time there was grape as well as shot, and MacAndrews heard the whining of the smaller iron balls as they passed high over his head. The earth around the hilltop battery was lashed and pummelled, and for a while the guns there went silent. A few skirmishers still squibbed with muskets at the 106th and the sailors manning the carronade.

'Lie the men down,' MacAndrews told Pringle and Wickham. The sailors had some protection from the bank topped with sandbags, but the redcoats were in the open and there was no sense in exposing them unnecessarily, and so the men could lie down until they were needed. MacAndrews and the other officers could not hide in the same way, for their job was to betray no sign of fear, and so they walked along behind the lines, chatting in a falsely relaxed and exaggerated way.

In an hour the boats took some eight hundred men back on board the warships. That was all that was left of the 89th, the Chasseurs, the Toledo Regiment and the gunners, and as far as MacAndrews could judge the rest of Lord Turney's expedition was either dead, wounded or captured. From what Hanley told him and what he could see, all this loss had been inflicted by a much smaller force – half a battalion of Polish infantry and a few French cavalry. There was still no sign of the vanguard of General Sebastiani's column coming from Malaga, and the major began to hope that they could evacuate before they arrived. Several thousand enemy would be much harder to keep back, even with the protective fire of the warships, which in truth was more intimidating than deadly.

Quite a few of the men who embarked no longer carried muskets, and some were injured. Hanley was worried because he could not find Williams, and MacAndrews could only hope that the lieutenant had been carried back on board one of the boats with the wounded, for the captain was sure he had seen him fall.

All the while the gunboats, the great ship of the line and the frigate pounded the shore. The battery replied sporadically, and then the two big cannon on the castle's eastern wall opened up again, and the *Rodney* changed its aim to slam shot against the ancient stonework. Heavy thirty-two-pound balls gouged deep holes in the sandy-coloured wall, and MacAndrews was puzzled as to why the general had not waited until he was ready to bring such firepower against the little castle.

It took another half-hour to carry off the remaining troops. MacAndrews had the sailors spike the carronade, tip their reserves of powder into the sea and then sent them and the Light Company into the boats. He pulled Jones and his marines back and took them and the Grenadier Company on to the sand of the beach itself. The gunboats edged in closer to fire canister at the low rise around the abandoned carronade battery, for the sight of the retreat had emboldened the Polish infantry and they were pressing closer. Pairs of skirmishers came warily over the mound of shingle at the edge of the beach, fired at the lines of redcoats and then fled back out of sight when bursts of canister flicked through the long grass. Three times they came on at a low crouch and three times the gunboats flayed the shingle with canister and the skirmishers vanished. One of the grenadiers was shot through the heart and died within moments, before the Poles were driven back, and another had his left arm broken by a ball. At last the boats approached to carry them off.

'Mr Jones, would you be kind enough to take your marines and board.'

For once the lieutenant closed a mouth which seemed perpetually open. 'Sir, it is the peculiar skill of my corps to operate from boats. I suggest it would be more fitting for your soldiers to go first.'

MacAndrews gave a slight bow. 'As you wish. Captain Pringle, take the Grenadier Company to the boats.' It reminded him of a story he had heard about the evacuation of one of the forts in Cadiz harbour. It had been held for weeks under terrible enemy fire, and when the time came to leave there was an argument between the commander of the garrison and the senior engineer. Each wanted to be the last to leave, and as they debated the issue a French shot killed the engineer and badly wounded the other officer. MacAndrews was not sure he felt much pride when he heard the story, and genuinely could not make up his mind whether a man should weep or howl with laughter at such antics.

None of the Royal Marines died because of their officer's insistence that they form the ultimate rearguard, but Jones got a ball through his hat as the Poles risked the fire of the gunboats to send a last defiant message to the retreating enemy. For another hour and three-quarters the warships bombarded the coast, concentrating mainly on the castle. The gunboats were out of ammunition and withdrew, but the larger ships sent shot after shot into the east wall, leaving half the parapet knocked down and the wall itself pockmarked.

Major MacAndrews felt the hull of the *Rodney* shudder under his feet as another broadside raced along from gun to gun on the two main decks. He was not sure whether all this spite was achieving very much, but understood that it was hard to pull away and admit failure.

'Well, gentlemen, there is the question of what we should do,' Captain Burlton said to the others. As captain of the *Rodney* he was now the senior naval officer, taking over from Captain Hope, just as MacAndrews was the senior soldier – the Navy apparently assuming that the colonel of a Spanish regiment must rank lower than a British major. '*Circe* is in sight, and so we are stronger than ever before, at least at sea.' The additional thirty-two-gun frigate, which was supposed to have joined the squadron before it sailed, had at last arrived.

Captain Hope lived up to his name with one last attempt at optimism. 'The main French force is here.' Lookouts had reported the approach of several hundred cavalry, followed by a strong body of infantry. 'If Sebastiani is here, then even in these light airs we could reach Malaga and take the place half a day before he could return.'

The sailors looked at MacAndrews. He did not think that either of the captains felt real conviction in favour of the proposal. Perhaps they wanted a soldier to confirm the ruined condition of all of the brigade apart from the 106th, or perhaps they simply wanted someone else to state the impossibility of continuing with the plan and to take the blame if there were need. Either way it did not really matter.

'Perhaps we could take it, but I doubt very much that we could hold it,' he said, and only a fool would have given another opinion. 'I can only rely on my own battalion – and of course on the marines and sailors,' he added, both because it was true and because few compliments were ever wasted. 'The other soldiers are spent, at least for the moment, and in no condition to fight. As importantly, the commander of the expedition is lost.' MacAndrews did not add that it would be presumptuous for a mere major to assume a general officer's command and initiate a new landing, for surely that was obvious – though he would not have hesitated to do so if there was value in the operation and a decent prospect of success. In this case there was neither.

The sailors raised no more objections. Both their ships were crammed with soldiers, and it would take time to ferry them to the transports, but for the moment the crews were busy working the guns. Burlton had already ordered food to be served to them before they left.

A little after five o'clock the bombardment stopped when lookouts spotted a white flag raised and men in red walking on the rampart of the castle. A close inspection through telescopes revealed that one of the redcoats was Lord Turney himself. A Polish emissary appeared on the beach, and when a boat was sent in he presented a list of the officers taken prisoner and instructions for the general's baggage to be carried ashore. This last request had been anticipated and the impedimenta was waiting in the cutter. Williams was not on the list of prisoners, and as yet had not been found among the men brought off the beach.

At five thirty Captain Burlton ordered the *Rodney* to weigh anchor and the whole squadron stood out to sea. Boats began ferrying all save the wounded back to the transport ships. With such high losses, there was plenty of room and so the flank companies of the 106th went to a vessel called the *Waltington*. The rest of the battalion would be taken from the Spanish two-decker and sent to this and another merchantman in the morning.

'Better to have our only fresh regiment in ships which do not require towing,' Burlton said, and MacAndrews was glad of the decision.

For two days they cruised off the coast, moving slowly in the light airs and coming abreast of Malaga. There was no attempt to revive the idea of landing, and it seemed no more than a gesture to worry the French and to postpone the inevitable.

The next day the squadron split, with *Topaze* and some of the smaller naval ships escorting the transports back to the Straits of Gibraltar. The *Rodney* set off to tow *El Vencedor* to Port Mahon in Minorca, although Captain Burlton was doubtful that even the yards there would be equal to the task of rendering her genuinely seaworthy.

As the convoy neared Gibraltar, MacAndrews felt a brief yearning for a longer voyage to spare him and the 106th a return to the monotony of garrison duty on the Rock. There was so little for the soldiers to do apart from drink, and he began to think of ways of creating interest in sport and exercises in the hope of distracting his men. He wondered whether Esther and Jane would come to join him now that Lord Turney was gone. The prospect was an exceedingly happy one, but that only reminded him of an unpleasant duty he had yet to complete.

Williams was not on any of the ships and was not among the French prisoners. Perhaps he had escaped somehow and found refuge with the partisans, but it was equally possible that he was dead. MacAndrews liked the young lieutenant, who reminded him a good deal of his own younger self. Williams was a good soldier, and had skill and luck far beyond the ordinary, so that he seemed invulnerable, able to triumph whatever the odds. MacAndrews had known a few men like that before. They were rare, and some were decidedly odd, but they won battles for you, and you came to believe that they could never fail and never be touched. For one or two it was actually true, and they received never a scratch and lived on to the ripest old age. The rest lived as if this were true, and then just died, at the hands of the enemy or sometimes disease or simple accident. It never quite seemed real, but it happened all the same and they did not come back. The character of a whole company or regiment could change when they were lost, and never be quite as good again.

Williams was gone, and he did not know whether he would come back. He had begun a letter to tell his wife and daughter the news, but after a few simple statements to say that he was well, he had found the words drying up. Simply saying that the young officer had vanished did not seem enough. From all Esther had said, his daughter's affection for the lieutenant had grown far beyond mere friendship. He would be the first to confess that the emotions of both mother and daughter often baffled him, but would swiftly add that it did not matter what he thought for they would do what they damned well pleased regardless of his wishes. Yet the growing bond between Jane and Williams had somehow turned into something which felt natural and permanent, indeed almost inevitable. He could not remember when he had suddenly taken to thinking of it in that way, but it was at least a year ago, and now it might well be over.

MacAndrews did not know what to say to make it less painful, so wrote little more and resolved to send the letter on with Hanley when he was carried to Cadiz in the *Sparrowhawk*. What was there to say save that it was war, and terrible senseless things happened without rhyme or reason? The day after the 106th landed in Gibraltar word reached him that *El Vencedor* had come adrift in a storm and sunk with all hands. He thought of its elderly captain doing his best, and of the welcome given to the regiment by its overworked and willing crew, and it was very hard to believe that they were gone. On land, battalions suffered losses, but some were wounded and plenty of men survived. At sea a few moments could snuff out the lives of hundreds. Weather and wave, as well as war, made no sense, and it was folly to expect otherwise.

20

'Nothing is certain,' Hanley said, knowing that he was repeating himself. 'He has vanished and that could mean several things.'

Miss MacAndrews looked at him with her big blue-grey eyes. Her expression was impassive and he could not read her thoughts, which only made him more awkward. Hanley wished that Pringle were here with him to take the lead. Pringle had sisters, and was more at ease in company in general. For all his bluff, cheerful manner, Billy would have known what to say. Instead Hanley sat alone with the girl in the room she and her mother used as a parlour, and he felt out of his depth.

'Do you think he is dead?' she said at last, her voice clear and flat.

'I do not know.' That was the truth, and for once reason failed to provide him with a clear answer to a question. Hanley felt himself to be a clever man, fond of toying with ideas and arguments. Soldiering itself still held many mysteries for him, but he revelled in the deception and intrigue of gathering information, finding out what the enemy was planning while confusing him as to your own intentions. It was a game, a dangerous and intoxicating game, where the stakes were infinitely higher than at the richest table, which only added to the thrill. He had not always won, but did more often than not, and was confident in his facility for guessing the truth from poor or misleading reports, and yet he was not sure what to think.

'I do not know,' he repeated when the young lady said nothing and simply stared at him, no doubt trying to read his expression.

'The French say they do not have him. Two soldiers from the foreign corps report seeing a British officer shot down, and I suspect that it was Williams.'

He had not meant to say that. It was only a guess on his part, but as far as he could tell there was unlikely to have been another officer in a red coat on that part of the hillside. Was he trying to convince himself that his friend was truly gone, and that as a rational man he should accept the truth no matter how unpleasant? Williams was an odd fish, but he was Hanley's friend. Along with Billy Pringle and old Truscott back with the 106th, the serious-minded Welshman had become closer to him than anyone else. He felt at ease in their company, enjoying not just the conversation, but a kinship that was odd because each of them was so different. In part it was reliance, a knowledge that they would risk their lives for him and that he would do the same for them.

Hanley had never relied on others since he was a child. Unwanted bastard of an actress and a rich man, he had received a good education, but the only affection came from his grand-mother. Friends were few, and came and went without any strong bonds forming. When he was older and discovered love it was an intense fire, burning brightly and briefly, and if he were honest more about his own needs and emotions than the woman's. Such things soon passed, and most of his time was spent in competition to seem more sensitive and clever than the other would-be artists who formed his circle. With Williams and the other two there was trust and never a hint of rivalry.

'You think he is gone, do you not, Mr Hanley?' There was an intensity about Jane MacAndrews' gaze that had not been there before.

'I fear it.' Hanley instantly regretted the words, for the girl seemed to sink, a slight drop of the shoulders the physical expression of some deeply sad and irrevocable shift in her soul. He knew how much this young lady had meant to his friend, watching with some amusement their turbulent courtship and sensing that over time his admiration was returned with growing strength.

'But I do not know it,' he added in some haste, although as he spoke he suspected that he really did. 'There is still hope.' The words were feeble and it was obvious that she knew it.

'Thank you for your candour, Mr Hanley.' The reply was distant and formal, and part of him was angry because she did not call out in despair or collapse into tears. Did he not mean more to her that that? A brave and good man who idolised her, and still felt himself so bound by honour that he must walk away once he learned that the girl had become rich and should not ally herself to a poor subaltern.

Hanley's despair overwhelmed him, coming in a flood as he knew that he had accepted his friend's death. If friendship was a recent thing, the grief of loss was newer and raw. Even the loss of his grandmother had not made him feel so low, since a guilty part of him had felt relief that he could set off to study abroad without worrying about the old lady.

He wanted to talk, and wished that Billy or Truscott were here – or Williams, he added to himself, before the absurdity of that thought struck him and the sadness bit all the more deeply. His friend was gone and would not come back, and part of his own life had gone with him. It was real, not imagination or fear, and he would not wake up from a dream to find the world restored. Hanley felt tears pricking at his eyes and wanted to throw off restraint and weep. Was it his imagination or had Miss MacAndrews gone glassy as well? The sight made him realise that he had forgotten her feelings in his own sorrow.

They were saved by the arrival of Mrs MacAndrews, leading in an excited young Jacob.

'We have seen a cat.' The lady offered a translation of the enthusiastic squeals and gestures. 'Good day to you, Mr Hanley, I take it from your expression that there is no good news. Yet I trust there is also no definite bad news?'

'No, ma'am.'

'Well, that is something, and one never knows what will

happen.' She forced a smile and reached down to ruffle the little boy's hair. 'After all, today no one would have guessed that we would see anything so wonderful as a tomcat with a bushy tail.'

The sound of the bells was loud, carrying across the red rooftops of Seville, and Marshal Jean Soult gestured to one of his ADCs to close the window and shut out some of the noise. It was Sunday morning, and soon the Marshal of France, Duke of Dalmatia and commander of the French armies in Spain would attend mass at the cathedral with its high tower, dome and ornate decoration where the Moorish elements blended with the more recent Gothic. The draught from the window had provided a pleasant relief in the already hot chamber in the palace, and Capitaine Jean-Baptiste Dalmas had been glad of it. Portugal in November had been cold and wet, but here in Andalusia the summer still seemed to reign.

Dalmas was amused by the willingness of the marshals and generals stationed in Spain or Italy to rediscover the Catholicism they had so publicly rejected during the Revolution. The marshal's name was really Jean de Dieu, but everyone knew he had pruned it to Jean. Dalmas wondered whether he would begin to employ his former name again, just as he had started going to mass. There were persistent rumours that a year ago the marshal had manoeuvred to have himself declared king of a conquered Portugal. Now he was effectively viceroy in the south of Spain, and relished the role. As they spoke, the grenadier and voltigeur companies of every battalion in the garrison were parading in their finest uniforms, so that they could line the road from this palace to the cathedral. A glittering staff would escort him, followed by the grandees of the city and other important men from throughout Andalusia. Dalmas was unsure whether these men would find the marshal's piety convincing, but at least these public shows helped to ease their conscience when they supported the rule of Napoleon's brother and his occupying armies, whose commanders were busy plundering the country.

Soult was not the worst of them, but was clearly determined not to return a poorer man when he finally went back home.

'So what you are saying,' the marshal said impatiently to Major Bertrand, the engineer who had accompanied Dalmas to the city, 'is that the old smuggler is stuck outside Lisbon and not going anywhere any time soon.'

Bertrand gulped nervously. 'The Prince of Essling' – mere majors of engineers did not refer to marshals of France and princes of the empire as old smugglers even if that is what Massena had once been – 'has pushed the British back to within ten miles of Lisbon and the sea, forcing the enemy to shelter behind a line of fortifications. These are formidable, Your Grace, truly formidable, for apart from the fortified batteries they have blocked all routes through, digging away at cliffs to make them steeper, diverting the course of rivers …'

Soult held up a hand. 'Yes, yes, but all that just adds up to the fact that he is not moving and not about to move.' The marshal was forty-one, and the active life of an army commander was now beginning to lose ground to his inclination to plumpness, especially around his neck, which was today constricted by the tight collar of his blue coat. A rich pattern of gold leaf covered the collar and cuffs, and ran in a broad stripe down its front. Soult did not have the face of a strong man, but his thick eyebrows gave a force to his gaze which hinted at the powerful will of one of the ablest of the Emperor's senior officers. If he commanded little affection there was plenty of respect, and Dalmas believed that it was well deserved.

'The Prince ordered the army to begin realigning itself around Santarem on the fourteenth of November,' Bertrand explained.

'So he has gone backwards.' Soult did not hide his amusement. The Emperor's marshals were notorious for their jealous rivalries and hatreds, and Dalmas suspected that this was deliberate, for it did not matter much when Napoleon led them in person and imposed his iron will to quash such petty bickering. With the Emperor in Paris and apparently weary of a war which dragged on interminably in Portugal and Spain, it was a weakness and one that Dalmas hoped would not prove fatal.

'Oh yes, I know, he remains close to the enemy,' Soult continued, ignoring the engineer's stammering justification. 'And he intends to stay there for weeks or months, but in itself that means nothing. What matters is whether in those weeks and months he can break through those lines and force Milord Wellington to take to his boats and sail away.' The marshal spoke with the complacency of a man who had chased Sir John Moore's British army into the sea at Corunna. 'The English like getting their feet wet, probably because it rains so much in their Goddamned country.'

The marshal's ADCs smiled dutifully. Their master was a man of few jokes.

'The fortifications are formidable,' Bertrand insisted, showing more spine than Dalmas expected, although not quite enough to mention that there had been no such defences at Corunna, or that the marshal's job had been to catch the English rather than just chase them away. Some of those same soldiers were now back sitting outside Lisbon.

'Dalmas, give me a soldier's opinion,' Soult said impatiently to the cuirassier officer. Even though this was a conference, not a parade, Dalmas was wearing the polished front and back plates of his cuirass. Most men dispensed with the heavy and uncomfortable body armour at any opportunity, but he did not, wearing it as a badge to show that he was a fighting soldier and not some ornamental staff man.

'If the Prince had enough heavy guns and another thirty thousand men, then he could force the lines and beat the British if they dared to face him.' Dalmas gave the answer readily, for it was the nub of the whole question. Bertrand looked a little surprised, but did not contradict him, and may have known that Massena had said as much himself. Marshal Ney, on whose staff Dalmas served, had a reputation as one of the boldest of all generals, and even he doubted that they could succeed with anything less.

Since he and the Prince of Essling agreed on so little, it was hard to argue against their judgement on this issue.

Soult grunted. 'And that assumes he can feed them for as long as it takes.'

It was a statement rather than a question, but Dalmas nodded in confirmation. 'Yes, Your Grace, that is the main reason for the withdrawal to Santarem. The land there is a little less devastated.' The ruthlessness of the British general was both impressive and chilling, for he had stripped the land of food, destroying everything that could not be taken. Most of the population were either forced to seek refuge behind the lines or were fighting as irregulars and harassing Massena's army. The complex arithmetic of food, fuel and fodder for three corps of more than sixty thousand men and tens of thousands of animals was not in favour of the French. 'The Prince believes that he can stay there three or four months, but something must be done to shock the enemy and make them get their feet wet. Our spies report that Lord Wellington keeps enough merchant ships and warships off Lisbon to carry away his entire army and the Portuguese troops if necessary.'

An ADC gave a polite cough and interrupted. 'Your Grace, it is twenty past the hour.'

'The bishop will not start without me, and this will not take long.' Dalmas, Bertrand and their tired and dusty escort had arrived late last night when the marshal was already asleep, and this was his first chance to hear their news and give a reply. Dalmas was not sure what the orders he had carried meant for his own fate, although Ney had hinted that he might be away some time. He was a supernumerary ADC, picked for his skill rather than his connections or decorative value, but he had failed to catch a British spy several months before and suspected the marshal was uncomfortable with any taint of failure in his headquarters. Detached service seemed likely, rather than promotion that would put him a step closer to command of his own regiment. Six hundred cuirassiers was a weapon he longed to wield in his hand, but Dalmas needed a victory to restore his superior's faith.

The Emperor liked lucky men, not men who, however talented, fell just short of victory.

'If I concentrated all three of my corps,' the marshal spoke with an air of decision, 'then it would be weeks before I could march to Portugal. It would mean abandoning the siege of Cadiz, probably abandoning all of Andalusia and everything we have gained. The partisans would flourish and murder anyone who has smiled at a French soldier let alone served us, and throughout all of Spain men would fear to join us in case they too were abandoned. And even if we paid that price, I doubt that I could keep enough of my men fed to make a difference. We had to improvise a siege train for Cadiz by fishing out guns lost by ships sunk at Trafalgar and from the Spanish magazines. It would take an age to carry them to Portugal and batter at the enemy's forts to open the way to Lisbon.

'All that would be a sacrifice to no useful gain. If the smuggler needs thirty thousand more soldiers then he must find them elsewhere. I cannot give up all the ground we took at the start of this year. Andalusia will be the heart of the new Spain and we must show that it will remain ours. I could perhaps assemble twenty thousand men for a few weeks, but not for any longer. There are too many threats which cannot be ignored – Romana inside Portugal, Blake in Murcia, and the British and Spanish at Cadiz and Gibraltar. We have beaten Blake and last month a few companies of brave Poles routed a landing force ten times their number – thanks in part to the cunning of the *chef de battalion*.' Soult waved his hand at an officer wearing the green-faced yellow coat of the Irish Legion – or mere regiment as it was supposed to be called these days. Two battalions of them were with Massena's army and Dalmas had seen a little of them. As far as he could tell few of the soldiers had any connection with Ireland and the regiment had become a useful dumping ground for foreigners of all descriptions who had no other place in the army. Many of the officers were Irish, hated the English, and spent most of their time duelling, usually with each other.

'We must hold what we have and that means having enough

soldiers to chase away the raids that will keep coming. We cannot expect to be as lucky as Sebastiani assures me we were at Fuengirola. We must also press the siege of Cadiz. If we can take it then the last vestige of a rebel Spanish government will be gone. That might be the very blow that frightens the English into their ships. What else would the Prince of Essling have me do?'

Major Bertrand hesitated, and then his words were halting. 'The Prince asks for all aid ...'

'Attack in the south.' Dalmas was the most junior in rank in the entire room and yet spoke with confidence, and if some of his ADCs were horrified Soult looked pleased at his interruption. 'Take those twenty thousand men and strike hard and fast against Romana. Take Badajoz, take Elvas if you can, and open the southern road into Portugal. That would give Milord Wellington plenty to think about.'

'As easy as that.' The marshal gave a rare smile. 'Thrash an army and take two strong fortresses.'

'Do any one of those things, Your Grace, and it would help Massena. Do three and it might well win the war.'

'Leave us,' Soult commanded, and gestured for only his chief of staff to stay, along with Dalmas and the *chef de battalion* in the green coat.

'What you suggest is the best we can do in a bad situation, and so we must try to make it happen. Dalmas, you are now attached to my staff as supernumerary. Ney says that you are clever and know how to fight, but he is an Alsatian and they are all mad, so I will judge for myself. We do not have enough men to do these things and to protect all that we must hold. So you need to help me confuse the enemy so they do not see this and hit us hard where we are weak – and then I need you to find me ways into Cadiz, and Badajoz, and Jerusalem and any other damned place that springs to mind.

'Good, now I will let you arrange that for me and I am going to church.' Soult and his chief of staff left, but a moment later the marshal of France's head reappeared around the doorway.

'Oh, I forgot. Dalmas, you are promoted to major in the

Thirteenth Cuirassiers, whoever and wherever they are. Effective from the start of the month, so I shall expect you to earn your higher pay. And don't trust this Irish rogue – he has a commission from King George!'

'Truly?' Dalmas asked as the door slammed closed again.

'Truly. Although the old bugger hasn't paid me for months.' The French was good, but there was a slight overemphasis that betrayed the Englishman – or in this case presumably the Irishman. 'But it means they think I am on their side and so I tell them things and let them send me money and muskets and anything I ask for.'

'Perhaps we should ask for the keys to the back door at Badajoz?'

'Might be worth a try, but in my experience the key is usually made from gold. There's enough men out there thinking that the war is lost and that they had best make their peace with King Joseph and make sure they are wealthy enough to enjoy the rest of their lives. When we can, we have been sneaking money into Cadiz to pay a fair few who might be persuaded to join us. Would have been a lot more,' the Irishman added ruefully, 'but the English Navy decided for no reason at all to raid an out-of-the-way little fishing port named Las Arenas just at the time when a little ship was bringing us a cargo of gold.'

'Did they know what they were doing?'

'Didn't look like it. They just swept in and took that, although they burned or left other vessels. We nearly got it back, but they were lucky and got away. By now they're even luckier and some fat admiral is a richer man by far. Still, it slowed our work.'

Dalmas rubbed his chin. 'Money might help at Badajoz. The governor is good, but one or two of his senior officers are less honest men from what I hear. It would be nice if the governor would drop dead, but these old birds tend to be tough.'

'I have a man who might be of use. He deserted from the English at Fuengirola, and from us before that, and I suspect from half the armies of Europe. But he's a killer if ever I saw one, and a fine shot. The English gave him one of their rifles, so now he's deadly at two or three hundred yards – or so he claims.'

'Could be useful, if the chance arises and we can get him into the right place – if and if and if ...' He trailed off.

'I know,' the Irishman said. 'Oh, and I haven't introduced myself, so had better remedy that. The name is James Sinclair, and it's an honour to meet you, Major.' The Irishman grinned as he held out his hand. 'Now it seems to me that the best way we can start is to make some mischief. The partisans are the eyes and ears of the British and Spanish alike, so let us see if we can make them blind and deaf. Now it just so happens that as a brave and handsome officer of the British army, I have visited a fair few of their bands in the mountains. Some of the chiefs will kill anyone if they are paid. With them, a couple of battalions and a regiment of cavalry, I think we could give them a very hard time.

'So while I see about that, how about you go and take a look at Badajoz?'

'A good start,' Dalmas said. 'A very good way to start.'

'An even better way is to find something to drink and raise a glass to mischief.'

Dalmas laughed. 'Mischief and money,' he said.

21

The year did not end well. Massena's army sat at Santarem and showed no signs of retreating. Wellington remained behind the shield of his forts and half the officers in his army sent letters home which ended up in the London newspapers and predicted the inevitable evacuation of Lisbon. Hanley knew that Napoleon in Paris and even his brother Joseph in Madrid got most of their news about what their own armies were doing from the English papers. Irregulars harassed stragglers and detachments and it was rarely safe for French messengers to move without an escort of at least a regiment. Yet the French still occupied almost all of Spain and Portugal and neither the partisans nor the remaining active armies had any prospect of driving them off. The newspapers did not seem to realise that it was a great achievement for the mauled Spanish armies to remain in the field and to fight on. Expecting great victories was to expect the moon, and yet when Hanley read the papers, usually within a week of their being printed, he felt that they were describing a different war.

At Cadiz the French laboured on their batteries and siege works or built gunboats and landing vessels so that they could contest control of the bays. Admiral Keats responded by adding to his own fleet of gunboats and harrying the French whenever they put out any distance from the bank.

'On the fourteenth the admiral thought that the little ships of each side would fight a grand fleet action,' Chaplain Wharton told Hanley during one of his visits late in November. 'But the French decided on discretion and rowed back into the inlets to hide.' The mouth that seemed so large in his thin face broke into a roar of laughter. 'Who knows, perhaps in a few weeks we shall have our Trafalgar!'

'It does put me in mind of Carthage,' Hanley said, 'in the last war.'

'Ah yes, with fleets built by both sides to contest the great harbours of that city. If I recollect much the same happened with Caesar in Alexandria. Odd how the great seafaring powers can be reduced to fighting at such a Lilliputian level.' The talk of Carthage led them to a pleasingly diverting half-hour speaking of Cadiz and its Punic origins, and then of the wider influence of all the peoples who had passed through Spain. 'Physically there seems little trace of the Visigoths,' Wharton said, 'at least assuming they were of the usual Germanic stock.'

They were interrupted by a midshipman sent by the admiral and were called on deck, but during the long bombardment of one of the French building yards, there was some opportunity to renew their discussion. By the time Hanley visited the flagship again, the French had gained an advantage.

'Unable to bring their fleet together by sea,' Wharton explained, 'they have dug a canal and concentrated them in perfect safety by this means or by dragging them over the land on rollers. Rather unsportingly they have taken to working during the night, which makes it hard to see them.'

Between them, they tried to organise a group of spies to go and observe the enemy works, but some were prevented from landing and the remainder found it almost impossible to evade detection in a landscape full of busy French troops. When none had yielded anything of value and two were caught and hanged on the shore, they decided that the cost was not worth the negligible gain.

Hanley was beginning to wonder whether the same might prove true of their work with the guerrilleros along the coast, and felt that each report he gave in Cadiz was more pessimistic than the last. At the end of November several French columns launched fast-moving drives through the main passes in the mountains. The enemy had obviously learnt from early mistakes, for they seized the most formidable positions before sufficient serranos could arrive to hold them off. A lot of the crusaders were killed, and far more driven off and dispersed. Smaller parties fanned out from the main columns, and some of these were Spanish irregulars who knew the country well, and these were ruthless in their depredations. By Christmas two partisan chiefs had been captured and another killed. Several more bands were dispersed or forced to flee so far into the mountains that they abandoned their supplies and could not strike back for some time to come.

'It seems El Lobo is a wolf in truth,' Sinclair said when Hanley met him not far from the mountain-top town of Ronda, 'and his pack of wild beasts are ravening across the land in the service of King Joseph.'

Hanley was used to the Irishman's taste for the dramatic, but in this case there seemed some justification, and it made the night seem darker and more sinister. It was a sorry tale to hear, although Sinclair spoke as lightly as always.

'I was at the camp of El Pastor's band five days ago, when the man and half a dozen of his ruffians rode in and asked to share the warmth of the fire.' There was a famous El Pastor – the shepherd – further north, but among the little groups of fighters in Andalusia there were several chiefs whose nicknames aped those of more celebrated partisans.

'Of course, I know the man, have spent time with him, and trusted the bugger, so when El Pastor was none too friendly I launched into a great speech about how we are all on the same side and should be friends. They still weren't keen, but I used my Irish charm and after a while we were all sitting down and drinking. My, those mountain folk can take their wine, and that's an Irishman who says it, but after a while El Pastor *passed out*' – the irony was heavy – 'and most of his band were so merry they didn't know what was going on.

'That's when they did it, for all the while the rest of the wolves had gathered, and a few of the ones with El Lobo had sidled up to the sentries. They cut their throats, and El Lobo just stood up and shot a man through the chest, as easily as kiss my foot, and his ruffians came on at a rush, shooting and slashing. There wasn't a chance, not a chance in hell, of doing anything to stop them.'

Hanley looked down into the valley below and saw a great tongue of flame leap up from the lower slopes of the far side.

'That'll be Don Antonio Velasco's house. Well, one of his houses, for the family is rich – or was before a lot of it was confiscated.'

'They seem to know just where to hit us.'

'Well, did you think they were fools, and would never learn from their mistakes?' Sinclair said. 'But I don't think burning down the family home will make El Blanco love the French, do you?'

'I'm not sure he has much cause to love the British either these days.'

'Don't follow you, old boy. I know he has never cared much for old James Sinclair, but since I cannot claim such an opinion is unique, I have never held it against him, or thought it extended to a universal hatred of Britannia as a whole.'

Hanley did not care to talk about the attack on the partisan chief's wife. He had not met with Don Antonio since it had happened – the one arranged meeting proving impossible when a French patrol camped around the inn where they were to talk. There were rumours that his wife had vanished, and Hanley did not know what to make of them. She had certainly been hurt in the fall, possibly badly, and perhaps was still recovering in the convent or some other safe place.

Sinclair watched him, clearly eager to press the matter, and so Hanley instead asked the obvious question. 'It is fortunate indeed that you escaped the attack, is it not, Major? Or is this no more than further proof of the good fortune of the Irish?'

'That it was, and no doubt of it, and I have found it odd that you have not asked.' Smiling, the Irishman turned round, lifted up his coat tails and bent over. A long line of fresh darns stretched across the seat of his trousers. 'I nearly did not get away, and El Lobo gave me this cut across the buttocks to remember him by.

Can't say it is the stuff of heroic poetry, and I dare say it won't be a story I'll tell my grandchildren around a crackling fire, but all in all a sword-slice to the bum for Sinclair is a narrow enough escape from a decidedly nasty situation. Can't say I've enjoyed riding much – or for that matter sitting down – in the last few days. Sadly the road to glory seems an uncommonly bumpy one!'

Sinclair pressed him to have more supplies sent. 'To start rebuilding what we have lost,' he said, but his reports were not encouraging. One of his sources did tell him about a wounded British officer hiding with one of the bands, but when Hanley rode to the area and made contact he discovered that it was Captain Miller of the 95th. The man had a gift for working with the guerrilleros, and it was good to confirm that he was well on the road to recovery after suffering a bad kick from a horse, but the brief hope that he had been wrong and that Williams was still alive died and plunged him into deeper despair.

Hanley was back in Cadiz at Christmas – his third Christmas since becoming a soldier and letting the war absorb his life. As usual he called on Major MacAndrews' family, but found the experience even less comfortable than before. He was sure his friend would have wanted him to be a support, and so he did his best even though he came to hate the awkward sessions sitting in the parlour and trying to think of diverting things to say. In the past he had enjoyed Miss MacAndrews' company, for she was lively, had wide interests and a considerable talent for making herself agreeable – most of all to gentlemen, listening and laughing when it was flattering, then talking or teasing lightly. Now the spark seemed to have gone, and if her mother managed to stir up the embers at times, it was rarely for long, and usually only when she made her daughter play or sing. Hanley was forced to venture a song or two to her accompaniment, and that was not pleasant for his voice was a thin one and he had always done his best to shun invitations to sing.

'Come, you must, Captain Hanley, for we insist upon it,' Mrs MacAndrews declared, and as usual would not be gainsaid. 'Why, I am instructing even the major to practise.'

Thus Hanley sang, and it was even more of a relief when he was able to excuse himself to go to his meeting on the flagship. Edward Pringle arrived as he left, and it seemed the naval officer was a frequent visitor whenever *Sparrowhawk* stopped at Cadiz. In the hallway leading to the stairs Hanley heard Miss MacAndrews laugh – a light, genuinely happy laugh of a kind he had not heard for months. Then he caught a pleasing tenor voice launching into 'Annie Laurie' and felt the resentment surge up within him as he damned their joy, which seemed treacherous to the memory of his friend.

'You seem on edge, my dear fellow, quite on edge.' Wharton brimmed over with sympathy and for the moment was simply the kind, harmless country parson and not the admiral's chief of intelligence. 'Are things truly so bad?'

'They are far from good,' he replied, shaking off the mood, and told of the recent French attacks, the activities of turncoats like El Lobo, and the losses to the guerrilleros. 'Without the organised and more skilful bands it is becoming harder for the peasants to gather and perform the bigger ambushes. From all I hear, the French convoys are getting in and out of Ronda and the other mountain garrisons with little or no difficulty.'

'Some large-scale advances by our armies would no doubt help,' the chaplain told him. 'Whether Romana, Blake or some of the brigades at Gibraltar. Something like Lord Turney's expedition, but with greater fortune. As I am sure you are aware, the governor and other great men who dispatched him have been busily writing reports which allot the general all of the blame. You would know better than I whether this is fair, but I would judge it inevitable when he is a captive and they are not. However, from all that I have heard no criticism has been aimed at your own corps or Major MacAndrews. He is shortly to take the One Hundred and Sixth to Tarifa, both to guard it and to launch raids against the French outposts.'

'Will they be there long?' Hanley asked, thinking of the major's family and feeling an unexpected and very strong desire to remove them from this city and the visits of Billy Pringle's brother. Tarifa lay inland a short distance from Gibraltar, but he was not sure whether it was sufficiently secure for MacAndrews to summon his family.

'A month or two, I should think, and they will be contributing in their small way to giving the French a few problems and forcing them to pull men away from the mountains to meet such fresh threats. There is talk of a larger expedition from Cadiz itself where the Navy would land a force several times the size of the Malaga expedition. General Graham is keen, but as yet has struggled to persuade the Spanish and we should need them to find the necessary numbers.

'In the meantime there is talk of a smaller raid, intended as a diversion so that the Spanish can secure the main crossing from the Isla to the mainland. I believe your battalion will play a role in this, although in the main it will be a Spanish affair. We should also endeavour to encourage and supply the irregulars. A stock of arms and powder is being gathered. Would it be best if you were landed first, so that you could arrange where they are to be dropped and ensure men and mules are waiting?'

Hanley nodded. He had hoped for a rest, but this afternoon had left a sour taste in his mouth, and, even though he knew he was being unfair, he no longer cared to stay in Cadiz.

'*Sparrowhawk* will carry you – Captain Pringle has had plenty of practice in this business.' Hanley smiled in satisfaction, which Wharton no doubt saw as a mark of confidence. 'However, you shall not go for several days, and I trust that you will be able to carry some good reports with you.' Wharton beamed at him, once again the meek country parson. 'Admiral Keats has arranged a little present for Marshal Victor.'

On Christmas night, the entire squadron of British gunboats gathered together with the Spanish ones in the bay. At one o'clock in the afternoon of Boxing Day, when the tide was at its height, the Spanish began a bombardment of the fort at San Luis, which protected the main concentration of French vessels. Bomb ships fired at other forts to keep them occupied, and then the British gunboats led in more boats packed with marines and sailors to burn the enemy's little fleet.

Hanley watched from the shore outside the city, early on spotting Edward Pringle and Miss MacAndrews and joining them. 'It would help my understanding to be guided by your experience, Captain Pringle,' he announced with the most innocent expression he could muster.

In the event it was difficult to see very much, as low cloud came in from the sea, bringing showers of rain. An elderly Spanish lady and her companion invited Miss MacAndrews to share the canopy erected by her servants, and the two officers stood near by. It was in a little depression, which offered protection from the wind at the expense of a significantly worse view. They could hear the muffled sound of the guns, with now and then the deeper booms of the bomb ships' great mortars. Yet the low gunboats were hard to see at a distance in such conditions, even with the aid of a glass.

For an hour and a half the action went on without their becoming any the wiser as to its course. Hanley wondered whether he was being unfair. Pringle joked and flirted with enthusiasm, much in the manner of his younger brother. Perhaps such conduct was unusual in a widower who had had so little time to mourn, but was it possible that he and the girl sought each other's company because they found comfort in someone who had also experienced a great loss. Hanley thought that there was more on Pringle's part, the hint of a harder, desperate edge behind his flirting. He could not tell whether Miss MacAndrews wanted more than mere friendship.

'Captain Pringle is to escort me to the New Year's Day races on the Isla, Captain Hanley,' she said once it was clear that the action was over. 'Would you care to join us?'

He was not sure what answer Miss MacAndrews hoped to receive, but suspected that events would intrude whatever he said. 'If my duties permit, it would be an honour and a pleasure.'

With two hours to spare before he was due to meet Wharton, he asked to walk with them to the young lady's home. 'I would like to give the greetings of the season to your mother,' he said, 'and to young Jacob.' Edward Pringle excused himself, saying that he was sure he could entrust the lady's protection to this escort, but when they parted he held Miss MacAndrews' hand just a little longer than was necessary. The girl said little to Hanley on the walk back.

'Twelve,' Wharton told him happily when he reported aboard the flagship. 'Twelve gunboats or other small vessels sunk or burned, and with little loss to us. Sir Richard is confident that they will not risk putting out into the bay in force, still less chance any attempt to land troops on the Isla or the city itself.

'For the moment we are safe, unless Bonaparte risks all and lets his fleet out of Toulon. He'd need to be lucky, but no blockade can overcome tide and weather so fully as to be complete, and he could get out, and could reach here and attack from the sea. For the moment that is the only serious threat to Cadiz, and it is a distant one. And much as the Regency Council and the new Cortes bicker, they are too busy passing laws banning ladies from wearing short sleeves or white shoes to think of talking to the French.'

'Have you discovered the story behind the gold captured at Las Arenas?'

'In part, although it is so difficult to be sure since it was taken by us and so not used by the enemy. There is something larger and darker at work. I have little doubt that it was intended to persuade notable men here in Cadiz to offer allegiance to King Joseph. We have a fair suspicion as to who they are, but they are unlikely to move through spontaneous enthusiasm or on mere promise of reward.

'I do wonder if Soult's attention is shifting away from us, and his money may well precede his army if it marches in another direction. He could go east and smash Blake, overrunning Murcia and so bringing even more of Spain under French control. In truth that would leave very little free and might make many lose heart. But it is more likely that he will go west and do something to aid Massena. We have captured dispatches from Napoleon telling Soult and the other marshals to do everything they can to aid the invasion of Portugal – and also to do everything they can elsewhere. It is our good fortune that Bonaparte does not return to Spain, for from such a distance his orders lack their usual ruthless concentration.'

'The frontier fortresses?'

'Perhaps,' Wharton said. 'Assuming that it is not all a bluff and he is hoping to lure an expedition out from Cadiz so that he can destroy it and break the will of the Spanish government. There is some game at work, I do not doubt, and we must hope to see it before it does real harm.'

'The attacks on the guerrilleros do hint at greater knowledge than in the past,' Hanley said, voicing a concern which had grown stronger and stronger. 'They know more, which suggests someone has been telling them more.'

Wharton rubbed his chin. 'Yes, that is the most likely answer. It may be gained from prisoners, but if so it has come remarkably quickly and in a manner which seems too convenient. Such men rarely tell you all you would wish to know.'

'A traitor – or several of them.' Hanley did not make it a question.

'It fits best. All sorts of men end up with the partisans, and since some have changed sides they would know more than the French, but it seems they are gaining more information all the time, and so someone is still at work. He could be Spanish, but we should not consider all of our own officers as entirely above suspicion.'

So open a statement surprised Hanley, and then he instantly felt disappointed in himself for the implied greater confidence in one nation over another. He did not like to think that he was so innately patriotic.

'Some of the officers with the partisans appeared early on in the war, and we really know so little about them.'

'Sinclair?' Hanley said. 'There is something odd about that man.' He felt foolish for saying that, since everyone – including himself and this outwardly simple parson – involved in such work tended to be peculiar.

'It may be unfair, but there is a natural tendency to suspect an Irishman. After all, many of Tone's men were true believers in their cause, and such belief can well survive the worst of defeats. But it could as easily be someone else, and dealing with him could just as easily distract us from the real source. We do not know enough to act, so keep your eyes open.'

'When do I go?'

'You will sail on the twenty-eighth. Come again tomorrow at this time and I will provide you with any new information.'

Hanley stood up. There was little chance of Edward Pringle being in Cadiz for New Year, and he decided against calling on the MacAndrews family for another uncomfortable half-hour.

'Oh, I had forgotten, there is a report via Gibraltar of yet another injured English officer being hidden by the partisans. This time with El Blanco. I thought that I would tell you in case it is your missing friend.'

Hanley felt himself reconciled to Williams' death, although deep down he knew that he was not. Spending so much time away from the battalion, it was easier to forget and pretend that his friend was still there, awaiting his return with Billy Pringle and Truscott and the others. Wharton's news forced him to think and brought gloom rather than optimism. Every rational part of him was convinced that his friend was gone for ever.

'Thank you,' he said flatly. 'We can still hope.'

'Sir Richard has ensured that his name will remain among those to receive prize money for Las Arenas in spite of the agent's eagerness to strike him from the list.'

'Thank you,' Hanley said again, and left the cabin.

22

The man winced as he dropped the roughly fashioned crutch and let some of his weight rest on his left leg. That weight was a good deal less than it had been, for he had lost two and half stone in the long weeks of fever, but his frame was large and he was a tall man. He hissed again as he shifted more and more of the burden until he was standing naturally. There were a few flecks of sleet amid the rain, but he did not feel the cold as it soaked into his shirt.

He stepped forward with his right leg, the good one, but that meant that all his weight fell on the left and the pain seared him almost as if the surgeon was once again probing for the ball that had buried itself near his hip. Somehow it had missed the blood vessels, and not done any real harm to the bone, but then the wound had been sewn up to heal and a week later it had gone bad. It had taken the doctor a long time to find the distorted ball and remove it, and then check nothing else was buried inside him. He had never known such agony, and would have screamed and screamed had the girl not held his arms, all the while speaking to him as if he were a child, soothing and calming. It did not take the pain away, and he did not know whether it was calming or whether foolish pride in front of a kind and attractive woman had kept him from crying out.

'Oh, damn,' the man said under his breath, 'damn, damn, damn.' He brought his hurt leg forward and then stopped. His shirt was clinging to him and he wished that he had worn jacket or cloak, but was not about to run and fetch them. He shivered and the hot wind of earlier months no longer seemed so oppressive.

The man walked on again.

'Dear God,' he said, but forced himself to go on even though his left hip screamed in angry protest. The scar on his head throbbed in sympathy and he felt giddy. A bullet had left a bloody welt across one side of his head and made a little notch at the top of his ear. At the time it had bled profusely and knocked him out, and even half an inch closer and it would have killed him, but since then it had given little trouble. The surgeon had felt his skull, but found no sign of fracture or depression and declared himself unconcerned. Three months on, the scar was fading.

Another step and another, each one as agonising as the last, and he told himself that this was good because it was not getting worse, and forced himself on. Then his right boot slipped on the wet grass and he fell forward, just managing to turn so that he dropped on to his right side, but still the jet of pain was savage in its intensity. The man screamed, a long cry without words, but he did not pass out.

When he had been wounded he had woken and then crawled because he knew that he had been left behind and did not want to be a prisoner. He had crawled and crawled and the sun had gone down and come up again and still he had dragged himself onward, fainting time and again from the pain. Later they told him that he had gone for two miles, but at the time it had seemed more like two hundred, as he went up and down the rolling hills, avoiding the village and heading for the convent he had never seen. He was almost there when the peasants found him and took him in. Tired, covered in filth which had got into his wound, the man had been aware of very little and soon fell into a fever. He was ill a long time.

Once again the woman was beside him, one hand slipping underneath his head and the other holding one of his. She kissed him on the cheek, the touch delicate, and he went quiet.

'You will die,' she said. 'The wound will open and turn bad and then you will die.' There was sadness in her voice, a deep sadness of past hurts, and also rebuke because he was reawakening the memories. Without her care he doubted that he would have lived, for the fever had been a bad one and yet she had stayed, mopping his brow, holding his hand. More than once he would have given up, for he felt so weary and so hopeless that it seemed too much effort to cling on, but she was there, a desperate longing in her eyes. It would have hurt her if he had died, and looking back he was sure that only the horror of causing her more suffering had pulled him through.

'I am sorry,' he said, for what else was there to say. He was upsetting her now, and could see the pain in her eyes, but he fretted at the idleness and was determined to recover as fast as he could. He started to push himself up, only just restraining another gasp as his hip complained.

'No you are not,' she replied, but still helped him, looking hurt when he gently freed himself from her grip.

'I must do this alone,' he said, standing for a moment to steady himself, and then he began to pace once again. With her watching he did not cry out, although his cheek still twitched with every spasm and he was sure she would see it.

The young woman watched him for a while, her black hair plastered down tightly against her head with the rain. It was longer now, covering her ears, and even wet it framed her face. She was very pretty and so very sad, but more often these days there was a new light which brought out her beauty. It was not quite happiness, and though it made his heart leap to see her smile, he was afraid that it would not last and that he might take it away.

' 'Amish,' she said, rolling the first letter and placing all the emphasis on it. 'Do not stay here too long. You need to rest or you will make yourself ill.' Guadalupe stood on tiptoes to kiss his cheek again, and Williams felt her brushing against him. Then she was gone through the field gate and back to the shelter of the farmhouse.

He kept walking, and for a long time was so absorbed with thinking about the girl that he barely felt the pain.

The rain stopped in the afternoon, and when the sun went down it left a sky bright with stars. They were up in a little valley high in the mountains, reached only by a few difficult tracks. The farmer and his family were poor, but kept sheep and goats and somehow eked out a living on land rented from Don Antonio's family. They had welcomed the British soldier, their landlord's sister-in-law and the two guerrillerros who escorted them up here ten days ago, and made them as welcome as they could. It had been an excruciating journey for Williams, jolting on a mule over mountain paths, and had left him flat on his back for forty-eight hours. When he woke from an exhausted sleep the girl had once again been by the bedside, waiting and watching.

At noon today El Blanco's entire band had arrived, and although they posted sentries on the only paths in and out, the rest prepared to mark the coming of the New Year with a great bonfire, food, drink and music. There was no sign of the French near by, but from what Don Antonio said, the enemy had been pressing them for weeks, forcing him to keep moving. They had never been close enough for shots to be fired, but they kept seeing the French, especially one regiment of dragoons who seemed to follow like bloodhounds. They had a leader with them, who wore a much paler green jacket than the cavalrymen and had the shako of an infantry officer with a tall white plume. No one saw him from up close, but when Williams listened it reminded him of a similarly dressed man watching from the shore at Las Arenas.

'It has been a bad month,' the guerrilla leader said. 'Just a week ago Jorge Hernandez and his band were ambushed south of Ronda. He was shot dead by a French marksman, and half of his men killed or taken.'

Don Antonio's wife was with him, looking very different in a dress rather than her usual trousers and riding boots. The dislocated shoulder had been reset and in the last months her broken arm had healed well. She was still pale, and said little, but gave a faint smile when she saw Williams.

'It is good to see you well,' she said, looking at the ground. Her sister appeared, and she had replaced her breeches with a flowing skirt in bright red which stirred as she walked. Guadalupe embraced Paula, and Williams was close enough to see that both were crying.

'I am glad that you are recovered,' Don Antonio said. 'I owe you more than I can ever repay, but know that you will always have a friend in Don Antonio Velasco.'

'And in his cousin,' Carlos added. 'And not just because it is reassuring for any physician to encounter a patient who remains alive. Now walk for me.' He watched closely as Williams took a few paces, and saw the obvious pain. 'There you are, as good as new. Mind you, no dancing tonight!' He patted the tall officer hard on the shoulders.

As night fell two pigs and a sheep were slaughtered and roasted over the fire.

'Nothing to the years of peace, but still a feast to enjoy,' Don Antonio told Williams, who was to sit beside him in a place of honour. There was a little cured ham. 'You must try it, it is the finest in the world.' The Welshman was watched closely as took the slice on a piece of bread, and it seemed that all the conversation and laughter around the fire had died down. The taste was rich, the meat tender, although he was not sure there was anything especially remarkable about it.

'It's good, isn't it,' Carlos said.

'Very good,' he replied as they continued to stare at him.

'The best.'

'Undoubtedly,' Williams agreed, and that was met with a great cheer. They laughed when he refused wine and continued to drink only water. 'My stomach,' he explained, rubbing it. 'Wine does it no good.' They roared with laughter, but did not begrudge the foreigner this eccentricity.

Early in the evening someone produced a guitar. Carlos played well, and his cousin was skilled with the flute, and as the hours passed most were filled with music. Some of the men sang and others danced on a square of planks laid down outside the barn.

'Come, sing us something English,' the guerrilla leader said.

'I know one.' Carlos Velasco began to pluck out the tune of 'Hearts of Oak'. 'Come cheer up my lads, come cheer up my lads …' he began, struggling to remember the words. Williams stood, steadied himself and then waited for him to reach the chorus.

> *'Hearts of oak are our ships, jolly tars are our men,*
> *we always are ready, steady, boys, steady.*
> *We'll fight and we'll conquer again and again.'*

He sang all the verses he knew in his deep voice, his Welsh blood coming to the fore as he relished the chance to sing to an audience. The partisans cheered, and began to join in with each 'steady, boys, steady', although not always at the appropriate moment. It took little urging for him to give them another, and he soon launched into the 'Minstrel Boy', letting Carlos pick up the tune as he went along. Then they tried to teach him some Andalusian songs and there was much merriment at his efforts.

'Señora, please dance for us.' The cry began and was soon picked up. 'Please, señora, please.'

'Don Antonio's wife is truly excellent,' Carlos whispered to Williams. 'The men love it when he lets her dance for them.'

Paula shook her head and looked uncomfortable.

'Please, El Blanco, beg your wife this favour.' The partisans persisted, and the farmer's wife appeared with a pair of castanets and a tambourine hung with bright ribbons. Don Antonio smiled and whispered to his wife. She shook her head again and whispered something back. The exchange went on for some time, as the men kept calling for her to dance. The partisan chief looked surprised at his wife's reluctance. 'Do not make me, I cannot.' Williams was close enough to hear the whispered words and to see her distress.

The bells on the tambourine rang as it was flipped with great vigour, and then the castanets began to click. There were gasps from all around the great fire.

'*Jesús, María y Joseph*,' Carlos said when he saw that Guadalupe stood on the wooden boards, arms raised ready. 'She has not since …' He did not finish and simply stared, until the young woman glared at him.

Carlos began to play and the girl began to dance. Her face seemed frozen in terror, some small hint of what this cost her, and at the start her movements were stiff. No one spoke, and there was only the sound of her shoes on the wood, the guitar and the clicks and jingles as her hands twitched. Don Antonio reached for his flute and took up the tune.

Guadalupe danced, a little faster, and a little faster, and all the while the life seemed to grow within her. Her movements took on a grace that had not been there before. Williams did not know this dance, and could not judge the correctness of each step and gesture, but even to his untutored eyes this was something truly special. The partisans were clapping now, that rapid clapping which seemed to come naturally only to the people of the south. The pace changed, slowing and then returning at redoubled speed as her heels pounded the wooden planks. There was an energy, an agility, a grace and passion of a sort he never seen elsewhere. He watched, feeling himself absorbed by each beat. More than at any other time he noticed the fine form of this unhappy young woman. He watched when her skirt flicked up and revealed her shapely legs, watched when she spun, took in the shapely rear, out-thrust bosom, and the proud head and straight back and neck. On and on Guadalupe danced, no longer a person, but part of the music, and Williams felt his pulse racing, and if some of his thoughts were of Miss MacAndrews with her dress flying in the breeze or held tight in his arms, they were driven away by the here and now, by this music and by the lithe figure who stamped and whirled.

The dance rose in a crescendo, the men cheering as well as clapping, and Guadalupe spun and slammed her heels down. Her face was still expressionless, but perhaps this was part of the dance, for when she finished at last she flashed a brief smile at him as the guerrilleros shouted their praise. Paula Velasco wept, but only Williams and her husband noticed, and Don Antonio embraced her.

'It is a new year indeed,' he said to Williams a moment later, as Guadalupe retreated to the house, refusing the pleas to dance again. 'There may still be hope,' he added. His wife was shaking as he held her close.

Soon afterwards they too went back to the house. Some of the guerrilleros were already rolled up in their cloaks and sleeping beside the fire. Others drank or ate, or sang softly as Carlos played to them. As far as Williams could judge it was well after two in the morning, and yet he did not feel tired. He sat and listened to the guitar and stared into the flames, struggling to remember his own world, the one outside these mountains. Thoughts came of staying here, of fighting the French by stealth and ambush, with a woman by his side who was beautiful and also a warrior as brave as any man. It was romantic nonsense, fit more for a novel than real life, and he despised himself for entertaining so foolish a dream at all.

He loved Miss MacAndrews, even if treacherous thoughts kept coming to his mind as he wondered about touching the skin of the Andalusian girl, of pressing her close, and clamping his mouth against hers. Yet he loved Jane and only Jane, even though he knew that he could not make her his wife and be with her. Guadalupe was lovely and kind, and he owed her his life. His heart swelled with pity for someone who had endured so much and had not been destroyed by it. He pitied her, was fond of her, and was stirred by her beauty, but did not love her. He was sure he did not.

'I think I will take a walk,' he said as Carlos noticed him getting up.

'Good. A patient should get plenty of exercise.' The former surgeon was showing the signs of his prodigious drinking and waved him a cheerful farewell before resuming his playing.

Williams was cold and stiff, and for the moment felt only a dull ache. He rubbed his hands, although the night was not really so very chill. As he wandered away from the fire, life came back to his limbs and the pain increased, but he walked on, trying to push through it. It was a truly beautiful night, and the absence of the moon made the great field of stars even brighter. After a while he stopped and stared up at the sky, wondering how anyone could see such wonder and not believe in God. He thought of Hanley, that clever man who said that nothing in the world suggested purpose let alone goodness behind it, and he could not understand him.

He heard the soft footsteps, but did not turn, for he was not sure what to say. An arm came and looped through his as she stood beside him.

'You should rest,' Guadalupe said. Neither of them moved, and they stood for a long while looking at the stars.

'Your dancing is wonderful,' he said after some time, wondering whether he got the compliment right. His Spanish was now good, but many subtleties still escaped him.

'It has been a long time. A very long time, and I never thought that I would dance again.'

Silence followed, save for the distant sound of Carlos' guitar.

Williams turned and looked down at her. 'You feel gratitude to me,' he began. 'Gratitude because I was in time to protect your sister from the worst, and there was no one there to help you.'

She did not speak, but she pressed close to him and he did not pull back. Her head rested on his chest, her hair against his chin.

'I am sorry no one was there,' he continued. 'It was wrong and it was terrible, but there was no one. Now you have helped me to live when I would surely have died, and you have cared for me as if I was a child. It is not love, not real love, at best the love of brother for sister.' He hoped the words were right.

'You did and you did not save Paula.' Her voice was muffled, for her head still leaned against him.

'I do not understand.' Williams patted her head and tried to make the girl turn her face to him, but she would not. 'I thought I was in time,' he said.

'For the first men, you were. They hurt her and frightened her, but you stopped them before they did more. Then you left another officer to guard my sister, and he raped her.'

Williams groaned, pulling away from her and feeling a pain greater than any his wound had caused. He had failed, utterly and completely, for as soon as she spoke he knew that she was telling the truth.

'I'll see him hang,' he said in English. He was shocked to learn that Hatch could do so foul a thing. 'Or if they won't do that then I'll call him out and blow his bloody head off.' It was rare for him to swear, but he felt the anger surging within him, a fury that burned bright. Then all at once it turned into sorrow and pity for this poor young woman, her own childhood and innocence cut short in so brutal a manner, and now no doubt living again all of those horrors.

He sprang forward, flinging his arms around her and pulling her close to him.

'You poor child,' he murmured, 'you poor, poor child.' She pressed tighter against him, and he felt her tremble as she wept, and he almost cried because there was nothing he could do to change what had happened. He kissed her on the top of the head, feeling her wiry hair, and when she turned her head he pecked her again on the cheek, mumbling words of sympathy.

Their lips met, and there was a desperation, even an anger, in the way she kissed him. One hand ran through her hair, smoothing it, and the other ran along her back, but hers were at the back of his neck, pulling him ever closer.

Guadalupe shook as they kissed, her whole body quivering. Williams' face was damp as the girl sobbed uncontrollably, the horrible memories all coming back. She gasped as if in pain. He tried to pull away, but her grip was so tight that it was painful. They kissed again and he was drawn back into the moment, grabbing her almost as tightly.

A shot echoed up from the edge of the valley, and only then did they part, the army officer and the partisan both alert.

'The French,' she hissed. They looked down to the southern path and saw shapes moving where their sentry had been. There was a scream, very short, before it was cut off.

23

The thatched roof of the barn collapsed in a great shower of sparks. Beside it the house itself burned steadily, flames licking out from the windows. On the coast the sun was already coming up, but the steep-sided valley remained in shadow lit only by the fires consuming the buildings. It was lighter on the ridge top, and Williams and Guadalupe found that they were no longer alone as Carlos and two more of the partisans scurried up to join them, crouching so that they stayed behind the crest.

'You left this behind,' the former surgeon said, handing Williams his sword. He had taken to wearing it even though it rested against his injured hip, forcing himself to accept the discomfort in his impatience to get well. During the feast he had unbuckled it to sit more at ease.

'Thanks. I thought that I had lost it.' He suspected that his pack with all his other possessions had either been looted or was burning away in the farmhouse.

Carlos shrugged. 'Not much of an armoury between us.' One of the guerrilleros had a musket and the other a pistol in his belt. Each also had a knife, and after a short discussion they gave one to the girl and the other to the former surgeon, who were both unarmed.

'Has anyone seen my sister or Don Antonio?' Guadalupe asked, to be greeted by shaking heads.

'There may be more of us scattered over the hills,' one of the men suggested. 'The first I knew of it was the shot, but poor Ramón died to give us that warning, and then they were among us.'

The light was growing, and Williams counted seven corpses sprawled around the fire and the buildings, as well as a circle of a dozen or so prisoners sitting under guard. There was no sign of a woman, but there had been shots and sounds of fighting from all along the valley floor and there were probably more dead where they could not see.

Williams reckoned that the French had consisted of a full squadron of dragoons and three companies of voltigeurs, the skirmishers of a battalion and men chosen to move quickly and use their initiative. Such men had yellow and green epaulettes and tall plumes to mark their status as elite, and one of the companies also had the yellow-fronted jackets of the Polish regiment which had fought so well at Sohail Castle. They had come first, slipping forward through the darkness, and only the vigilance of the man on guard had allowed him to spot them in time to give a warning. Then the voltigeurs surged through the defile and opened a path for a score of the cavalry to charge towards the bonfire. Another company had marched all the way round to seal the valley off from the other side. It had been neat and efficient.

'Didn't think they knew this place,' Carlos said, 'but we were wrong.' He sighed. 'Don Antonio will miss Francisco. He was very fond of that horse.' All of the mules and horses of the partisans were tethered in a row, being inspected by a dragoon officer. If others had escaped, then they would be on foot.

'That's if he is alive to care,' one of the guerrilleros suggested.

'They won't get El Blanco.' Carlos' face belied such optimism, but then reddened with anger. 'Ramirez is with them.' They saw a man dressed as a partisan riding a piebald horse with a couple of dragoons. He had a musket slung on his shoulder and was clearly not a prisoner.

'Whore-bastard,' hissed one of the men.

'Don Antonio threw him out for robbing anyone whether or not they sided with the French. No doubt he is being well paid.'

'We will pay him properly,' the other partisan said, fingering the lock on his musket.

'We will, we will indeed,' Carlos said, 'but there is nothing we can do here, so we had better go.'

'Just a minute.' Williams was staring down as an officer joined the traitor and the dragoons. The man was mounted on a grey, had a plume in his shako, and wore a light green jacket. None of the voltigeurs wore green and this looked like the commander of the force. 'I am sure I know that man.' He wished he had his glass to be sure, but there was something about the way the man sat and gestured that looked very familiar.

'You can wave to him later,' Carlos said, and led them off down into the next valley. They moved with care, keeping amid the scrub as much as possible, before climbing up the far side and then dropping down into a ravine leading to a path which climbed like a snake up to a big peak. They had not seen any French coming up the side of the valley, but that did not mean that patrols were not roving the hills. Williams struggled to keep up, and his hip complained at every step. Guadalupe clung to him, giving support, and he could tell that she needed the comfort of touch, afraid not for herself, but for her sister. She never spoke during all the long hours they climbed. After a while, Carlos became even more wary, scouting ahead every few hundred yards before he beckoned them on.

'This is Buera country,' one of the men explained. 'El Blanco and Don Juan fell out a few months ago. He wanted the chief to come under his command and the chief said no.'

'Good thing too,' said the other man. 'Too many damned foreigners fight with Buera, and I don't trust the buggers.'

Williams did not see any point in commenting, and soon afterwards Carlos waved for them to come on. The man was grinning broadly, and when they came over a low rise they saw why, for he was not alone. Guadalupe pulled free and ran to embrace her sister. El Blanco patted her on the back and welcomed them all. There were eleven men with him, and most of them still had muskets or carbines.

'We are being watched,' he added more quietly, 'but I do not think it is the French.'

He was right on both counts, for a quarter of an hour later a circle of men surrounded them, coming out from behind bushes or boulders. They were stocky mountaineers, all in broad-brimmed hats and with cloaks slung from their shoulders, and heavily armed. They did not look any different from El Blanco's men, and did not show any signs of hostility.

That night Don Juan Buera entertained them around a fire lit in the mouth of a great cave opening out on to a hidden ravine. The red light cast tall flickering shadows on the rock and Williams could not help thinking that things would not have looked so very different when ancient man lived in such places thousands of years ago. The mountain chieftain was friendly from the start, but as the evening wore on his manner became even warmer. Williams guessed that El Blanco had agreed to serve in his band, at least until he could rebuild his own numbers. In a way this was the very thing that Hanley and other officers were urging, wanting the separate bands to merge and act together.

The thought had hardly crossed his mind when Don Antonio beckoned for him to come over.

'We are to see your friend tomorrow,' he said.

'So Sinclair sends word.' Don Juan Buera was an older man, balding on the top of his head. He was broad shouldered, wide chested and short like many of his men, but had a quick glance and bright eyes which spoke of considerable intelligence. 'More importantly, this Hanley is bringing us ten mules carrying powder and muskets. I would like to know more of this man, for these days it is hard to know who to trust.'

'He is a good man,' Williams said. 'I have fought beside him for three years and trust him with my life.'

'But should I trust him with my life and the lives of my men just so I can arm those who come to me without the means to fight?' Don Antonio ignored the jibe. Paula and her sister had withdrawn for the night to a little alcove shielded by a curtain, and the partisan leader seemed to have relaxed. It might hurt his pride, but he needed Buera's protection.

'Then trust, but not blindly.' He could not remember where

he had heard the expression and wondered whether it was something another guerrilla leader, the famous El Charro, had said back in Ciudad Rodrigo.

Don Juan Buera was pleased with that. 'Spoken like a man of the mountains. So I will speak to you like one. If your friend Hanley plays us false, then I will have you shot.'

'As I said, I trust him with my life.' Williams admitted to himself that there were some qualifications to that, for if he trusted his friend he did have doubts about his judgement. Something else was nagging him, something about the officer who had led the attack. 'Festina lente,' he added.

One of Buera's lieutenants chuckled. He was a thin man with a sallow complexion and the scars of disease on his face.

Don Juan glared at him. 'One does not need to be a priest to have a little education, Xavier,' he said. The lieutenant hung his head. He was dressed as the others, but Williams had heard that there were many monks and priests with the partisans, fighting the war until they could go back to their calling.

'A saying of Caesar Augustus, I believe,' Buera continued. 'From Suetonius, perhaps, but the sense is an apt one for an emperor or a man who fights the little war. Yes, we shall "hurry slowly".'

They left before dawn. 'Better to be there first, and better still not to let them see your own country too closely,' Don Juan told them as they set out. Williams and Carlos Velasco went off with the young priest and five partisans. 'Take a look at the place before we arrive,' they were told. 'If anything is wrong fire three shots and run fast because you will not catch us.'

The meeting place was a cluster of five little houses and a small church set on the crest of one of the foothills. They rode on mules and the priest took them on a long route to approach from the far side. Williams was fortunate to find his mount sure footed and compliant by the standards of its race, but even so the jogging motion hour after hour was an ordeal. Carlos noticed, but could do nothing.

'Don't die on me, Englishman. I have so few patients who are still alive.'

An hour before noon they were in an olive grove looking up at the houses. Three horses were tethered outside the church, and a guerrilla stood beside them.

'There's someone in the tower,' the young priest said. There were no other signs of life. 'People tend to be nervous when they see soldiers – any soldiers,' he added.

They waited for half an hour, Williams very glad to be off the mule and able to massage his leg. 'Is Don Juan here?' he asked.

'Of course, that is why you cannot see him,' the priest replied. Carlos rolled his eyes.

Ten minutes later a partisan on a donkey rode up the track towards the little village. He stopped, staring up the gentle slope, and waited. A man came from the church, dressed in a cocked hat and grey jacket.

'Sinclair,' the priest grunted.

The Irishman swung himself up on to a grey horse and put her into a walk. He rode with one hand folded back and resting on his hip in the proper posture for a gentleman on horseback.

'It looks fine.' Carlos sounded satisfied, and clearly he was not alone, for the partisan swept his hat in a great circle. A little column emerged behind him, with three more irregulars leading a string of ten mules. Ahead rode an officer with his drab cloak thrown back to reveal his red coat. Williams smiled; it was the first time he had seen Hanley or anyone else from the battalion or the army for three long months.

Sinclair kept his grey at a slow pace, and lifted his arm to wave. Something about the gesture sparked a memory, and then it seemed so very artificial, not a casual greeting but a signal. Williams was thinking of a horseman in a green jacket watching from the shore at Las Arenas and riding through the valley past the burning farm. He could not understand why he had taken so long to see it.

'Fire the shots,' he said.

'What?'

'Sinclair is false,' he insisted. 'He is with the enemy. Fire the shots now!'

284

'Are you sure?' Carlos asked, but he had unslung his carbine. Williams had wanted a musket, but feared that it was too awkward to carry and so instead drew the pistol from the belt and ran back towards the mules at the back gate to the olive grove. Cocking the gun, he pointed it in the air and fired. Carlos let off another shot and then one of the partisans raised his own musket and pulled the trigger.

Williams dragged the reins free and jumped on to the mule, kicking it forward. He was too far away to shout and needed to warn his friend. Reaching back, he slapped the beast on the rump so that it trotted along the wall of the grove. When he came out into the open he saw that everything seemed to have frozen in place. Sinclair was some thirty yards from the scout and as far again from Hanley and the mules. Everyone was looking around, trying to understand what was happening, and then Sinclair gave a shout and spurred his horse forward. Men came rushing out of the church and houses, men with tall yellow and green plumes in their shakos and yellow fronts to their blue jackets.

'Run!' Williams shouted as loud as he could. 'Run, you fool!'

The scout had his musketoon resting across the neck of the donkey, and now he aimed and fired at the Polish voltigeurs. The bullet went high and frightened his mount, which bayed in alarm and began to buck. Two voltigeurs stopped to fire, and a ball slapped into the panicking beast's neck. The rider fell to the ground.

'Run! Get away!' Williams yelled as he urged his mule on.

'Bills?' Hanley saw him and forgot everything else in his shock. The voltigeurs were spilling down the slope, at least half a company with more coming from the houses furthest away. Sinclair spurred past the dying donkey and its fallen rider, heading towards Hanley and the mules.

'Bills, is that you?' His friend was waving, and a great smile spread across his face.

'Who do you think it is, Lord Wellington? Run, you damned fool! Run!'

More Poles stopped, dropped down on to one knee and raised

their muskets. A ball flicked through the long grass just ahead of Williams. Another took the partisan scout in the shoulder, flinging him back down as he tried to rise. Sinclair's grey reared up and the officer sprang from the stirrups and fell rolling on to the ground.

Williams saw Hanley head towards the fallen major. 'Leave him! Run!' he shouted. Shots flicked past his friend and one struck the leading mule in the head, so that it sank down on its haunches and died, the bell around its collar tinkling.

Hanley turned and fled. Williams longed to follow him, but there was the rocky path of a fast-flowing stream at the bottom of the fold in the ground between them and he doubted that his mule would make it. Another bullet plucked at his long hair, and the Poles were getting close now. He turned the beast around and slapped it again to make it go. There were shouts and more shots, but the mule kept running and streaked back to the stone wall surrounding the grove. The priest was there, with one of the partisans, and both had raised muskets aimed at him. Williams wondered whether they would think he had played them false and fulfil Don Juan's threat, but the priest was calling him on.

'They have got Sinclair,' he said. Four or five voltigeurs clustered around the Irishman, lifting him. Two more held the scout down on his knees. About twenty more formed a skirmish line, while the rest doubled back towards the houses.

'They have always had Sinclair,' Williams said, wondering whether they still did not believe him. His mule, so sure footed up until now, stumbled and dropped its shoulder, making him lose his balance and fall. Something whizzed through the air where he had just been and slapped into the chest of the priest. There was a sharp report.

'The tower,' the partisan said, as the priest staggered, blood pumping out over his body. He was choking, but could say no words as he fell. Williams saw a wisp of smoke drifting from the window of the church tower, which must have been almost three hundred yards away. It was an incredible shot, and both the sound and the accuracy made him sure that the man had a rifle. The dying man slid down, leaving him wet with his blood.

'Come on, English,' the partisan called, and hit his mule hard to drive the beast on. Williams' animal began to follow and he managed to grab the saddle and haul himself up on to its back. Carlos and the others met them on the far side of the olive groves.

The sun was setting red beneath the mountains before they reached the rest of Buera's band. Don Juan questioned two of his men for some time before he called Williams to him. El Blanco was beside him, and with him were Paula and her sister, clad once again in breeches and boots. That is a shame, thought Williams, although he was pleased neither had yet cut her hair short again. His own was longer than he had ever had it in his life, and it would be good to be rid of much of it when there was an opportunity. Barbers seemed rare in the mountains.

'The warning saved us, and I hear it was you who gave it. For that you have my thanks.' Don Juan spoke very formally.

'Major Sinclair is a traitor or a French spy pretending to be a British officer.' Williams could see no other explanation. 'Either way he fights for them. It would explain a good deal,' he added, stating the obvious.

'Never did care for the man,' El Blanco said.

'I think he has a rifleman with him, perhaps a deserter from one of our foreign corps. The man is an excellent shot, and it was not chance that the bullet struck Xavier.' He did not add that he was sure it was Brandt, plying his trade for yet another army. It would do no good to mention Paula's attacker – her first attacker, he reminded himself, and promised once again that he would see Hatch brought to account.

'Sinclair can do less harm now that we know his true colours,' Don Juan said. 'But anything he saw and anywhere he went is not safe. We must look for new campsites and places to hide stores.'

'I must tell my commanders,' Williams said.

'Won't your friend Hanley do that? He should have got away.'

'He does not know. French soldiers appeared and Sinclair fell from his horse as he tried to escape. There was nothing to see that showed his guilt if he was not looking out for the signs. Sinclair can still do us harm, so I must make sure that they know about him in Gibraltar and Cadiz.'

'Write a letter, and we will see that it gets through,' El Blanco said, and the other leader nodded his approval.

'They might not believe a letter. I must report in person.' Williams also thought of Lieutenant Hatch. He could not put that in a letter.

'Are you up to the journey?'

'I shall have to be.' In truth he had forgotten all about his wound when he had smoked Sinclair and gone to warn his friend. On the journey back the pain had returned, but in spite of all the rigours of the last few days it was getting better.

'Gibraltar is closest,' Don Juan said, glancing at El Blanco. 'We will get you there.'

24

Near the end of January Marshal Soult, the Duke of Dalmatia, gathered his twenty thousand men and led them north-west towards the border with Portugal. Dalmas went with him, and took Brandt.

'I think he might be useful,' the cuirassier had said to Sinclair, 'that is if you can spare him.'

The Irishman was happy to agree, since with many battalions stripped away from the divisions left behind there was little chance of any more drives through the mountains or ambushes set to catch the partisan bands. He was also well satisfied with the havoc he and Dalmas had wrought. Bribery and threats had produced a good few informers from among the prisoners, and with Sinclair's knowledge of the guerrilleros they had dealt a succession of savage blows against the irregulars. The Frenchman was the better soldier, the Irishman had a more naturally devious mind, and the two of them proved a very effective team. Some of the raids into the mountains had marched far and fast to no result, wearing out boot leather and spirits without ever seeing the enemy. Yet more than half had worked, and they had inflicted heavy losses, dispersing those bands they did not destroy. For the moment the survivors were too scattered and wary to cause much trouble.

The marshal was pleased. 'Now, Dalmas, find me a way into Badajoz,' he commanded when the pair were summoned to Seville. 'And you, Sinclair, make sure that Andalusia stays ours while I am away. Do the British still think that you are one of their own?'

'For the moment.' He was sure that was true, and was pleased with his performance, pretending to flee from the Poles, then making his horse rear and taking an artful dive. It was a shame Brandt had missed the red-coated officer who was with the partisans. If it was Williams then he must have seen through the charade. 'In a few weeks they will probably find out.'

'Then use those weeks to fool them, and make sure they do not fool you.'

Dalmas had an idea for that, a bold idea, and the more Sinclair thought about it the more he enjoyed its impudence.

'They want to come out from Cadiz.' The cuirassier major had just heard the Irishman's latest instructions from Admiral Keats. 'Good. With the sea and ramparts to protect them we cannot get at them in Cadiz, so we want them to come out. Then we can fight them in the open and crush them.'

'What about the risk? Marshal Victor's corps is weaker than it was.'

'Not by that much. The duke has only taken a few of his regiments and he still has the bulk of three divisions. At best the English and Spanish will match him in numbers, and there is no Milord Wellington here. The rest of the English generals are children without him, and from all you say La Peña is an old woman. I'd back Victor and his veterans against any of them.'

'It's still a risk,' Sinclair said, but without conviction.

'It's war,' Dalmas replied and shrugged – an odd movement since as always when on duty he was wearing his cuirass. 'Draw them out. Tell them how weak Victor is and how afraid we are of being raided. Then make sure he knows where to find them and can meet them on ground of his own choosing. Smash them in the open, and the city itself might fall.'

'Is that your key into Badajoz?'

'Maybe. If I'm lucky.'

'You should have been born Irish,' Sinclair told him, and knew that he would miss the big man and his reassuring competence. That night he went south, already planning the messages he would write to Cadiz. The key was to convince, and that was best done by subtle modifications to the truth. He had a list of the regiments in Victor's corps and their current strengths. Reduce them by a fifth, and add to the numbers given for those in hospital or on detached service, and it would give the English and Spanish exactly what they wanted to see. An enemy still strong enough to blockade, but one bluffing them to look stronger than he was.

There was another letter to write, one explaining his remarkable escape in case Hanley was already back by the time his messages got through. Experience said that ridiculous and unflattering details were one of the best ways to sell a lie. He had used being shot in the bottom before, and wondered whether this time he might claim to have sneaked out hidden in a dung cart.

As he rode south, Chef de Battalion James Sinclair was happy man, his mind alive with possibilities.

January was wet all along the Andalusian coast, and much of the time it was cold. Near the end of the month Major MacAndrews led one wing of the 106th and a few dozen Spanish cavalrymen to raid a convent held by the French. The intention was to distract the enemy and let a much larger Spanish raid take the town of Medina Sidonia, which in turn was meant to draw their attention and permit the Spanish to throw a bridge of boats across the river separating the peninsula of Cadiz and the Isla with the mainland.

'Let us hope the French are as confused by all this as we are,' MacAndrews told his officers when he explained the plan, and Hatch had laughed along with the rest. The remnants of the Chasseurs had been disbanded, with many of the men going to the allegedly Royalist French *Chasseurs Britanniques*, but he had remained in command of a half-company of riflemen attached to the 106th.

Hatch did not care much for Tarifa, and cared even less for a week spent sleeping in the open with only a boat cloak to keep out the rain. Yet in every other way he could not remember a time when he had felt happier – if he was honest, even when his best friend Redman had been alive. Revenge was far sweeter than he had ever guessed, and the knowledge that he had won so complete a victory over his enemy without anyone realising. Sometimes, sitting in the mess of the 106th, he had burst out laughing at the mere thought, especially if Pringle or Truscott or any of the others from the old days was there. No one paid him much notice, for they all knew he was a sot and a queer sort of fellow, and no doubt spending time with foreign soldiers would only make him worse. There was amusement at his odd ways, and that only made it all the more hilarious.

The woman had been an impulse. Hatch was not a bold man and knew it. He had served well enough in half a dozen actions and had played his part, but no more than others in the regiment. Not a coward, then, and yet he did not have the reckless courage of men like Williams or the quiet confidence of the likes of Pringle. Taking the woman had changed that. It had all happened so quickly and then it was done and no one shouted at him or called him to account. Hatch realised that the world was there to be seized by anyone spirited enough to do it.

During the chaos of the next day he had known that he could not be touched and that he could do anything. When his men were sniping at the castle he had picked up a rifle dropped by one of the wounded and begun to fire. He was sure that he had hit at least one of the defenders. As the chasseurs fled around him and the Poles surged up to the battery, Hatch went through it all without ever fearing for his own safety. The brigade was in rout, but he was safe and had waited, resting his back against some boulders as men fled to the beach. He saw Williams, running away from the crowd and up on to a little rise, and another impulse came so naturally that the rifle was at his shoulder before he knew it.

Hatch aimed carefully, feeling a thrill of power, let out half a breath and squeezed the trigger so that the rifle slammed back into his shoulder. Smoke blotted out the view and he ran to the side and saw Williams – terrible, invulnerable Williams – with blood on his side and then the Welshman's head jerked back as he was shot again. The French had completed the job for him, his enemy had gone, and he felt free. Hatch was sure that he would enjoy the rest of the war, at least once they left this miserable hole of a place.

His men were compliant enough, and had a talent for making themselves comfortable in the field through energetic and well-organised theft, whether from local civilians or the rest of the army. With his new-found boldness Hatch encouraged them, as long as he was given an appropriate share, including plenty of bottles of spirits they were lifting from the mess stocks of the 106th. Once he found three of his soldiers with an officer's valise and let them keep the contents after taking half of the thirty guineas they found inside. Part of him still missed Brandt's roguish spirit, but on the whole it was more comfortable without the murderous Pole. The only real shadow in his bright existence was Sergeant Mueller, who watched him with evident disapproval and tried to rein the men in. Hatch longed for some pretext to break the man to the ranks, but the German was the consummate soldier, always efficient, never crossing the lines imposed by discipline. The lieutenant found it easier to ignore the dull fellow as far as was possible. His lately acquired funds allowed him to frequent the gaming table, and in two nights he gambled and lost all fifteen guineas.

The raid gave everyone a lot of marching and discomfort to little purpose. MacAndrews took them to the convent, but it was too strong to assault without heavy loss and his orders were only to threaten it, so Hatch deployed his men alongside the Light Company to harass the place. He carried a rifle all the time these days, and cheerfully popped away at the slits in the fortifications.

This was all very amusing, until news arrived of the advance of a battalion or more of the enemy which meant that the detachment would soon be heavily outnumbered by the French. MacAndrews withdrew his men, looking for a good spot to defend where his smaller numbers would not place him at a disadvantage. The Scotsman had lately developed the irritating habit of humming or singing softly to himself, always the same song.

'We'll ne'er see our foes but we'll wish them to stay ...'

'It sounds as if the major is longing to join the Navy,' Hatch said to Ensign Derryck.

'Last night I thought we had!' Every night without fail the heavens had opened, and at the last bivouac they had been flooded out by an overflowing stream.

An elegant Spanish officer on a spirited Andalusian came through the French lines to bring a report to the major.

'The Spanish have not moved,' MacAndrews told his assembled officers, 'but I am assured they will move today. If the fellow who brought the message is anything to go by, then they certainly do not lack courage and want only organisation, so I expect that they will advance.' The staff officer had ridden back to carry his assurances to his superiors, and it took a cool hand to ride in full uniform past the French garrisons.

Hatch took a party of chasseurs out on patrol while his sergeant led out another group. The lieutenant let the men disperse when they came to a farm so that the buildings could be searched thoroughly. There was little to find, for no doubt the French had been here often enough before, but then he heard a woman screaming. A couple of his men had found a peasant girl and cornered her in a pigsty. No doubt the girl was dirty enough in the first place, but after being thrown down in the mud she was filthy. Hatch doubted that she was very pretty, but there was something about her fear and helplessness that thrilled him. His new-found boldness was about to surface when a shot split the air. Sergeant Mueller appeared – goddamned Sergeant bloody Mueller – with his patrol to restore order and announced that a larger French detachment was approaching. They left the girl – perhaps the French found the bitch – and went back to MacAndrews' force. Just once the sergeant's impassive veil dropped, and Hatch saw his expression of contempt. Well, damn the man, he would break him or, failing that, shoot the bugger just as he had shot Williams.

At noon the next day the French battalion retired, which suggested that the Spanish had indeed moved, and so MacAndrews led his men back to the convent. Forty-eight hours had failed to make it any more susceptible to attack, so the skirmishers resumed their old occupation of shooting at the high walls and hoping luck would carry a ball through one of the narrow firing slits.

'We shall weary them with the noise, if nothing else,' MacAndrews declared, leaving Hatch's men and a detachment of redcoats to keep up the fire while he took the remainder along the Medina road. They surprised a foraging party of dragoons and infantry and quickly put them to flight, capturing twenty men. A little later a column of black smoke curled up into the air as the French burnt a storehouse filled with forage rather than let the British capture it. At the end of the day MacAndrews was back, retreating as the French battalion advanced against them once again. This time the Spanish main force was ready, and they pushed into Medina against little opposition, only to abandon it as the enemy battalion returned and more troops came to reinforce them. The same staff officer once again crossed the lines to inform MacAndrews that bad weather had prevented the attack from Cadiz and so there was no point holding on against superior numbers.

'Well, it has all been a pleasant winter ramble,' the major told them as he marched his force back to Tarifa.

Hatch was glad to be back under a roof and by a warm fire even if it was in the drab surroundings of Tarifa. That night the mess was even more convivial than usual, and soon stirred by two pieces of news. The first was that Lieutenant Colonel FitzWilliam was recovered and would soon arrive from England to take back command of the battalion. Hatch had never met the colonel, but heard that he was a decent, gentlemanly fellow. There was a fair chance that the remaining chasseurs would be posted elsewhere, and he was not sure whether to ask to return to the battalion or seek a posting elsewhere, perhaps with the Portuguese. Much depended on whether he would keep his lieutenancy if he went back to the 106th, and on FitzWilliam's attitude towards him. Hatch had no desire to be an ensign again, and part of him wondered whether his new-found confidence would find better opportunities elsewhere.

At that point, MacAndrews requested and was granted an invitation to enter the mess.

'Gentlemen, I have some remarkable and very pleasing news, which I am sure many of you will be delighted to hear.' The Scotsman cleared his throat, drawing out the moment before he continued. He had their attention, and Hatch suspected nothing.

'I am glad to be able to tell you that our errant boy has been found. Mr Williams is alive, apparently well, and with the irregulars in the hills.'

There were murmurs and then cheers led by Pringle and the Welshman's other friends, and MacAndrews let them die down. 'Captain Hanley writes to say that he has seen him, although he is at a loss to explain why our comrade has gone all gypsy on us. No doubt we shall find out when he returns.'

Pringle pushed back his chair to stand and then raised his glass. 'Here's to the gypsy, and to the One Hundred and Sixth.' He paused, looking around the room. 'And commiserations to all those junior to Williams on the list!'

A roar of laughter filled the room, the major chuckling with them. When an officer was killed the men junior to him received a step in seniority, edging them just a little closer to promotion. If Williams had died then the most senior ensign would have been raised to lieutenant.

'Just my luck!' Derryck said, grinning from ear to ear.

Hatch tried to laugh, eager to be a good fellow even when it was well known that he and Williams were not friends. It would not come, and he had to trust that his grimace would be taken for a smile.

He could not believe it, for he had seen the man fall and known in his heart that he was dead. The bullish confidence of the last months crumbled away as fear seized him. Williams had been looking the other way when he fired. He could not have seen who it was, even if he realised that the bullet had come from his own side, and then the other ball had struck and that must have been fired by an enemy. Williams could not know – could not even suspect.

What about the girl? The question forced itself unbidden into his mind. He remembered standing above her after it was over, the knife again in his hand, and wondering whether one swift thrust would ensure her silence. The woman had passed out, and no eyes stared up at him, but he was appalled that he had even thought such a thing. He felt fear then, not of the consequences, but of what he had become. Hatch had never wanted to be a saint, only a brusque and dangerous English gentleman. That he could even consider murdering a woman had sickened him, and he threw the knife away into the corner with bitter disgust. He was almost tender when he covered her with Williams' cloak, and only after he left did the elation come.

Even fear did not make Hatch regret the decision. He was not that sort of swine, but nor did he fancy the prospect of court martial and disgrace – if not worse. Surely they would not take the word of some foreign slut over an officer with a proven record? That was a thin hope, and at the least his name would be damaged.

Williams might well know what he had done. After all, the man was with the partisans and they were not folk to forget a wrong. What would the Welshman do? Hatch could still picture Redman's body, the wound over his heart, lying pale and naked after the attentions of the looters. He must get away.

The next morning he requested permission to see Mac-Andrews and submitted a letter applying for transfer to the Portuguese service.

'I will forward it, of course,' the Scotsman said, for he was acting governor of Tarifa and thus Hatch's superior even though he no longer served with the 106th. 'However, I cannot say how quickly anything will happen.' Hatch tried to read the major's expression and failed.

'Good luck to you, Hatch.' MacAndrews offered his hand. 'I

am sure the colonel will support your application as strongly as I would.'

FitzWilliam arrived that evening, and the next day the Scotsman left for Gibraltar, leading away the Grenadier and the Light Companies. They were to go to Cadiz to be combined with the flank companies of two other corps to form a temporary flank battalion and the major was given this command. Opinion in the mess saw it as a well-deserved reward for the skill with which he had handled the 106th during the colonel's absence.

Hatch spent less time in the mess and instead drank on his own – at least his chasseurs continued to supply him with plenty to drink so his empty purse was not called upon to pay for this relief. FitzWilliam promised to expedite his application, had even made a half-hearted if polite attempt to persuade him to reconsider and remain with the 106th, but the days turned into weeks and nothing happened. Williams began to stalk his nightmares on those rare occasions he managed to sleep.

At Cadiz the admiral and the generals waited on the weather. January ended with storms and February was no better. For the first time in his life Hanley felt the stirrings of seasickness when he attended another meeting on board the *Milford*, the big ship riding at anchor. Its motion was oddly unpredictable, which meant that the big lurches of the deck kept taking him by surprise. The outer harbour offered only a little shelter from the wind, which caused a deep swell and sent rain hammering against the stern windows. Everywhere on the ship was damp, the wood slick underfoot and he had slipped and fallen after coming aboard.

'We are ready, apart from the weather,' Sir Richard told Hanley and Wharton. 'And the Spanish assure us that they are ready, but it will have to get a good deal better before they are able to put to sea – a very good deal better. I have been a sailor all my life, and even on the calmest day I should not care to be in some of the barges they have to carry their troops.

'La Peña is to command. General Graham is convinced that

298

was the only way to get the Spanish to take part, and he is probably right, much though I regret the necessity. The Spanish have some fine regiments here, very fine, and several of their brigades are led by stout fellows, but La Peña is a nervous fool. Most of his own officers call him the "Dowager".'

'There is no choice, Sir Richard,' the chaplain reminded the admiral. 'Without them there are not the numbers. Graham can muster little more than five thousand men, but La Peña will bring at least twice as many. Sinclair reports that Victor has somewhat over eight thousand soldiers in or near the siege lines, excluding some of the gunners manning batteries. That is correct, is it not, Hanley?'

'Other sources suggest similar figures, some a little higher and some a little lower. If he is playing us false it does not seem to be in this respect, at least not by any great margin.'

'Have your doubts about him grown stronger?' Wharton's avuncular manner slipped to reveal the keen-sighted and calculating master of spies.

Hanley considered his answer. 'Yes, though not for any very clear reason. The more I think about it the more I believe him to be a French agent. I do not know why, and I may be in error, it is just that I feel him to be false.'

'If so, then what is his purpose?' Sir Richard asked. 'Soult has taken a strong force away, and so there must be fewer men here along the coast, and fewer to besiege Cadiz. Does he inflate their numbers to deter an attack?'

'Or hide them to encourage one?' Wharton suggested.

'Either way the attack will happen, for the generals are decided on it, the politicians support it, and whatever the risks it seems to me the best thing to do. With Soult gone north there is all the more reason to make trouble here in the south and so relieve the pressure on Lord Wellington.'

The plan was straightforward, the admiral punctuating his explanation with fingers jabbed at the map of the coastline from Cadiz to Gibraltar. Escorted by the navy, transport ships and barges would carry all of Graham's men and most of La Peña's to

Algeciras near Gibraltar. From there they would march overland back towards Cadiz. When Victor pulled his men out of the siege lines, the remaining Spanish regiments would attack from the Isla. At the least they would overthrow some of the enemy's works, but the principal aim was to force Marshal Victor to battle.

'Break his army, and thus break the siege,' Sir Richard concluded, slamming the palm of his hand down on to the table.

'Perhaps we can use Sinclair, and at the same time test him,' Wharton said.

'I am all ears,' the admiral replied, spreading his hands.

'Let him know of the expedition, say that he is to muster irregulars, but let him believe that our numbers are fewer. If he tells the French then they will be more willing to fight and that is all to the good.'

Hanley snapped his fingers as the idea came. 'Why not tell him that the commanders mistrust each other, are hounded by the Regency Council and so may be rash, while the soldiers are inexperienced?'

Wharton was pleased. 'Yes, that would convince and should encourage them to boldness. They say Marshal Victor is longing for a chance to beat the British after the repulse at Talavera.'

'Well, he may get his chance soon, God willing,' Sir Richard said. 'And God willing Graham can make sure that La Peña does not make a hash of it all.'

25

The luck went against them from the very start, when one of the mules bucked off its rider, kicked another animal so badly that its leg was broken, and then sprang over a precipice. That left them with three mounts between five of them, and so they walked the rest of the way, winding around the mountain as they climbed.

'It is not so fast, but it is safer,' Carlos Velasco explained. 'There is nothing up here to attract the French.' Don Juan had provided a local guide, although Carlos seemed to know the country quite well. Another of El Blanco's men came as escort and so did Guadalupe. The brief intimacy she and Williams had shared was not repeated, and for most of the journey she said little.

There was no reason for the French to be up so high, and yet, on the third day, the guide hissed a warning and they pressed back against the rock wall beside them, holding the mules tightly and praying that they would not bray. The path was only a couple of yards wide before the ground fell away in a slope so steep that it was virtually a cliff. In the valley beneath them a strong force of infantry – two companies at least – was slowly climbing, skirmishers to the front, flanks and rear.

Carlos tapped Williams on the shoulder and pointed higher up to a line of figures standing out dark on the crest.

'We cannot go through the pass,' the guide told them. 'We must go back or go over the top.'

Williams wondered whether he should have agreed to go back, but the man was sure the path was not closed. It meant giving up the mules, for they would have to climb as often as they walked, and so El Blanco's man led them away. Carlos told him to meet them at a village on the far side of the peaks.

'If you are not there by Sunday, we'll go on.'

It proved a hard climb, far harder than Williams had expected. These mountains were not so very high, but the land was broken by ravines and cliffs so that walking even a short distance as the crow flew meant precarious descents and hard climbs. They went for two days without seeing any more French, or indeed anyone at all. The Welshman's leg hurt and became stiff, and Carlos made them stop earlier than the guide wanted because there was the prospect of shelter in a shallow cave – little more than a hollow in the cliff face. Wet snow fell, and a bitter wind howled among the rocks, but they had carried some dry kindling and found enough fuel for a small fire. Huddled together, the thin soup seemed the most wonderful of all foods.

So much of Williams' time in Spain had been spent in the wet and cold that these days he laughed at the thought that once he had believed it to be a place of eternal sunshine. The next day the snow became heavier, and they had to be even more careful not to lose the way and stray from the path. Williams was sure that he was going more and more slowly. Guadalupe also found it harder going, and it was odd how he had taken her strength for granted in the past. As he looked at her now, he could see she was a slightly built young woman scarcely out of childhood, and even a year spent with the guerrilleros had not prepared her for so arduous a journey.

They pressed on, but he and the girl were flagging. The guide's assurance that they were on their way down cheered them only a little, for it still seemed the same routine of scrambling down rocky scree and then clambering up slopes the other side. Snow turned to rain, but the wind was still cold and it did not feel very different. There was no more kindling and that meant cold camps and no hot food. At the end of the fourth day, the guide took them up again, leading them slowly along a precarious path until they reached a deep cave sunk into the side of the slope.

It was pleasantly sheltered, even warm out of the wind, so that their cold food tasted better.

Carlos was on watch when the shouts echoed up from the valley below. He woke them, and they crept to the mouth of the cave from where Williams saw a big fire a few hundred yards below them. Figures moved around the fire and the men did not seem to care about being seen.

The sun rose, breaking through the clouds to give the first dry and bright day since they had begun. Williams could see that the men camped beneath them wore no uniforms and were instead clad in the drab blacks and browns of partisans. There were fifteen of them, and as many horses and mules, and they did not seem in any hurry. Most slept late, and the two sentries paced in a leisurely manner as they circled the camp. It was late morning before the others rose, and as they stretched and stamped their feet Williams felt Carlos tense beside him.

'El Lobo,' he whispered, which settled any thought of leaving the cave in daylight. At noon some of the partisans began to climb the slope towards them, so the guide took them back, crawling through a crack in the rocks to reach a natural chamber, where they lay and waited. Time passed slowly. There was only dim light filtering back from the mouth of the cave. Guadalupe lay beside Williams and her hand pressed his tightly.

They heard men's voices, at first faint and then echoing as they stepped into the cave. The accents were strong, and even after months with El Blanco's band Williams could understand only a few of the words. It did not seem as if they were hunting for them or anyone else. A long sound of splashing made it clear that one of them had decided to use the cave for another purpose. Then there was laughter and the voices receded.

In the near-darkness they lay and waited. Guadalupe kept a firm grip on his hand, and moulded herself close to him. Eventually Carlos crept forward and peered through the crack. He watched for a while, seeing and hearing nothing, before he went through into the main cave. The guide followed.

'I love you, 'Amish,' the girl whispered in his ear, hope and desperation in every word, but she was so close that she must have felt the change in him.

What could he say? Williams admired her and pitied her, and could not deny that she was lovely and there beside him, soft to the touch and so very warm and alive. He did not love her.

She needed a good man who loved her and would love her forever. Someone who would justify the newfound hope kindling within her after so much pain. She did not need a man who would take her only to leave her and plunge her back into despair. His head told him all this, but still had to struggle as his flesh thrilled at her softness.

'I am sorry,' he began, and in an instant felt her withdraw, the whole sense of her body beside him immediately different.

She shook off his attempt to help her up and left him. Williams followed, feeling himself a miserable worm, but not knowing what else to do or say. At the mouth of the cave Carlos and the guide lay, peering out.

'Smugglers,' the former surgeon said in a low voice. There were more men down below them, seven of them with a string of heavily laden mules. El Lobo went out to greet them, giving the leader a hug and lifting the man off the ground. 'The old rogue is not letting the war interfere with the chance of making money.'

The two bands mingled, sharing wine and food with every sign of friendship. Their guide was the first to spot the soldiers, dressed in long coats and coming in file down a path on the far side of the valley.

'French,' he said.

It was a few more minutes before anyone down in the valley saw the infantrymen. Someone shouted and Williams watched as El Lobo whipped a pistol from his belt and discharged it into the man he had hugged. One of his men clubbed another of the smugglers to the ground and all the others had weapons in their hands. A smuggler was hacked about the head. The rest threw up their hands. By the time the French soldiers reached them the fight was over.

'Some French general has gone into business with the bandits,' was Carlos' judgement. Not that it mattered to them, but since the partisans and soldiers had camped in the valley tor another night it meant that they must wait in their cave. Guadalupe said nothing apart from short acknowledgements when someone passed her something. She never looked at Williams and he was glad when darkness fell and it was impossible to see anyone inside the cave. Sleep eluded him, and he lay on his back hating himself for hurting so fine and brave a young woman.

El Lobo's men left in the morning, the voltigeurs following them an hour or two later. They waited for a few more hours before risking leaving the cave. It was another dry day, and they made good progress for a while, but it was already Monday and so they had missed the rendezvous. In fact it took them another day and a half to reach the mountain village. Carlos went ahead to see someone he knew there, found that the man with the mules had never arrived, and that French soldiers had passed through the day before. It was a gamble, but they risked staying the night in one of the little houses, glad of warm food and proper shelter.

For the next week they went slowly, wary alike of enemy troops and the irregulars of El Lobo. Williams was glad of the slower pace, and felt that his leg was getting better, but worried that it was taking so long for him to carry word of Sinclair's treachery. He wished now that he had written a letter as El Blanco had suggested, although whether that would have travelled faster and more safely was hard to say.

When they came nearer to Gibraltar their path was blocked again and again. The country was less sheltered here, and something seemed to have stirred up the French, for there were large detachments marching and countermarching across the country, while patrols seemed to be everywhere. A dozen dragoons with yellow fronts to their dark green coats and drab covers over their brass helmets surprised them as they were leaving the shelter of a straggling pine forest. They fled, seeking cover, and for the next three hours the French horsemen hunted them through the driving rain. Such a small group of soldiers would normally be wary of guerrilleros lying in wait.

'Must be a lot more of them around,' Carlos gasped as they lay panting in a dense thicket, after having to run for half a mile. Only the broken ground had stopped the horsemen from catching them.

At long last the dragoons gave up, but they were too weary to go any further and rested in a dell surrounded by thick thorn bushes. 'Either you're a Jonah or the French just do not like you, Englishman,' Carlos Velasco suggested. Guadalupe would still not meet his gaze. The former surgeon obviously sensed something was wrong, although he said nothing.

The next day they saw more patrols, and drifted steadily north and west to evade them. In the end they gave up trying to cross the lines and reach Gibraltar, and instead made towards Tarifa. They were weary, filthy from their journey, and running low on food. Yet it was like finding the natural grain in a piece of wood, and they found themselves going faster and faster. The guide left them to visit an isolated village and came back with bread and fruit, and that night they had a better meal than they had had for days. As they ate Guadalupe looked at Williams for the first time in a week. He wanted to say again how sorry he was, how he hated to hurt her, but the others were there, and what would the words really have meant? Instead he offered a weak smile. The girl did not return it, but she did not look away, and that at least was something.

They were close now, and on a drab day when heavy showers rolled in from the sea every hour or so, they headed for where they hoped to find the Allied outposts. The land was rocky, with low sandy hummocks and patches of marsh, and they felt very exposed. No one was in sight, and they tried to take what cover they could as they went towards a low ridge topped by cork trees. Williams unslung the musket he had carried throughout the journey. It was French and felt awkward in his hands.

'What is wrong?' Carlos asked. Surviving as a guerrilla had given him a healthy respect for men's instincts.

'I do not know.' Williams took the wine cork from the muzzle of his firelock, thinking once again that this partisan habit was a good one, and then pulled off the rag covering the lock. Flicking open the pan, he saw that the powder was there and it looked dry.

They went more slowly now, his wariness spreading to the others, all of whom drew their own weapons. Guadalupe had a pistol in one hand and a curved sabre in the other, with the haft of a clasp knife sticking from her sash.

When it came the shot sounded dull in the heavy damp air. The ball went nowhere near them, and it must have been a signal, for enemy dragoons appeared from the trees. There were five to their right about a quarter of a mile away, and seven or more further to their left. The Frenchmen whooped and spurred their horses at the fugitives.

They ran. No one needed to shout the order, the four of them just sprinted for the trees, splashing across the waterlogged ground. It was bad going for horses and that slowed the dragoons, but the closest was within a hundred yards when they burst through the first line of trees. The hill had a wide top and they kept going, dodging between the trunks. Williams stumbled, his weight falling so awkwardly on his bad leg that he cursed in pain. Carlos stopped to fire back at the leading dragoons, and Guadalupe took the Welshman's arm as he pushed himself up. There was warmth in her eyes as he thanked her, and they ran on, going down the far side of the ridge where the cork trees were thinner. They came into the open, and there was a wide field leading to another, denser wood. It seemed their best chance, so they sped towards it.

The guide was at the back. He was one of those tough, stocky mountaineers, so common in these parts, but he was not made for sprinting. Hearing the pounding of hoofs coming closer, he spun around and took aim with his carbine as two of the green-coated cavalrymen bore down on him. When he pulled the trigger the flint sparked and powder flared, but the main charge must have been wet or shaken out because the gun did not fire.

The leading dragoon hacked down with his straight sword. Its edge was blunt, for French cavalry were taught to thrust, and so the blow bludgeoned the man, knocking him into a crouch. The second horseman had to lean low to spear the tip of his blade into the man's forehead, the momentum of his cantering horse driving the steel through the bone. With only a grunt, the guide fell, the dragoon pulling his sword free as he rode on.

Puffs of powder smoke sprouted from the line of trees, and one of the horses reared, screaming in pain. A dragoon following behind was plucked from the saddle, dark blood on the yellow front of his jacket. Another shot followed, flicked Williams' sleeve and gouged Carlos Velasco's side. The former doctor was spun round, a puzzled look on his face. Williams went back to him, raising his musket up to his shoulders. The threat and the presence of who knew how many more enemies in the trees was enough to make the dragoons retreat. One lingered to fire a pistol at an absurdly long range.

Carlos' hand was red as he felt his side just below the ribcage. He glared angrily back at the French and then at Williams. Guadalupe ran to help him, but he pushed her away and lurched forward.

'It's nothing,' he hissed.

The three of them staggered on towards the trees.

'Fire, damn you, fire!' A shrill voice was calling from somewhere in the shadow of the wood, yelling out in English. Williams knew the voice from somewhere, but could not place it. 'Shoot them, you bloody fools, shoot them!' The man was almost shrieking.

Another voice, louder and deeper, shouted over the first, and then blue-uniformed soldiers appeared, and one of them was calling to him.

'Lieutenant Williams!' The man had white chevrons on his right sleeve and Williams recognised the face a moment before the name came to him.

'Sergeant Mueller.'

The German nodded, and barked an order for two of his

men to help cover them as they came in. It must have been the sergeant who had ordered the outpost to stop firing.

'We fetch the dead man when French are gone,' the sergeant explained, nodding in the direction of the corpse of their guide.

They walked into the shadow of the trees, Carlos striding more confidently and still refusing any aid. The two chasseurs stood with levelled rifles to deter any renewed enthusiasm on the part of the dragoons. No Frenchman appeared.

An officer stood under the trees, in shadow until they were close.

'Well, you have turned up after all,' he sniffed.

It was Hatch. Williams caught a tremor in the usually supercilious voice, and in an instant he knew that the swine had wanted to kill them. The lieutenant scratched at the broad scar across his face, and held a rifle low in his other hand, as if pretending that it was not there. Williams was sure the bullet that had hit Carlos had been aimed at him and fired by Hatch, and perhaps too it was the lieutenant who had tried to kill him at Fuengirola.

Without conscious thought, the Welshman realised that he had twitched the muzzle of his musket up to point at the lieutenant's belly.

Hatch licked his lips. 'We had heard that you were with the irregulars, but were not expecting you to appear. If it was not for your red coat we might have shot you all down.' He was talking much faster than was natural.

Williams stared at him. Carlos looked puzzled, and then ignored them as he dropped his carbine and used both hands to examine his side.

'Hanley told us, d'ye see. Or at least he wrote to MacAndrews, who told us. You were toasted in the mess.' The lieutenant kept talking.

Williams brimmed over with hatred and contempt and said nothing.

'He's back, you know. In charge of a flank battalion with the army come from Cadiz.'

Guadalupe stood beside him, and he remembered that she had

not seen her sister's attacker, so did not know who this was. She had sheathed her sabre, and stuck the pistol back into her sash.

Hatch kept rubbing his scar. 'General Graham has come here with an army, only the Dons have not arrived yet and so he waits and hopes that they will turn up.'

Williams wondered what to do. His musket was in his hands and it was loaded, and that offered the simplest of all solutions. He remembered how close he had come to killing Brandt and the others; how easy it would have been to snuff them out. He had not done it, and the corporal had escaped to join the enemy and commit who knew what viciousness in the future.

'Well, I suspect it's his fault for trusting in our glorious allies. You remember Talavera, and how they ran and left our wounded behind? I only just got away thanks to some friends.' There was rebuke in the last few words, a trace of the old scorn. Williams' own friends had been carried away in a carriage, but there had been no room for Hatch.

Williams took a pace forward and then stopped as fear flickered in the lieutenant's eyes. The muzzle of his musket was no more than a yard away from the man's stomach. Or the Welshman could strike him, laying down a challenge which Hatch must accept or live with the shame.

'You have missed a lot,' Hatch went on, the malice growing in his words. 'I do hear old Pringle's brother is now engaged to Miss MacAndrews. There's a peach for you – and rich as well as comely.'

The Welshman did not move and said nothing.

'Wouldn't mind being in his shoes. I'll wager you would too – but then of course you tried and didn't get anywhere.' The old Hatch was back, sly and full of mockery.

Williams made up his mind and lowered his musket.

'Sergeant Mueller.'

'Sir.' The German stiffened to attention, although the stamp of his foot was quiet against the sodden ground.

'The lieutenant is relieved of duty, pending court martial for an assault on a woman.' Williams had no idea whether or not he had the authority to do this. He did his best to sound as if he had not the slightest doubt that his order would be obeyed.

'Sir?'

'The attack happened at Fuengirola, on the lady we had rescued from Brandt and his companions.'

Carlos looked up, frowning. Mueller kept at attention, his eyes flicking from one officer to the other.

'That's a damned lie!' Hatch had gone pale. 'You might have done it. What proof do you have?'

'The lady has written a statement.' That was certainly a lie, a bare-faced lie, although Williams hoped that Paula Velasco would supply one in due course. 'And this young lady is her sister and will also testify.'

'Bastard!' Horrible realisation was dawning on Carlos Velasco's face. His hand reached for his knife and found that it was no longer there, no doubt dropped during their flight. His eyes flicked to the carbine lying beside him.

'He will swing for it, I promise you,' Williams said, trying to calm him, and then he spoke quickly in Spanish to Guadalupe, telling her who this was. The girl walked forward, face rigid, and went right up to Hatch. He was not a big man, and so it was an easy matter for her to spit in his face. Carlos asked her whether it was true and her expression told him everything he needed to know.

'Bastard,' he said again, and added more in his own language.

'She is a witness,' Williams said, once again bending the truth, but doing his best to sound confident and fully in control. He needed to have Hatch placed in custody now. If nothing was done then the matter might be forgotten or postponed. It needed to start now.

Rifle shots shattered the peace. There were shouts from over to the left, and then more shots.

'French!' Mueller called out, and pointed to the nearest chasseurs, gesturing for them to run in the direction of the noise. 'I must go, sir,' he said, and beckoned the remaining men to come with him.

'I will guard the prisoner, Sergeant,' Williams told him. The Welshman hefted his musket once more, and felt to check that it was still cocked.

Guadalupe's hand moved quickly, whipping the clasp knife from her sash and flicking the blade open with the same motion. She slashed from left to right, slicing through Hatch's neck just above the stiff collar. Blood gushed on to his jacket and sprayed over her face and body.

Hatch's eyes opened wide and then started to flicker, as his head dropped to an unnatural angle, and he folded down on himself, slumping on to the wet ground.

Mueller swore a long oath in German, but then barked at the chasseurs to follow him into the trees, for shouts and more shooting kept coming from further along the outpost line. The men gaped at the dead officer and the bloodstained girl, and the sergeant had to bellow again before they went with him, faces pale. They vanished into the wood, and there were a few more shots before it went quiet once more.

The girl wiped the blade with the loose tail of her sash and then flicked it shut.

'Good,' Carlos said.

'He should have hanged.' Williams stared down at the lieutenant lying in a pool of his own blood and struggled to take it in. Guadalupe wiped a hand across her face, smearing the blood as it began to dry.

'Waste of rope,' the surgeon concluded. 'If she had not killed him then I would have done it.'

It was over, and not in the way he had hoped, but Williams felt more sad than satisfied. Guadalupe prodded the corpse with her boot and then spat on its face.

She looked at Carlos. 'We should go.'

He nodded and they walked away, heading back towards the enemy outposts.

'Goodbye, Englishman,' Carlos said, but the girl was silent and did not even look at him.

'You should stay,' Williams called. They did not answer and kept walking. 'At least let a surgeon take a look at your wound.'

Carlos stopped for a moment and grinned. 'One of those butchers – certainly not!' He spread his fingers over the wound and when they came away there was no fresh blood. 'It is nothing, just a scratch. Goodbye, my friend.'

The two guerrilleros walked on. Williams could see no sign of the dragoons, but even so he feared they were walking to their deaths.

'Lupe.' It was the first time Williams had used the diminutive. 'Wait.'

They stopped and she turned.

'Stay here where it's safe.'

The girl started walking again. Carlos shrugged and gave a smile. 'I do not think this is a matter for discussion. We will be fine.' He waved a hand and hurried to catch up with her.

Williams watched for a moment and felt his eyes glazing over.

'Lupe,' he called after the young woman, 'I'm so sorry,' and the pathetic, indulgent uselessness of the words had him despising himself once again.

She did not look back, nor did either of them stop. Williams scanned the ridge ahead of them and could not see any sign of the enemy. It was hard to tell how many dragoons were out there or what they would do. He had the loaded musket in his hands, but the thought of using it to stop the partisans never occurred to him.

The pair walked on, Guadalupe staring straight ahead, until they disappeared into the woodland on the ridge. Williams watched the girl every step of the way, not really knowing what he felt about anything.

There was the sound of someone pushing past the low branches of the trees.

'Good God.' A mounted officer in the dark green uniform of the 95th walked his horse towards the body. 'What's happening?'

'French dragoons. They caught me coming across to our lines. Thankfully our piquet was here.'

The rifleman looked him up and down. He had not shaved for days, and his jacket was patched, repaired and long faded from its original scarlet.

'I am Lieutenant Williams, One Hundred and Sixth Foot, returned from service with the Spanish irregulars.'

'Have you, by God.'

Mueller appeared and saluted the officer. He gave a brief report in his stilted English. The dragoons had attacked as Williams and the others came into their lines, but were driven off after a fight. The sergeant looked at each of his men in turn, none of whom showed any inclination to question this version of events.

'They killed the Spaniard out there and the lieutenant.' The sergeant did not so much as glance at Williams. The Welshman's mind went back to Roliça, and Dobson's wooden expression as he reported that the French had killed Mr Redman.

'Bad business,' the rifleman said. He did not sound especially concerned. 'Mr Williams, I had better take you to the general, and he can decide what to do with you.'

After four months, Williams was back with the army, and from what Hatch had said with the regiment as well – or at least some of it. He had dreamed of this as soon as he recovered from the fever, and at last it had happened.

Hamish Williams felt flat and empty.

26

The Spanish were late, and although it was not their fault, Lieutenant General Graham was on edge. The sixty-one-year-old remained unfailingly courteous to all, and frequently genial, but Hanley and the rest of the staff could see the small signs that the Scotsman was worried. There was enough news from further north to dampen anyone's spirits. Massena clung on in Portugal, and Soult had taken the town of Olivenza and already begun the siege of Badajoz. At the end of January, the Marquis of Romana, commander of the Spanish army supporting the border fortress, had died of a heart attack. Hanley had met the marquis several times, while General Graham had known him quite well, and the news had made the Scotsman aware of his own advancing years. Romana was a cautious, steady fellow, proud of his country, but willing to work with his allies for the common good. To make matters worse, his successor was generally held to be a fool.

It was scarcely encouraging, although it did make the purpose of the expedition all the more important. The British were four days on board ship, and at the end of that could not land where they had intended or with any of their artillery. It took a day's march over muddy goat tracks barely visible in the driving rain to get the battalions from Algeciras to Tarifa, where there was some shelter and they were at least reunited with their guns. The Spanish were held back by the weather – Hanley learned later that their soldiers had been left on board the uncovered barges for days at the mercy of the storms.

'They're tough,' one of La Peña's officers told him. 'They are used to hardship.' He supposed the men had to be when their officers treated them in so casual a manner.

Graham had five thousand men and was on his own for four more days, and the old Moorish town of Tarifa was very crowded. Truscott told him that the mess of the 106th had so many guests that they went through two thousand bottles of wine and spirits in less than a week.

'That seems a good deal, even by my standards,' Billy Pringle said.

'Yes, a mere half would be sufficient for your needs,' Truscott responded with some spleen. As president of the mess he faced the gargantuan task of keeping track of all this.

Hanley enjoyed seeing his friends again, and was even more pleased when Williams had turned up on the second day the army was at Tarifa.

'You look like Robinson Crusoe's poorer brother,' Pringle told him, when the Welshman arrived, long haired, unshaven and covered in grime. 'If that is what being dead does to a fellow, I cannot see it ever becoming popular.'

Williams looked spent, with no energy to reply, but he insisted on drawing Hanley aside at once.

'It's about Major Sinclair,' he said, and launched into a description of the ambush. 'He was there, waiting with the French infantry.' There was a trace of disappointment when Hanley accepted it all so readily.

'I was already more than half convinced.' He wondered whether Williams had expected instant action. 'We have been sending him misleading letters so that he will pass the false information on to his superiors. In a few days that will not matter any more, and I can send word to all the guerrilleros that he works for the French. I imagine they will soon catch him if he keeps trying to ride among them, for he must have guessed that the game is up.'

Williams lingered, and it took a while to coax the rest of the story from him. Hanley heard about Hatch, what he had done at Fuengirola, and how Guadalupe had murdered him.

316

'Probably for the best,' he told the Welshman. 'I certainly cannot say that I blame her.'

Williams was staring at the ground. 'I should have stopped her,' he said at last.

The 'why' died on Hanley's lips as he decided that this was no time for recriminations or the morality of revenge.

'Well, you didn't,' he said brutally. 'And it is too late now, so the best thing is to forget about it. We are all likely to have enough to concern us in the coming days.'

Hanley was never quite sure what went on in his friend's head, but this seemed to satisfy him. Before nightfall Williams was snapped up by Major MacAndrews to serve in the Flank Battalion. Smooth chinned, hair cut so that it only just covered the top of his collar, and the man and his clothes cleaned as well as was possible, he went to join the Light Company of the 106th, which was short of officers. Pringle loaned him a cocked hat to replace the one he had lost.

'You look almost human,' Billy said, before deciding some qualification was necessary. 'In a poor light at least.'

Hanley saw little of either of them in the next few days as they waited for the Spanish to arrive. It would have been easy enough for Marshal Victor to bring two or three times their numbers against them, and Tarifa was not a modern fortress but an old Moorish town with decaying walls. It was thus a great relief when Captain General Manuel La Peña and his two Spanish divisions arrived on 27th February and raised the total number of Allied soldiers to more than sixteen thousand. At the very least they should have parity with the French, and perhaps a significant advantage. Victor had three divisions, but Hanley was still unsure how many men were left in each after the detachments were taken by Soult, and then there was the question of how many men would be left behind to guard the siege lines.

The general's cheerfulness readily spread to his staff and the army as a whole. Even bad news from the north failed to dampen spirits. Yet it was bad enough, for Romana's successor had risked a battle with the French about a week ago. Thoroughly outmanoeuvred and out-fought by Soult and his veterans, the Spanish army had been cut to ribbons, and so Badajoz was isolated.

'All the more cause to press on,' General Graham told them, and on 28th February the entire army set out, with the Spanish in the lead and the British bringing up the rear. It was chilly, and the waterlogged fields were proof of weeks of wet weather, but they covered twelve miles at a good pace and camped for the night just before the road divided.

'Medina,' the general announced when he returned from a conference with La Peña. 'The coast road would only take us towards the French outposts and to Victor's main camp at Chiclana. It would invite him to concentrate where he is rather than draw him away from Cadiz. So Don Manuel rightly intends to go north and follow the road to Medina Sidonia.'

As Hanley listened the name sparked a dim memory of a treaty signed in the town, but the details eluded him, and soon he and the other officers were too busy to think of anything save the task in hand. At Tarifa General Graham had divided his force into two brigades under General Dilkes and Colonel Wheatley. His two squadrons of King's German Legion Hussars were attached to the more numerous Spanish cavalry led by General Whittingham. Hanley was still surprised to find an English officer serving in the Spanish army, but it seemed Whittingham had raised his own regiment and been rewarded with rapid promotion. In return for the hussars, La Peña generously placed two of his own infantry battalions under British command, and Hanley was sent to them to make sure that they understood their orders.

There were about two hours of daylight remaining when the cavalry left camp at five o'clock in the afternoon.

'The captain general believes a night march will help confuse the enemy as to our intentions,' Graham informed his staff, and Hanley was unable to read his expression. The opinion of MacAndrews was a good deal more obvious when he encountered the major and his Flank Battalion marching as part of Dilkes' Brigade.

'Are they mad?' The major had his cocked hat tied on tightly with a piece of yarn because a biting easterly wind was gusting over the plain. 'At this time of year the plain is half under water. We went over it back in January, and even during the day it was none too easy to follow the road and not end up in a bog.'

Given the time the 106th had spent in Tarifa, Hanley suspected the major was speaking the truth, but there was nothing that he could do, and since they were at the very rear of the army it was dark by the time the Flank Battalion moved out. Marching feet, the hoofs of horses and mules, and the wheels of limbers, guns and carts had churned the route into deep mud which sucked at shoes as MacAndrews and his men trudged on their way after the others.

Hanley had the freedom of a staff officer to ride along beside the column, and spent the night going back and forth. More often than not he passed troops who were standing still, hunched against the wind as they waited for some delay further ahead to clear. Each time the column started they went quickly, eager to get warm and frightened of being left behind.

'Hurry up and wait, hurry up and wait,' a captain of the 2/87th said to him as he rode back past the Irish regiment on his way to the Spanish serving under Graham. Hanley grinned at the man, remembering him from Talavera. It was one of the few battalions which had seen any service, and the men in the other units all seemed so very young. A long march in darkness and foul weather was new to them, and although they set to with a spirit, he could see that it was adding to the slow, staccato progress of the column. Officers kept hurrying the lead companies on without giving time for the rest to catch up, so that the ones in the rear ran and stopped, ran and stopped. By the look of them, most of the young soldiers were wearier than they had ever been in their lives.

'Hurry up and wait!' the captain yelled after him as the 87th started off at the double. 'Damned staff officers!' he added with a cheerful wave.

There was a wide lagoon to the left of the main track, and

rivulets and streams flowed down from the little hillocks to feed it. After all the rain, the lagoon was wider and the watercourses faster and deeper. The wind drove the water across the fields, and it would have been hard in the light of day to tell the difference between an inch or so of puddle over a solid track and pond with several feet of water.

MacAndrews was his usual calm self, keeping the Flank Battalion at a steady pace, and getting Billy Pringle to ride back and forth to make sure that they did not lose contact with the rest of the column. They spent more time waiting than moving, and when Hanley carried an order for them to about-face, the major showed no surprise.

'Second time in less than an hour,' he remarked.

'The guides went astray,' Hanley explained, 'and so we must go back on ourselves for half a mile.'

'Nice change to be in the lead,' the Scotsman said, and ordered his battalion off. Hanley rode with them for a while, and saw Williams leave the column to walk beside the marching men. The Welshman strode along, a musket on one shoulder and with his few gleaned possessions rolled in a blanket strapped over the other shoulder.

'Evening...' Williams raised a hand in greeting as he spoke and then his feet slipped from under him and he slid down two yards of bank to splash into a pool. There was much amusement from the Light Company and anyone else who had seen his rapid descent.

The Welshman emerged, muddy and with water streaming from him as he climbed back up the bank.

'If my poor mother could see me now!' he called out, and that produced an even more open roar of laughter. It seemed his friend was settling in with his new company.

The general himself rode back to stop the Flank Battalion when they had gone far enough. Then they stood and gave time for the units ahead to turn around and follow the proper path.

'Hurry up and wait,' Hanley said under his breath, 'hurry up and wait.'

When the sun rose he felt a little more cheerful, although the cold wind robbed it of most of its warmth. At least they could see where they were going a little better, but Hanley was dismayed to realise that they had not even come level with the far end of the lagoon. The column kept going – or at least stopping and starting every ten or twenty minutes.

Hearing that MacAndrews knew the ground, Hanley accompanied the general to see him. It was nearly noon and they had been going for nineteen hours.

'I reckon about twelve miles, sir,' the major said when asked how far he thought they had gone. 'The convent at Casas Viejas must be four or five miles further on, and Medina twelve miles or so beyond that.'

No one had any good maps of the area, but Hanley could tell that the general had expected the answer.

'Much obliged, MacAndrews,' he said. 'Then I had better take a look.' Graham set off for the head of the column, driving his horse on at such speed that it was a struggle for his two ADCs and Hanley to keep up.

By the time they arrived, the advance guard was a couple of miles past the convent on the road to Medina Sidonia.

'Generous to march past the garrison of the convent and make it easier for the Frogs to count us,' one of the aides muttered with ill-concealed contempt. The general was a good deal more tactful, but it took well over an hour to convince the captain general that they should deal with the Frenchmen in the convent. By then almost the entire army had marched on within sight of its walls. MacAndrews was told to select two companies to storm the place, but as soon as the grenadiers and light bobs of the 106th formed up to assault, the defenders bolted from the back gate.

A squadron of German hussars led the chase, and Hanley rode with the flank companies which followed as fast as they could. There were about one hundred and fifty of the enemy, and when their commander saw the horsemen and realised he could not outrun them he formed his men into line.

'Can see us coming, otherwise he would have gone into square,' Pringle suggested.

The trumpet sounded the charge, and the KGL hussars went from walk to trot, and then canter, swords raised high ready to lunge. They were close when the French officer gave the order and a volley rippled along the line. A rider was pitched from the saddle, and two horses went down, but the hussars did not stop.

The French dropped their muskets, raising their arms to surrender.

'They've left it too late,' Pringle said as the German hussars spurred into them, heavy curved sabres chopping down. 'You can't shoot a man one minute and expect his friend to spare your life the next. If they wanted to quit they should have done it straight away.' Hanley watched in horrified fascination as the hussars cut down again and again. The French did not resist other than to cover their heads with their arms. As the survivors were brought back to the convent Hanley thought that he had never seen such ghastly wounds.

'No point treating that lot,' the surgeon announced, and had half the wounded laid out in a line while he treated the few who had any hope of survival. Hanley spoke to the handful of unwounded, and some of them shook as he spoke to them. They all told the same story. There was a brigade at Medina Sidonia, so substantial a force that Marshal Victor was bound to come to its aid if the Allies attacked.

The plan seemed to be working, until it became clear that it was no longer the plan. La Peña had changed his mind, and had decided to march instead back towards the coast, heading towards Victor's main force at Chiclana. Hanley was there when General Graham used all his charm and diplomacy to persuade the captain general to press on to Medina instead. Don Manuel would not be shifted, and his only concession was to delay the march from 5 p.m. to eleven. A second meeting and even longer bargaining postponed the movement until six the next morning, an hour before sunrise. In the event there were more delays and they did not start until eight. Hanley could only wave when the whole army marched back along the track, watched by the Flank Battalion, which had been left behind as rearguard.

A few cavalrymen appeared about a mile away on the heights to the north, too far to pick out the details, although no one was in any doubt that they were French. As the army swung southwest to take the road running along the edge of the lagoon, the horsemen shadowed them, more appearing as the day went on. At one point they came closer – Hanley remembered MacAndrews telling him that if you could see faces and cross-belts with the naked eye then they were within half a mile. That was not all he saw. Leading one of the patrols was an infantry officer riding a grey. Even at that distance his green coat was a good deal lighter than those of the dragoons beside him.

'Sinclair,' he said to the general.

'Impudent fellow, ain't he?' Graham replied. 'But there is nothing we can do about him at present. If I send out the hussars they will not catch them and there are not enough of our own horse to shield the whole column.'

There was the same stop-start progress until the latest stop stretched into a half-hour. Graham rode forward to discover the delay.

'The causeway is lost,' La Peña announced. They were at the point where the road went along a narrow piece of solid ground between a river and the lagoon. Today the land was flooded and it was invisible, the wind making waves across the surface of a veritable lake. A few of the stakes marking the causeway stood out of the water at crooked angles, but most had gone, rotted or swept away by the flood, and there were not enough to give a good idea of the route.

'We are searching for a crossing point,' the captain general assured his British subordinate. All around, the leading Spanish battalions had spread out on the low rises either side of the track before it came to the water. Some were standing, some sitting as they waited. A few were wading out into the water, carrying boots and stockings and with their trousers rolled up. They went with great care, for it was too cold for any sane man to relish being drenched. Hanley saw one officer being carried on the back of a sturdy private, the gallant leader of men complaining like a dowager if any water splashed on to him. There was no sense of urgency, no officer taking charge.

General Graham said nothing, and simply set his horse straight at where he guessed the trackway led through the water. The staff followed, although Hanley had trouble persuading his gelding to risk stepping into the lake. For the next ten minutes they all rode up and down, the flood past the horses' bellies and soaking their boots where it was deeper. It was a couple of feet less deep and the ground far more firm when they struck the causeway. The general was busy calling out soldiers from the waiting battalions. The Spanish infantry came willingly, striding into the cold water, and then standing to mark the causeway. Hanley thought that they were happy to be doing something. There seemed a far greater sense of purpose among the soldiers and junior officers than among their commanders.

Soon the infantry were marching across by companies, and Graham cheered them on and joked with them in Spanish as he sat on his horse, the waves lapping against its chest. La Peña sent one of his aides out to say that he was worried that the causeway would not carry guns, given that it was being churned up by the men's feet. Graham sent one of his staff to hurry the closest British battery to the spot. It took twenty minutes, and the escorting party of riflemen from the 95th were sweating from keeping pace. At the general's command the greenjackets went through the water, keeping step as if on parade even where it reached their waists. The artillery drivers used their whips to push the trace horses into the flood, and soon the first and the second teams of six horses, a limber and a gun were through to the other side. The next one skidded when a horse took fright, and the nine-pounder cannon lurched off the causeway, a wheel sticking fast in the mud as it sloped away.

The grey-haired general was at the spot in a moment, kicked his feet free of the stirrups and jumped down into the water. By the time Hanley and the rest of his staff joined him Graham was grinning at an Irish bombardier as they both pushed with all their strength to shift the wheel. A couple of Spanish ADCs arrived, their gold-laced blue jackets quickly soaked and covered in mud as they too strained to push the nine-pounder. The commander of the leading division was now wading along the causeway, chivvying his men to keep moving. Senior officers and artillerymen clustered around the nine-pounder, straining until they felt it move, and with a jolt the gun rolled back on to the causeway. The bombardier whooped and slapped one of the Spanish ADCs on the back. Hanley was worried for a moment, but then the aristocratic young man gave the NCO a polite bow and went off to remount.

Captain General La Peña watched.

It was midnight before the army halted. Everyone was soaked and there was no hot food – indeed little enough food of any sort. News arrived that the garrison of Cadiz had launched its sally on the previous night as arranged, since the message telling them that the army would not be in position on time had yet not reached the city. 'They took the French by surprise and overran their first line, but then French reserves struck back and they were tumbled back to the Isla,' an ADC told Hanley.

The captain general proposed another night march, but Graham and his own divisional commanders convinced him that the men were exhausted and in need of rest. They spent a cold night with no fires and only the wet ground as a bed. On the next day scouting patrols were sent out, and Hanley rode with the general on a reconnaissance of his own. French dragoons were about, and although they kept their distance he spotted Sinclair more than once. Confusion over who was to give the orders meant that no cavalry had been sent out to look at the ground or search for the enemy, but La Peña proposed dividing the army so that the British marched on one road and the Spanish on another, nearer the coast.

'It will help us to move faster,' he said, but Graham was unconvinced, and so Hanley went out with two of the ADCs and was able to confirm that the road allocated to the British was impassable to artillery and difficult for everyone else.

On the way back they weaved between the fir trees of a straggling forest. Hanley's gelding was close to exhaustion, and soon lagged behind the thoroughbreds of the other two officers. It was a gloomy day, the light in the wood poor, and so it was a shock when he came to a clearing and found Sinclair sitting on his horse.

The Irishman was alone, but he was also quicker off the mark and whipped a pistol from one of his saddle holsters before Hanley had even got his fingers around his sword hilt.

'Why, it is Captain Hanley. Good afternoon, sir,' Sinclair said with a pleasant smile. He pulled the hammer back and the click seemed appallingly loud in the stiller air under the trees. 'I take it you are not surprised to see me in this uniform? You certainly seem unimpressed.'

'We know you are a traitor.' The words sounded foolish and rather pompous, but it was hard to think of anything to say. At this range the man could not miss.

'The pistol is another clue, I suppose. Good little British officers are not meant to point weapons at one another, except of course in a matter of honour. As to treachery, does that not depend on your point of view? Would you believe me if I said that I have held true to a cause all my life, or would you prefer to hear that I sold my own mother into slavery to buy a bottle of brandy? What does it matter what you choose to think of me?'

There was the sound of hoofbeats near by, but Hanley could not tell more than that they were somewhere ahead and had no idea whether it was one of the ADCs or a Frenchman coming to find Sinclair.

'I don't think I'll kill you today,' Sinclair said, and backed his grey horse away.

'Conscience?' Hanley asked, and tried to edge his sword out so slowly that the other man would not see it move. His heart was pounding and his throat dry as sand-paper, but he tried to keep his voice steady.

Sinclair levelled the pistol at the Englishman's head. 'Maybe that, or maybe they are not paying me enough.' He wheeled the horse and sent it cantering away among the trees. He was gone by the time one of the staff officers appeared.

'Thought we'd lost you, old boy.'

'I'm still here,' Hanley replied, and followed him back to the army. His back was drenched in sweat that had not come from the day's hard riding.

The idea of splitting the army was discarded at Graham's insistence, and at five in the afternoon of 4th March the Spanish once again led the column off. They were heading for Conil, a village on the coast about eight miles away. The British general was worried by a night march so close to an enemy whose precise strength and location were unknown, but Captain General La Peña dismissed his concerns.

'We shall keep Marshal Victor guessing,' he declared. 'And by tomorrow we will have him trapped between us and Cadiz, or force him to leave the road open.'

Hanley could see that General Graham was unconvinced, and understood why. It was very hard to see how the French would be trapped unless they wanted to be. Nor was it easy to understand what would have been achieved if they were able to march straight to the Isla and Cadiz without fighting. He thought back to Fuengirola, and that nagging sense that no one in charge was quite sure what they were hoping to achieve.

Soon all the aggravations of the earlier night marches returned, the immediate personal discomfort and annoyances driving away the bigger concerns.

'Hurry up and wait, hurry up and wait,' he found himself muttering again and again as the column kept halting, sometimes every few minutes. He had not had time to mention the encounter with Sinclair, but since the French would have to be blind not to have a fair idea of where the Allies were going it probably did not matter.

The men in the lead took the wrong path in the darkness. Hanley told the general that he was sure they had left the path to the coast so that the British were heading directly for the main French camp. Graham halted his own troops and rode to see La Peña and sort out the confusion.

'*Voilà ce que c'est que les marches de nuit*,' the general said in exasperation when they reached the Spanish commander, and Hanley wondered whether La Peña spoke French. If so, then he did not appear moved by the rebuke. One of the Spanish ADCs insisted that this was the wrong road and the British were on the right one. Hanley insisted the opposite, as did the local guides, and eventually this fact was accepted by everyone. There was more argument about what to do, until after a good half-hour fresh orders were agreed.

With the sun rising, the army marched on towards the enemy.

27

Williams felt the noon sun on his face and was glad of its warmth. His leg was troubling him, and felt stiff, the wound to his hip throbbing as if it might burst open again after the succession of night marches on slippery tracks. It was pleasant to be warm and have nothing to do.

'The firing has stopped,' remarked Lieutenant Black, the senior lieutenant in the first battalion of the 106th and acting commander of the Light Company in the absence of Major Wickham. The latter had secured a staff posting with one of the brigade commanders in Wellington's army and had left for Lisbon before the Flank Battalion was formed. The Light Company boasted an ensign, but he had fallen sick and was in hospital at Gibraltar, and so Williams was attached to assist Black.

'Dons must have pushed the French back,' Billy Pringle said. The noise of fighting coming from the direction of Cadiz had got quieter in the last hour or so, which suggested that the advance guard had forced the French back. He was lying on the grass, a rolled cloak as a pillow and his hat pulled down over his face.

'There is no need to look quite so interested,' Black told Pringle, and began to prod him with his boot.

'God save us from restless and imprudent youth.' Pringle tipped his hat up with his finger and peered myopically at the lieutenant. His glasses were folded neatly in his inside pocket to keep them safe while he rested. 'Not in your way, am I?'

Black grinned, but was still restless and soon began to pace up and down, watched with tolerant amusement by the men of his own company and the grenadiers. The lieutenant had gained his promotion from ensign by volunteering from the militia and bringing thirty recruits with him. Four years on, there were still a dozen of these men with the Light Company. Black was a capable and popular officer, who had served in Portugal and on the retreat to Corunna. Around half of the men of his company had come through those campaigns, and even more of the grenadiers of the 106th had served there and at Talavera. The redcoats sat or lay along the slope of the low ridge, enjoying a rare moment of idleness. To their right were the two companies of the 9th Foot with yellow facings on their jackets, and on the other side was the contingent from the 82nd, also with yellow cuffs and collars.

'Can you not stand still and dream of all the captains who may get shot before the day is out?' Ensign Dowling suggested. He and Lieutenant Richardson were under Pringle's command.

'Thank you for such a kind and disloyal thought,' their captain told them. 'Now stop chattering and let me return to dreams of wine, women and song.'

'Cheer up, my lads,' Richardson said, and Dowling giggled. Major MacAndrews' recent obsession with 'Hearts of Oak' had become a joke in the 106th and now in the Flank Battalion as a whole.

Pringle glared at him. 'Haven't you got a hoop to play with, boy?' Richardson was twenty, but his curly hair and smooth, innocent face made him look younger. Dowling was only eighteen, was born with heavy jowls and the serious frown of an ancient, and still acted like an infant. Williams knew that Pringle was fond of them both, rather in the manner of an indulgent man who kept puppies.

It was good to be back with the battalion – or at least its flank companies. The rest of the 106th was half a mile away with Wheatley's brigade. There had not been much time or leisure to speak to his friends, although Pringle had assured him that he knew of no engagement involving his brother. 'Would not put it past the rogue to try, but I am positive that Miss MacAndrews has superior taste.'

A nagging doubt remained, at least when the fatigue and the throbbing in his leg gave him any time to think about the world beyond this hillside and the here and now. His head kept telling him that a battle was likely today, since otherwise he could see little point to the whole expedition. The rest of him felt sluggish, as stiff in spirit as his leg was physically. There was none of the familiar tension, fear and excitement mingling until all a man wanted was for the waiting to be over, whatever the horrors to follow. Hatch, Guadalupe and the months with the partisans seemed distant memories. Williams wished he felt some of Black's impatience, for at least it seemed to keep the man busy.

'Something's up,' the lieutenant said. 'Bramwell is coming over.' Even Pringle began to stir.

'Form your companies. We are to move to the top of the hill,' the acting adjutant of the Flank Battalion told them.

'And what then?' Black asked.

'Major MacAndrews will inform you once he returns from meeting with General Graham.' Lieutenant Bramwell of the 82nd struck Williams as a good officer, but he was not an affable man and gave every impression of seeing his new role as a sacred trust.

The officers walked to their companies and found the sergeants waiting for them, ready to turn their instructions into reality. Grenadiers and light infantrymen stirred, some knocking out their pipes, a few moaning in a half-hearted manner. Many had to be shaken awake, having fallen asleep almost as soon as they lay down on the grass. Within a couple of minutes all six companies were formed up and then the battalion marched to the top of the ridge. They did not have far to go, because the high ground, with its straggling bushes, low trees and red-brown sandy soil, was no great height.

'Hanley tells me the locals call it "Cerro del Puerco" – the Pig's Hill,' Williams told Black when the battalion halted near a half-ruined farmhouse on the top of the highest part of the low ridge. 'It's supposed to look like a hog's back.'

The lieutenant grinned. 'Typical bacon-bolter of a grenadier to be thinking of food,' he said. Williams remained a stranger to the Light Company. The light bobs and the grenadiers were the elite companies of a battalion, and existed in a perpetual state of rivalry as cordial as most civil wars. At times they might unite to prove their superiority to the other eight companies of the 106th, just as they would in turn join with those same men to disparage the rest of the army. His orders were obeyed, but a few days was far too little to admit Williams into the family of the company. The men were less free in speaking to him than they were to Black, and he was unsure whether or not he had the confidence of the sergeants, especially Sergeant Tom Evans, the short, heavy-browed man with a fiery temper who was the biggest character in the Light Company.

Evans was from North Wales, a man whose English was spoken from the back of his throat in the way of those who grew up speaking Welsh. Williams doubted that his being half Scots, half Welsh and from Cardiff would encourage any fellow feeling. There were a few other Welshmen in the Light Company, just as there were only a handful in the other parts of the 106th, in spite of its official designation as the Glamorganshire Regiment. Only one of his fellow countrymen – a rogue with ginger hair named Pryce – belonged to the dozen or so intimates of the sergeant. All were men who fought hard and lived as well on campaign as was permitted through cunning and an utter disregard for the property of anyone outside the Light Company.

'What's for dinner today, Pryce?' Black asked the light infantry-man as he and Williams walked along the rear of the company.

Pryce shook his head.

'Sorry,' Black said. The officers kept going on their way to report to MacAndrews. 'Oh, that is bad,' the lieutenant added when they were further along. 'If that parcel of rogues are going without then I dare say we officers will fare even less well. Let the men rest, Sergeant.'

'Sir.' Sergeant Evans was in his place at the far left flank of the company's line.

'Light Company!' His voice did not sound as loud as that of

many NCOs, and yet the words carried clearly. 'Light Company, fall out.' Two ranks of redcoats turned to the right as one man, and then their shoulders slumped and each shape slipped from the formality of parade. The same order was being given to the other companies and soon the five hundred men of MacAndrews' battalion sat or lay on the ground, a low murmur of conversation rippling along like a light wind through the grass. Within minutes a good third of the men were asleep. They were wise to regain as much strength as they could, but even so Williams never liked to see soldiers asleep in the daytime, for unconscious men too easily fell into postures very much like those of the dead.

Major MacAndrews waited for his officers not far from the old farmhouse, the sunlight gleaming on the great sweep of blue Mediterranean over to the west. The major stood beside his horse, nuzzling its head.

'As you can see, our battalions are now setting out to follow the Spanish,' he said. Most of Wheatley's brigade had already vanished under the cover of the pine forest ahead of them. Dilke's brigade was following, a succession of scarlet columns threading along the track into the trees.

The major stepped past his mount's head and pointed down the coast. 'They are moving to take up a new position there, where you can see that spike above the beach. That is another of these towers.' A round tower, its top decayed with long years, stood on the slope of the hill near the sea. 'This one is the Torre de la Barrosa and that is the Torre Bermeja. Beyond that is the road to Chiclana and beyond that is the Isla and Cadiz itself. General La Peña's Spanish have driven the enemy back from their works nearest to Cadiz. Some of the garrison of that city have thrown a bridge of boats across the inlet and joined up with our vanguard. The French – from what I hear, about a division in strength – have retired along the road to Chiclana to a stronger position, and thus the path to Cadiz itself is open.' He paused, looking from face to face to gauge whether or not they had understood him. Since no one was disposed to ask a question, he went on.

333

'For the moment, the baggage of the entire army is in front of this hill, waiting to follow when the tracks are clear. The cavalry under General Whittingham protects them, and guards the coast road and our own flank. Two Spanish regiments, the Walloon Guards and Ciudad Real, are here, waiting with us on Barrosa Hill, although for the moment they will stay on this northern slope. Gentlemen, we are the rearguard. This hill is the strongest position for miles around, and if anyone put guns up here they could dominate the plain and the coast road. Our guns have gone, so we are to stay here and make sure the French don't try putting some of their own pieces up on top. I am assured that three more Spanish battalions are on their way to reinforce us.'

This time when the major stopped there were questions.

'How long will we be up here?' a captain from the 9th Foot asked.

'Until they tell us otherwise. I was unable to gain more information and apparently the situation ahead of us remains uncertain.' The major put sufficient emphasis on the last word to make his low opinion of such vagueness very clear.

'Any news of food, sir?'

'I regret to say no news and no food.'

'What about the French?' said the commander of the 82nd's Light Company, and from the expression on his face it was obvious Billy Pringle had been about to ask the same thing.

'With the exception of the troops forced back by the Spanish, no one appears to have any idea where the rest of them are. Hence General Graham's insistence that we hold on to the high ground.

'We may as well take full advantage of the chance to rest. I want a corporal's piquet from each of our three corps alert and on the far slope. Mr Williams, you will arrange that and stay with them until relieved. Keep a good watch, and report if you see hide or hair of a Frenchman. I'll come and inspect you presently.'

As the officers dispersed, they saw a column of Spanish infantry coming back down the coast road to reinforce them.

MacAndrews was especially pleased to see a half-battery of guns moving with them.

By half past twelve Williams had his line of sentries stationed in pairs along the edge of the ridge looking back the way they had come. It was Pryce of the Light Company who first spotted the French dragoons.

'Cavalry, sir!' he said in a voice that was oddly high pitched.

They were at the end of the ridge, furthest from the sea, and the horsemen had emerged from the fringe of the great pine forest, some way to the east. There were only a few of them, a thin line of vedettes scouting for the main force, but they trotted out from the trees and soon a formed body of a squadron emerged.

'You.' He turned to the other redcoat. 'Run back to Major MacAndrews and tell him that there is at least a squadron of French dragoons coming towards us. Stop,' he commanded, as a second column followed the first. 'At least a regiment in strength.'

The man ran off.

'Well done, Pryce,' he told the Welsh soldier.

'Sir.' The man seemed unmoved by the compliment, but Williams was sure men served better when their officers knew them by name, and were as ready to praise as reprimand. He wished he had his long glass, and thought for a moment how upset his mother would be at the news of its loss. She had saved from her meagre funds to buy it from a pawnshop. It was intended to be mounted on a tripod, and in truth was too big and bulky for a soldier to carry, but Williams had grown used to it and come to appreciate its high magnification.

The French cavalry were out in the open, easy to see on ground broken by a few folds and dotted with occasional pines and cork trees. They were not coming closer to the ridge, but feeling their way towards the coast road. A third squadron had followed the others, and Williams guessed that there were some three hundred and fifty to four hundred of the green-coated cavalry advancing to the sea. These days many dragoons had taken to wearing cloth covers over their brass helmets, hoping to hide the glint of brass and so make it easier to surprise wary Spanish irregulars, but this regiment was not hiding itself today. Even without his glass Williams could see the light catching on well-polished Grecian helmets, the long black horsehair crests streaming behind whenever a man pushed his horse into a trot. This regiment had red fronts to their dark jackets.

MacAndrews arrived, and with him were Whittingham and two Spaniards in the dark blue and heavily laced coats of senior officers. Yet the Englishman outdid them for gaudiness, his collar and cuffs a riot of gold embroidery, the white plume running along the top of his cocked hat thicker than theirs, and his horse a good few hands taller. Whittingham wore the red cockade of Spain rather than the black of Britain, and Williams wondered what rank he had held in King George's army before he was elevated so high in the Spanish service.

'They're trying to get around behind us and cut the coast road,' the general said in English, and then repeated the words in Spanish for the benefit of his colleagues. 'We must move smartly, very smartly indeed, to prevent it.'

Whittingham had six squadrons of cavalry under his command, two of them KGL and most of the rest the Spanish troops he had raised and trained. From what Williams had seen of them they looked well mounted and disciplined, and greatly outnumbered the dragoons – at least the ones they had seen so far.

'Major MacAndrews, what do you intend to do?' Whittingham asked, once again speaking in English, and this time not bothering to translate for his Spanish colleagues.

'Do, sir, do?' The Scotsman frowned, and Williams was unsure whether he was genuinely surprised or hoping to remind the general of his duty. 'What do I intend to do? I intend to fight the French.'

Whittingham stared at the French through his telescope, and when he took it from his eye it was clear that his mind had not changed. 'You may do as you please, Major MacAndrews, but we are decided on a retreat.'

Williams was not sure the Spanish had been consulted, for he heard one ask what was happening, and so he began to translate for them.

'Very well, *sir*.' There was a pointed emphasis on the last word. 'I shall stop where I am, for it shall never be said that Alastair MacAndrews ran away from the post which his general ordered him to defend.'

By the time he reached this point in his translation Williams could sense that the Spanish officers were unhappy, but they were also under Whittingham's command. Even so one asked the Englishman to leave some support for MacAndrews' men. The general agreed.

'If you will not come with us, but wish to retire on General Graham's brigades, I shall give you a squadron of cavalry to cover your retreat,' he said.

MacAndrews did not acknowledge this, and simply wheeled his horse and went off at a canter back to his battalion. Whittingham and the Spanish set off a moment later.

Williams waited to be summoned back.

'Do you hear that, Pryce?' he asked a few moments later. There was a burst of shouting from behind them, as the Flank Company formed up and the Spanish prepared to move off. They waited until there was silence again and Williams began to wonder whether he had imagined it. Then it came again, a faint tinny sound of music drifting towards them. The enemy was marching with a band playing.

'Cocky fellows, aren't they,' the officer said, and was rewarded with the faintest of smiles. Williams saw the head of a column of infantry appearing from under the shelter of the trees.

They were called back to the battalion and found it formed up next to the farmhouse. MacAndrews had deployed into three sides of a square, with the fourth made up by the stone building.

'If there is time, I'll have the wall loopholed,' he told Williams.

The Welshman reported seeing the French infantry and hearing their martial music. He looked down the far slope and saw the rear of the Spanish columns already some distance away.

There was a good deal of confusion as the mule train was chivvied to the rear.

By this time the dragoons had reached the coast road, and one squadron had already wheeled to face them. It came on slowly, with a screen of skirmishers trotting ahead of the main body. A second squadron moved to support them on their right and echeloned a little back, and within a few minutes the third conformed to the new advance. They came on steadily, the skirmishers already almost within musket shot. Then the regiment halted as their colonel decided what to do. It did not take him long, and soon the flanking squadrons extended from column into line – lines which extended to either side of the square.

'Damn it,' MacAndrews said softly. 'They have guns.'

The teams were visible, still some way back, but throwing up plumes of dust from hoofs and wheels as the drivers flogged the horses forward. Further to the left, the blue ranks of French infantry were pressing on towards them. Williams could see one battalion wholly out of the shelter of the trees and another was following.

MacAndrews turned to his adjutant. 'Mr Bramwell, get the men out of the farm and form the battalion into column at quarter-distance.' The major stared down at Williams and gave a thin smile. 'And now you will see Alastair MacAndrews running away from a post his general ordered him to defend! Back to your company with you.'

The men of the Flank Battalion ran quickly to their places. A column at quarter-distance had one company behind the other, separated by only a short gap. It was a dense formation, and if the men on the flank halted and turned outwards it was almost as good as a square to fend off cavalry, but if the enemy brought their cannon within effective range, then the column would be a death trap. As they formed up, the dragoons were still busy extending their lines, but the infantry kept coming. Williams counted three battalions and was sure that there were more.

'Forward march!' Bramwell called out the order and walked

beside MacAndrews as the major rode at their head, taking them down the hill towards the track which the rest of Graham's troops had followed. None of them was in sight.

Williams marched in his place behind the Light Company, close to the middle of the column, and even with his height he could see little. They stepped off briskly, and at least the rolling ground and trees dotting the hillside would help to slow the cavalry down. Near the bottom there was a gully, and although it caused a brief disorder as men scrambled down one side and up the other, it was another awkward obstacle to horsemen. As he clambered up the bank, Bramwell appeared.

'Williams, take ten men and form in loose files to cover the left rear corner of the column.' It was not quite an order from the drill book, but the sense was clear. He called to the end five files to follow him and jogged ten yards out from the formation. Further would have placed them at great risk if the French charged, for they might not be able to run back to the shelter of the column. Isolated men on foot were at the mercy of fast-moving cavalrymen in the open. So was a column, if it lost order and began to break up or scatter. Ahead of them was an open field with hundreds of yards to go before they came to the shelter of the trees.

The French skirmishers had pulled back and a half squadron was formed in line low down on the slope. Another was over on the other flank, and more were moving up in support. They were waiting for the infantry to make a mistake, when they could spur their mounts forward, long swords ready to jab down with all the momentum of a galloping horse behind them. Williams could see the Frenchmen's faces, the ones nearest to him wearing tall bearskin caps rather than the usual helmets. They had red plumes and red epaulettes which marked them out as the elite company, grenadiers just as he was – not that it was any consolation to think that he was about to be killed by the best soldiers in a regiment.

'Keep pace, lads,' he told his men. They could not afford to be left behind. 'Rear rank men, back!' Five of the men ran back twenty yards and then knelt, muskets raised. 'Front rank men!' he called, and sent the others running past them. Williams went with them, but stopped when he came abreast of the kneeling soldiers. The front rank men kept going another twenty yards before they stopped to cover the others.

Williams was surprised that the French were not pressing more closely, and then he heard the brass notes of a trumpet, and the drumming of hoofs. He saw movement over the heads of the column as some thirty hussars of the King's German Legion charged past, curved sabres held high, with the tips pointing forward. More of the cavalry in their round fur caps and gold-braided blue jackets appeared on his side of the column, led by an officer on a magnificent black horse.

The French gave way – not far, but they did not wait for the charge and simply turned about and cantered back a short distance. There were too many of them waiting in support for the hussars to chase, and so they in turn halted and came back. Five times the Germans charged by half-squadrons. Williams had seen other KGL hussars in action in Spain and Portugal and knew he was not alone in thinking them the best cavalry in the army. It was like watching an expert fencer, probing his opponent, feinting, forcing him back, but never dropping his own guard. The French knew the game too, and so the horsemen chased each other back and forth as the infantry marched steadily on towards the trees.

A few French voltigeurs were now arriving to aid the dragoons, and soon there was a popping of musketry. As one half-squadron of the KGL pulled back from another charge, one of the horses slumped down, the tendon in its right hind leg smashed by a ball.

'Come on, Kelly,' Williams called to the nearest Light Company man, and sprinted to help the dazed rider up just in case the French chose this moment to mount their own charge. The nearest line of dragoons were walking their horses forward. The German hussar had tears in his eyes as he unclipped his carbine and cocked it.

Williams flinched as the shot rang out and the ball drove deep into the animal's skull. He wondered why seeing an animal killed was often more upsetting than seeing a man fall, but then he saw one of the dragoons spurring towards them.

'Kelly!' He shouted the warning, and the Irish soldier swung his musket up to aim at the Frenchman. Williams unslung his own firelock, happy to be carrying the familiar Brown Bess rather than the foreign weapon, and the threat of two loaded muskets was enough to deter the dragoon from his bid for glory. The man brought his sword up in salute and then wheeled back the way he had come. Two hussars reined in beside them, one reaching down to pull his dismounted comrade up behind him. With grunted thanks to the infantry, they trotted away, and Williams and Kelly ran back to the other skirmishers.

The head of the column reached the woods, and Bramwell shouted the order for them to turn about and form into line on the edge of the trees. It was enough to deter the dragoons, who soon pulled back and headed towards the coast road. The KGL shadowed them, trying to keep them from pressing too close. Barrosa Hill, the Pig's Hill, was dark with French infantry. The enemy had the high ground which dominated this wide, wooded plain, and the rest of the army was strung out on the march. Williams did not know where they were, or how many more French regiments were waiting to appear. MacAndrews had sent a German hussar with orders to find General Graham, and hopefully the general could bring order to this mess before it turned into a disaster. The French were not generous to enemies who made mistakes.

The Flank Battalion stood in line with the branches of the trees above them and waited. From the plain they could no longer see the Mediterranean, but Williams could still smell the salt in the air. His leg was sore and the wounds he had taken at Fuengirola had shattered the naive belief that somehow he could not be hurt. He did not want to believe in luck, but an insidious idea came that he was bound to die near the sea because he had grown up beside it. Hamish Williams did his best to push the

341

thought away by reason and then sheer stubborn determination, but it would not go away, and he felt vulnerable. A breeze picked up, and the branches sighed softly as they stirred.

28

Sinclair offered a silent prayer that he be right. Ashamed of himself, he tried to turn it into a secret jest by ostentatiously making the sign of the cross. Everyone knew he was Irish, and everyone assumed that meant he was a Catholic. Yet although he was raised as a Presbyterian, he had rejected both denominations when he read of the intoxicating atheism of the revolutionaries in France. He had shouted and fought for the emancipation of his Roman neighbours at home purely because it was fair, and because a united Ireland led as a republic was a golden dream worth a man's life.

It was a distant dream these days, and he thought of it less and less. Revolution had become empire, but France had welcomed him, and there was still much that was new and good about the rule of the Emperor. Best of all, the Emperor gave him enemies to outwit and beat, and it was all the more precious because these enemies were English and that would make winning all the more joyous.

He just hoped that he was right. Marshal Victor was like a man fighting for his life in a pitch-dark cellar. He did not know how many enemies he faced, or where they were. Sinclair was sure that the British had been deceiving him in the last weeks and that they had more men than they claimed. The marshal had asked him how many men the enemy had and so he had taken what he had been told and guessed at the truth.

'Six thousand British and nine or ten thousand Spanish, Your Grace. Perhaps a thousand of that total are cavalry. But they are all spread out over ten miles of country and not ready to fight.'

Marshal Victor, the Duc of Belluno, had hesitated for just a moment. He had one weak division holding the Spanish advance guard with barely three thousand men. That left him with two divisions, Ruffin's and Leval's, who between them mustered around seven thousand bayonets. The regiments were all French, for he had left all his foreign regiments in garrisons scattered around the south. What mattered even more was that they were all veterans. So was their commander.

'Sinclair, where the hell are the enemy going?'

Over the last few days what he had seen and heard from other patrols had left the Irishman baffled. The Allies kept changing direction and doubling back on themselves.

'Back to Cadiz?' Sinclair suggested. It was hard to reach any other conclusion, but equally hard to understand why they would go to all this trouble simply to march their army back to where it had started. They had driven the French away from a small section of the siege lines and that was little more than a nuisance. No vital position had been lost and the damage could be repaired in a few days.

'Why?'

All Sinclair could do was shrug, prompting a snort of laughter from the duke.

'Well, it does not matter.' Marshal Victor had served before the Revolution as a private soldier. He was proud of what he had done, enjoyed the wealth and lifestyle of power, and yet in his heart he had not changed. 'Gentlemen, we attack. General Leval, strike north-west towards the main track through the woods.' Leval had six battalions, one of them an elite force of grenadier companies gathered from their parent regiments. 'Ruffin, come with me and we will take Barrosa Hill and then see what we see.' The other division also had six battalions, two of them composed of grenadiers, but all of the units were a little weaker than their counterparts serving with Leval.

'Have them play "*La Victoire est à nous*",' the marshal told one of his staff officers. This was to be an occasion and the duke was determined that it would look and sound like one. Safely camped in one place for the last few months, he had ordered all regiments to parade in their finest uniforms. Gone were the loose coats and cloth covers for helmets and shakos and instead men marched off with polished buttons and plumes nodding.

At Talavera the Rosbifs had held off his men and eventually driven them back. This time it would be different, and the Emperor back in Paris would chuckle with delight when he read the dispatch.

The French attacked, and Sinclair hoped that the march the band played was prophetic and the enemy was as vulnerable as he had claimed. As they rode off through the trees, the Duke of Belluno was pom-pomming along to the hearty beat of the band.

Major MacAndrews heard the horses coming along the track and felt a momentary fear that the French had got behind them. It was a great relief to see a rider in scarlet weave his way through the trees, and an even greater pleasure to see that it was Captain Hanley.

'Yes, sir,' his former subaltern shouted back the way he had come, 'it is the Flank Battalion.'

The rest of the general's staff came along the track, Graham streaking along at their head, a good two lengths ahead of his young ADCs. His face was angrier than MacAndrews had ever seen, and he pulled hard on the reins and leaned back to stop his horse abruptly, flinging up mud from a puddle.

'Major, did I not give you orders to defend Barrosa Hill?' The Highland accent was stronger than usual, a clear sign that his countryman was barely restraining his annoyance.

'Yes, sir, but you would not have me fight the entire French army with just four hundred and seventy men?' Officers made the total nearer to five hundred, but the convention was to count only the rank and file.

'Had you not five Spanish battalions, together with artillery and cavalry?'

345

'Oh, they all ran away long before the enemy came within cannon shot.' MacAndrews knew that he was being unfair. The soldiers had marched off under orders, and if he felt bitter it was at Whittingham for retreating so quickly.

General Graham remained angry, but at least it was no longer at him. 'It is a bad business, MacAndrews,' he said. 'The French have wrong-footed us, and I do not know how quickly the Spanish can be turned around, so for the moment it is up to us. There is at least a division ahead of you, and another over there to the left. Perhaps fifteen thousand of them all told, so we are outnumbered, but at least the woods mean that they probably do not appreciate their advantage.

'The entire division has turned about and is coming back as fast as they may, but for the moment you are all that I have and so you must instantly attack.'

'Very well, sir.' MacAndrews made an effort to keep his voice steady and hoped that he succeeded. He and his men were being flung at the enemy to buy time, their lives offered up to the gods for the common good. 'Am I to attack in extended order as flankers or as close battalion?'

General Graham looked across the open field up at the French lining the hill. 'In open order.' The general took off back down the track to hasten the rest of the army.

MacAndrews took a deep breath. 'Lieutenant Bramwell, be kind enough to order the battalion to attention.' The closest men had already heard the order and were waiting expectantly. He saw Williams behind the Light Company, and the man's straight back and large frame, even after his wounds and months spent in the wild, were reassuring. The Welshman must have heard and would understand what they were about to do, but he did not show it.

'By the right, forward march!' Bramwell gave the order at his signal, and the acting adjutant had a good voice on him. The six companies marched out of the trees and into the open, two hundred and twenty-four men in each of the two ranks, with sergeants, drummers and officers forming a sparser third rank. Their uniforms were in better condition than was usual for men marching into battle, for all had come only recently from garrison, but the rigours of the march had left their white trousers spattered with mud.

MacAndrews halted them once they were properly clear of the trees.

Bugles sounded the call, and Bramwell repeated it as an order. 'Half-companies deploy as skirmishers!'

The drills were familiar ones, and alternate platoons split out of the line and doubled forward to form a chain of skirmishers about eighty yards ahead of them. He watched as Williams took half of the Light Company out, the men moving in pairs, and he thought back to the time when the Welshman had not long joined the battalion and he had insisted that his Grenadier Company drill in extended order as well as shock troops. Pringle, as was proper, stayed with the supports of his own company, and MacAndrews looked at the men he had trained and wondered how many would be left standing or even alive in half an hour's time. He did not know the officers and men of the 9th and 82nd as well as those of his own battalion, but a few weeks' acquaintance had made him fond of them all. The Flank Battalion responded readily to his orders and he was proud of them.

The supports remained in two ranks to act as a more solid reserve and, when required, feed fresh men forward to replace losses and add weight to the line. The new deployment made the battalion less of a target, although the formed men were still vulnerable to the enemy guns, but less so than in a continuous line.

He was about to order the advance when General Graham came galloping up again.

'Major MacAndrews, I must show them something more serious than skirmishing,' he said, and it was evidently the sort of order he preferred to give in person, for he looked him straight in the eyes. 'Close the men into compact battalion.'

'That I will, and with pleasure.' MacAndrews met his

commander's gaze. 'As a former grenadier, it is more to my way than light bobbing.'

'Good, I knew I could rely on a fellow Scot.'

MacAndrews nodded to the bugler from the 9th who was tasked with standing beside him at all times, and the nineteen-year-old sounded the call to re-form.

'Do you wish me to manoeuvre and move on the hill from further to the right?' The slope was steeper there, and it would be harder for the French to fire down at them as they climbed it.

'There is no time.' General Graham understood, but his order was clear. 'Attack to your front, and immediately.'

'Sir,' MacAndrews said, and then allowed himself a smile. 'Though I do wish I had a piper to play us off.' The sound of French band drifted down from the ridge, thumping out a brassy and confident tune.

'Aye,' the general replied. 'Good luck to you,' and with that he was gone, his horse flinging up earth as it went off in a canter.

MacAndrews walked his own horse around the flank of his battalion to the front and kept going until he was at the centre of their line.

He raised his hat to them, scanning the faces beneath the black stovepipe shakos. They were good men, whether they had the green plume of a light bob or the white of a grenadier.

'Gentlemen,' he announced, his white hair stirring a little in the gentle breeze. 'I am happy to be the bearer of good news – General Graham has done you the honour of being the first to attack those fellows.' He let that sink in, while he sought for words fitting for the moment and knew that there were none. Better to keep it short. 'You are the finest companies in this division and now you will prove it. Now follow me, you rascals!'

There was no cheer, but he had not expected one. There would be a time for that if they ever got close enough to charge, and for the moment there was no need to puff up their courage.

There were veterans in the ranks, especially in the companies from the 9th and his own 106th, and those men would know what they were doing. The others would guess, unless so stupid as to lack all imagination. MacAndrews could not help envying anyone who was still in such a blissful state of ignorance.

'Bayonets,' he said to Bramwell.

'Fix bayonets!' All along the line men reached back to draw the slim triangular blades from their scabbards. They pulled them free, eased each one around the muzzle of their muskets, twisting it until the ring locked on the lug designed to hold it in place. Then the men brought the firelocks back to their shoulder. Eighteen inches of steel spike made the weapons feel different, and the knowledge of the blades' purpose always brought home the seriousness of what was about to happen. Yet they also made men confident.

The Scotsman nudged his horse around and let her walk off.

'Forward march!' He shouted the order himself, not bothering to ask Bramwell, even though the adjutant and the bugler were there by his side. The Flank Battalion stepped out behind him, the sound of the French music still in his ears, and he wished for some of their own not to let the enemy have it all his own way. It was an insult to have an enemy tune to accompany the slaughter of his command. An idea came unbidden, and if it was a foolish one then that was fitting enough as fewer than five hundred men advanced to attack five or even ten times their numbers of steady veteran soldiers. Major Alastair MacAndrews began to sing.

'Come cheer up, my lads, 'tis to glory we steer, to add something more to this wonderful year.'

Every letter from Esther and Jane reminded him to practise the song, and usually urged him to learn others as well. His family's new-found obsession with music was admirable in its way, and it was always good to know that they were passing the time pleasantly, but it had proved a greater burden to him than he had expected, for he must become musical as well. MacAndrews liked a tune as well as the next man, but doubted that his thin tenor voice would give pleasure to anyone else.

The Flank Battalion marched across the open field towards the end of the ridge furthest from the sea. Sergeants watched the dressing from behind the second rank, pushing men back into place where necessary.

'To honour we call you, as freemen not slaves, for who are so free as the sons of the waves?'

The thought of his wife and daughter reminded MacAndrews that they were not far away – perhaps fifteen miles, or was it a little more? Probably too far for them to hear the guns when they began. Being made to sing would be a small price to see them again, and somehow it made it worse to think that he might die when they were so close.

'Heart of oak are our ships, jolly tars are our men, we always are ready; steady, boys, steady!'

A few voices joined him – one was certainly Williams with his rich bass-baritone. It was good to have the man back, safe and sound, although whether that would still be true in half an hour's time was less certain.

'We'll fight and we'll conquer again and again.'

Please God, let that be true, MacAndrews thought. He kept walking his horse on, for there was nothing he could do save go forward in front of the line. They were across the open ground, coming to the start of the slope, and at this point the gully they had crossed further down was no more than a slight dip.

'We ne'er see our foes, but we wish them to stay.'

The French were there on the crest, each battalion in a column with a two-company frontage so that they formed a succession of smaller lines, one behind the other. Closest on their left was a unit of *Legère*, the French light infantry who wore blue jackets and trousers with short black gaiters. These days such regiments rarely skirmished as entire units, but they tended to be better than average soldiers.

'They never see us, but they wish us away.'

The light infantry did not worry him half as much as the line of eight field guns deployed beside them and almost directly in front of his battalion. They were silent, as were the infantry, but all that meant was that they were letting the redcoats come into the most deadly killing range. Gunners scurried around their pieces. He was close enough to see them push charges and projectiles down the muzzles of each gun. A man stepped forward and thrust them down the barrel with a long wooden ramrod. Then he stood back, and though MacAndrews could not make out the detail, he knew another man was pricking open the bag holding the main charge and then thrusting a reed of fine powder down the touch-hole, before he too stood back. The French gunners waited, standing to attention around their green-painted gun carriages, each gun captain holding a linstock with a slow-burning match, waiting for the order to put it to the touch-hole and set off the fuse. Sometimes one of them would blow on to the match cord to make sure the flame glowed strongly.

'If they run, why we follow, and run them ashore.'

Three hundred yards to go and still the French waited as the Flank Battalion stepped closer and closer. They were half-way up the slope now, and the going was easy, although there were a few scrubby bushes dotted along the side of the ridge in their path. Redcoats stepped around them, breaking up the line until the sergeants shouted and forced them back into their ranks. Their equipment rattled and slapped softly against them as they marched, with that noise peculiar to infantry on the move.

A French band still belted out a stirring march, and now that they were close the music was drowning out everything else. The Flank Battalion was two hundred and fifty yards away.

'For if they won't fight us, what can we do more?' MacAndrews' voice cracked as he bawled out the words, not believing them for a moment. The irrelevant thought came that perhaps he should have learned a song about the army rather than the navy, but he simply liked the tune and had known most of the words before his family began to nag him.

They were one hundred and fifty yards away and still below the French, and he hoped that this would give them some protection when the enemy finally did fire. Troops on a hill tended to aim too high when they tried to shoot down a slope. It was a thin hope, for the slope was gentle and good artillerymen knew how to adjust – and the French gunners were always very good at their job, proud of the fact that the Emperor himself was one of their own.

'Heart of oak are our ships, jolly tars are our men.'

MacAndrews' throat was dry, his lips felt raw and cracked, and now they were barely one hundred yards from the French and still the enemy waited. A group of senior officers in plumed hats sat on their horses behind the gun line, watching the redcoats approach. The band was even louder now, and perhaps it was his imagination, but they seemed to be playing faster as they urged their comrades on.

The front of the *Legère* rippled and seemed to turn to the right as the first and second of the three ranks brought their muskets up their shoulders. They were to the left of the guns. To the right of the artillery was a battalion of line infantry with white trousers and white fronts to their jackets. MacAndrews doubted that they were at a favourable angle to fire at his men, and evidently their colonel thought the same thing, because the front of their column wheeled a little to face them and then brought muskets up to the present.

'We always are ready; steady, boys, steady!'

The last word was lost and the French music blotted out as the gun captains touched match to fuse and a fraction of a second later the main charges exploded. Six eight-pounders and two six-inch howitzers slammed back on their trails, flinging metal canisters and the wooden sabots on which they were mounted from the muzzles in a gout of flame and thick white smoke. The tins disintegrated, flinging out scores of musket balls and scrap iron in a great swathe.

For MacAndrews it was like walking into the teeth of a gale, as the air all around him was ripped by a hail of metal. The canister swept into the line, so that it twitched and writhed as men were flung down like rag dolls. One blast killed one of the 106th's grenadiers outright, two balls driving through his ribcage into his chest, and another smashing the bridge of his nose. Seven other men dropped around him. None of the canisters missed altogether, and each scythed great holes in the line.

The infantry fired, the noise less appalling than the great roar of the heavy guns, and more men were snatched from the line of redcoats. A light bob from the 106th screamed as he was hit in the groin, and, as he fell his rear rank man was shot through the forehead and died with no more than a gentle sigh. Further along, the Light Company of the 1/9th was badly hit by the *Légère*'s volley. Its captain was on the ground, his pelvis shattered by a musket ball, and a third of his front rank was hit.

In the battalion as a whole a dozen men were dead and some seventy wounded, and none of them had yet fired a shot. MacAndrews could not believe that he and his horse were untouched.

'Steady, lads!' he called, no longer singing. Behind him sergeants and officers bellowed out encouragement and orders to re-form, and behind all the cries were the moans and screams of the wounded and dying.

'Close up, close up!' Redcoats stepped forward on their own or were pushed to take the place of the fallen. The line drew in on itself, closing up towards the centre. It still rippled like a live thing or a banner in the wind. Ahead of them the French reloaded. The band had stopped, shocked by the roar of fire, but now it started again. Smoke drifted slowly towards the Flank Battalion.

'Come on, follow me!' MacAndrews called, daring to look back over his shoulder to satisfy himself that enough order had been restored. 'Forward!'

The Flank Battalion went on up the slope. Its line was less

neat, with little gaps opening up between the companies and wider ones between the different corps as men instinctively shuffled together with those they knew best. Some had the blood of comrades spattered over their jackets and showing bright on their white trousers. Most looked pale, staring blindly ahead, but they went forward, muskets still on their shoulders.

'Steady, boys.' MacAndrews held his sword high, and could not remember when he had drawn it. He saw gunners ramming down the charge and fresh canisters. The infantry were already bringing muskets back up to the present.

This time he was close enough to hear the shouted orders, as the French columns fired a second volley, the balls punching into the flanks of his line. More men dropped, with the companies from the 9th and the 82nd the worst hit because they were nearest to the fire. Then the guns boomed, the sound coming almost at the same instant hundreds of canister balls flayed the line. Eight more men from the 106th's grenadiers were flung back, limbs suddenly flying wildly like those of dangled puppets. Two bursts hit the Light Company, snatching away ten men. Pryce was dead, half of his face carried away. Lieutenant Black was sitting on the grass, hands pressed against his belly to hold in his own entrails. Gaps opened all along the line, as men fell or sprang back in horror.

Again MacAndrews was not hit. There was a graze along the neck of his horse, but it was no worse than if it had been scratched by a branch, for otherwise it was untouched. He struggled to accept that the storm had passed him to strike with such horrible fury against his men.

'Mother, Mother!' a man was screaming.

'Help me,' another pleaded, while more simply moaned or howled in pain.

'Come on, my brave boys, close up, close up!' MacAndrews turned to the side to call back at them. The carnage was appalling, but the NCOs still responded.

'Mother, oh, Mother!'

'Close up!' That was Dobson, shako gone and a cut to his

forehead. Other sergeants echoed the shout. Much more slowly this time, they harried the men back into ranks, closing up around the piles of dead as the wounded were dragged or crawled to the rear. 'Close up, close up!' The men of the Flank Battalion moved as slowly and clumsily as sleepwalkers, stunned by the horror around them. All the while the French reloaded and their band kept playing.

'Come on!' MacAndrews bellowed the order as loud as he could and urged his horse up the slope. 'Charge!'

They cheered then, with the defiance of a wounded beast, and muskets came down from the shoulders to thrust out in front, long bayonets reaching for the enemy. The Flank Battalion ran forward, its still shaky order loosening further as they went at their own pace. There were no more volleys from the French infantry, each man firing as soon as he was ready, and so balls began to come one or two at a time. Ensign Dowling had pushed his way through the ranks of the grenadiers, a mix of terror and excitement contorting his face so that he looked even older than usual.

'Follow me,' the eighteen-year-old squealed in a voice as high pitched as a little boy's as he circled his slim sword above his head. A musket ball smashed into his ankle and the shout turned to a scream as he slammed forward on to the grass.

Five of the eight guns fired, their captains not willing to wait for the others, and the canisters seemed to fling the whole of the redcoat line backwards. Two balls hit Dowling, one in the shoulder and another in the hand, and he screamed all the more. A grenadier fell on top of him, the man's kneecap shattered. The smoke was so thick that MacAndrews could not see the French.

His battalion had gone. Another forty or so men were down, and all the rest were scattered, going back down the slope in ones and twos, not running, but moving as if they had no will of their own. They went back, companies jumbled together, and most of them stopped when they were still a hundred yards from the French.

MacAndrews had felt balls pass inches from his face, pluck his sleeves and the long tails of his coat, and yet none had touched him. He patted his horse, avoiding the cut to its neck, and turned her to go after his men.

29

There was a good deal of confusion in the woods as the British division turned about and hastened back to seek the enemy. The French were advancing from the south-east as well as occupying Barrosa Hill, and so General Graham ordered one brigade to face the enemy attack and the other to re-take the hill. There was not time to make this happen neatly. Voices were shouting orders and all the time harrying the men to hurry, but the pines made it hard to see any distance and often the track split or grew faint. A pause of only a few moments often meant the troops ahead vanished into the woodland. Companies strayed from their battalions and battalions from their brigades.

'I reckon it'll break, sir,' the sergeant in charge of the drivers assured Hanley. General Graham's staff had been sent out to do what they could to bring order to the confusion, and he had found himself tasked with guiding the guns back to where they were needed. In the Royal Artillery, gunners served the guns and their officers were in overall charge, but the limbers towing them were handled by soldiers of a separate corps, who wore Tarleton helmets like the Light Dragoons instead of shakos.

'I'm sure it'll work,' the sergeant insisted, the three gold chevrons bright on the right sleeve of his blue jacket. As they hurried along through a more open patch of the forest, one of the teams had turned too tightly and the left wheel of the limber had hooked around the sturdy trunk of a sapling, bringing horses, carriage and gun to an abrupt halt. Three pairs of horses could not be made to walk backwards and it would take time to unhitch them and manhandle gun and limber clear, and so

357

the sergeant suggested driving the horses forward in the hope of snapping the tree.

'Go ahead,' Hanley told them, for he had long since reached the conclusion that sergeants normally knew what they were about. A gunner subaltern looked as if he was about to disagree, but deferred to the staff officer.

'Now!' the sergeant shouted, and each of the drivers kicked hard at his own beast and cracked his whips as he struck the horse beside him. The NCO was at the front, pulling at the collar of the lead trace horse. Together the animals pulled and took a step forward before the chains stretched taut. They strained, eyes wild, and the drivers kept jabbing with their spurs and beating with their whips, until the sapling started to bend forward. Hanley saw blood on one of the horses from the driver's spur and felt a pang of conscience, but then with a sharp crack the trunk snapped and fell. The whole team shot forward, limber and gun rolling over the stump and shaking the branches of the fallen tree as the iron-rimmed wheels rolled over it.

'Keep going,' he shouted, and at least the ruts left by the wheels of the rest of the guns made it easy to follow them. The gunners ran to keep up with the speeding limber, and a moment later they saw some of the redcoats from the 2/47th who were tasked with escorting the artillery.

They came into the open suddenly, on the eastern side of the forest, and saw the other guns already deploying. Major Duncan waved at Hanley, and pointed for the team to take this last gun to the left of the position.

'I'm having to pack them closer than I would like,' the artillery officer explained. Duncan was in charge of the two batteries with the force that fielded a mixture of nine- and six-pounders, and a couple of howitzers. 'Look at it,' he added, disappointed with the efforts of nature. 'Flat as a pancake, but we shall do our best.'

There were thick gorse bushes all around, and horses had to go carefully not to trip. Men and animals had already trampled patches of the gorse down around each gun and team, but it still covered the ground ahead of them, which sloped up gently.

Half a mile ahead of the gun the French columns of Leval's division were advancing, and Hanley heard their band playing. He counted four battalions in column and there looked to be another one or two behind them in support. There was no sign of any cavalry, but artillery teams were pulling guns up on the enemy's left.

'Six, I make it,' Duncan said, 'and I doubt there is any better position for them either.'

Gun captains were raising their hands to show that their pieces were ready to fire. Duncan waited for the last gun to finish loading and then began to call out fire orders, telling them to aim at the closest columns.

'Fire!' Gun captains set off the priming tubes almost as one, and the guns leapt back with deep-throated roars as they belched flame and smoke and sent roundshot to bounce in front of the enemy formations and then skip through them, smashing flesh, bone and anything else in their path. The force of the detonations flattened more gorse bushes in front of each gun, while pieces of burning wadding dropped down in the scrub to smoulder.

Hanley went to the left as he saw greenjackets of the 95th emerge from the trees. There were some men in blue with them, and he recognised the uniforms as Portuguese. Most of them were formed up, acting as supports for the riflemen in the skirmish line, and he watched as the pairs of soldiers moved forward through the scrub.

The guns fired again, some at the columns and some at the French artillery. Their barrels warm, the British gunners had switched to spherical case shot. Hanley saw one of the shrapnel shells burst in the air just in front of an enemy column. It shook, men dropping from the front rank, but it still came on, the living stepping over the dead and wounded. The band kept playing and the French formations advanced as if on parade. Hanley had rarely seen anything quite so magnificent in terms of martial pomp. Yellow plumes topped with green bobbed as the voltigeurs advanced to form their own skirmish line. The tops of their shakos had a yellow rim, and there were green epaulettes on their shoulders. Many of the men wore long black gaiters reaching above the knee, and all of them had all their brasses polished so that they gleamed whenever they caught the sunlight. Behind them the main columns marched with shouldered arms and uniforms just as immaculate. They were getting closer now, some six hundred yards away, and coming on steadily.

Muskets and rifles coughed as the rival skirmishers began to fight their own battle as precursor to the main action. The British rifles sounded different, sharper somehow, and they were more accurate than the smooth-bore muskets. Hanley could already see a few bundles of blue rags stretched out in the long grass and scrub. The voltigeurs stopped, searching out any fold in the ground to use as cover while they fired back. Duncan's guns thundered again, ignoring the light infantry and firing instead at the main bodies.

The greenjackets pressed their advantage, going forward a little way before they stopped to aim and fire. Slowly the voltigeurs gave ground, and for a while even the columns behind them paused. Hanley looked behind him and saw patches of red amid the trees. The rest of Wheatley's brigade was approaching. He wondered where the Spanish were, for Graham had sent to ask the captain general to bring his troops to support the British.

Hanley headed back towards the artillery, just as horse teams steered between the gaps in the guns. Crews lifted the trails and pushed on the wheels to turn them around and hitch them on to the backs of the limbers. Major Duncan was streaking off, riding to the point where he intended to set up a new gun line a couple of hundred yards further forward. The greenjackets and Portuguese were ahead of him, driving the voltigeurs back towards their battalions. As the British guns rolled out of the scrub and into long grass, Hanley saw that the French artillery was deploying on a gentle rise some way ahead. It was a race now, for a team of six horses towing a limber and gun was a far better and more fragile target than a battery of artillery spread in a line and waiting to fire.

Duncan was hurrying his men on, and soon two guns were

already unhitched and in place, and the rest moving into position. The French fired, three guns almost together, and then the other five one at a time. Hanley heard a tearing sound as shot passed over his head. All ten British guns were in the new line, the gunners toiling to load them.

'What the deuce?' Duncan was looking at the nearest battalion of French infantry, which had halted and was hastily forming square. He looked back towards the forest edge, but could see nothing to explain it. 'Well, I'm damned,' the artillery major said. 'They must have mistaken our donkeys for cavalry. No offence, old girl,' he added, patting his own dappled mare.

Offered so wonderful a target, Duncan had all of his guns laid to fire at the dense formation of infantry. They were already loaded with shrapnel, and even if he would have preferred ball, the well-cut fuses exploded the shells above the square, spraying it with carbine balls. Hanley saw the battalion quiver as men fell, and then its commander realised his mistake and ordered the companies to wheel out and once again form column. The closest riflemen were also pouring fire into the column and the British guns fired twice more as the battalion manoeuvred. When it moved off, it left behind a smear of blue and white bodies.

The French gunners had found the range. A cannonball took the foot off the spongeman from one crew, moments before another struck a gun captain at the waist, flinging his trunk through the air to knock over a man carrying ammunition. The grey-painted gun was splashed with red, and the legs stood on their own before collapsing. A gunner vomited, but wiped the mess off his jacket and went on with his job. The Royal Artillery talked of gun numbers, each with their own task in loading, and when one was maimed or killed, there were drills so that someone else immediately took his place.

A musket-sized ball threw up a spark as it nicked the iron rim of a wheel and another made a splinter in the wood of the wheel itself.

'Must have changed to canister,' Duncan remarked. 'The Frogs tend to use it at longer range than any good Christian.' He set four guns to returning the French fire, but kept the other six pounding the columns. The French were advancing once more, but the voltigeurs had run back to join the formed battalions and as they got closer these opened fire. Riflemen were elusive targets, but there were a lot of Frenchmen firing and some balls found a mark. A column would fire, all save one of them at the pace of each soldier rather than as an ordered volley, and then after a while the officers would make the men stop and the whole formation would advance a bit further before it fired again. The odd man fell as he was struck by a bullet or they dropped in clusters as shrapnel balls exploded above them, but still the columns kept coming.

The greenjackets retired. They went grudgingly and stopped to fire, but they did go back and the French came slowly forward. Hanley looked behind and there were still just a few groups of redcoats at the edge of the forest, and he realised that he had seen only a few leading companies rather than the main battalion. He wondered whether to ride and look for them, but he had not been told to do that, only to watch the guns, and felt that he should not abandon them. There was nothing to do apart from stay and try to appear confident.

A dull sound, somewhere between a slap and the noise of an axe biting into wood, and Hanley's horse let out a long breath and went down on its front knees. Its tongue lolled out between its teeth and he saw a jagged hole just above the eyes. He managed to get his feet free of the stirrups and, as the animal sank, he pushed himself off and rolled in the grass. The landing was awkward, making his left shoulder hurt, and it was tempting to sit and recover.

'What beautiful music,' said a voice, and Hanley looked up to see a red-faced major in Portuguese uniform. The man was polishing his spectacles with the fringe of his sash, and was obviously one of the many British officers now seconded to their allies.

'I don't know the name of the tune,' Hanley said, pushing up with his right hand.

'Oh, I do not mean that blasted band.' A musket ball snapped through the air close to the major's face. 'I mean that,' he said. 'Ain't it beautiful music?'

'Delightful.' There was no accounting for someone's peculiar taste, but Hanley felt he might as well be polite. Further out on the left, the 95th were pushed back almost to the edge of the wood.

'Should we conform, sir?' asked the English captain in charge of one of the Portuguese companies.

'No, let 'em go,' the major replied. 'Keep pouring it in, lads,' he called out, and then remembered that his men were not English and so yelled the same sentiment in badly accented Portuguese.

Voltigeurs had run forward again, tall plumes nodding as they eagerly pursued the greenjackets and pressed harder around the Portuguese.

The major grunted, blood bright from the bullet which had driven deep into his side. He swayed in the saddle, was hit again, and fell.

'I knew those bastard English would get us killed!' The speaker was another officer, Portuguese this time, and he called to his men in their own language. 'Run for it, lads!'

The blue-coated infantry ran as they were told. A few carried their major, who groaned with the movement, but most of the two companies pelted back towards the trees. It was their first real action and the noise and chaos were all the more unnerving. The British captain grabbed one soldier by his cross-belts and yelled at the man to stand firm. He stopped, glanced back at the enemy, and a musket ball smacked into his forehead. The Portuguese bluecoat dropped like a stone. The captain stared at him for a moment, mouth gaping, and then went after his men, calling on them to come back.

He ran back past hundreds of redcoats who were now emerging from the trees. The main force of Wheatley's brigade was here at long last, but the French were close now, so that Major Duncan had his cannons firing canister to hold the nearest battalions at bay. All of the guns fired at the infantry, even though the French artillery still knocked down gunners one at a time.

The two companies of the 47th had come forward to guard the battery's flank now that the skirmish line had withdrawn.

Orders were being shouted as the battalions began to form in front of the forest. A few men had already fallen to well-aimed shots by the voltigeurs. A captain of the Foot Guards clapped an immaculately gloved hand to staunch the wound to his arm, but did not stop encouraging his men to hurry into formation. Wheatley's brigade had arrived, but they were still outnumbered and the enemy was close. Hanley wondered whether it might all be too late.

30

Williams ran from the shelter of a clump of bushes to a dip in the ground, musket balls flicking the grass as he went. Sergeant Evans and two men were crouched in the dip. One of the soldiers had the yellow facings of the 9th Foot, and Britannia on his brass belt-plate. The Flank Battalion was now a thin line of men lying or crouching behind any cover they could find.

Evans put his head over the top and took a moment to aim before he pulled the trigger and fired up the slope. He ducked back, handing the firelock to one of the two redcoats and taking the man's loaded weapon. He gave a curt nod to the lieutenant as he pulled the hammer back to full cock. The grass just above him twitched as a bullet clipped it. The sergeant winked at the man from the 9th, and then bobbed up again to fire at the enemy.

'Don't know why they haven't chased us away, sir,' he said to Williams once he was back down in cover. Evans handed the firelock to the other redcoat. 'Reckon I'm the best shot,' he added in explanation.

'They must think our supports are near,' Williams suggested, for he knew as well as the sergeant that the Flank Battalion would crumble and flee if the French came forward. 'Or they want to hold on to the high ground and meet any attack there.' He could not think of any other reason, and experience had taught him that it was rare for the French to give the enemy any relief when they had them at their mercy.

'So what are we to do?' the sergeant asked him.

'Stay as long as we can, let 'em know we're still here, and wait for supports.'

'And they're coming?' Evans' eyes flicked to the two redcoats. The man from the 106th's Light Company was young and clearly stunned by all that had happened.

'They're coming. The Guards and the Sixty-seventh.'

'Huh, bloody Guards, I've shit 'em,' the sergeant said gruffly. He did not appear to have any particular opinion of His Majesty's 67th Foot.

'Hang on, and we'll beat them yet,' Williams said, as much to the privates as the gruff Evans, but he thought he saw approval in the sergeant's grim face. He sprinted away, hoping that he would be a poor mark for any voltigeur at this long range. Each time he found a couple of redcoats he stopped and encouraged them. The companies were mixed all together, and half the officers were down along with quite a few NCOs. He recognised only a handful of the men, but they were glad to see someone and be assured that they were not fighting a lost cause on their own.

'Supports are coming,' he kept telling them. It was hard to tell how much time had passed since the Flank Battalion's attack had been so savagely ripped to shreds. Twenty minutes at least, and maybe half an hour, but to men clinging to any scrap of cover it seemed like most of the day. Some did not fire, but simply cowered like animals in a storm, hands gripping their firelocks so tightly that their knuckles were white.

'Come on, lad, fire!' he called to one boy, lying on his own behind a bush which had already lost branches to musket shots. 'Load your musket.' The boy was a grenadier, and had the red facings of his own regiment, but he must have joined after Williams was sent back to Spain. He struggled, and then it came to him. 'Come on, Flattery, load.'

The use of his name stirred the lad from his horror. Williams smiled, patting the young soldier on the back. 'Well done. That's it, draw cartridge.' The officer was smiling and standing up straight above the thin shelter of the bush. The French had not closed, and with all the smoke drifting on the hillside, he would just have to hope that no one was able to hit him. Now and then a ball flicked through the air near enough to feel the wind of its passage, but neither man was hit.

Step by step he went through the drill for loading, giving each order in turn. The boy's confidence came slowly, as the movements brought back memories of hours of training, safe and secure with his comrades around him rather than alone on a bare hillside.

'That's it, Flattery, well done. Slide the ramrod back. Now pull back the hammer. Present!' The young grenadier knelt behind his bush. 'Fire!'

The boom was bigger than normal, a blow to the ears, and Williams guessed that the firelock already had a ball and charge in it. He had not thought of that, and was glad there had not been more otherwise the barrel could easily have exploded.

'Well done, you're a good soldier, now do it again.' He went through each order a second time, and by the end the lad was anticipating them, but he kept on talking for the boy needed to know that he was not alone.

After the second shot, Williams told the grenadier to follow him and he ran on another ten yards to where a Light Company veteran was resting his musket on a boulder to take careful aim.

'Ryan,' he said. 'This is Flattery, another gallant Irishman like yourself. He can serve as your rear rank man – the man's a demon shot.' The youngster glowed with pride and knelt down beside the older soldier.

Williams went on, going along the thin skirmish line that was all that was left of the Flank Battalion. The French infantry kept firing, but they did not advance and the enemy guns had been silent for a long time, waiting for better targets. Then a cannonball tore through the air above his head and he followed the noise to see it bounce on the edge of the field and skip upwards to knock a branch off one of the trees. Infantrymen in red were coming from the forest.

MacAndrews appeared, still mounted and still unscathed. 'They're here,' the Scotsman said. 'They've taken their damned time about it, but they are here.' A musket ball struck the ground by his horse's feet and the animal shied away.

'Good. You stay and keep the men shooting, Williams,' he said as he cooed to calm the beast. 'Pringle is to your right, and Captain Douglas of the Eighty-second is to the right of him. A lieutenant from the Ninth is to your left, and the Lord only knows where everyone else is. Still, that is one and a half Scotsmen, counting yourself, two and a half if you include me, and that should be enough to keep back all the hosts of Midian put together.'

Williams grinned. 'Yes, sir,' he said and could see the major was encouraging him just as he had been encouraging the men. No doubt as they spoke the general was telling his colonels how lucky he felt to have them with him – and the French were doing the same.

'I need to make sure the Guards and the others come up on our left, where the approach is more sheltered. Look after the lads, and I'll be back.' MacAndrews leaned down to pat his shoulder, and then set his horse running down the slope. The animal streaked away, happy to flee from the noise.

The lieutenant went back to checking the line, talking and praising as he passed each little group, and leading any man on his own to find companions. He thought the French fire was slackening, and that meant they were preparing to meet the new attack. It would have been good to push the skirmish line forward and distract them, but he could see the men would not move. This time he walked – if MacAndrews could ride then he could surely walk – to the left until he met a subaltern from the 9th. The Flank Battalion was still there, battered and stunned, but it was still there and it kept firing up the low hill.

'Hot work, sir,' a familiar voice said as he went back down the scattered line. Dobson was there, his head bandaged, but like Evans with several men loading for him. Williams did not recognise any of them, and two of the three were from the other regiments.

'Hotter for the Frogs up there,' he replied.

'Oh, aye, bet they're really scared now.' The sergeant fired up the slope. 'One less to worry about.'

They could barely see the French through the drifting smoke. 'You'd be lucky to hit the hill,' Williams told him.

'The cheek of the man. Do you know this young rip used to be my rear rank man?' The redcoats were wide eyed and disbelieving.

'It's true. The sergeant taught me everything I don't know.'

A ball ripped the officer's cocked hat from his head.

'Well, I didn't manage to teach you to keep your bloody head down, did I, sir,' the veteran told him.

'I cannot have paid enough attention.' He bent forward and scooped the hat back up, but could not resist sticking his finger through the holes. 'Right through,' he said ruefully. 'Stay with the sergeant, lads, and he'll see you through.'

'That's right.' He heard Dobson's deliberately loud whisper as he moved on. 'Stick with me and if you're smart you'll be a sergeant before long. If you're stupid you might even become an officer.'

The French battery boomed from above him. The noise sounded different, and he wondered whether the enemy guns had moved. They were firing at the First Foot Guards, but the redcoats were not an easy target as they weaved their way up the slope, dipping down into gullies and behind folds in the land. MacAndrews must have reached them, or their own officers seen the safer path, because they were advancing to the right of the Flank Battalion. Further beyond them was a smaller unit without Colours, and more redcoats next to them.

A few guardsmen fell – Williams saw one file collapse in ragged ruin as a roundshot smashed down both men, but most of the cannonballs bounced over their heads. The line was two deep, some six hundred men strong, and when they crossed the steep gully to begin climbing the slope, the ranks fell into disorder. As they went up the slope there were more ditches, boulders and bushes in their path, and short stretches where a few men had to go round or almost scramble up on hands and knees. It must have broken the sergeant major's heart to see such disarray, but the Foot Guards made only brief pauses to redress their ranks and then pressed on, the formation bent and crooked. In the centre, their crimson Colours dipped as the young ensigns struggled to bear their weight.

Beyond them three companies of the 3rd Guards were not to be outdone by their sister regiment, and pressed on just as quickly. They were part of a composite battalion, but the men of the Coldstream Guards had gone astray as they hurried back through the forest and were now not far from Hanley, about to advance against another enemy with the other brigade. One wing of the 2/67th, with yellow facings on their coats, moved up on their flank, and they had a skirmish line of riflemen shielding them.

Some 1,400 redcoats advanced uphill against 2,000 Frenchmen, and the latter were determined that they would meet the charge. The enemy battery began to take more of a toll as the First Guards reached the more open slope, but then the French guns fell silent as the columns went forward to sweep the impudent British away. Drummers beat the *pas de charge*, and behind them the band still played. There were four battalions, two of them grenadiers with ornate shakos topped by high red plumes, and other companies wearing tall bearskin caps. The Emperor had ordered the expensive and old-fashioned headgear withdrawn, but regimental colonels jealously hoarded the ones they had or employed dark arts to hide the fact that they were buying new ones. The fur caps made the wearers look taller, just as the red epaulettes on their shoulders made them look broader. Moustached, suntanned, tall and square, the grenadier battalions looked just like the veterans they were. Beside them came two battalions of line infantry, and if less of an elite, these were still men who had humbled the armies of Europe.

'*Vive l'empereur!*' Williams heard the chant he had heard so many times before. The drummers gave two beats, then a roll, then another beat, and as they paused to begin again the French soldiers yelled out praise for the man who rewarded victory so generously. Marshal Victor and General Ruffin rode just behind the four battalions, next to a fifth which came on in support. All were in column of divisions, with two companies in line three deep, then another pair of companies thirty yards behind them, and a third pair the same distance further back. From the front it looked like a succession of lines coming forward, as strong and inexorable as the breakers of an incoming tide.

'*Vive l'empereur!*' The chant was loud, for the moment drowning the music of the band. It was a concentrated attack, with neither room nor time to let the voltigeurs snipe at the enemy and weaken them. The ragged lines of redcoats were two-thirds of the way up the hillside, still disordered from the climb, and Marshal Victor would strike before they had a chance to recover. He had seen the English run before, when his men drove back the first line of Rosbifs at Talavera, including some of their King's Guards, but then his columns had been stopped by the few reserves the English general had scraped together and placed in their path. Today, the Duke of Belluno could see that the redcoats had no reserves and so he would crush them.

'*Vive l'empereur! Vive l'empereur!*' The drums went silent as the two battalions in front of the First Guards halted at their commanders' orders. A shouted command, and the leading companies fired a volley down the hillside. The already untidy line of redcoats shook as men were flung down. One of the Colours dropped for a moment, but was quickly picked up and raised aloft. Sergeants pushed men forward to fill the gaps in the front rank, and Williams could imagine the shouts as they did their work.

'Present.' The line of redcoats rippled as muskets came up to shoulders.

'Fire!' This time it was the columns that quivered, as the white fronts of men's blue jackets blossomed red and soldiers dropped or were pitched back into the ranks behind.

Further down the hill, the 2/67th and the Third Guards fired at almost the same instant at the grenadiers bearing down on them.

'*Vive l'empereur!*' The drums started again, officers yelled at their men to go on, but the men were more interested in loading and firing at the enemy. Shouts and drumbeats died, and there was eerie quiet as soldiers on both sides went through the routine of loading. Half a minute later there were new volleys, less perfect this time, but more men were falling on either side. Then it was back to the old drills. Drop the musket's butt to rest on the ground. Reach back for a cartridge. Some of the veterans had shifted their pouch round more to the front of their hip to make it easier. Take the paper cartridge and bite off the ball itself. Pull back the hammer to half-cock and flip open the pan, pouring a pinch of powder into it. Then the rest went down the muzzle with the paper as wadding. Spit the ball after it. Draw ramrod, thrust once to drive ball and charge down. Retrieve the ramrod, and turn it to slide back into place. Pull back the hammer to full cock, musket levelled again. Pull the trigger and feel it pound back against the shoulder, as the flint sparked, the powder in the pan went off and sometimes flung burning pieces against the cheek, the main charge going off in noise and smoke, and then drop the butt to the ground, reach back for the cartridge, on and on until the drills drove everything else from a man's mind.

A man's throat grew parched, dried by the saltpetre in the gunpowder from all the times he bit a cartridge, and his shoulder was sore. The enemy was a brooding presence somewhere behind the clouds of smoke, and he would never know if any of his balls struck home. Comrades he had messed with for years fell around him, dying with a grunt or sigh, or sometimes with a look of surprise. Wounded men moaned or screamed, and still he went on loading and firing, loading and firing, sorry for them, but glad it was not him.

'*Vive l'empereur!*' Marshal Victor himself rode to the front, waving his plumed hat and yelling at his beloved soldiers to charge and win the day. The two nearest columns stopped firing, and the men walked forward, drums beating a confused rhythm, but then some of the bluecoats were flung back as they were struck, and the leading companies stopped, men reaching for cartridges.

It hung in the balance, everything on a knife edge. Williams could remember how men were left stunned from the noise of their own and the enemy's fire, confused and lonely even when surrounded by other men in the same uniform. All it would take was a bold charge by either side and if their officers or any brave men could just persuade them to run hard at the enemy then the other side would give way.

'Bills!' Pringle called. Williams had not seen him coming along the line. 'Mr Williams,' the captain continued more formally. 'We must form the battalion and advance. Give those fellows something else to think about. Gather as many men and form them in close order here. You will be the centre of the line and everyone else will dress off you.'

He was off, shouting at men and pointing for them to join Williams. A handful responded, pushing themselves up warily and walking towards the Welshman. To his relief MacAndrews cantered up the slope to him, the sides of his horse now flecked with sweat.

'Splendid,' he said. 'Just what I was coming to order.'

'Pringle's idea, sir.'

'Then well done, Billy.' The major walked his horse to stand in front of the half-dozen men. 'Round up some more. I'll stand out as a better marker. Flank Battalion,' he roared. 'To me!'

The sound of heavy firing came from their right, the French columns and British lines little more than twenty or thirty yards apart, but neither able to push on those last steps. Instead they kept firing, and men in blue and red kept falling on either side.

Williams found Evans, still with the other two loading for him.

'Battalion is to form up,' he said. 'Over there by the major.' The sergeant looked surly, but then he did most of the time, and Williams ran on to the next group as if to imply that there was no question of his order being disobeyed. He found Flattery and Ryan, the veteran with a piece of torn shirt tied around his thigh, but both got up and went back to rally with the others.

Six men grew into ten, then fifteen and then thirty, and more were coming. Sergeants Dobson and Evans were both there, as was a young but confident NCO from the 82nd. Pringle returned with still more men, and an ensign from the 9th came from the other direction with more. Soon there were two ranks apiece of twenty-four men with a sergeant at each end of the front rank. A corporal and the sergeant from the 82nd along with all the officers save Pringle and MacAndrews stood behind the little line. Williams was at the far right, trying to work out what was happening in the great fight further along the slope.

'Flank Battalion!' The major called out the warning order so that men were waiting ready to respond to the command. It was no more than an under-strength company, but they had begun as a battalion and would end the battle that way, for good or ill. 'Forward march!'

The smoke cleared, and Williams saw General Graham riding along the front of the First Guards. The grey-haired Scotsman was using his sword to flick up the muzzle of any man about to fire. Williams had read of such things, but had never seen anyone doing so bold and dangerous a deed. French bullets kept knocking men down all along the line, but as the redcoats fell the old general rode on without a scratch.

The Flank Battalion went up the hill. There was an enemy column some way ahead and to their right, waiting to support the main attack, and a line of cannon pointing along the slope, but still masked by their own men. A thin line of skirmishers was in front of them; as soon as the line started moving, bullets snapped towards them. Ryan fell, blood gushing in a fountain from his throat, and Flattery stepped over the fallen man, walking stolidly up the hill. Men in red began to appear, coming out from cover. Redcoats fell, but the Flank Battalion grew bigger as it climbed the slope. Now there were seventy men, the newcomers shoved into ranks regardless of their regiment or company.

A cheer – a British cheer so different from the sound of a French attack or indeed one by Spanish or Portuguese troops – came from the right. The First Guards surged up the slope towards the columns, and beyond them the other Guards and the 2/67th charged as well, bayonets down.

Williams watched, letting the little Flank Battalion go on ahead, for he knew this would decide the day. If the British stopped to fire again, then they might never manage another charge, and there were more Frenchmen and they had the advantage of height. It was always easier to charge down than up a slope; in fact for a man burdened with his pack it was difficult to stop at all once he began running down a hill.

The French broke. Marshal Victor screamed at them, but the men in the rearmost companies could not see what was happening. They heard the great roar of a cheer and imaginations filled with thoughts of vengeful enemies coming through the smoke. They ran, and then the companies ahead of them crumbled into a stream of bluecoats flowing to the rear, and finally the companies at the front of each column followed them. General Ruffin was down, pinned by the weight of his dying horse, and the redcoats rushed up the slope, bayonets glinting, and General Graham rode with them, cheering them on. The enemy had gone. Some began to cluster together again in line with the supporting battalions, and so the Guards and the 2/67th halted and began to fire. The bluecoats went back.

A cannon fired, leaping back with the violence of the explosion, and a tin of canister swept through the nearest files of the Guards. Another gun captain touched the match to the priming tube and more of the redcoats were tumbled over, but artillery officers had seen the approaching Flank Battalion and shouted out orders to limber up and retire.

MacAndrews had one hundred and thirty-five men in his little line. Williams had caught up, and he could not understand how the Flank Battalion men appeared as if from nowhere. Some must have hidden well, and not bothered to fire at the enemy, for he had thought far more were dead or gone, and yet here they were, coming to rejoin the ranks.

'Fix bayonets!' MacAndrews must have suspected that a lot of men had dispensed with the clumsy blades while they were shooting. They made a musket ungainly, and worse still could take the skin off the knuckles of a clumsy man as he reloaded.

'Charge!' The Scotsman urged his horse on, his own sword thrusting out ahead of him as he led them towards the nearest cannon. He had not given the men time to fix their bayonets, but that did not matter because the gunners were in no mood to fight. A few voltigeurs fired, and a grenadier from the 9th was hit in the shin and fell forward on to his face. Most of the skirmishers fled, but one stumbled as he ran. Two men in the yellow facings of the 9th clubbed him with the butts of their muskets as he lay, and kept striking until the man stopped moving.

The gunners were hauling the heavy eight-pounder back to the low limber as MacAndrews reached them. His horse reared as an artilleryman in shirtsleeves swung a heavy ramrod. The mare went back, but MacAndrews drove it to the side and slashed down before the man could raise the clumsy weapon again. The gunner dropped the ramrod and clutched at the gaping wound across his face. Dobson was there, and shot one of the crewmen before driving his bayonet into another. The rest raised their hands as the drivers took the team and limber away at a jerky canter.

Men cheered, but MacAndrews was shouting at them to re-form in front of the captured gun. A company of French *Legère* had wheeled away from the main battalion and were forming to face his men.

'Get back in line,' Dobson shouted, and Evans was pushing redcoats back into place, snarling at them when they did not respond immediately.

An officer's sword swept down, and the *Legère* vanished behind a bank of smoke. The range was long, and most of the shots went high, but Murphy hissed in pain as a ball nicked his arm. Another shot threw up cotton and a puff of wool as it burst through the shoulder wing of a light bob from the 82nd. The man gasped in surprise, and then there was a deeper grunt from the man in the rear rank, another light infantryman but this time from the 9th, as the bullet punched through his ribs and into his lungs.

'Present!' MacAndrews' horse stirred, its ears flicking back and forth and its eyes rolling.

'Fire!' he shouted. About half of the men were loaded, and the volley was more like the crackle of burning wood than a roll of thunder.

'Charge!' he called. Men lurched forward through their own smoke, all feeling suddenly tired, but still they went with the Scotsman and they managed a thin cheer. Williams shouted as loud as he could, drawing out the cry, and others were yelling with him. It was less a formation than a scatter of men, only a few of them still able to run, and the rest jogging or lumbering along.

The *Legère* went back. Their battalion was giving way as the Guards closed on them, and the isolated company did not want to be left behind, so their captain shouted at them to retire. MacAndrews took his men to where the French had stood and halted. They were all breathing hard, even though they had not come very far.

To their right the First Guards were re-forming, with the other units beyond them. The French were retreating, some of their battalions grudgingly and others fleeing with no real order. The Guards had taken another of the guns, but the remaining six went back with the infantry. Some of the redcoats were cheering as General Graham galloped along the lines and went to see how his other brigade was faring. Even the Flank Battalion jerked from their exhaustion and yelled out as the Scotsman went past, raising a crop in acknowledgement.

For the moment the British were in scarcely better order than the retreating French. Six hundred of the redcoats lay forever still or moaning softly on the top and slope of the hill, more than a third of the men who had attacked. There were almost as many dead and wounded Frenchmen scattered in the grass, and now that the sound of firing had faded the air was full of cries for help, cries for mothers or friends, and wordless whimpers of pain.

Pringle looked around him and then at Williams. It had been

so close, so very close and it could so easily have been the French who had charged on to glory.

'Bills,' he said, 'how the hell did we get away with that?'

31

Major Duncan's guns kept firing through their own smoke and the blacker smoke of the grass fires started ahead of them by their wadding. None of the cannon was still manned by all the crewmen who had been there at the first shot. Behind the battery was a long row of wounded, and there were redcoats from the 47th helping to drag the heavy cannon back into place before firing and drivers from the artillery train were filling the places of the dead and wounded. Hanley saw the sergeant who had knocked down the pine tree ram the charge down one barrel and wondered whether it was the same gun.

'Pour it in, keep firing!' Duncan had little to do, for the targets were obvious and the enemy columns now little more than eighty yards away. They had hesitated when the British battalions of Wheatley's Brigade first appeared at the treeline, but the long pause as the redcoats sorted themselves out had given the enemy the chance to press closer. Musket fire ripped along the front of the nearest column, pitching a man from the 47th into the muddy puddles made by the constant rolling back of the gun. A gunner pulled the man out of the way, before the gun captain set off the charge and the heavy carriage sprang back again.

There was nothing for him to do here, so Hanley headed towards the formed infantry in time to see the angry Major Gough of the 2/87th telling the commander of the Coldstream Guards to 'Damn your precedence, sir. My regiment will lead off!' The major's battalion was in the centre of the line, and still numbered six hundred and fifty men even though several dozen of the Irishmen had been cut down while the senior officers bickered.

To the right was the other wing of the 2/67th in their yellow facings. To the left of the Irish Battalion were the neat ranks of tall Coldstream Guardsmen, two hundred of them in two companies. On the far left Hanley saw the red cross on white Regimental Colour of his own 106th. Before he knew it he was jogging towards them, seeking comfort in the familiar faces.

'*Vive l'empereur! Vive l'empereur!*' It was the first time today he had heard the French chanting. Four battalion columns were bearing down on the thin British line, with two more following in support. Leval's Division marched confidently and kept good formation, the men resplendent in their best uniforms. Hanley saw a group of senior officers riding ahead of the supports. A man on a tall bay with an abundantly plumed hat was no doubt the divisional commander, and near him was a shorter officer wearing a green uniform and riding a grey horse.

Hanley wondered what to do. Sinclair was over there and he was sure Wharton and the admiral would be very happy to hear that the Irishman was taken or dead. He wished Williams was here, or better still Dobson. He was sure they could find a way to reach the man in all the confusion of battle.

'*Vive l'empereur! Vive l'empereur!*' The drums were beating the hypnotic sound of the charge. For a moment three of the leading columns halted and fired, but then they were moving again, coming ever closer.

Men had fallen all along the British line, but the redcoats were also marching forward at last, feet swishing through the long grass and stirring the fallen pine needles of many years. They walked in silence, save for the sergeants rebuking any man who lost his dressing.

'*Vive l'empereur! En avant, mes amis!*' Ahead of the closest column a French officer was almost dancing as he went at the enemy, swinging his sword around in great circles and shouting to his men of honour and glory.

'Steady, lads!' British officers tried to sound calm, as if victory was only to be expected.

The drums kept beating, and three of the columns stopped again to fire.

'Close up!' the sergeants called. Only the French battalion marching at the 2/87th kept coming on and held its fire. It was ahead of the others by twenty yards or so. Hanley hurried on, but kept looking back over his shoulder to watch the enemy until he loped up behind the far right flank of his own 106th. The right was the place of honour, where the Grenadier Company would have stood had they not been a mile away with MacAndrews on Barrosa Hill. Instead Truscott tipped a finger to his hat in greeting.

His words of welcome were lost when a great rippling volley drowned out everything else. The 2/87th had stopped some sixty yards from the French column and fired. Men in blue jackets with white fronts were flung back in the leading two companies, but then the survivors steadied the line and brought muskets up to their shoulders. The volley was not quite so loud, for fewer men were firing. Yet it fell mainly on the centre of the red line, and there men staggered or jerked as they were struck by the heavy lead balls.

'Halt!' Lieutenant Colonel FitzWilliam was normally a soft-spoken man, but now his voice carried easily over the shouts and firing to their right. There was a French column no more than fifty yards ahead of them, its two leading companies delivering an irregular fire. One of Truscott's men yelped as a ball drove into his leg. He fell on the grass, screaming.

'Quiet, you rogue, it's nothing,' shouted a sergeant. 'Don't show us up in front of the Frogs.'

The man looked more angry than abashed, but stopped anyway.

'Fix bayonets!'

Hanley drew his sword. It always felt odd to hold the thing, some remaining pacific impulse stubbornly resisting his martial calling. Truscott and his subalterns drew their own blades. The young ensign whose name Hanley could not remember swished it back and forth until he noticed one of the sergeants glaring at him. The boy blushed like a child caught scrumping by his schoolteacher.

The French were trying to form line, the companies in the second and third lines parting so that they could march and deploy on the flanks of the leading division.

'Present!' With a long series of rattles and slaps the muskets of almost seven hundred men came up to their shoulders.

'Now, my boys, be sure to fire at their legs and spoil their dancing!' Men chuckled, looking at each other in surprise at their colonel's words.

'Silence in the ranks!' bawled the sergeants as they stood in the rear, half-pikes ready to straighten the dressing by forcing men back into place with their six-foot staffs.

'Fire!'

Smoke blotted the French from sight, but from the end of the line Hanley saw a glimpse of the enemy formation as dozens of men fell.

A howl – there was no other word for it – burst out from the centre of the army, as the 2/87th flung themselves at the enemy. The cry turned into what Hanley thought were words, but he could not make them out. All along the British line the battalions were going forward, but none went as fast as the Irish.

'Charge!' FitzWilliam spurred his horse into the smoke and was gone.

The 106th cheered and followed him. It was the first time that their lieutenant colonel had led them into battle, but the men liked him and were confident in themselves. Hanley charged with them, but then a man was pitched back from the company, tripping the officer, so that he landed hard on the ground. He was winded and had let go of his sword – Williams was always telling him to wind the cord around his wrist so that he would keep it even if his fingers let go.

Musket shots rattled like the sound of a child dragging a stick along a rail fence. Hanley pushed himself up, chest still sore. His sword was stuck in the ground, its blade a little bent. He grabbed it and saw that the regiment was only thirty yards or so ahead of him, Truscott standing beside his company as the men reloaded.

Hanley caught up, and saw that the French had gone back but rallied and now were a misshaped mass, neither quite a column or a line. They had given way, but not run, and they were loading and firing as each man was ready. The young ensign was calling encouragement to the men when a ball hit his fist as he raised it to wave his sword. He screamed, a horrible piercing scream, and as he was helped to the rear Hanley saw that it had driven into his knuckles.

'My sword,' the boy sobbed. 'I must not leave my sword.'

'Do not worry, I shall preserve it,' Truscott told him. 'It will be waiting for you when you return.'

A man twisted as he fell back from the rear rank, blood and pieces of tooth spilling out from a hole in his cheek. The 106th fired at the enemy and all across the field there were shouts and shots as the British advanced and the French clung stubbornly on. Hanley saw General Graham, horseless and hatless, urging the Coldstream Guards to pour more fire into the French. The elderly Scotsman must have just arrived which suggested that the fighting was over on the hill.

Hanley did not hear the order, but again the men around him started to cheer and the 106th lowered their bayonets and charged. He joined in the yell, running beside Truscott, and he saw the French give way a little more, what little was left of their formation seeping away.

Yet once again they did not go far, and when they stopped the irregular mass still would not give in and resumed its heavy fire. A man in the front rank of the company was hit in the belly and flung back, knocking down his rear rank man, who cursed him until he saw how badly his friend was hurt. Beside him a redcoat turned his head just before he was struck and the ball smashed his left eye and broke his nose.

'My man, you should not have stayed behind.' Truscott spoke to a greenjacket lying in the grass with his rifle at the ready. The

383

95th had long since retired after their noble efforts holding up the enemy advance and it was curious to find one still here.

'Do you hear?'

Hanley knelt beside the rifleman, and the movement saved him because a ball sang through the air where his head had been an instant before. The greenjacket still did not move, but there was not a scratch on him. Hanley patted his shoulder, and the motion was enough to make the man's shako fall to the side. A ball had entered his forehead and the back of his skull was gone, a ghastly mixture of grey matter, bone and hair pooled in his cap.

'Good God,' Truscott said. 'And he looked so lifelike.'

'The rifle appears to be loaded.'

'Thomas,' Truscott called to one of his men. 'You are the finest shot. Take this rifle and see if you can take revenge for its poor master.'

Corporal Thomas stepped out from the rear rank, slinging his musket over his shoulder.

'How about that bold fellow?' Truscott suggested, gesturing with his sword at a French officer near the front of the mass ahead of them. The man was brandishing a gilded eagle on a blue staff, making the tricolour flag flap as he tried to get the men to rally and attack. Each French regiment had an eagle, given to them by Napoleon, and carried by the first battalion.

'No, the green rascal on horseback!' Hanley said, and made sure that Thomas could see Sinclair with another mounted officer near the flank of the enemy battalion. 'Knock that treacherous bugger down and I'll give you ten guineas.'

Thomas laid his own firelock down and raised the rifle, hefting it to get a sense of its balance. Shots whipped past or flicked through the grass, but he ignored them and took careful aim.

Hanley saw Sinclair turn, recognise him, and his mouth opened to shout. Then Thomas fired, his discharge muted with all the other shots close and far. The officer beside Sinclair fell back in his saddle, arms flung wide as a dark stain spread above his heart.

Sinclair grinned at him – Hanley could see the mocking triumph even at this distance – and then spurred away.

'Charge! Come on the One Hundred and Sixth!' This time Hanley caught FitzWilliam's shout and he began to yell as all the redcoats somehow found the strength to go forward again. The French mass dissolved at last as the British rushed at it – one moment solid and the next instant a crowd cascading to the rear. Hanley saw a group of men led by the colonel going for the eagle, but before they were close it was spirited away and dipped, so that it could no longer be seen in the press.

The slow and the reluctant stayed and a few were caught, the long bayonets doing their work, but most surrendered and the rest escaped. Everywhere the French were giving way.

Sinclair knew the battle was lost. He was still not quite sure how it had happened, for he had not seen any Spanish and he was sure the French outnumbered the redcoats. Somehow they had still been driven back. He galloped back to find General Leval in the hope that the reserve battalions could still save the day, although he knew in his heart that the chance was gone.

'*Faugh A Ballagh!*' The shout was so unexpected that he reined in violently, his horse twisting its head in discomfort as he tugged at its bit. '*Faugh A Ballagh!*'

A battalion of redcoats with deep green facings were yelling the cry as they drove back a column of the 8ième Ligne. The French infantry had left it to the last minute before they broke before the onslaught, but when the second battalion ran they went straight into a confused mass of their own first battalion. Men collided, pressed up against each other, and it turned into a tightly packed mob, unable to move.

'*Faugh A Ballagh!*' It was so odd to hear the Gaelic, a tongue to which he had not been born, but had learned and come to love. 'Clear the way!' they shouted, and the men of the 2/87th cleared the path with bayonets and the butts of their muskets. The Frenchmen could not run and so the Irishmen killed them, and went on killing them.

'*Faugh A Ballagh!*' The men of the 87th had been mauled by the French before Talavera, and now they saw that enemy at their mercy and found that they had little. Sinclair saw a man whose musket had broken grab a Frenchmen and wrestle him to the ground, where he pounded his skull with a rock.

The eagle of the 8ième Ligne was in the press, Sinclair could see it protected by a knot of moustached veterans who were not running. It was just a plain blue staff, for the regiment had left the flag in store, but the men who protected it were NCOs chosen for their courage even if they often lacked the education to command. A surge of Irishmen led by an ensign came at them, and the lad dodged the halberd of one of the eagle guard and thrust his slim sword through the body of the officer carrying the precious standard. The man died, and for a moment the young ensign had hold of the blue staff. One of the guards fired a pistol, which missed the officer and killed a private running up to help him. Then another Frenchman jabbed with his bayonet, and the ensign arched his back away as he screamed, until another bayonet took him in the throat.

A big sergeant came at them, wearing the shoulder wings and white plume of a grenadier, and he jabbed with his half-pike and ran through one of the men who had killed his officer. He ripped the blade free and swung the staff, tumbling another enemy with the blow and forcing the rest back.

Sinclair tried to urge his mount through the press, but could not tell what he hoped to do for he both loved and hated these fierce countrymen of his. Another of the eagle guard fell, his thigh gouged deep by the spearhead of the pike so that blood pumped from the wound and sprayed across the sergeant's white trousers. He recovered his balance, stamped forward and killed the man who had picked up the eagle.

The crowd split apart. Suddenly there was enough room to run and so hundreds of men fled, and as they pushed by his horse, Sinclair found himself being carried with them. The slowest still fell to the Irish bayonets, but they were few and the remnants of the 8ième Ligne escaped. Behind them they left the big Irish sergeant holding the eagle aloft in triumph. There was a wreath fastened over its head as a battle honour, but now the Irish had taken this symbol of pride and the regiment would have to live with the shame.

'Bejabers, boys, I have the cuckoo!' Sinclair heard the cry in so familiar an accent and he laughed amid the bitterness of defeat.

EPILOGUE

It had been dark for hours by the time the men of the Flank Battalion felt the wood planks of the bridge of boats beneath their feet. After so many miles of mud and earth the springiness was an odd sensation, especially when the boats shifted under their weight and with the tide. Williams heard the cables creak and hoped that the Spanish engineers had done a good job when they made the crossing. The Light Company proceeded in silence, too tired even to complain about another night march or the uselessness of their allies. It was almost midnight on a day when they had fought a battle and lost so many comrades. There were Spanish soldiers holding torches to guide them across the bridge, and in the flickering light Williams thought his men's faces looked blank, eyes staring without seeing as they shuffled along, struggling to take each new step. The bridge led to the Isla, and if a man kept on this road he would come in time to Cadiz.

They had won the battle, driving the French away, and the two squadrons of KGL hussars had done sterling work chasing the fleeing enemy, and driving back the dragoons who tried to screen the retreat. The Germans took prisoners, and two more French cannon, but they could not prevent Marshal Victor from following the road back to Chiclana. Whittingham, the Englishman in charge of the Spanish cavalry, had done little. Captain general La Peña had done even less, sitting with ten thousand men faced by a quarter of their number of French soldiers. He could easily have driven them back, as easily have cut off Victor as he retreated, but he had not. Instead the regiments under his command had chafed and sat idle.

Two hours ago a Spanish colonel, no less, had come up to Williams, a mere lieutenant, and apologised. 'The man should be shot,' he had declared of his own commander. 'He is a useless coward and we must be rid of his kind if we are to win this war.'

The Walloon Guards and the Ciudad Real Regiment had reached Barrosa Hill a mere ten minutes after the British had captured it, having force-marched back as soon as they received the order. Williams' men had joined the other redcoats in jeering the approaching soldiers. It was unfair because they were good and willing regiments, but with so many fallen comrades the men of the Light Company were not inclined to be fair.

There was a rumour that General Graham and the Spanish commander had argued, and whether or not it was true the British had gone back to the Isla. The Spanish had not, although it seemed unlikely that they would stay on their own. Victor's men were driven off, but their regiments were not crippled, and so once the Allies crossed back to the Isla, the French would no doubt resume the siege as if nothing had happened.

'We've lost twelve hundred men,' Hanley had told him earlier on, 'and the French at least two thousand,' and yet for all that blood they would all soon be back where they started.

Their friend had been able to bring them news of the battalion, which had done well under FitzWilliam's leadership. 'He is mentioned in the dispatch, as is MacAndrews. Stanhope tells me that the general is sure there will be a brevet for him.'

Hanley saved the best news until last. He must have known that the story had spread around the little army with the speed of the electric matter so talked about in recent years and demonstrated on the London stage. 'The Eighty-seventh have taken an eagle. It is to go with the dispatch back to England. A sergeant took it and he is promised a commission.'

Their friend had said more, assuring Williams that he was due a substantial sum of prize money from the Navy. He had said as much before, when the Welshmen had come through the lines to Tarifa, and yet it did sound far-fetched. Jane MacAndrews was not far away, probably asleep in her bed as anyone of sense ought to be at this hour. Their last meeting had been one of joyous hope, cruelly interrupted, but the long months had not altered the essential truth that she was rich and he was not. Prize money brought fortunes for admirals and considerable wealth for captains. While pleasant enough, he doubted it would make him the girl's equal and so the hope could be no more than a daydream.

Love was not enough without honour, although he could imagine Pringle struggling to understand and Hanley filled with baffled incredulity if he dared say such a thing aloud. The thought brought memories of Guadalupe, of the love she had declared for him. He did not know whether she had escaped back to join her sister and the partisans, or what would happen to that beautiful, sad girl. The little war had horrors that even the bloody hill of Barrosa could not match.

Williams remembered the slow growth of happiness in the young woman's face, the tenderness with which she had watched him, and felt honour was a cheap word by comparison. He also recalled her dancing, the graceful sensuous movements as her skirt twirled and her shoes pounded the floor, and then the feel of her in his arms, the softness of her lips. The voice of the man he aspired to be told him that it was just as well that they had been interrupted. The man he was had no such certainty, and he found himself thinking of her touch and her smell. Tired as he was, the thrill coursed through his body and led his mind back to Jane.

'Bravo, boys, bravo!' An engineer officer was waiting as they stepped off the planking on to dry land. 'Welcome home!' The man must have greeted each unit in the same way, and his voice was hoarse from cheering them.

Williams and the Light Company marched back on to the Isla, and he could not help wondering whether it had all been worthwhile. His leg, which had behaved itself for the rest of the day, started to ache again.

'Come on, lads, step lively and we'll soon have hot food and a good night's sleep.' That, at least, was something worthwhile.

Tiredness threatened to flood over him – not just the long marches and the day's battle, but the months spent away from the regiment. The time with the partisans was already fading to seem unreal. Williams marched on, too weary to feel or think anything.

Six days after Graham's British division crossed back to the isthmus of Cadiz, a Spanish army came out of the main gate of another city. There were almost eight thousand of them, dressed as well as brushes and polish could make them in their old and faded uniforms. Each battalion had two Colours held proudly before it, and a large band played as they marched in step through the Trinidad Gate at Badajoz, following the road out of the fortress before wheeling into a field and forming up as if on parade. With them went two heavy guns, the limbers pulled by mules.

Major Jean-Baptiste Dalmas watched them with a deep sense of satisfaction, smiling as, company by company and regiment by regiment, the Spanish soldiers laid their firelocks on the ground and went into captivity. The governor of the fortress had insisted on the ritual as a mark of honour, and the French had cheerfully granted the empty symbols of a bygone age.

Marshal Soult would rightly take the credit for the capture of the fortress, although he would not have the leisure to enjoy it for tomorrow the main body of the army must return south to restore order in Andalusia. Massena was retiring from Portugal, his army starved to the point where it could no longer hold on, and that meant that the conquest of the country had failed for the moment. With this surrender, the French held three of the four great border fortresses between Spain and Portugal. The road to Lisbon could be opened again, whenever sufficient force could be gathered to do the job properly, and in the meantime the routes leading to Spain would be held against the Allies.

Dalmas had made it happen. In February he had found the route through the hills so that the French cavalry could take the Spanish army in the flank. Ten days ago, the cuirassier had waited in a hidden pit not far from the city walls, knowing from one of his paid sources that the Spanish were about to launch a sortie against the French siege lines. Brandt was with him, his British rifle carefully loaded with loose powder rather than a cartridge, and the ball wrapped in a leather patch so that it gripped the barrel tightly. His spy told him that General Rafael Menacho, the commander of the garrison, planned to watch the attack from the ramparts to encourage his men.

He did not tell anyone except Marshal Soult what he planned, and when the Spanish attacked some Frenchmen died as they overran the forward trenches. Dalmas let the fleeing French and the advancing enemy pass before he propped open the roof of their hide. A close inspection of the ramparts soon revealed the governor, peering through an embrasure.

Dalmas let Brandt take his time. There was enough room for him to be some feet away from the Polish marksman so that he could see what happened without being hindered by the smoke of the discharge. The man now wore the green uniform of Sinclair's Irish Regiment and had a sergeant's yellow stripe on his sleeve.

Brandt fired, and Dalmas saw Menacho jerk back and vanish behind the wall. They pulled the cover back over themselves and waited for the sally to be repulsed. His source soon confirmed that the governor was dead, and the next most senior officer was a timid man, lacking confidence and easily swayed by those around him. The promise of more money to another officer, who had already been generously rewarded, convinced the man to say the right things. The French pressed on with their siege, and when they sent in a summons to surrender, the new governor found a way to convince himself that capitulation was the only sensible course.

'Well done, Dalmas,' Soult said as they rode past the rows of prisoners and headed into the fortress. Its walls were formidable, the little breach the French guns had made narrow and steep. 'It would have cost us two thousand men to get in and even then we might have failed.'

'Instead it cost us thousands of gold coins,' Dalmas said.

'King Joseph's money, and he can afford it.' The marshal

spurred ahead, for he must lead the procession into the town, but Dalmas was happy to lag behind. The war would go on, and in the years to come the French would win. In the meantime there would be plenty of opportunities for an able soldier to gain high rank and fortune. Dalmas was a very happy man as he rode through the Trinidad Gate into Badajoz.

HISTORICAL NOTE

Run Them Ashore is a novel, but the story is firmly grounded in fact and I have done my best to describe the real events and people as accurately as possible. The 106th Foot is an invention, but I have tried to make its officers and men act, speak and function like their real counterparts. This is the fifth story in the series begun in *True Soldier Gentlemen*, and it opens at a time when Allied fortunes in the Peninsular War were at their lowest ebb and ends just when things were beginning to turn around. Even so, it would be another year before the balance openly shifted in their favour.

The title comes from a song about the Royal Navy, which played an essential if often ignored role in the ultimate success of Wellington and his soldiers. British intervention in Portugal and Spain would have been impossible without the Navy's capacity to land them there. Continuing the war would have been equally impossible without British control of the sea routes to and from the Spanish Peninsula. Wellington's complex series of fortifications, the lines of Torres Vedras, are justly famous for stopping the French invasion. Yet they relied on his army as a mobile reserve to block any breakthrough. That army could not have been fed without constant shipments of grain and other supplies brought by sea. Sufficient transport ships and escorts were kept at Lisbon so that the entire army could have been evacuated if it became necessary. Without this assurance it is doubtful that Wellington would have stayed where he was, and it is certain that the ministers in London would not have let him risk Britain's only field army.

We remember Trafalgar and Nelson, but can easily forget that British naval supremacy over the next decade was maintained only by immense effort. There were no more fleet actions on that scale, and much of the work was unglamorous, maintaining a blockade year in year out around ports like Brest and Toulon. The Navy was expensive – far more so than the army – and it needed to keep growing, for there were never quite enough ships to perform all its roles without risk. Several of the ships featured in the story were quite new at the time – HMS *Rodney* had been launched only in December 1809 at Deptford. Each year Napoleon was building more line-of-battle ships than Britain – in part because he controlled more of the resources necessary for shipbuilding. The French would struggle to man them, particularly to man them with well-trained crews, but over time the numbers would swing more and more in their favour. Hence the deep worries of admirals and ministers alike that the French would seize the remnants of the Spanish fleet and its dockyard supplies.

There was more than a little irony in Cadiz becoming the focus of so much naval activity just a few years after Trafalgar. A strong British squadron was stationed there, alongside the Spanish and French ships they had so recently been blockading. The French ships became prison hulks – the dramatic escapes of men on two of these mentioned in the book did occur, and it was only with some effort that I resisted the temptation to alter the real chronology and have these episodes happening during the story. By 1810 most of the Spanish ships were in a very poor state. In real life as in the story the seventy-four-gun *El Vencedor* had to be towed by the *Rodney* when it carried British troops to Fuengirola, and sank with all hands soon after that operation.

Keeping the army supplied and reinforced meant the protection of transport ships, which in turn involved the Navy in the difficult and unpopular business of escorting convoys. The burden of these fell on the smaller ships, such as frigates, sloops and brigs, and the principal threat was not the French Navy, but the privateers which were encouraged to establish themselves in the ports of southern Spain. Some French generals even invested in these little ships and their crews as a moneymaking enterprise as well as a contribution to the war effort. Their prey included not only British transports and the smallest Navy vessels, but Spanish and other ships coming from the New World. Most captains far preferred orders allowing them to cruise in search of these privateers rather than the dull routine of convoy escort. Yet the privateers were numerous and the Navy was overstretched, so that at best they controlled the problem and could not solve it. 'Cutting out' raids to take or burn privateers and any enemy merchant vessels were common whenever the Navy was able to find the ships and men to undertake them. The attack on Las Arenas in the story is as fictional as the place itself, but is based on real operations. Casualties in such attacks were often one-sided, and if they went well the Navy suffered little loss while inflicting serious damage on the enemy.

In the autumn of 1810 most of Spain was under French control apart from a few coastal areas. The French would most probably have taken Cadiz had it not been for the swift action of the Duke of Alburquerque – who was subsequently attacked by his rivals, sent to London as ambassador and died there a few months later. If Soult had taken the city and the last remnants of the Spanish government, then the rest of the country might well have collapsed. With Wellington fallen back to the lines of Torres Vedras it was very hard for anyone to be optimistic about the Allied cause in these months. The Navy's control of the sea meant that he could cling on there, allowed some support to be sent to Spanish enclaves on the coast, and permitted Cadiz to be reinforced.

Cadiz lay in a naturally strong position, but modern historians have been a little too ready to see it as impossible for the French to take without strong naval forces. This is certainly not the impression gained by reading Graham's letters from the time or indeed the comments of naval officers who were concerned about the poor state of defences on the Isla. The race to build flotillas of gunboats and other small vessels to dominate the

Inner and Outer Harbours suggests a serious threat. The fighting there is described faithfully in the book, and involved the use of Congreve rockets and bomb ships. As the months passed, there was a steady growth in confidence, and only occasional scares. On one occasion Graham ordered a mortar to fire from just outside Cadiz itself to prove that the French batteries on the other side of the harbour were out of range. The French lacked many of the things they needed – some of the heavy guns they used were dredged at low tide from cannon belonging to ships driven ashore and wrecked after Trafalgar. Marshal Soult had others, including some mortars, cast in Seville and taken south with great effort. Some of these were able to fire on Cadiz itself, although in the event they achieved very little.

Cadiz proved secure, and was packed with politicians and refugees so that for a while it became one of the most populous cities in Spain. Many Spanish as well as British observers were shocked by the impression of a community too busy with politics and with celebrations to worry about the dire state of the war. One officer from the 79th Foot – later the Cameron Highlanders – noted in his journal that he attended one party where '... common decency seem'd laid aside. Some of the Ladys [sic] appeared in Men's Clothes, and the men again in those of the Women. One great piece of wit amongst the Men was the dropping of handfuls of a very small sweet meat down the backs and Bosoms of the Ladys who though of course much annoyed took it all in good humour'. Thus the indignities inflicted on Jane MacAndrews have their basis in fact, but I did not feel Williams would be inclined to show such 'good humour.' Similarly there are many stories of hired assassins prowling the streets to seek vengeance for real or imagined slights. No doubt these tales exaggerated the frequency of such things, but they are common enough to justify this episode.

The French never attempted a real assault on Cadiz, but the siege lasted until 1812 and thus with hindsight it is easy to see its outcome as a foregone conclusion. Yet allowing the Regency Council and Cortes to stay secure and holding on to this enclave were ways of staving off defeat, much like Wellington's strategy in Portugal, and Allied leaders were keen to find ways of striking back. It was rightly considered essential to encourage and support the irregulars fighting the guerrilla – the little war. On several occasions Spanish regular troops launched what were effectively raids into enemy-held territory, sometimes coming by sea or setting out from the shelter of Gibraltar or other coastal towns still held by the Allies. The most successful were probably those operations where they never encountered serious opposition and withdrew before the French caught them. In such cases the gain was making the enemy gather a field force, drawing troops away from other duties. The French were left frustrated and tired, and usually it meant that other areas were stripped of troops and so offered better opportunities for the irregulars.

The landing at Fuengirola was a slightly more ambitious attempt at similar ends. It was dreamed up by the governor of Gibraltar and his naval counterpart, won the backing of the Spanish, and happened even though its objectives were never very clear. In real life command was given to Major General Lord Blayney, who left a lively account both of the operation itself and his subsequent captivity. I have not based the character of Lord Turney on him, wanting a fictional leader, but in every other respect I have tried to present a faithful account of what actually happened. It is hard to know whether the intended objective of Malaga was ever feasible. Perhaps it might have been taken, but it is less likely that it could have been held. The real-life Blayney seems to have abandoned it quickly, but did not decide what he wanted to do instead and became obsessed with taking Sohail Castle. Although a brave man with a long record of distinguished service as a subordinate, his performance as a commander was much less impressive, in spite of his personal courage. The castle – which has been restored and can be seen today – might have succumbed to the heavy firepower of HMS *Rodney*, but since she did not arrive until too late, there was no means of breaching its walls. Instead Blayney seems to have expected the garrison to give in, in part because he dismissed them as poorly motivated foreign auxiliaries.

The Polish soldiers of the Fourth Regiment of the Grand Duchy of Warsaw – a recent creation of the Emperor Napoleon, who stopped short of reuniting all Polish territory into one kingdom – proved him wrong. There were 153 of these men in the castle at the start, reinforced by 63 who sneaked in during the first night of the siege. Another force of some 200 infantrymen along with some 80 men of the French 21st Dragoons launched the bold attack to relieve the garrison. It was not good cavalry country and the dragoons played only a minor if significant role. Blayney had four companies of the 2/87th, the Imperial Toledo Regiment, the short-lived foreign regiment referred to as Chasseurs (and formally named the Foreign Recruits Battalion), as well as artillerymen, sailors and marines – more than 1,600 men in total. Two flank companies of the 82nd Foot – whose shoes are filled by my fictional 106th in the story – landed near the end along with some marines, so that the grand total was probably nearer two thousand. In spite of these odds, the Poles comprehensively trounced Lord Blayney's expedition, and captured the general as well as large numbers of his men and a lot of stores. Blayney's ornate sword remains in the collection of Krakow Museum.

The sources for the combat at Fuengirola are poor and often in conflict, and I confess that I do not have the linguistic skills to access the Polish accounts directly. I have tried to be accurate, and, when I could not find the information, to represent it in a way that was at least plausible. The sources for the uniform worn by the Fourth Regiment in October 1810 are contradictory. There is even less readily available information about the chasseurs, other than to say that they were raised from prisoners and deserters.

If Turney's real-life predecessor Lord Blayney offers an example of poor British generalship, La Peña's performance during the Barrosa campaign was even worse. As described, the Allies were carried by sea down the coast, and then marched from Tarifa back towards Cadiz. The Spanish general kept moving at night, which meant that the column strayed on several occasions, tiring his own and the British soldiers. He does not seem to have been at all clear about what he hoped to achieve. The Spanish regiments under his command performed as well as his dismal leadership permitted. The division commanded by Zayas would fight with great distinction later in the year at Albuera. At Barrosa on 5 March 1811, they were kept idle by their commander and thus unable to support their allies in any meaningful way.

Barrosa is an odd battle in many respects, not least because both the British and the French were convinced that they were heavily outnumbered. The totals were closer to roughly 5,000 British against 7,000 French. Victor's men were veterans, and the sources all claim that they fought the battle in their finest uniforms, and mention the French bands. In contrast few of Graham's men had seen much active service. Several of the units were second battalions, generally composed of younger soldiers, and others served in detachments, such as the composite battalion composed of companies from the Coldstream and Third Guards – who in the event ended up fighting separately.

The attack on Barrosa Hill by the Flank Battalion occurred as described apart from the inclusion of my fictional characters. It was led in reality by Brevet Lieutenant Colonel Browne of the 28th Foot, who did indeed ride ahead of his men singing 'Heart of Oak'. The exchanges between MacAndrews and General Graham follow a subaltern's account of what was really said. Browne came through the action unscathed, but his battalion lost 236 men from the 514 who began the climb and for a long time became no more than a thin skirmish line. Their advance gave the rest of the brigade the chance to deploy and launch a bigger attack. The British were deployed in line and opposed the French in column, but the advantages of the former formation in terms of firepower do not in themselves explain the outcome. Accounts suggest that this was a very hard-fought action, and that it would not have taken much for either side to break. Something kept the less experienced British soldiers in the fight longer than their opponents, and it was the French who gave way. The same was true of the fighting between Leval's division and Wheatley's brigade.

In many ways the French army remained a more sophisticated machine than the British, and it was certainly more experienced, especially in large-scale operations. As one Guards officer put it – 'For 360 days in the year, the Frenchman is a better soldier than an Englishman. Their movements compared to ours are as mail coaches to dung carts ... But at fighting we beat them and they know it.' At Barrosa the margin between success and failure was probably tiny, but the British somehow won, even when they were in a bad position and there was no Wellington to lead them. General Graham had turned his army round and showed inspirational courage. Yet in the end the battle was a series of fights won by the individual battalions and companies.

Sinclair is fictional, but Napoleon did maintain a green-coated Irish Legion and most of their officers were Irish, even if the rank and file were not. Parties went around trying to recruit redcoat prisoners and were not too fussy about soliciting Scots and English as well as the Irish. In the event there were few volunteers, and so they became a repository for all the army's strays. Far more genuinely Irish was the 87th, which was granted the title of 'the Prince of Wales' own Irish' after taking the eagle of the 8ième Ligne at Barrosa. It was the first taken in battle by any British soldiers and was paraded in London and made to dip before British Colours. Ensign Keogh was the first to take the standard, but was killed, and it was Sergeant Masterson of the Grenadier Company who took and held the eagle. He was rewarded with a commission, although in a foreign corps stationed in the unhealthy West Indies. The 8ième Ligne claimed for some time that the eagle had been knocked off by a cannonball and merely lost, but were eventually forced to admit its capture. Such reticence over lost symbols of pride is common enough in all armies, but Napoleon was especially sensitive to such things.

Barrosa was a tactical victory, but the subsequent withdrawal to Cadiz rendered it of little or no strategic value. The news probably hurried Soult on his way south, but the loss of Badajoz far outbalanced any damage inflicted on the French cause by their defeat in what was a relatively small action. General Graham was disgusted by his Spanish allies, and especially a campaign fought out in the Cadiz press over what had happened. He was very glad to go and join Wellington in Portugal. Some of the troops from Barrosa went with him, and that is where the 106th will also soon go.

After I had finished the book it was pointed out to me that the word shrapnel was not used until the middle of the nineteenth century for the spherical case shot invented by an RA officer called Henry Shrapnell. For a while I wondered about changing the word, but in the end decided that it has too great a resonance and so it is used once or twice. I will try to prevent any of the characters using it in speech in any future stories, but suspect that I will not be able to resist including it in descriptions.

Finally, with the bicentenary of Waterloo coming in June 2015, I would recommend that anyone with an interest in Wellington's men visit the website of Waterloo 200 – http://www.waterloo200.org – which has a lot of information about the planned commemorations.

CAST OF CHARACTERS

Names underlined are fictional characters.

The 106th Regiment of Foot

Captain Billy PRINGLE – Born into a family with a long tradition of service in the Royal Navy, Pringle's short-sightedness and severe seasickness led his father to send him to Oxford with a view to becoming a parson. Instead Pringle persuaded his parents to secure him a commission in the army. Plump, easygoing, and overfond of both drink and women, Pringle has found active service easier to deal with than the quiet routine and temptations of garrison duty in Britain. Through the battles in Portugal, and the arduous campaign in Spain, Billy Pringle has won promotion and found himself easing into his role as a leader. Part of a detachment whose ship was driven back to Portugal after being evacuated from Corunna, Pringle served in the 3rd Battalion of Detachments at Talavera and was wounded in the last moments of the battle. After a brief spell in Britain, he returned to Spain, serving at Ciudad Rodrigo and the River Côa in 1810.

Captain William HANLEY – Illegitimate son of an actress and a banker, Hanley was raised by his grandmother and spent years in Madrid as an aspiring artist. His father's death ended his allowance, and reluctantly Hanley took up a commission in the 106th purchased for him many years before. He served in Portugal in 1808, suffering a wound at Roliça. Since then his fluency in Spanish has led to periodic staff duties. Even so, he was with Pringle and the Grenadier Company throughout the retreat to Corunna. Captured by the French, he escaped and has found himself involved in intelligence work. He was wounded at Talavera. In 1810 he was once again employed on detached service, gathering intelligence and often operating behind French lines.

Lieutenant Hamish WILLIAMS – Williams joined the 106th as a Gentleman Volunteer, serving in the ranks and soon proving himself to be a natural soldier. He was commissioned as ensign following the Battle of Vimeiro. During the retreat to Corunna, he became cut off from the main army. Rallying a band of stragglers, he not only led them back to the main force, but thwarted a French column attempting to outflank the British Army. He was praised by Sir John Moore for his actions, and was beside the general when the latter was mortally wounded at Corunna. In 1809 he was promoted to lieutenant and commanded a company in the 3rd Battalion of Detachments and fought with distinction at Talavera. Returning to Spain, he was left in charge of a small party of redcoats and Spanish infantry when the French besieged the frontier town of Ciudad Rodrigo. He also saw action in several border skirmishes and at the River Côa. Fervently in love with Jane MacAndrews, Williams' cause seems to be continually thwarted by her unpredictability and his clumsiness, and most recently by her acquisition of a considerable fortune.

Captain TRUSCOTT – A close friend of Pringle, Hanley and Williams, the slightly stiff-mannered Truscott was wounded at Vimeiro and suffered the loss of his left arm. A slow recovery kept him from participating in the Corunna campaign. He served in the 3rd Battalion of Detachments and by the end of the Battle of Talavera was its commander.

Major Alastair MACANDREWS – Now aged fifty, MacAndrews first saw service as a young ensign in the American War of Independence. A gifted and experienced soldier, his lack of connections or wealth have kept his career slow. Raised to major after decades spent as a captain, he took charge of the 106th at Roliça, and led the battalion throughout the retreat to Corunna. Given the temporary local rank of lieutenant colonel, he led a training mission sent to Spain and became involved in the border fighting in 1810, fighting with distinction at the River Côa. He has now returned to the battalion as a major and its second-in-command.

Lieutenant Colonel FITZWILLIAM – The new commander of the 106th, fresh from the Guards. He has some connection with Wickham, although the two do not seem close.

Lieutenant BLACK – Subaltern in the Light Company, and its acting commander in the absence of Wickham. Black was promoted from ensign when he transferred from the militia and brought thirty recruits with him.

Ensign DERRYCK – Senior ensign in the battalion, he served in Portugal and Spain in 1808–09.

Sergeant DOBSON – Veteran soldier who was Williams' 'front rank man' and took the volunteer under his wing. The relationship between Dobson and the young officer remains quietly paternal. However, at Roliça he displayed a ruthless streak when he killed an ensign who was having an affair with his daughter Jenny. Repeatedly promoted and broken for drunken misbehaviour, he has reformed following the accidental death of his first wife and his remarriage to the prim Mrs Rawson. He was wounded at Talavera, and served with Williams in Ciudad Rodrigo and at the River Côa.

Ensign DOWLING – Eighteen-year old subaltern in the Grenadier Company.

Sergeant Tom EVANS – NCO in the Light Company, Evans is an experienced but somewhat surly soldier.

Private FLATTERY – Young soldier in the Grenadier Company.

<u>Private KELLY</u> – Soldier in the Light Company.

<u>Sergeant MURPHY</u> – A capable soldier, Murphy and his wife suffered a dreadful blow when their child died during the retreat to Corunna. He fought at Corunna, and was with Williams in Ciudad Rodrigo and at the Côa.

<u>Lieutenant HATCH</u> – Former lover of Jenny Dobson, the frequently drunk Hatch was a close friend of Ensign Redman, the officer Dobson murdered at Roliça. Hatch falsely believes that Williams was the killer and has done everything he can to blacken Williams' reputation. Wounded in the face at Talavera, he remained in Spain when the other members of the 106th returned to England. After briefly rejoining the battalion, he transferred to a newly raised foreign corps and was promoted to lieutenant.

<u>Private PRYCE</u> – Welsh soldier in the Light Company and intimate of Sergeant Evans.

<u>Lieutenant RICHARDSON</u> – Twenty-year-old but boyish subaltern in the Grenadier Company.

<u>Private RYAN</u> – A veteran soldier in the Light Company.

<u>Corporal THOMAS</u> – Experienced NCO serving in Truscott's company.

<u>Brevet Major WICKHAM</u> – Handsome, plausible and well connected, Wickham continues to rise in rank and spends as little time with the 106th as possible, preferring staff appointments. Williams and many others have come to doubt his honour, honesty and courage.

Their families

<u>Jenny DOBSON</u> – Older daughter from Dobson's first marriage, Jenny has ambitions beyond following the drum and flirted

with and let herself be seduced by several of the young officers. During the retreat to Corunna she abandoned her newborn son to the care of Williams and Miss MacAndrews and left in search of a better life. She is currently the mistress of a French officer.

Mrs DOBSON – Herself the widow of a sergeant in the Grenadier Company, the very proper Annie Rawson carried her lapdog in a basket throughout the retreat to Corunna. The marriage to Dobson has done much to reform his conduct.

Jacob HANKS – Son of Dobson's daughter Jenny. His father killed and his mother run off to seek her fortune, the baby was protected by Williams and Jane. He is now being raised by Major MacAndrews' family.

Clara PRINGLE – The wife of Billy Pringle's brother Edward, Clara has recently died soon after giving birth to a baby who also perished.

Mrs Esther MACANDREWS – American wife of Major MacAndrews, Esther MacAndrews is a bold, unconventional character who has followed him to garrisons around the world. More recently, she managed to sneak out to Portugal, bringing her daughter with her, and the pair endured the horrors of the retreat to Corunna. In 1810 they once again travelled to Spain in the hope of joining her husband and the battalion.

Miss Jane MACANDREWS – Their daughter and sole surviving child, the beautiful Jane has a complicated relationship with Williams. During the retreat to Corunna, she was cut off from the main army and rescued by him, becoming involved in the desperate fight he and a band of stragglers fought to defend a vital bridge against the French under Dalmas.

Miss Ann WILLIAMS – Oldest of Williams' three sisters, Anne is an intelligent and prudent young woman.

Mrs Kitty GARLAND (née WILLIAMS) – The middle sister, Kitty is bright but impulsive, and her marriage to the light dragoon Garland occurred only after Pringle had fought the cavalryman in a duel. Garland has subsequently died of wounds received in the summer of 1810.

The (Royal) Navy (This phrase was rarely used at the time and it was more often known as the Navy)

BENNETT – Captain Pringle's coxswain on HMS *Sparrowhawk*.

Captain Sir George BURLTON – The experienced captain of HMS *Rodney*.

Thomas CLEGG – Able seaman and a topman on HMS *Sparrowhawk*.

Mr CASSIDY – Master's mate and acting lieutenant on HMS *Sparrowhawk*.

DICKINSON – Sailor aboard HMS *Sparrowhawk*.

Captain HALL – Commander of the six gunboats sent from Cadiz to join the expedition to Malaga.

Captain Henry HOPE – Son of a Royal Navy captain, Henry Hope went to sea at the age of eleven and was a captain by the time he was twenty-one. He took command of HMS *Topaze* in 1809 and has already led several successful raids and cutting-out expeditions. In later years he would win fame and a knighthood during the war with the USA.

Lieutenant JONES – The Royal Marine officer commanding the detachment of marines on board HMS *Topaze*.

John JULIUS CAESAR – Able seaman and topman aboard HMS *Sparrowhawk*, the experienced Caesar is of West Indian or African origins.

Rear Admiral Sir Richard KEATS – Took command of the squadron based at Cadiz in July 1810. Aged fifty-three, he had been in the Navy for forty years and seen extensive service in the American War of Independence and in the more recent wars with France.

MACLEAN – Sailor aboard HMS *Sparrowhawk*.

Corporal MILNE – Royal Marine NCO serving aboard HMS *Sparrowhawk*.

Mr PRENTICE – An elderly and hard-of-hearing warrant officer, he is the gunner of HMS *Sparrowhawk*.

Captain Edward PRINGLE – Master and commander of HMS *Sparrowhawk*, Edward is Billy Pringle's older brother and has followed the family tradition of going to sea. Smaller than his brother, and more sober in his manner, he has risen to command his own vessel by the age of twenty-eight. However, professional success has been marred by personal tragedy and a few months ago his wife died in childbirth.

Lieutenant REYNOLDS – The only other officer currently on board HMS *Sparrowhawk*, Reynolds is middle-aged and experienced, but unlikely to rise higher in rank.

Midshipman TREADWELL – A young midshipman on HMS *Sparrowhawk*.

The British

Mr Ezekiel BAYNES – A merchant with long experience of the Peninsula, now serving as an adviser and agent of the government.

Lieutenant BRAMWELL – A subaltern in the 82nd Foot, currently serving as adjutant to MacAndrews in the Flank Battalion.

Corporal BRANDT – Polish deserter serving with the rifle armed company of the Chasseurs.

Lieutenant General Colin CAMPBELL – Appointed governor of Gibraltar in 1810. He also sent a garrison to Tarifa and helped to inspire the attempt to take Malaga.

Major General William DILKES – One of the brigade commanders in Graham's division.

Captain DOUGLAS – Company commander from the 82nd Foot serving in the Flank Battalion.

Major DUNCAN – Officer in the Royal Artillery commanding the guns with Graham's division.

Major GOUGH – Acting commander of the 2/87th Foot.

Lieutenant General Thomas GRAHAM – Born in 1748, Graham became a soldier in his forties after the coffin carrying his late wife was desecrated by French revolutionaries claiming to search for weapons. He served as a volunteer at Toulon in 1793, raised a regiment at his own expense – the 90th Foot – and saw considerable service, notably in Egypt in 1801. A close friend of Sir John Moore, he served on the latter's staff in Spain. He has recently been appointed to command the British and Portuguese troops at Cadiz.

Major GRANT – Commander of the detachment from the 2/89th Foot forming part of the landing at Fuengirola.

Captain HARDING – The senior engineer in the force landed at Fuengirola.

Richard HENEGAN – An officer in the commissariat currently serving in Cadiz. He later wrote a lively account of his service in the Peninsular War and at Waterloo.

Private JORGESEN – Danish deserter serving in the rifle company of the Chasseurs. He is a close comrade of Brandt.

Captain KEITH – Company commander in the 2/89th.

Captain MILLER – An officer from the 95th Foot on detached service as liaison with the partisans in Andalusia.

Lieutenant General Sir John MOORE – One of the most widely admired British commanders of the era, Moore had been sent with an army into Spain in the autumn of 1808. As the Spanish armies were overpowered by strong French forces led by Napoleon in person, Moore was eventually forced to retreat through the mountains to Corunna. He was mortally wounded in a battle fought outside the city, but his army was able to embark without serious interference from the French.

Mr Daniel MUDGE – Confidential clerk to Lieutenant General Campbell, the governor of Gibraltar.

Sergeant MUELLER – Veteran NCO serving in the rifle company of the Chasseurs.

Captain MULLINS – Brigade major in the force landed at Fuengirola.

Captain SAMSON – British officer operating with the partisans.

Major James SINCLAIR – A Protestant Irishman, Sinclair holds a commission in the Chasseurs, a corps formed from enemy deserters and prisoners. Little is known about him or his former military experience, but he has spent much of the year with the various bands of partisans along the coast. Not always popular, the Spanish have nicknamed him 'Sinclair the bad'.

Captain James STANHOPE – Guards officer currently serving on General Graham's staff. He produced a journal which has survived and recently been published.

Major General Lord TURNEY (formerly Jack Stevenson) – An experienced officer given command of the expedition to take Malaga. Well into his forties, Lord Turney remains an active man and attempts to look younger than his years. He has a reputation for bravery and as something of a rake.

Lieutenant General Viscount WELLINGTON – After several highly successful campaigns in India, Wellesley returned to Britain and several years of frustrated ambition before being given command of the expedition to Portugal. He managed to win the battles of Roliça and Vimeiro before being superseded. Along with his superiors, Wellesley was then recalled to Britain following the public outrage at the Convention of Cintra, which permitted the defeated French to return home in British ships. Cleared of responsibility, Wellesley was given command in Portugal and honoured with a title for his victory at Talavera.

The Reverend Joseph WHARTON – Sir Richard Keats' chaplain is also in charge of coordinating the gathering of intelligence, performing for the admiral the same role undertaken for Lord Wellington by Ezekiel Baynes.

Colonel William WHEATLEY – One of the brigade commanders in Graham's division.

The French and their Allies

Giuseppe BAVASTRO – A Genoese privateer who operated under a letter of marque from Napoleon and was both praised and decorated by the Emperor. From 1810, he commanded a squadron of small raiding vessels operating from ports along Spain's southern coast.

Major Emile BERTRAND – An engineer officer serving with Massena.

KING JOSEPH Bonaparte – As Napoleon's older brother, Joseph has reluctantly been moved from the comfort of his kingdom in Naples to Spain, where he finds himself less welcome. A man of strong literary and philosophical tastes, he has done his best to win popularity. Recently he has lifted a ban imposed on bullfighting by the chief minister of his Spanish predecessor.

<u>Private KAMINSKI</u> – Polish soldier in the garrison of Sohail Castle. He has previously served in the Russian artillery.

Marshal Andrea MASSENA – Prince of Essling, Duc de Rivoli. Born at Nice in 1758 (which was then part of the Kingdom of Sardinia and not in France), Massena was the son of a shopkeeper and served in the ranks of the French army for fourteen years, but did not become an officer until the Revolution. From then on, his rise was rapid, and he was a general by 1793. He served with great distinction, particularly in a succession of campaigns fought in Italy. Napoleon dubbed him the 'spoiled favourite of victory' and was willing to trust him with independent commands. In 1809 he helped to stave off utter defeat at the Battle of Aspern-Essling. The rigours of campaigning and an unhealthy lifestyle made him appear even older than his sixty-one years, and Massena hoped to retire to the comfort of his estates. Alongside his reputation as a soldier, he had earned another as a rapacious plunderer, and loot had supplemented official rewards to make him an extremely wealthy man. Although perhaps past his best by the time he came to Spain, Wellington had immense respect for Marshal Massena's skill. After capturing Ciudad Rodrigo and Almeida, he has advanced deep into Portugal.

Marshal Michel NEY, Duc d'Elchingen – Born in 1769, the red-faced Ney was the son of a barrel-cooper in the Saar country on the border with the German states. He enlisted in the ranks of a hussar regiment, and was another gifted leader who was rapidly promoted after the Revolution. In four years he rose from sergeant major to general. His courage was never in doubt – Napoleon would later dub him 'the bravest of the brave' – but his judgement was less certain. He was certainly experienced and at times showed great skill. Yet he was also readily offended, and inclined to lose his temper or sulk, and proved a difficult subordinate. He commands a corps in Massena's army.

General Andoche JUNOT – Born in 1771, Junot was a law student who volunteered to join the revolutionary army in 1793.

He caught Napoleon's eye at the siege of Toulon, and received successive promotions in the years that followed. Prone to outbursts of temper, he proved less capable when made a general and given charge of the invasion of Portugal in 1807, and was defeated by the British at Vimeiro a year later. He commands a corps in Massena's army.

Capitaine Jean-Baptiste DALMAS – A former schoolteacher, Dalmas was conscripted into the army and took readily to the life of a soldier, serving in most of the Emperor's great campaigns and winning promotion. Since 1808 he has served as a supernumerary ADC to Marshal Ney and proved himself to be both a brave and an intelligent officer. The only blemish on his career has been his failure to seize a bridge so that the French could outflank Sir John Moore's British army as it retreated towards Corunna. On that occasion he was repulsed by a ragtag band of stragglers led by Hamish Williams. In 1810 he was tasked with capturing or killing Hanley. The British officer escaped, but during the pursuit Dalmas uncovered the vulnerability of General Craufurd's Light Division and helped Marshal Ney drive the British back across the River Côa.

General LEVAL – Divisional commander in Marshal Victor's corps, Leval has already encountered British troops at Talavera.

Captain MLOKOSIEWICZ – Officer commanding the company of the 4th Regiment of the Grand Duchy of Warsaw garrisoning Sohail Castle. He was subsequently decorated with the Cross of the Legion of Honour for his part in the siege.

Marshal MORTIER – Born in 1768, Mortier became a soldier early in the Revolution and saw extensive service in the years that followed. He belonged to the marshals promoted when the Emperor created the rank in 1804. In Spain he commands the V Corps and is subordinate to Soult.

General RUFFIN – Divisional commander in Marshal Victor's corps, Ruffin has already encountered British troops at Talavera.

General SEBASTIANI – Like Napoleon himself, Sebastiani hailed from Corsica. He became closely associated with the future Emperor early on. In his career he has mixed diplomatic with military posts, but has proved a capable if unexceptional soldier. He has also acquired a reputation as a voracious plunderer.

Marshal Jean-de-Dieu SOULT, Duke of Dalmatia – Born in 1769, he served in the ranks of the Royal Army before rising rapidly in the revolutionary army, and was a general by 1799. He served in Italy and on the Rhine, and was chosen as one of the first batch of marshals in 1804. He played a distinguished role at Austerlitz, Jena and Eylau, before being sent to Spain. He led the pursuit of Sir John Moore's army, but was evicted from Portugal by Sir Arthur Wellesley later in 1809. In 1810 he led the invasion of Andalusia, and has been placed in command of the French armies in the south.

Marshal VICTOR, Duke of Belluno – Victor originally served in the ranks of the artillery, and then won rapid promotion during the Revolutionary Wars so that within three years he led an entire division. He has fought and beaten the Austrians, Prussians, Russians and recently the Spanish, and is a capable, if extremely aggressive, commander. At Talavera his divisions gained some success, but were eventually repulsed by the British of Lord Wellington and he is eager to gain revenge.

Sergeant ZAKREWSKI – An NCO in the 4th Regiment of the Grand Duchy of Warsaw who took charge of the two heavy guns in Sohail Castle.

The Spanish

General Joaquín BLAKE – One of many descendants of Irish exiles to rise to high rank in the Spanish army, Blake commands the army in Murcia. He is also a member of the Regency

Council. Although his commitment to the cause is unquestioned, there is less confidence in his military ability.

Don Juan BUERA – The successful leader of a band of guerrilleros.

General Rafael MENACHO – The experienced and energetic commander of the garrison of Badajoz.

El PASTOR – 'The shepherd', leader of a small band of guerrilleros.

Don Manuel La PEÑA, Captain General of Andalusia – The senior Spanish officer at Cadiz had a poor military record and was considered more of a politician than a soldier.

Marquis de la ROMANA – An experienced soldier, Romana proved more capable than many of his peers at concerting his operations with his British and Portuguese allies. In 1808 he commanded a division of the best Spanish regiments stationed by Napoleon in the Baltic, but with the aid of the Royal Navy was able to bring the bulk of his men back to Spain. He commands the Spanish army supporting the fortress of Badajoz.

RAMIREZ – Partisan expelled from El Blanco's band for looting.

RAMON – Partisan serving with El Blanco's band.

Don Julián SANCHEZ García/El CHARRO – One of the most famous of the guerrilla leaders, El Charro operated from Ciudad Rodrigo. A former soldier who had served in the ranks of the Spanish army, over time his band has developed into a regiment of irregular lancers.

Lieutenant VEGA – Officer originally from Fuengirola sent with Hanley and Williams on a mission to the partisans in that area.

Carlos VELASCO – Former surgeon in the Spanish navy, he

now serves as a lieutenant in the partisan band of his cousin, Don Antonio.

Don Antonio VELASCO, El Blanco – The leader of a band of partisans in the mountains around Ronda, Don Antonio's nickname comes from his white hair.

Paula VELASCO – Wife of Don Antonio, she and her sister ride and fight with his partisans.

Guadalupe – The younger sister of Paula, she was living in a convent when it was stormed by the French and the inhabitants killed or raped. Saying little, she fights the invaders with a cold hatred.

El LOBO (aka Pedro the wolf) – A former bandit turned partisan. He is not popular with the other guerrilleros.

Colonel (later General) WHITTINGHAM – British officer serving in the Spanish army. He commands the cavalry with La Peña's force.

XAVIER – A priest who has set aside his robes and his calling to fight in Buera's band of partisans.

For literary discussion, author insight,
book news, exclusive content,
recipes and giveaways, visit the
Weidenfeld & Nicolson blog and
sign up for the newsletter at:

www.wnblog.co.uk

For breaking news, reviews and exclusive competitions
Follow us 🐦 @wnbooks